# Poison Weeds

Other books by the author

*Writing as Marty Slattery:*

Diamonds are Trumps: A Pitcher's First Novel

*Writing as Edward Bear:*

The Dark Night of Recovery: Conversations from the Bottom
of the Bottle

The Seven Deadly Needs

The Seven Deadly Fears

Tyler and the Twelve Traditions: The Legacy, the Lore, the Wisdom

Tyler and Edward: Relapse and Recovery

The Cocktail Cart

# Poison Weeds

## a novel

**Marty Slattery**

White River Press
Amherst, Massachusetts

First published 2011 by White River Press

White River Press
P.O. Box 3561
Amherst, Massachusetts
www.whiteriverpress.com

ISBN: 978-1-935052-40-1
eBook ISBN: 978-1-935052-57-9

Library of Congress Cataloging-in-Publication Data

Slattery, Marty, 1933-2006.
Poison weeds : a novel / Marty Slattery.
    p. cm.
ISBN 978-1-935052-40-1 (pbk. : alk. paper)
1. Prisoners—Fiction. 2. Prisons—Fiction. I. Title.
PS3569.L267P65 2011
813'.54—dc22
                    2011006763

This is a work of fiction, but like most works of fiction, it is based on
some real events and real people. The names and details have been
changed in most instances to protect the privacy and reputation of
those on whom this work is based.

For

**My brother, Gene**

**My sister, Mike**

# Poison Weeds

The vilest deeds like poison weeds,
Bloom well in prison air;
It is only what is good in man
That wastes and withers there. . . .

Oscar Wilde, *The Ballad of Reading Gaol*

# CHAPTER 1

## 1965

Fremont was an old prison, nearly as old as San Quentin, a stone and steel fortress built in 1867 (the date chiseled on the archway above the infamous East Gate) to house California's most dangerous criminals. Constructed with massive granite blocks from the Folsom quarry, the architecture dark and ominous, it faithfully reflected nineteenth-century attitudes toward crime and punishment. Nearly a century after it was built, it remained virtually unchanged. The only new construction was a gun tower added to the north wall in 1936. But there was still no hot water in any of the cells.

The fourteen-foot granite walls that defined the prison towered over the surrounding fields of lettuce and squash like an evil presence. At each of the four corners, high above the Yard, armed guards in circular gun towers cradled carbines and kept watch over the State's murderous children. Further out, fifty yards from the walls, the perimeter was secured by two rows of cyclone fences spaced fifteen feet apart. Atop the fences, spirals of concertina razor wire lay coiled like giant slinkies, discouraging trespass. German shepherd dogs and slow moving state vehicles patrolled the perimeter day and night.

The prison was located east of the Santa Lucia mountains and west of the Sierras in the fertile San Joaquin Valley, far from civilized centers of commerce. Until the advent of the automobile, it was accessible only by rail or horseback or by the stagecoach that traveled the rough road between San Francisco and San Luis Obispo twice a month. Now, Highway 127 ran north and south only a mile from the East Gate, the connecting road a ribbon of blacktop lined with elm trees and tidy staff housing, the manicured lawns tended daily by Honor Block inmates. Still, there were few visitors.

The day Manny Vargas died started out like all the other days at Fremont. At six A.M. the klaxon horn pulsed noisily through the cellblocks, destroying sleep, unraveling dreams, rousing from slumber the community of three thousand felons, rekindling the flames of rage and hostility that spread through the prison each day like a deadly virus.

Hog Beaumont, Voodoo Jefferson and Dave Leonard awoke and went about their separate tasks with a callous efficiency learned in the long years behind the walls.

The Mess Hall prepared to open and serve the morning fare— cream chipped beef on toast already congealing into a tasteless suet, powdered eggs tinged with green, coffee that was weak and metallic tasting. Sgt. Melvin Pollard, Poison Pollard to the convicts, ample stomach straining the buttons on his khaki shirt, thumbs hooked in his belt, toothpick dancing across his mouth, stood by supervising the activities. Outside, the gun tower guards shook off the night and watched for early signs of movement on the Yard.

Manny was a shriveled old Mexican who had been locked up since 1923 following his conviction for setting fire to an orphanage that resulted in the deaths of twelve children. He had been in the California prison system longer than anyone—forty-three years (even longer than Billy Whitehorse, the unrepentant Indian who was approaching his fortieth year for killing a Catholic priest)—though his only crimes were being a Mexican and having the bad luck to be in the vicinity of an orphanage that was burning. (There were those in power who knew of his innocence, but felt that it was not politically expedient to release him after all this time.)

Manny never saw his killer. He was walking alone near the Welding Shop when he felt an arm tighten around his chest. A moment later there was a stinging sensation across his throat. At first there wasn't much pain; he didn't think he had been hurt badly. But when he saw the blood spray out against the wall, he knew. In that awful moment before the real pain began, he realized what had happened. When his assailant released his hold, Manny sank to his knees, both hands to his neck, trying to stop the flow of blood that gushed through his fingers.

He tried to speak, but all that came out were bubbles of blood. He wanted to say that he had never set fire to that building, had never killed anyone. Not ever. And certainly not children. He had children of his own. Why would he want to kill children? He wanted to speak so that someone would hear, so that someone would finally know the truth. But all that came out were those small red bubbles. His heart raced, trying to pump an ever dwindling supply of blood. He crawled toward the Welding Shop, but the shadows and the darkness came before he reached it. He did not feel the knife begin to gouge out his eyes.

# CHAPTER 2

The Watch Office was cold as slate: metal folding chairs, steel desks and filing cabinets, floor tiles hard as peanut brittle. Casual conversation created echoes. The slow, uneven clacking of a manual typewriter sounded like sporadic gunfire. There was no second hand on the big wall clock; the minutes ticked away in sudden, quantum leaps. Three of the walls were bare, solid reinforced concrete from floor to ceiling except for one small, barred window that looked out onto the Yard. A large plate glass window half way up the remaining wall separated the room from Control Central across the hallway. The sign over the door read:

**INMATE WATCH OFFICE**
**Authorized personnel only**

Greek Koumantakis sat at one of the desks reading a week-old newspaper held close to his face. Short and stout, with a fringe of dark hair resembling a tonsure, he had the look of a medieval monk.

A few feet away, Moose Rankin balanced his three hundred pounds on a rickety metal stool and explored the inner portion of his left ear with an index finger the size of a sausage. His face was an odd assortment of poorly matched parts—eyes too small, mouth slightly offset, a silly-putty nose, hair the texture and color of straw.

"Who'n the fuck'd want to kill Manny?" he said.

"Who knows?" said Greek, putting the paper down. "Place is full of crazies. Could'a been anybody."

Chuck Bledsoe, alias Count Dracula, leaned against the tall filing cabinet and checked the list of incoming convicts to see if any of his friends would be arriving soon. The deep lines etched in his face made him appear much older than his twenty-four years.

16

He had been dubbed Count Dracula by the local media because he wore a black cape during each of his nine rape attempts. His undoing came the night he was stopped for a faulty taillight wearing only his cape.

### NUDE DUDE SUSPECT IN CAPE RAPE

trumpeted the Santa Monica *Evening Outlook.*

Only in California, he muttered to himself, sitting alone and shivering under his cape in the Felony Tank.

Detective Tiller thought it was funny…Looks like you really stepped on your foreskin this time, Bledsoe. Should'a stuck to robbin' gum ball machines…

Identification was swift, conviction only a formality.

"Sounds like somethin' Popeye might'a done," said the Count.

"Popeye's in the Hole," said Greek. "Solitary."

The acknowledged leader of the group, Dave Leonard, a stocky six-footer, sat at the other desk playing solitaire. He wore large, horn-rimmed glasses on a face that was dark and square, a face that seldom smiled.

"Least he's got a good alibi," he said, pushing the glasses up on the bridge of his nose. Habit. He had eyes like an owl, eyes that never blinked.

"How about Doc?" said Moose.

"Doc did abortions, man," said the Count.

"Don't mean he can't kill people."

"So what the hell was Manny doin' out on the Yard after lock-down anyway?" said Greek.

"Maybe he was lookin' for Mexican whores," said Moose.

"Manny was old," said Greek. "Sixty-somethin'."

"Hey, don't hurt to look."

"No hookers on the Yard," said the Count. "I been checkin'."

"I bet you have."

"Maybe somebody was out practicin'," said Greek.

"Practicin' what?" said Moose, cracking his knuckles. "Killin' people?"

"Sure. For when he gets out…For when it counts."

"It don't count in here?" said Moose. "Killin' people in here don't count?"

"Nothin' counts in here," said Leonard, looking up from the cards. "You know that. This is all make believe. Disneyland without the rides."

"Red four on the black five," said Moose, looking over Leonard's shoulder.

"Don't-work-the-cards, Moose," Leonard said evenly. "Didn't I tell you that? Don't work the fucking cards, and don't look over my shoulder. It's called Solitaire for a reason."

Moose nodded and moved away with a slow, simian gait, his face revealing little emotion—only his eyes narrowed briefly.

"...And stop crackin' your knuckles."

"How about the Iceman?" said the Count. "He prob'ly wouldn't mind getting' in a little practice takin' people out."

"Ice could be a possibility," said Greek.

"Shit," said Moose. "Maybe the spooks did it."

"It's not Voodoo's style," said Leonard.

"Voodoo don't own all the niggers, man."

"Don't kid yourself," said Leonard. "Nothin' black goes down on the Yard without Voodoo's okay."

"I hear the guy who did it cut Manny's throat and drank all the blood."

"Jesus," said Greek. "Now I suppose we got vampires on the Yard."

"Then cut his eyeballs out."

"Who told you that?"

"Magoo," said Moose.

Greek shook his head.

"Magoo. Guy doesn't have one single brain cell that works, Moose. Not one. Might as well ask Jimmy the Face. Or Stoney. They don't know shit either."

"Could be the truth," said Moose.

"And I could be Jesus Christ," said Greek.

"Not likely," said Moose. "If you was really Jesus, you coulda worked a miracle and got yourself out on parole by now. Jesus had some juice, man."

"And if you was really Jesus," said the Count, "you prob'ly wouldn't a been out there squeezin' widows and old people for rent money."

"I suppose you were tryin' to get a suntan on your dick," said Greek. "Wavin' it around like it was a flag. You and your hot cape disguise."

"You don't know shit, Greek," said the Count. "You know that?"

"Give it a rest," said Leonard. "You guys are givin' me a headache."

The silence didn't last long.

"Terrible class of convicts here," said Greek. "I ever do time again I'm goin' back to a Federal joint."

"I heard Federal time's better," said Moose. "More like a country club."

"Terrific," said Greek. "It was so fuckin' good I hated to leave. Steak and lobster every night. Blow jobs from the guards. They had to actually force me out the gate."

"Nobody get killed in Leavenworth?" said Leonard.

"Some," said Greek. "But a guy like Manny? Never. Manny was a stand-up guy, for chrissakes. Forty-three years in the joint gotta count for somethin'. What happened to respect? You don't take out guys like that."

"Any vampires there?" said the Count.

"Gimme a break," said Greek.

"You know there's people do that kind of shit," said Moose. "Drink blood. Eat stuff you wouldn't believe…There's people eat brains and termites and sheep guts and balls, man. Real balls. Everything. Snails. Toads. Monkey brains. There's people eat monkey brains while the fuckin' monkeys are alive, man. Drinkin' a little blood's like a day at the beach. No sweat."

"Jesus," said Greek.

"Maybe he drained it and put it in the soup."

"What kinda soup we have for lunch?" said the Count.

"…Tomato."

"See," said Moose. "Perfect. Nobody'd even notice. You have any soup?"

"I never eat the soup," said the Count. "Half the time they piss in it."

Greek picked up the paper and squinted trying to get it in focus.

"Hey, Leonard, *The Wizard of Oz* is playin' at the Rialto."

"One of my favorites. Maybe we can get a pass for a couple of hours."

"…Doubtful," said Greek.

"Even if we promise to come back?"

"I don't think they trust us all that much."

"What's *The Wizard of Oz*?" said Moose.

"A movie."

"I know it's a movie, man…I mean what kind of a movie?"

"It's a movie about a wizard, Moose. *The Wizard of Oz*. And a bunch of guys who go to the Wizard to get somethin' they want."

"…Like what?"

"Lemme see," said Greek. "The Cowardly Lion wants some courage, the Scarecrow wants a brain, and…"

"Hey, I'll tell Paulson about the brain," said Moose. "Anybody could use a brain, it's Paulson."

"…and the Tin Man wants a heart."

"Don't forget the girl," said Leonard.

"Right. The girl. Dorothy."

"Who's Dorothy?" said the Count.

"Dorothy is Judy Garland."

"…So who's Judy Garland?"

"You don't know who Judy fuckin' Garland is? How old are you?"

"Twenty-four."

"Jesus…"

"Jesus what?"

"No wonder the world's so fucked up."

"Why? Because I don't know who Judy fuckin' Garland is? I got news for you—I don't care who Judy fuckin' Garland is."

"I think I'll pass on the show," said Leonard. "I don't like the seats in the Rialto. No leg room."

"Suppose there really was a Wizard, Moose," said Greek, "and you got to ask for anything you wanted."

"Depends on who it is," said Moose.

"What's the difference? Any Wizard. Use your imagination."

"Don't kid yourself. It makes a difference."

"Okay…Say it's the new warden. What's his name?"

"Quinlan," said Leonard. "Robert T. Quinlan."

"Why would I ask that prick for anything?" said Moose.

"Might be a nice guy," said Greek. "You don't know."

"Guy's a prison warden, man. How nice can he be?"

"Okay, let's pretend it's Leonard. Leonard's the Wizard."

"And I can ask for anything I want?"

"Anything but a parole. That's too simple."

"Then it's a no-brainer," said Moose. "We ask for some dope. Some reds, whites, yellows, rainbows, sleepers, keepers, some speed to do the deed. There's no hope without dope, man. Everybody knows that."

Moose Rankin had been standing in the unemployment line in Venice, California, poring over the racing form (penciling in Big Daddy for his hunch bet in the third race), when he was arrested by two undercover agents acting on a tip furnished by a rival drug dealer. Possession of marijuana, second offense. Judge Abernathy (feeling poorly that morning due to ongoing hemorrhoid problems) sentenced him to the maximum term of two to twenty in state prison.

"How about you, Count?" said Greek. "What'd you ask for."

"The keys to the women's prison in Frontera," he said. "Then we got the chicks and the dope."

"You ever see those women in Frontera?" said Leonard.

"You just get me the keys. I'll worry about what they look like."

"And finally, the leader of the band," said Greek. "What'll it be for you, Leonard?"

"How about a phone in my cell so I can keep track of my…business interests."

"Done," said Greek.

"And you, Greek?"

He cleared his throat and thought of all the things he could ask for. His teenage son, Rocky, was into drugs (what ever happened to shots and beers? he wondered), his wife was on the verge of divorcing him, and the time he had to do on his latest conviction stretched out in front of him like thirty miles of bad road. Getting any of those things off his back would be a big relief. But he didn't mention any of them.

"Get me an extra key to the women's prison," he said.

"What for, old man?" said Moose.

"Just get the extra key," said Greek. "Let me worry about the rest."

"Old man dreamin'," said the Count.

"Hide and watch," said Greek. "You might learn somethin'."

No one spoke for a time.

"Hey, Boss," said Moose, "you decided on the prize for the Fly Killin' Contest next year?"

"All I know," said Leonard, "is it'll be better than this year's."

"Hard to beat that, man," said Moose.

"Just wait," said Leonard.

"… Must be time for chow, eh?" he said. "I'm starvin'."

"You're always starvin'," said Greek.

"Hey, I'm still growin'. Anyway, here's what I think," said Moose, getting up from his stool and heading for the door. "Fuck the Wizard. And Judy Garden. And the Warden. Let's eat."

# CHAPTER 3

Just getting booked into the Old County Jail took nearly twenty-four hours. Friday nights it was a zoo. The recently arrested shuffled aimlessly around the holding cell like zombies, vomit drying on filthy shirts, scabs beginning to form over fresh head cuts. Some shouted obscenities and demanded to be released, but most were silent, sullen, brooding over bad luck and hard times. Several tried to sleep, sprawled on the floor in odd postures like broken dolls. Many were still drunk. One was already dead. Nobody noticed.

"Amateur night," said Officer Baldwin, wrinkling his broad black nose in disgust.

A single seatless toilet at the rear of the cell looked like a giant stained teacup; it was occupied by a series of transients with loose bowels, adding still another unpleasant odor to the rank smell of sweat and unwashed bodies. There was no toilet paper.

"Flush that thing, willya?" someone grumbled.

"Drop one, drown one," said another. "That's the way we do it in the jailhouse, man. Drop one, drown one. Send it to Long Beach."

The back wall of the cell, once a pale institutional green, was now grimy shades of gray, laboriously penciled or etched with messages about sex, drugs, despair, and that old standby, Jesus.

Officer Baldwin kept a handkerchief filled with orange peels balled up in his left hand, periodically put it under his nose and took a deep breath. He made a mental note to ask Sgt. Wymans if he could transfer back to Traffic. Six months working Intake at the Old County Jail was about all he could take. Even Traffic, which was no picnic, was beginning to look good—at least it was outside. Anything would be an improvement over Intake.

Stan Smith drifted back to consciousness on a wave of nausea. He turned, pressed his face against the bars and stared blankly at

Officer Baldwin's desk...His head throbbed painfully and a foul taste filled his mouth. Moments later he gagged and swallowed, then gagged again.

"God," he said.

Though his senses hammered home the message that he was in jail, he had no idea why, or any memory of how he had gotten there. He closed his eyes, counted to five and opened them. The scene was unchanged. He fingered the cuffs of his tan safari shirt (was that blood on the right sleeve?), looked down at his pleated denim trousers and shook his head.

"...God," he said, fighting the rising tide of panic that was making it difficult to breath.

"Sally makes the good times roll," said a man with a deep gash across his cheek. "Sally bakes the bread." He smiled. "Sally blows my horn." He seemed unaware that the cut on his cheek was still oozing blood.

A drone of voices addressed no one in particular. Solitary minds tethered to memories as old and useless as snake oil complaining about hard times and the treachery of certain women. Of worthless bitches. Of two-timing, money-grubbing bimbos. And of course the po-lice.

Stan felt a hand on his hair.

"Nice," said a gravelly voice behind him.

Stan jerked his head away, turned and looked into a battered face laced with ruptured capillaries. One eye was swollen shut. Stan smoothed his hair and frowned. The man reached for it again.

"Nice," he repeated.

"You better get the fuck away from me," said Stan, his voice high and strident, not like his own voice, not like a man's voice.

Fingers smiled unpleasantly; his teeth were yellow like an old dog's teeth, and his one open eye had the same red roadmap that webbed the rest of his face.

"I fix your hair, boy."

Stan struggled to his feet and moved away. The man with the gash on his cheek looked up when he passed.

"Sally blows my horn," he said. Then he laughed. "...Frank's, too... Maybe everybody's."

Stan continued on to the other side of the cell, carefully stepping over bodies. He found a spot on the floor and sat with his back to the bars. He found it impossible to think clearly. Why couldn't he remember anything? He fished through his pockets and discovered that he had no money, no wallet, no keys. Had he been robbed? In his shirt pocket he found two folded slips of paper. The first he recognized as a list of his personal property (wallet, money, keys, etc.). The other was marked Booking Charge:

### SMITH, Stanley 187 PC

He knew that drunk driving was section 502, because he had been booked on that before. But what was 187? He stared at both slips for a few moments, then folded them and put them back in his shirt pocket. It didn't make any sense. Any of it. Why was he in jail? What had he done?...And what did 187 PC mean?

The backs of his hands began to itch. He scratched them until they were raw and bleeding. He wished he could stop shaking. The clock over Officer Baldwin's desk indicated that time had stopped.

Sometime later he was fingerprinted, photographed, herded to the showers and sprayed with DDT from an old flit gun...(Bend ovah and spread 'em, said a black trustee, his eyes the color of mustard... Keep 'em spread til I tells you else.)...Did Stan only imagine that he was bent over in that awkward position longer than the others?

Another few hours and he was taken out of the holding cell and questioned by a salt and pepper team of detectives who wanted to know about the murder.

"...Murder?" said Stan.

The two detectives exchanged glances.

"Section one eighty seven of the penal code, Mister Smith. Murder in the first..."

Neither detective was smiling.

"Murder..." said Stan, his stomach churning.

"Loughlin died," said Salt.

"...Loughlin," said Stan, as if the name were new to him.

"Jeffrey Loughlin," said Pepper. "The guy who was bangin' your old lady. Remember him?"

"God," said Stan. How did they know about that?

"You wanna tell us about it?"

Stan shook his head.

"You got a lawyer?"

Stan shook his head again.

"Better get one. This is Murder One, Mister Smith... Welcome to the big time."

...Murder, he thought as they led him back to the cell. Jesus... Murder. Was it possible?

He was issued a tin cup, a blanket and a mattress not much thicker than the blanket. He and several others were escorted to the D Wing on the eleventh floor in the early morning hours. There were no bunks available. Four men were assigned to each of the two-man cells. He stumbled over sleeping bodies (Watch way yo steppin', fool!...) until he found a bare spot on the floor. He unrolled his mattress and lay down. The smell was damp, primal. It reminded him of caves, of animals in the rain, of decay and of fear. Especially fear. He had to breathe through his mouth.

His heart thumped noisily in his chest; it seemed to be skipping beats. He wondered if he might be having a heart attack. If he was, he was sure nobody would come to help him. Nobody would even notice. The fact that Uncle Frank died of a heart attack in his late twenties was part of the Smith family lore. Bingo, he was gone, his father said. Heart seizure. He snapped his fingers. Just like that... Just-like-that.

Murder?...Of course he remembered Jeffrey Loughlin—WWII Marine hero Jeffrey Loughlin. How could he forget? But could he have actually killed him? Stan Smith kill somebody?...He searched his memory for clues, for the last remembered moment, but most of the previous evening was lost in an alcoholic haze. He remembered drinking the Heaven Hill Kentucky Bourbon. He drank it like his father did—out of a small Kraft cheese glass. Straight, no chaser. But that was early. He saw himself loading and unloading the gun, but he had often done that in the preceding weeks, thinking of what he would do if Jeffrey were there. He accidentally shot a hole in the floor one night. That scared him, but only for a few days. Then he went back to loading and unloading the gun at night, his imagination fueled by scenes of retaliation.

Sometimes he pictured himself as James Cagney in *White Heat*, one of his favorite gangster movies. Cagney was Cody Jarrett—high style and the essence of cool. Cody would have taken care of someone like Jeffrey Loughlin without a second thought—just drilled him and walked away…Bingo. Just-like-that…Stan saw himself as Cagney—cool, mean, streetsmart, dealing swiftly with those who dared betray him. But he knew he wasn't Cody Jarrett. Cody was tough. Stan was…Wimpy Stan, same as he'd always been.

They ran off together, Bonnie and Jeffrey Loughlin. That's what happened. Just ran off. His wife, Bonnie Aldridge Smith, who had promised to love, honor and obey him forever less than three years before, ran off with Jeffrey Loughlin, WWII Marine hero. That was the real story. Stan turned to the Heaven Hill for solace. Not the first time he had found comfort in a bottle. The bottle and the pills.

In the aftermath of her disappearance he took to shedding his clothes and making long incoherent speeches to the mirror on the back of the bathroom door. He wrote his last will and testament, then destroyed it after reading it the following morning. Then did it again the next night…Being of sound mind and…The only peaceful times he knew were the twilight zones of drugs and alcohol…But there were evenings that he couldn't remember, hours that vanished from his life without a trace. What had happened after eight o'clock on the evening in question? In truth, he had no idea. Could he have killed Jeffrey during one of those times? It hardly seemed possible.

He never thought of himself as a violent person, though he recognized it in his father. Carl Smith was given to periodic outbursts of rage (mostly when he was drinking, though not always), times when he picked up things and people and carried them from place to place, from room to room; sometimes threw them if they were light enough. Just did it without telling anyone why he was doing it or why he was angry. It seemed to satisfy some primitive need for control. No one dared ask. If he was really angry, he would lift the big easy chair and carry it across the room, set it down and stare at it as if he expected it to say something. Then a few minutes later pick it up and move it back, his face red, veins bulging in his neck, grunting from the exertion. The chair was clumsy and heavy. Sometimes he picked up Stan or his mother if they were sitting on one of the dining room chairs, carried them around, moved them to another part of the room like they were human chess pieces. They learned not to struggle, to just let it happen. They were no match for King Carl. Several times he picked Stan up and threw him across the room. "There," he said, as if that was an explanation. Stan was terrified of his father.

The sounds and smells of the cellblock assaulted his senses; he buried his face in the rough wool blanket to muffle the sobs. He listened to the blubbery wheeze, the hack and cobble of men disturbed even in sleep. He tried to think of a prayer, but none came to mind. All those years in Catholic school and all he could remember was mea culpa, mea culpa, mea maxima culpa. Maybe he should have become a priest after all. He'd thought about it when he was twelve or thirteen (just before he discovered those exciting things he could do with his penis). Even talked to Father O'Connell about going into the junior seminary. But it all came to nothing because Father O'Connell told his parents and that ruined it. Telling his parents about anything always ruined it.

He closed his eyes and tried to shut it all out, wondering if he would make it through the night. And then what? How many more nights? How many years?…God…

Men died in the Old County Jail; he learned that early on. The frail fared poorly, abused with monotonous regularity. Most endured the indignities because the will to survive was strong, dodging cellmates bent upon penetration, carrying scars that would not show, each assuming a stance for the dance that would carry them through till tomorrow. Buying time. But some did not survive. Rabbit Marshall died there, dirty tee shirt stuffed in his mouth, some evidence of sperm in his hair. A cursory investigation turned up several suspects but no witnesses. The usual situation. Two days later Bible Joe hung himself with strips of cloth from his own shirt, the words of Jesus fresh as strawberries on his bruised blue lips. Rag Man said that Bible Joe could talk to Jesus in person now, now that they was both dead…Jesus died for everybody, man. You know that? You an' me an' everybody…He made it sound like a good deal.

Stan, with his stylishly long blond hair and slight build moved carefully through the maze, seldom speaking. He locked his face into a scowl and tried to appear threatening.

For no apparent reason, a man he knew only as Speed smashed him in the face one day as he was walking along the tier. Just walking along, hands in his pockets, minding his own business, Speed hit him and knocked him down. Stan thought his cheekbone was broken; the whole side of his face hurt for two weeks. Speed didn't say a word, didn't even look at him, just hit him and kept walking. One shot. Bam…And kept walking. Nobody else seemed to notice, at least nobody turned to look. It was like it never happened. Speed had a tattoo on his forearm—a heart with a dagger through it and the word HATE under it. Stan's sense of hopelessness deepened with each passing day.

They were allowed to shower once every eight days in the Old County Jail. A three-minute shower. Three minutes, then the water was turned off. Those slow to rinse had another eight days to ponder their lack of speed. The summer was long and hot, often exploding into violence. Black men trash-talked and strutted, slapped pink palms and displayed an abundance of manhood. They jabbered about the muffuckin' o-fays and the po-lices and the homeboys. They did pushups and situps until their rancid smell filled the cellblock.

I hope you die…That was the last thing Bonnie said in her letter…I hate you and I hope you die…The Jail Censor got a kick out of that. He showed it to his buddy, Morales. They both got a good laugh out of it. Morales said this guy must have one tough old lady. The letter was typed. That was like her. Neat. Precise. Everything proper. If she made a mistake she would type the whole page over. Never mind the CorecType.

He wrote back but the letter was returned, NO PROFANTY ALOWED scribbled across the envelope. Of course Bonnie hadn't used any profanity, hadn't said she was sorry, hadn't acknowledged her part in it. She blamed it all on him. Everything. That's what she always did.

Richard (Just call me Dick, pal) George, the lawyer provided by the Public Defender's Office, provided Stan with the missing pieces to the events of the night in question. When he finished he informed

Stan that the best they could hope for was Murder Two. The very best, and they'd be lucky to get that. He looked like he slept in his suit.

"They got you dead bang," he said. "No pun intended. Witness, gun, the whole nine yards. Frankly, Smitty, this is not the smartest caper I've ever seen. Unfortunately you took out somebody who was a War Hero. Very bad form. Prosecutors love that. Wave the flag, defend the country, all that crap…Only shot we've got is to prove it wasn't premeditated. Only shot. That'd make it second degree. Otherwise, it's the Green Room, pal…The cyanide pills in the bucket. Bye, bye, Smitty. I know a guy who was there when Chessman checked out. Said it didn't look all that tough. Breath in a few times and it's over. They say it smells like peach blossoms. Can you imagine that? Cyanide smellin' like peach blossoms. Wonder how they know? Well, see you later, pal. Gotta run."

He called all his young clients pal. And he seemed to be terribly busy, always in a hurry.

Stan was fingered by the hand that fondled him, condemned by the person who brought him such ecstasy. The lawyers lay their petitions before the Altar of Justice. The Assistant District Attorney sought the death penalty for the brutal slaying, citing the nobility of the deceased, the cruelty of the accused. The Public Defender countered with a portrayal of the defendant's nearly spotless record, painting a picture of infidelity, duplicity, betrayal, a chance encounter in the heat of passion. He implied the possibility of self-defense.

Stan sat at the long, mahogany table and tried to appear contrite. His expression was strained; a slight frown, pale skin stretched tightly across finely chiseled features. He clung to the unreasonable hope that the jury would find him innocent. Yet how could they, after the evidence? Bonnie took the stand and Told All, punctuating the grisly tale with heartrending sobs. She made it sound as if she had just gone over to Loughlin's house to deliver some important papers. A business meeting. Hardly. Stan knew what she had gone to deliver, how long she'd been there and how many previous trips she'd made. He often wondered if they sat around and talked about him, made fun of him. Of Wimpy Stan.

When asked to identify the man who shot Jeffrey Loughlin, she pointed to Stan without hesitation. Was she sure? She replied that she was.

"Let the record show that Mrs. Smith is indicating the defendant, Mr. Stanley Smith."

On the bench, Judge Kathleen Barker, parchment face wrinkled with age, appeared to doze at times. The trial was short, the deliberation even shorter. The verdict—Murder in the Second Degree. Judge Barker, elegant blond coiffure piled neatly atop her head, Ben Franklin glasses far down on her nose, sentenced him in the chilly confines of Superior Court Division 107.

"I have no choice," she said, her voice a faint, dry rasp, "but to sentence you as the law proscribes, to a term of not less than five years nor more than life in State Prison." She paused to catch her breath. "Defendant will be remanded to the custody of the bailiff for transportation."

The gavel fell, a sharp, final sound that lingered in the air. Judge Barker vanished with a swirl of her long black robes. Case closed. She had other fish to fry.

Richard (Just call me Dick, pal) George put a hand on Stan's shoulder. He smelled like stale bourbon.

"Well, not too bad," he said philosophically. "Could'a been worse, pal. A lot worse. Could'a been first degree. The Green Room."

He eased a breath mint into his mouth, gathered his notes, stuffed them in his briefcase and left without another word.

But Stan didn't see how it could be worse; didn't see how anything could be worse. Even the gas chamber, the Green Room. At least then it would be over. But five to life? Five years?...To Life?... In prison? He couldn't imagine what it would be like. Could it possibly be worse than the Old County Jail? Could anything?

Just a month before, the already overcrowded conditions had worsened considerably in the wake of the Watts riots. Six men were then assigned to each of the two-man cells; four slept inside and two outside on the narrow walkway euphemistically dubbed the Freeway. The incoming were mostly black, young and angry. They looked down from the eleventh floor of the Old County Jail and waited for their soul brothers (rumored to be marching toward the

31

jail) to come and set them free. Some said that this was the beginning of the muffuckin' Revolution. It had been foretold—the Nation
of Islam would rise. Praise Allah…But they waited in vain. Nearly
all the soul brothers were already in jail. Those still on the streets
were busy looting the stores. The ghetto enclave of Watts smoldered
in ruins. They had torched their own community. Thinking they had
set fire to the entire city, chants of Burn, Baby, Burn rocked the Old
County Jail in the long hot summer of '65.

Stan chewed on his lower lip and blinked away the tears. He
saw his mother weeping at the back of the courtroom, blue pillbox
hat perched on her head. He knew his father, Carl, was still in the
hospital. His heart, his mother had informed him a week before from
the visitor's side of the bulletproof glass, clutching the telephone
receiver in one hand, a damp Kleenex in the other. He couldn't take
it…timidly striking her breast in response to some hidden bell. The
strain, she volunteered. He nodded, sensing the recrimination in her
voice, the parenthetical (How could you do this to us?) unsaid but
heard. She sniffled into her Kleenex. He wished she wouldn't wear
that stupid pillbox hat.

He found himself wishing that his father would just die and
get it over with, yet knowing, even as the thought flashed through
his mind, that there must be something terribly wrong with him if
he actually wanted his father to die. He couldn't imagine a normal
person feeling like that. No matter what kind of a father he had.

He was haunted by Bonnie's memory. He wondered why no one
seemed to see her part in it. Her guilt. By some strange quirk of fate,
she had become the victim, the innocent. Yet she had orchestrated
the whole thing. Beginning to end. He saw that now. How could he
have misjudged her so badly? How could he have been so gullible?

> …*Do you, Stanley, take Bonnie*
> *to be your lawful…*

Stan was five-foot-five. She was three inches taller. She looked
straight ahead at Father Seabert, her fingertips pressed together at
the point of her chin. She was beautiful—he tried to memorize her
face. …in sickness and in health, in… God, how he loved her. How

he needed her. ...By this ring, taken and pledged... Martha Bates
played the organ and sang Oh Promise Me in her husky contralto.
...til death do us part...

Start to finish, it lasted less than three years.

After the sentencing, he was escorted back to the holding cell by
two burly marshals.

"Whad'ja get?" said Ace, one of his cellmates awaiting his own
trip to court.

"...Five to life," said Stan

"Law per-scribes," he said, shaking his hand as if he had just
burned all his fingers.

A big black man sitting on the bench chuckled.

"That sho'nuff hold a fella," he said. "Goin' to the Big Yard now,
boy. Bettah get yo mind right. You can't be doin' no big time less you
gets yo mind right." He shook his head and chuckled again. "Walk
slow, keep yo prune tight and yo back to the wall. Don't fo'get what
old Benjamin be tellin' you, boy. Gonna come in handy someday."

"Five to fuckin' life," said Ace, savoring the sentence as if it
were his own. "Jesus, man. That's a load."

Stan leaned against the bars, hands deep in his pocket.

"Shit," he said. "Five to life?...No big deal."

But he didn't believe it. Not for a minute.

# CHAPTER 4

Hoss Criner was angry; he moved across the Yard like a menace, bulldog face and no neck. If he wanted to look right or left, he had to turn his whole body. But he was quick for such a big man. Gimpy almost had to run to keep up with him.

Hoss knew where to find Reno. He turned the corner on the south side of the Laundry and there was Reno, shirt off, sitting on a bench, sunning himself as if he didn't have a care in the world. Hoss got to him quickly and threw a chopping right hand to the side of his head that knocked him to the ground. Gimpy stood at the corner making notations in a small notepad, keeping an eye out for the Yard bulls.

"You owe me two boxes, asshole," said Hoss.

Reno shook his head, then touched his ear and checked his fingers for blood.

"God damn, man," he said.

"Two boxes," said Hoss.

"Jesus," said Reno. "I know, man. I ain't forgot. I just need some time. I got it comin' in. Guys owe me, Hoss. You know that. I got four, five boxes out. Owed ...They be comin' in soon."

"That ain't what I heard," said Hoss. "I heard you ain't got shit loaned out and you're into the Organ Grinder for two boxes besides the ones you owe me. That's really dumb, Reno. Even for you."

"A week, Hoss. Gimme a week."

"You already had a week...Two weeks."

"A week," said Reno. "What's a week, man? We been walkin' the Yard a long time, you and me, Hoss. Right?...What's another week?"

"You think Leonard's running some charity deal here? He just gives them smokes away?"

"I'll make it right, man," said Reno.

Hoss considered that for a moment.

"Okay. One more week. But then you gonna owe me three boxes. Every week you don't pay it goes up a box."

"I'm good for it, Hoss. You know that."

"Better be," said Hoss. "I don't get 'em soon, I sell your debt to Voodoo. He make a hobby shop outta your asshole. Rent you out to the other jigs on the weekends. So they can party." He laughed mirthlessly. "Voodoo put a spell on you, man. Make you shrivel up and die."

"I'm good for it," said Reno.

"Better be," said Hoss. "Be a whole lot worse next time."

Reno touched his ear again.

"I think it's broke, man. Can't hear nothin' outta that side."

"That's why you got two," said Hoss. "Case one gets broke." His laugh was dry, mechanical. "I be lookin' for you next week. Don't forget."

He walked to the corner and held up three fingers. Gimpy nodded and made a notation in his notebook.

Reno got up, sat on the bench and slumped back against the Laundry wall. He had no idea where he was going to come up with three cartons of tailor-made smokes by next week. Hoss was right—nobody owed him shit. He could take a chance and bet on the fights Saturday night, but that's how he lost the first carton he didn't have. And the rest of them. The fix was supposed to be in. Easy money, they said. Some fix. They probably bet the other way and cleaned up. Couldn't trust anybody.

He eased a plastic cigarette container out of his pants pocket, removed one of the last two home-rolled Bugler cigarettes and lit it. He inhaled and blew the smoke down on his concave chest. It tasted good.

He hardly had time to enjoy it before Fat Tony Monza moved in and sat on the bench next to him.

"Great fuckin' day, eh?" he said.

Reno eyed him suspiciously.

"Fair," he said.

Fat Tony weighed a ton. Eyes as big and black as olives stared out of a round, pockmarked face. He had a hundred pounds on Reno. A hundred pounds easy.

"Gimme a smoke, eh?" he said.

Reno fumbled in his pocket, pulled out the plastic container and held it up for Tony to see.

"Only got one left," he said.

"Just right," said Tony, grabbing the container in a meaty fist. "One smoke. Must be my lucky day, eh? I need one smoke, you got one smoke. Like a fuckin' miracle, eh?"

He took the cigarette out of the container, examined it, then put it in his shirt pocket. He tossed the empty container back to Reno and got to his feet with an effort.

"Don't take no wooden nickels," he said.

"Bad luck to take a man's last smoke," said Reno.

"Not for me," he said. "Besides, you suppose to be a cat burglar. Go steal some."

Reno watched him walk away with that heavy rolling gait.

"Fat prick," he mumbled. "Take a man's last smoke." It wasn't fair. No way. First Hoss and then that goddam Fat Tony. He squinted up at the sun as if it might have an answer.

"Who's next?" said Hoss.

Gimpy checked the Book.

"Froggy over at the hospital."

"Fuckin' Froggy," said Hoss. "Some people never learn. What's he owe?"

"…Eight."

"Maybe he'd like to trade for some pills."

"You think Leonard would go for it?"

"Leonard don't have to know everything," said Hoss.

They started toward the hospital to see Froggy, Gimpy skipping along behind trying to keep up, more than a little worried by the last remark. Trouble was, Leonard usually did know everything. That was his business. And if you crossed Leonard, it could get ugly. Very ugly.

Voodoo lounged around outside the entrance to North Block, his shaved black head glistening in the sun, ropy muscles rippling under his white teeshirt. He passed the time talking to the brothers, palm slappin', hip dippin', though his mind was elsewhere, planning strategy, making preparations for the Revolution.

Newly released on the Main Line from Protective Custody, the young and talkative Bobby Burnside pranced across the Yard with Allan Mobley as if he didn't have a care in the world. Nick the Knife, taking it all in from his usual position near the Mess Hall, made a mental note to take care of young Bobby as soon as he could, thereby ridding the world of one more snitch. Maybe Allan, too, for even being seen with him.

Dave Leonard leaned against the wall near the handball courts and watched Hoss and Gimpy on their appointed rounds.

"Go get 'em, Hoss. Bring in the bread."

Preacher, tall and scrawny, his face a tale of woe, stood at his usual spot in the center of the Yard, floppy Bible held aloft like a limp-winged bird, index finger of his free hand punctuating the air with dots and dashes and exclamation points, exhorting repentance, warning of the perils to come:

> *...Vengeance is mine, saith the Lord. For it is close,*
> *the hour of their ruin; their doom cometh at great speed...*

He lowered the Bible and blew his nose.

> *...The doom cometh at great speed, homeboys...Be thee*
> *ready or be thee shit outta luck.*

# CHAPTER 5

The gray Department of Corrections bus idled slowly across the County Jail parking lot and shuddered to a stop at the EXIT sign. With a loud grinding sound, the driver muscled it into low gear and lurched forward onto Temple Street, barely missing a Volkswagen bus with a mattress tied on top.

"Stupid goddam hippies," said the Driver.

"Jesus H. Christ," said the Riot Gun.

"How 'bout grindin' me a pound," said one of the convicts.

"This fuckin' thing got a clutch?"

"Po-lices don't need no clutches, man," said another.

Stan looked out at the cloudy sky through the heavy steel grid that covered the window. The pains in his chest were back again. He tried to ignore them.

The early morning streets were bleak, deserted, as gray as his mood.

### . . .SPRING ST. . . MAIN ST. . .

Left turn on Los Angeles Street to the freeway onramp.

### SAN BERNARDINO FREEWAY
### RIGHT LANE

The bus groaned up the ramp, picked up speed and eased into the sparse Saturday morning traffic. Stan took a deep breath—bus fumes and the sour smell of unwashed bodies. He wondered if he could ask someone to open a window, then felt foolish even thinking about it. He bit his lower lip and stared out the window through the

38

cold rolled steel. On top of everything else, he had to go to the bath-room. God…

He wouldn't survive the penitentiary; he was sure of that now. Bonnie would get her wish. One more had died in the Old County Jail. Stan didn't know his name, but he remembered him because the backs of his shoes were broken down and the heels dragged when he walked. They made a strange hissing sound, almost like whispering. He was a Negro, but he didn't seem as bad as the rest. He even said hello to Stan once. Somebody strangled him; choked him until he was dead and left him out on the Freeway, his eyes wide open, the toe of a shoe jammed in his mouth. Probably somebody got tired of the hissing sound his shoes made. Most everyone seemed to be irri-tated about something, angry about something. Nobody knew who did it. The guards pretended to be interested, even questioned a few people, but of course nobody saw anything. They never did. Stan knew how easily it could have been him. Rag Man shook the dead man's hand and told him to say hello to Bible Joe for him. Bible Joe and Jesus both.

The bus sped quickly through the morning. A light rain began to fall. The Driver and Riot Gun talked quietly in front, the Shotgun sat alone in the rear compartment. The center portion, isolated by a heavy steel grid, was occupied by the prisoners, handcuffs hooked to iron waistbands, leg irons fastened to eyebolts in the floor. Not all were glum; a few appeared to be in a festive mood, reminiscing about the old days at San Quentin. Some remembered Boots Larsen (who did his top on a one to fourteen), Mississippi Sam (who killed three men on the Yard in Folsom) or Fat Frankie (hurled to his death from the fourth tier at Quentin for crimes unspecified).

"We goin' to the penitenchurry," chirped someone near the back of the bus.

"Well halle-fuckin-lujah…"

A young convict across the aisle had managed to get his pants unzipped and was nervously stroking himself. The chains that secured his wrists clanked softly with each short stroke. He looked at Stan and smiled. Stan looked away.

The man seated next to Stan nudged him.

"That guy's jackin' off," he whispered.

"Yeah."

"Prob'ly a punk."

"…Yeah."

"Jesus, man…Fuckin' punks. Somethin' else."

How had it all come to pass? he wondered. From the quiet, three bedroom house on Walnut Street, to a seat on a bus headed for prison. He remembered the night she left.

"I'm going, Stan," she said.

"Oh?" he said. To the store? he wondered. Out with Joanna? To the movies?

"Goodbye," she said.

"Where to?" he said.

"Goodbye, Stanley."

"…Goodbye?"

She walked out the door, bulky brown suitcase banging against her leg. He put the paper down and watched her. When had she packed a suitcase? And why?

He recognized her boss, Jeffrey Loughlin, taking the suitcase from her as they walked down the driveway. What were they doing? Neither looked back at the house. Jeffrey put the suitcase in the trunk, opened the passenger door of the small red car, then went around to the driver's side and got in. A throaty little vroooom and they were gone. Just like that. Vroooom…An MG?…A Triumph?… He wasn't good at cars, especially sports cars.

"…Bonnie?" he called.

The car, top down, sped away. They were both laughing. Bonnie held her hair with both hands to keep it from blowing in her face. She had long hair. Red. Like the car. Stan waved. It was like a movie, waving goodbye to friends. He could never understand why he waved.

He returned to the chair and picked up the paper. She's gone, he thought. She just left. With a suitcase. A big suitcase. She left with Jeffrey Loughlin…But why? He tried reading the paper, but he couldn't get through the first paragraph of Melvin Durslag's column. He drank a whole six-pack of Eastside beer in less than an hour. Tall cans.

She's gone with Joanna, he said, though he knew it was a lie. He went to the door several times, halfway expecting her to return. But she didn't. He had no idea what to do. He drank the last Eastside, took two small yellow pills and fell asleep in the chair sometime during the late news.

He called her at work the next day.

"It's over," she said.

"What's over?"

"Us...The marriage."

"Bonnie, what are you saying?"

"I'm saying it's o-ver, Stanley. O-v-e-r. Get it?"

"...How can it be over?" he said.

"It just is. Look, I'm really busy and..."

"Bonnie, we've got to talk about this. People don't just walk out on each other like that. We've got to sit down and talk about what we need to do to..."

"I'm tired of talking about it."

"How can you be tired of talking about it, for chrissakes. We haven't ever started talking about it. We..."

"That's the trouble," she said.

"What is?"

"We don't talk."

"Well, that's what we'll do," he said. "We'll start talking about things."

"You don't know how to talk about anything important, Stanley. Anything...meaningful. You talk about those stupid things you make at work. Those electric things. You know ...circuits. I don't want to talk about circuits. And you talk about movies, like they're the realest things there is. Especially gangster movies. You're obsessed with gangster movies. You realize that? Movies aren't real, Stanley. They aren't anything. They're make-believe."

"Don't you think I know..."

"And we don't communicate. We don't talk about anything important. Meaningful."

"We'll start. It's not too late."

"Yes it is," she said. "Way too late. You never listened when you should have. When it was important. Besides, there's those other things."

"…What other things?"

"I mean some of the things you do. They're not all that normal. You know what I mean. That's not a personal attack. Just a statement. I ever tell you I found those Polaroid pictures you took of yourself?"

"…You did?"

"Those things aren't normal, Stanley. The things you're doing in those pictures. With your clothes off. They're not normal. People don't take pictures of themselves doing things like that. I was shocked. You should get help."

"…When did you see the pictures?"

"Never mind, it's not…"

"Listen, Bonnie, we'll start over. This is new ground. We'll communicate. We'll…"

"And you never want to play cards with Earl and Marie when they come over. Never. I must have asked you a jillion times. You always have some excuse like you have to go finish some dumb book you're reading. You make fun of them. They're my best friends… And you think they're stupid. They're not stupid, Stanley."

"Well," he said lamely. "…Cards."

"You're the one that's stupid," she said. "Anyway, it's too late."

"How can it be too late?"

"Don't yell, please. That's really annoying. One of the most annoying things you do. Yelling. And don't harp on things. You're like a broken record sometimes, always harping on things…"

"We're still married and I want to talk to you…"

"And you whine about things, too. You ever notice? You're immature."

"Oh, I see," said Stanley. "And I suppose what's-his-name… Jeffrey is Mister Maturity."

"He's certainly not like…"

"This guy must be fifty years old, Bonnie. Fifty-five maybe. Your father's not that old, for chrissakes."

"There's no need to…"

"Are you fuckin' him?"

"That's crude, Stanley. Really crude. That just shows your immaturity."

"Fuck immaturity," he said. "We're married and you're sleepin' with some other guy. That's illegal."

She sighed.

"It's not illegal," she said.

"Well, it oughta be…And it's certainly immoral."

"I have to get back to work."

"…So you give him a blow job while he talks about world history? The Germans are invading Poland. Suck, suck…Important events that mature people talk about? You come yet, honey? That how it works?"

"God…I don't believe it. Don't call anymore, Stanley. You're disgusting. Absolutely disgusting."

"I'm disgusting?" he yelled. "I'm disgusting?…You're fuckin' somebody old enough to be your father, your grandfather maybe, and you tell me I'm disgusting?"

"I'm getting a divorce," she said tersely.

"Goddamit, Bonnie, you can't just up and…"

…click. . .

The phone went dead in his ear.

"Bonnie?…Bonnie?…"

The following month was hazy. He drank a lot, even more than usual. Took the pills she kept for painful menstrual cramps—they made his face burn. She wouldn't talk to him when he called at work. When asked if he would like to leave a message he would often say things like, Tell her to go fuck herself. Soon, when she began to recognize his voice, the receptionist would hang up before he had a chance to say much. Though he hadn't been to church since his marriage, he went to St. Catherine's every day and lit a votive candle under the statue of Our Lady of Perpetual Help. And put a dollar in the poor box. But nothing worked. His prayers went unanswered. Women, he muttered. They're all the same.

For a hundred dollars a day plus expenses, Norman Frank (Frank Investigations—Discreet & Dependable) followed the two lovers. He got pictures of them entering and leaving Loughlin's house, holding hands, kissing near the statue of the saber-toothed tiger at the La Brea Tar Pits. When Stan asked for more explicit evidence, Norman said that the flagrante delicto stuff would be extra, over and above the C note. Plus expenses. Dangerous work...Not for the slight of heart, he explained.

The movie in his mind played day and night, cinema verité versions of Bonnie and Jeffrey sliding all over each other like snakes in a barrel, Bonnie and Jeffrey engaged in oral sex, she bending to his root like an eager acolyte. And who was the Supreme Allied Commander in Europe during WWII, honey?... Oh, you just came all over my wisdom teeth...Don't talk with your mouth full, sweetheart...

Stan watched. That's what he had done all his life. He stood on the sidelines and watched while the real men played football and drank beer. He was too small for football. Besides, he was afraid. Of everything. He lived in books and in movies; only there could he sometimes find a link, a connection to a world and a reality that always seemed just beyond his grasp. Like an emotional moon, he remained in orbit, always distant, always separated, never a participant.

He read all the Winnie the Pooh books, read and reread *Pinocchio*, often hiding under the covers at night and reading by flashlight, following along with *Pinocchio* on his perilous journey, imagining his own version of the Blue Fairy who would someday wave her magic wand and make him a Real Boy.

> *I've got no strings to hold me down,*
> *To make me fret and make me frown...*

His favorite movies were gangster movies—*Angels with Dirty Faces, White Heat, The Maltese Falcon, On the Waterfront*...He was a history buff—military history. He could explain in detail how the archers were deployed at Agincourt, what went wrong at Waterloo, why the Union forces won the day at Gettysburg, give verbatim survivors' accounts of the Battle of the Somme. If only somebody would ask. He tried out for the Debate Team, but found out that he turned mute when an audience was present.

When he began to drink in his early teens, he discovered that his fear of people went away when he drank. It was like magic. He had been paralyzed by fear, and after one or two drinks it vanished. He would remember later that he never knew just how fearful he was till the fear went away for the first time. A few drinks and he became a taller, handsomer version of the hapless, inept Stanley Smith. He could talk to people. He could even dance. Pure magic. He never forgot how it made him feel.

He emerged from the gray landscape of college with a degree in engineering. He was more comfortable with AC Theory and Circuit Design than he was with people. And engineers were in demand. He went to work for Lockheed. Half the engineers in his class went to work for Lockheed; aerospace was the thing and the money was good. While the real men were out surfing and balling the beach bunnies, he was bread-boarding time-base generator circuits in the R&D lab. He was afraid of the water.

Bonnie was his finest hour. His triumph. She was the luminous jewel that brightened his otherwise undistinguished life. She legitimized his existence. He must be okay; he was with her. It did not occur to him till much later that she might have had motives other than pure love for marrying him. Had her abusive, tyrannical father driven her into marriage with the first passable prospect who had a decent job? Was he merely a brief stop on her way to a Better Life? Her ticket out of Tyranny Town? A Chump?

He didn't think it was possible to hate anyone as much as he hated Jeffrey Loughlin. He became obsessed with revenge, consumed by a desire to make Loughlin pay for what he had done. He drank more than ever, often falling asleep on the couch during the late news. Even so, he usually only slept a few hours. One day he threw a tray full of food across the cafeteria. The Lockheed Cafeteria. No one had ever done that before. Certainly not an engineer. Not at Lockheed. The other engineers and programmers watched obliquely and dutifully reported the incident.

His work suffered. He got and gates and nand gates mixed up with flip-flops, grounded the outputs of op-amps, carelessly fried five-watt resistors with excess current. His boss suggested he take some time off...*Get a handle on this thing, Smith, whatever it is...*

The threat veiled but real. Stan didn't care; a job was the least of his worries.

He went to Dr. Duvall to get something to help him sleep. Dr. Duvall gave him a prescription for Seconal. They didn't help; he took too many and drank too much. Then he tried Benzedrine. He saw little green worms crawling on the backs of his hands. He scratched them until his hands were raw and bleeding. Next it was his face. Worms. The same green ones. He got a tweezers and tried to pick them out. He thought he was losing his mind.

The prosecution reconstructed the evening in question for the benefit of the jury.

Stanley Wayne Smith appeared at the house on Mill Road at eleven P.M., fired several shots from a large caliber revolver into the deceased at close range, then calmly departed. That was the damning part—the fact that he was so calm. (He heard himself described several times as a cold-blooded killer.) And of course the fact that Bonnie was there as an eyewitness. The deceased clawed at his chest with both hands, his Orphan Annie eyes wide with surprise, then sagged to the green shag carpet where his life leaked away in a matter of minutes.

What Stanley knew about the evening was what they told him. Perhaps if he could remember firing the gun. Or seeing the blood. Something. Maybe then he could feel some remorse. (Didn't it count for anything that he didn't remember? Wasn't that important? His lawyer never mentioned it. Not once.)

He felt strangely separated from the incident. It was like a movie with a reel missing. Or picking up the morning paper and reading about someone with his name who had killed somebody. Murdered somebody. Stanley Wayne Smith…had killed someone. Murdered them. In cold blood, they said. Not me, he thought. Not me…How could it be me? I don't even remember.

He wondered what Bonnie was doing. He hoped that she was alone and suffering, hoped that at last she realized what she had done to him and how much he loved her. Had come to her senses finally. He hoped that, but he didn't really think it was so. He pictured her writhing in bed with a resurrected Jeffrey Loughlin, his gigantic Marine member stuffed between her thighs, three bullet holes in his chest, impervious to the pain. Bonnie moaned and bounced up and down on the object of her desire. Stan pressed his handcuffs into his crotch and shifted in his seat.

"That guy just shot his wad," said his seatmate, indicating the young convict across the aisle. "I knew a guy who could shoot all the way across the room. Ten, fifteen feet. No bullshit. Guy was a come freak."

"Yeah," said Stan.

He swallowed hard and looked out the window. He wondered how long it would take to get to the Guidance Center. And what would happen when they got there.

# CHAPTER 6

"What's for chow?" said Moose.

"You ever think about anything but food?" said Greek.

"Sure. Sometimes I think about pussy…"

Paulson ran his finger down the mimeographed menu that was taped to the wall.

"Friday," he said. "…Horsecock sandwiches and soup. Bean soup."

"What would the penitentiary be without beans," said Leonard.

"We just had horsecock sandwiches," said Moose. "Jesus Christ. Couple of days ago. Shit. The crap they feed us in this goddam place. You suppose things'll change now that we got a new warden?"

"Yeah," said Greek. "They'll get worse. Tough breakin' in a new warden. Takes time. Most of 'em aren't all that smart."

"Wonder what he's like," said the Count.

"Just your regular run-of-the-mill prick," said Greek. "Got a reputation as a head buster."

"Where's he from?"

"He was Craven's assistant at Quentin."

"Big Red?"

"The Iron Fist himself. Not a good sign."

"Well," said Moose, "I don't see how the chow could get any worse."

"Just wait. You could be the size of a jockey by the time you get out of here."

Dave Leonard sat at his desk leafing through the file cards on incoming convicts, arranging them in alphabetical order for the Watch Commander. He always looked like he needed a shave.

He pushed his glasses up toward the bridge of his nose with his index finger, then scrolled a stencil sheet into the old Royal typewriter and started typing the daily Movement Sheet. He tuned the conversation out. He was still fuming over his recent denial at the Parole Board hearing. Another goddam year, he thought bitterly. One more goddam year. At least one more. The Parole Board showed little inclination to release him. This year or next. Fourteen counts of grand theft, well over two million dollars involved. Charges of extortion (though never proved) lingered in the testimony. Many solid citizens ripped off while trying to greener their nests with what looked like Easy Money. They were outraged. They wanted their money back or they wanted Dave Leonard in prison. Or both, preferably. Despite the best legal defense that money could buy, he was convicted.

Each year when he was due for his parole hearing, the Board received letters from companies, foundations and private citizens whose net worth had been diminished considerably after dealings with Dave Leonard. His annual appearance before the Board amounted to fifteen minutes of accusations and denials. . .

> . . .*None of that money has ever been recovered, Mr. Leonard. But of course you know that, don't you? Worse yet, there seems to be no effort on your part to make restitution.*

Restitution—he knew it was the key. If he made restitution, even attempted to make restitution, just some good faith effort, they would consider him for parole. But he had already decided that issue. He had worked too hard for the money to give it back. Besides, there wasn't all that much left. His only hope was that public pressure would eventually lessen or the Parole Board would soften its stance. But neither seemed likely as the years went by.

There were other options. Escape wasn't out of the question, though it would be difficult. Not impossible, just difficult. It would mean running, possibly never seeing his two boys again. Still...

Each year, along with the letters urging the Department of Corrections to keep Dave Leonard in prison as long as possible, the Board always got a letter from Esther Leonard pleading for mercy and listing the many virtues of her husband. She declared that he was desperately needed at home, now that the two boys were teen-agers. She had no qualms about begging.

The Board received many such letters from desperate wives or mothers prior to parole hearings. A few were eloquent and flowery, though most were plain, full of pain and misgivings and misspell-ings. The Board ignored them all.

On Sundays Esther and the boys came to see him. Every Sunday. You could set your calendar by Esther. The khaki clad cops who patrolled the Visiting Room to enforce public morality and curtail the drug traffic knew her by name. Dave saw his sons begin to drift away. Once they had sought his wisdom and counsel. Now they seldom even looked at him.

They came to eat cookies and cake (Esther baked them herself). They came to talk and to eat. They were the clock that ticked his life away, the silence of his sons a strange counterpoint to Esther's nervous chatter. Esther believed that given enough food and enough talk, everything would be okay. She had always believed that. She learned it from her mother, whose own life had never been okay.

They came to pass the time as if nothing had happened, as if the most normal thing in the world was to spend Sunday afternoons in the Visiting Room at Fremont State Prison. He tried not to be angry at the boys, but didn't always succeed. After all (he told himself) they were growing up; they had their own lives to live. But he knew they were slipping away and he was powerless to stop it. That was the most painful part.

Then there was Esther. She waited. That seemed to be her spe-cial vocation—waiting. She knew about the other women; had known about them from the beginning. Dave was always traveling. Business, he said. He made phone calls from distant places; she could never remember the names. He always asked about the boys and said that everything was fine. Just fine…But of course it wasn't. Not for Esther. She wished he would ask how she was sometimes—not always just the boys. And never mind the flowers he had his secretary send. He didn't even sign the cards himself.

She discovered that it was hard being married to someone who was a little bigger than life; hard to know what to do, how to act. She'd never been very good at it. So she waited. She cleaned their spacious home and she waited. She brought cookies and cakes and two teenage sons to the Visiting Room. Waited to get in and waited to get out. Waited for the following Sunday. Waited for the Parole Board to decide when Dave Leonard could come home. It wasn't much of a life. She just wanted things to be okay. That's what she'd always wanted. It didn't seem like too much to ask.

Leonard slammed his fist down on the desk.

"You want somethin', Chief?" said Paulson.

"I want outta this goddam place," he snapped.

"No problem," said Greek. "I'll talk to the Watch Commander. Put in a good word for you. Who's on tonight? ...Wotek?"

"I think."

"Take me with you," said Moose.

Leonard shook his head.

"I'm travelin' light," he said.

"That lets you out, Moose," said Greek.

"Hey, fuck you," said Moose.

"I hear Carson's gettin' out next week?" said the Count.

"Yeah," said Leonard. "Which reminds me...We're gonna need another runner."

"How much time'd he do?"

"Fifteen and change. Murder one."

"Who'd he kill?"

"His mother."

"Jesus Christ," said Moose. "Carson killed his mother?"

"I got news for you—not all mothers deserve to live."

Paulson whistled.

"Fifteen," he said.

"By the time you get out, little man," said the Count, "they'll be wearing space suits and livin' on the moon."

Paulson smiled; he had never felt so loved and accepted.

Lenny Paulson was doing his second stretch for armed robbery (ten to life), both committed with a toy pistol in the friendly environs of Grover City. Born and raised in that small seaside town, he was married and the father of two in his early twenties. His brief history included evidence of marginal intelligence (some said his marriage to Margaret Hempstead proved that), but no violence. His neighbors considered him the mildest of men. It had somehow seemed appropriate at the time, the first time (though he could never say exactly why it had seemed appropriate), the first robbery, conducted in broad daylight, no mask, no disguise of any kind. Just the doughy Paulson face, the stubby little body, and the toy gun in the presence of those who knew him by name. Not enough insanity had yet surfaced in his life to make that a viable defense.

When he returned home from prison, Margaret had eaten her way into a size eighteen and the children had forgotten him. (She said that the thought of bringing the children to prison to visit was more than she could bear.) He sat by the front window and stared out at the cluttered yard: tricycles and deflated rubber balls, tub toys and broken suction cup arrows. Weeds. He drank beer and watched the lawn die; no one watered it. Eventually even the weeds died. Margaret urged him to get a job, to be useful, productive. But he was not able. He sat by the window and watched everything die. She submitted to his infrequent sexual advances with obvious reluctance, suffering his need with terminal sighs, her cloistered cranny rarely available. The children continued to ignore him.

Six months later he was back in the same Grover City Savon Drugstore with his toy pistol and this time a Frankenstein mask. Nobody was fooled. It's the Paulson boy, they said. Judge Granville Jarvis banged his gavel down and said he had no choice, no-choice, but to sentence him as the law proscribed to a term of not less than ten years nor more than life in State Prison. . .

"Maybe we can get Carson to change his mind," said Greek. "They say it's no picnic out there."

"Too late," said Leonard. "Somebody already told him about the topless bars."

"Jesus," said Moose. "Topless bars. Tits..."

"Man," said the Count. "All those tits...and I'm locked up in here."

"Check the list we made up last year," said Leonard. "See if we've got any prospects to take Carson's place."

"Done," said Greek.

Leonard leaned back in his chair and pushed his glasses up on the bridge of his nose.

"Hoss deliver today?" he said.

"Ten boxes," said Greek.

"That's low, eh? We got a problem?"

Greek shrugged.

"What's the word on the Yard?" said Leonard.

"…I hear maybe," said Greek.

"Well, that certainly would be a problem, wouldn't it? Check him out. We got the books. Talk to some people he's collected from. Lean on him if you have to."

"…Ice?"

"Yeah. Have the Iceman give him a little pep talk about loyalty and friendship…and staying alive."

"You wanna Creme Soda, Chief?" said Paulson.

Leonard shook his head.

"I'll take it," said Greek.

"I'm…savin' it," said Paulson.

"For what?"

"…For somethin' special."

"This is special," said Greek. "I'm thirsty."

Paulson walked over and looked at the menu again.

"We got Jello for desert," he said. "Lime Jello. That the green stuff?"

"Jesus," said Greek. "You don't deserve to be doin' time with us."

"I hope that fuckin' Nelson's not countin' North Block," said Moose. "That guy's a fuckin' moron, man. I mean he can't even count. He's always got it fucked up. You remember the time it took him an hour to clear the count? You must have to have an I.Q. of about fifty to be a bull. Maybe fifty's too high. Jeez…Wish to fuck they'd hurry up."

"For horsecock sandwiches?" said Greek.

"Man's gotta eat," said Moose.

"This is Nelson in North Block, Lieutenant. We seem to be nine short here."

"What does that mean, Nelson? We seem to be nine short?"

"It means…I'm counting nine fewer inmates than we're supposed to have. Sir."

"Did you get all the outcount?"

"Yessir."

"And did you add that number to the number you actually counted?"

"I. . .I think so," said Nelson.

"You-think-so," said Lieutenant Wotek. "We're not counting apples and oranges here, Nelson. We're counting convicts. Convicted felons. Murderers. Rapists. You know. Try to keep that in mind."

"Yessir. I'll count again."

"Yes, Nelson. Good idea. Why don't you count again? We'll wait."

"Don't Voodoo live in North Block?" said Paulson.

"Yeah," said Greek.

"Maybe he made himself disappear."

"You really fuckin' suppose," said Moose, "that Voodoo can make himself disappear?"

"I heard that," said Paulson. "Honest a God."

"Fuck," said Moose. "If Voodoo could make himself disappear, he'd be on the streets, man. Free. Use your head."

"Lieutenant Wotek?"

"Yes, Nelson?"

"I counted again, sir."

". . .And?"

"And they're all here." There was a note of triumph in his voice.

"You're sure now?"

"…Yessir. Absolutely."

"Good job, Nelson. I know the community will rest easier tonight just knowing you got the count right."

"Thank you, sir."

Wotek shook his head and flipped off the intercom to North Block.

"Where do we get these guys?" he said. "Anybody tell me that?"

The announcement came from the four bell-shaped speakers positioned atop the gun towers at each corner of the Yard.

*The count is cu-lear. . .*
*Re-lease for early chow. . .*

"'Bout time," said Moose. "Somebody oughta drop a pipe on that Nelson. Do us all a favor. Maybe teach him how to count. One, two, eight, twelve, forty-two…Jeez."

*The Protestant Choir will meet in the*
*chapel at five thirty for choir practice. . .*

"I was in the choir at Leavenworth," said Greek. "Reverend Stipple's old lady baked us a cake every Sunday. German chocolate cake. I can still see her sittin' in that wooden folding chair, cup and saucer in hand, pinky up in the air…her legs spread this far apart." He held his hands two feet apart. "We all sat across the room and looked up her dress. No drawers. Pure beaver. Patterson used to bend over and tie his shoes about every two minutes. The Reverend acted like he didn't notice."

"Awwww, Greek," said Paulson.

"I swear," said Greek. "On my mother's grave. No drawers."

"German chocolate cake," said Moose. "I seen German chocolate cake looked good enough to fuck."

"You'd fuck anything wasn't movin' too fast," said the Count.

"Jesus, look who's talkin'," said Moose.

Leonard pushed his glasses up on his nose, got up and headed for the door.

"Come on, ladies," he said. "Let's eat before the Main Line gets cut loose."

He wanted to get back and start gathering information about the new warden. He'd start with Reiner. He had an uneasy feeling about the whole thing; he didn't like the rumors he was hearing.

# CHAPTER 7

The bus sped along the freeway, labored up the long grade at Kellogg Hill, then settled in at seventy miles an hour for the ninety-minute drive to the Reception/Guidance Center. Stan looked down at the cars as they passed, envying those who were going where they pleased, when they pleased. Young people. Old people. People who were free. It didn't seem like he had ever been free. Or ever would be.

An hour and a half later they turned off at the Central Avenue offramp—from there it was only three miles south to the sign:

## S.R.G.C.
### Southern Reception Guidance Center

The bus stopped for a moment at the front gate, turned right at the fence, lumbered slowly through the double rear gate and hissed to a stop at the loading dock.

"Home sweet mothafuckin' home," said one of the passengers.

A few convicts out walking the Yard in the light rain turned to stare. Stan felt sick to his stomach. They filed off the bus as the leg irons were unlocked from the eyebolts in the floor. Three armed guards watched from one end of the dock. They were herded into a large room, relieved of the rest of their shackles and told to disrobe. Stan waited as long as he could, then hurriedly shed his clothing and took a seat on the end of one of the benches, clothes bundled awkwardly in his lap. Though it was not particularly cold, he could not stop shivering. An older man with a rose tattooed on his forearm sat next to him. He made a circle with his thumb and forefinger and held it by his knee.

"You got somethin' for Toasty, kid?" he said.

Stan pretended not to hear.

Toasty shrugged.

"Either way," he said. "Don't make me no never mind. Toasty knows how to get it anyway...And you ain't gonna like it one bit. Guaranteed."

The room buzzed with subdued conversation for several minutes before the door opened and Correctional Officer Stefanko entered. He was a big man, nearly bald, with the pale complexion of someone who spent most of his time indoors. He scanned the rows of naked convicts, took the cigarette out of his mouth and dropped it on the floor. He made no attempt to put it out.

"I'm Sergeant Stefanko," he said.

"Big fuckin' deal," came a muffled voice from the back of the room.

Ignoring the comment, he clasped his hands behind his back, looked up at the ceiling and launched into the speech he had been giving twice a week for the last seven years.

"Welcome to the Southern Reception Guidance Center," he said. "Ground ze-ro. The end of the line, amigos. If you've been waitin' to hit bottom before you straightened out, you can stop waiting. You're there. This is it. You have been sent here for your crimes, gentlemen. Your transgressions against the people of the State of California. You were apparently a danger out there, a menace to the people because you could not obey-the-rules. So here you are. The end of the line. You may have thought you could beat the system. Ha-ha-ha...Nobody beats the system. Nobody. Now you will be here with us at the Guidance Center for the next four to six weeks. Some a little longer. You will be tested, e-val-u-ated. You will be observed. Closely observed. The results of those tests, those evaluations, those observations, will determine where you will spend the next few years of your life. Might be San Quentin, Folsom, Fremont...Who knows, eh?"

He took a nearly empty pack of Camels out of his shirt pocket, shook one loose and lit it with a Zippo lighter. His hands were covered with thick blond hair. And bruises. He inhaled deeply and blew the smoke toward the ceiling.

"Now...prison is not a pleasant place. Most of you already know that. If this is your first trip, you should be aware that it can be your last. May not be, but can be. It is not necessary to return time and time again. If we are to believe the statistics, most of you, more than two thirds of you, will return. Something in the range of sixty-five to seventy percent. Give or take…Most don't get the picture the first time around. Or the second or third. Of course by then it's too late. They put you in CMC East with the other old men. Limber-Dick Valley, they call it. Guess why?

"So here's the picture, amigos. You do the crime, you do the time. That's the picture. It's no big mystery. You go out there and break the law, we come get you and put you back in here. Simple."

He paused for a moment, thumb and forefinger pinching his lower lip.

"Now, what you do with your time in here is largely up to you," he said, beginning to pace up and down in front of the benches. "There will be a course of action charted for each of you. Might be vocational training, maybe academics. Who knows, eh? But nobody's gonna make you go to, say…welding school, if you don't want to. Or bakery school. Or auto repair. Nobody's gonna make you do that. You can goof off," flipping his right hand up in the air to show what goofing off looked like, "lay in your sack. Sleep. Slap bones on the Big Yard. You can do that. Some do. But California has what is known as the Indeterminate Sentence law. Which means if you're doing, say, a burglary second and the sentence is one to fourteen, we can keep you for the whole fourteen. I'm not saying we would, but we could. If we wanted to. If we felt it was justified. If you couldn't seem to go along with the program, do something that would help you stay out. People have been known to do their top on a one to fourteen…Don't do that," he said quietly to a convict in the front row who had both hands wrapped around a large erect penis. Stefanko cleared his throat and continued.

"Now the Parole Board likes to see you doing things. Improving yourselves. Making some effort at rehabilitation. Getting with the program, so to speak. They like that. And if you're smart, you'll like it, too. Then there is the matter of discipline. Ve-ry important. Perhaps the most important thing. Disciplinary reports follow you wherever you go. If you can't follow the simple rules in here, how can we expect you to function out there in society?…The Parole

Board wants answers to those kinds of questions. If you can't get along with your fellow inmates, if you're consistently fighting and causing disturbances, how can we expect you to get along with your neighbors out there? In the free world?"

But he knew there was slight chance that any of them would get along. They would continue to maim and kill one another as they always had. Hatreds from the streets carried over to prison and the wars went on uninterrupted. Territory. Race. Revenge. He had learned in his years as a correctional officer that prisons were full of violent men who did violent things. It was no mystery. The convict code demanded vengeance; anything less was considered weakness. And the weak did not survive. He had seen men change, but seldom for the better.

"We have two types of disciplinary reports—one-fifteens and one-twenty-eights. One-fifteens for major infractions, one-twenty-eights for minor ones. Now if you're inmate Jones and you've got a bunch of one-fifteens when you see the Parole Board, you think you're gonna get any serious consideration? No chance, amigos. Inmate Jones is down for another year. Maybe two. You want some advice from Sergeant Stefanko, keep your nose clean."

He tapped the side of his nose for emphasis.

"…It costs the State of California over five thousand dollars to keep a man confined for a year. One man. Five thousand bucks. Lotta money. People go to college for less. Like Yale or Harvard. Big time colleges. The public pays that money, tax money, so they can feel safe at night. Safe from robbers, murderers, rapists…and so forth. From men who can't obey-the-rules, who think they can beat-the-system. Men like yourselves. The Parole Board members are appointed by the Governor who is elected by the people…who like to feel safe. So, number one, it's a very bad thing to come here with a crime of violence. Very bad. Two, it's even worse to engage in any kind of violence while you're here. You can extend your stay almost indefinitely."

"Big fuckin' deal." The same voice.

Stefanko could only tell that the comment came from the back of the room.

"You know, that's the trouble with some people—they don't seem to get the picture. Ever. They are mostly worthless cocksuckers, those people are. Like the person who just made that remark. They're the ones who are doing life on the installment plan. Little by little until they end up with the other old men in C.M.C East. They're the ones who can't make it out there in the free world. Gutless assholes. Can't cut it. Never could. Now I happen to know who made that comment. In the back there." He glanced toward the back of the room. "And I will pass that information along to the people responsible for placement. Count on it. I can almost guarantee that that person will end up doing hard time. So instead of going to the Camp Center or C.I.M. that person will most likely end up in Fremont or Quentin. Someplace like that…Your choice, men."

He cleared his throat and rubbed his hands together.

"Now, as your name is called, step through the door behind me. Leave your clothes on the bench. You'll be given state issue clothing and toilet articles, have your picture taken and be given your cell assignments. You will become a ward of the State until such time as you are judged fit to return to society…In the meantime, you can give your soul to Jesus, but your ass belongs to the State of California."

No one joined in his hollow laughter.

They filed out as their names were called, colors from white to dark chocolate, anglos with tee shirt tans, sporting tattoos about love and death and honor and mother and born to lose. One man had a fly tattooed on the head of his penis.

Stan left his clothes on the bench and hurried through the line. Fortunately, Toasty left long before they called Stan's name. The pants they gave him were too long, the size nine Santa Rosa high tops much too big for his size seven feet. The rectangular board they draped around his neck was slotted to receive the white plastic letters. They took his picture; he looked like a deer caught in the headlights.

**SMITH, Stanley**
**A-83534**
**S.R.G.C**

He was issued a small cloth bag containing a toothbrush, chalky tooth powder, a razor, one Gillette blue blade, a small sack of Bull Durham and twenty cigarette papers. At the end of the line he was given a slip of paper with his cell assignment. He clutched it tightly in his hand and walked out into the cavernous main corridor. Into another world. He wondered if Toasty would be somewhere waiting for him.

# CHAPTER 8

The lettering on the translucent upper part of the door was barely dry.

**ROBERT T. QUINLAN**
**SUPERINTENDENT**

Inside the office, Quinlan sat in a large swivel chair, his head resting against the high leatherback. He was dressed in a long-sleeved white shirt, dark blue trousers and matching tie. His shoes were standard black wingtips. His hair was dark, neatly trimmed, beginning to thin at the crown.

Only a small aluminum calendar indicating the day and date graced the large mahogany desk. There were no pictures, no papers. It was a desk without waste or compromise, well suited to the man behind it.

Robert Quinlan was pleased with his recent appointment; only forty-one years old and already superintendent of the second largest prison in the state. Political life might well turn into the reality he had always dreamed about. Governor Quinlan, he thought. It did have a certain ring to it. But first there was work to do; his brief time at the prison had convinced him that a firmer hand was needed. A much firmer hand.

He rose from the chair and walked to the big French windows that faced the outside approach to the prison. Were it not for the fences and the squat gray building used to screen visitors, it might have been a scene from almost any small American town; beautiful elm trees, lawns in front of the staff housing nicely kept by Honor Block inmates, sidewalks swept clean by trusted wards of the state. It was not unlike the view from the East Gate at Folsom. Two worlds, he thought, and only a few feet of concrete and some decent men to separate them.

Across the street was the Visitor's parking lot, filled on weekends with junk cars and lines of visitors queuing up to be cleared for entry, waiting to be scanned by sensitive metal detectors, purse and pocket searched by dull, mechanical guards. A portion of the screening building was devoted to the Inmate Hobby Shop. Hanging from the walls were paintings of sad-eyed clowns, thick oil seascapes painted from memory, thinly disguised revolutionaries in postures of defiance. There were hand-tooled leather wallets and belts, jewelry, spiders imbedded for all eternity in polished orbs of clear plastic. Many visitors were astonished that work of such high quality could be produced by such lowlifes.

A timid knock on the door interrupted his reverie.

"Come in," he said.

The door opened; officers Powell and Hebner entered. Hebner, slightly built with light hair and a thin wisp of a moustache, looked prim and official in his pressed khakis. Powell, a black man whose appearance ran more to flesh, always looked slightly rumpled.

Quinlan pointed to the two chairs on the other side of the desk with both index fingers.

"Gentlemen," he said, easing into his swivel chair.

"Yessir," said Hebner.

"Yessir," said Powell.

Quinlan waited till both men were seated.

"I have not had time to fully assess the situation here," he said, carefully choosing his words, "but it is already obvious that we have certain...problems that need to be addressed. Now my predecessor, Mr. Alexander, while a fine penologist, and I'm sure a fine person, allowed a certain laxity to exist. A certain softness that's not appropriate, given the circumstances. You follow me here?"

"Yessir."

"Yessir."

"There's no need to discuss the consequences of that type of policy. A glance at the monthly Incident Reports is sufficient to show how...counterproductive it is to pamper prisoners."

He paused to massage his temple with his fingertips.

"It is not my intention to criticize administrative policies from Sacramento. Far from it. Let me be clear about that. But I'm sure you'll agree that many of the recent programs have been …unsatisfactory. Shortsighted, to say the least. Work Furlough is a case in point, an example of giving an inmate freedom he is not yet prepared to handle. That he does not, if the truth be known, does not even want. He needs and wants discipline. He may not be aware of it, but that's what he wants. And that's the backbone of the entire prison system—discipline. There are other programs, in the works, so to speak, aimed at giving inmates freedoms that are not commensurate with their status as wards of the state. Unnecessary freedoms…Dangerous freedoms."

Hebner and Powell smiled and acknowledged their agreement with identical nods.

"Nineteen sixty-five will go down in history as a year of lawlessness," said Quinlan, warming to his task. "A year when the criminal element tried to take over this great country of ours. Ours, gentlemen; yours and mine. America the beautiful. The land of the free and the home of the brave. We can't let that happen. There are riots in the streets…Atlanta, Cleveland, Los Angeles. Almost every major city. So-called civil disobedience, and worse, in the name of civil rights. Civil rights…If I may be allowed the vernacular of the streets—bullshit."

His small audience chuckled appreciatively.

"Now you two men are in a unique position here. You will notice that Captain Greer is not here."

The two lieutenants glanced around the room as if to reassure themselves that Captain Greer was not hiding somewhere.

"I purposely did not invite him to our little conference. Captain Greer is a fine man. Let me be clear about that. A man above reproach. I know his record well. Exemplary. I know his wife and daughter. Fine family…You understand, of course, that what I am saying is to be held in strictest confidence."

"Yessir."

"Yessir."

"A fine man. But a man somewhat in the mold of Superintendent Alexander, with that same softness, that same…lack of resolve that's required when dealing with the men we deal with on a day-to-day basis. That is, of course, not a criticism. Captain Greer will be eligible for early retirement soon and I will urge him to accept it. Strongly urge him. Perhaps even insist if necessary.

"I believe that the Department of Corrections needs to return to the old traditional values of discipline, discipline and more discipline. As a point of information, confidential of course, there are plans to expand the force here; plans that include two captains. Two...Now you two, as senior program lieutenants, are the obvious candidates for those positions. Of course much will depend on what happens in the upcoming year. There are some new policies that will be initiated. We'll...discuss them. But the need is not so much new policy; we simply need to implement the policies we already have. Do you men think there's a gambling problem on the Yard?"

"...Well," said Hebner.

"A few minor infrac..." Powell said before he was interrupted.

"There most certainly is a gambling problem," said Quinlan, leaning forward. "A serious one. It's like Las Vegas out there for God's sake. Wake up. Football pools, baseball pools...God help us. And there's a drug problem in case you two haven't noticed. And a discipline problem and God knows what else. I believe it was Superintendent Smithfield at Folsom who said that if an inmate was ever brought to him for striking an officer, he wanted the inmate carried in, preferably on a stretcher and preferably suffering some serious physical damage."

He leaned back in his chair.

"Now all prisons have problems. We understand that. Comes with the territory, as they say. And not particularly surprising when you consider the type of individual we're dealing with. But we can minimize those problems, gentlemen. Yes. We can take a firm hand here. No question. That's our job. It's what we get paid for. I don't want some convict, or group of convicts running my prison. Let me be clear on that. It's like the animals taking over the zoo. Not a pretty picture. And I won't have it. You understand?"

"Yessir."

"Yessir."

"Looking over the Incident Reports for the last few months, Hebner, I noticed an inmate death as a result of alcohol poisoning."

"Yessir. Inmate Padilla."

"And what happened to those responsible for that? For getting the alcohol and killing inmate Padilla?"

"Eh…Nothing, sir."

"Nothing, Lieutenant? Nothing? Someone consumed that much alcohol and nothing happened? How can that be?"

"…We were unable to get sufficient evidence to…"

"Did you know who was involved?"

"We knew who two of them were. They left him on the hospital steps. As a matter of fact, we were trying to get Padilla to tell us the identity of those involved when he…expired."

"We have a liquor store here on the grounds, Mr. Hebner?"

"No sir…not that I know of."

"Not that you know of," said Quinlan, drumming his fingers on the desk. "Well, we either have a liquor store here, or a Pruno factory or they're having it delivered. I don't think we need those types of inmates here at Fremont. Wouldn't you agree, Mr. Powell?"

"Definitely, sir," said Powell. "Most certainly."

"We were unable," said Hebner, "to get sufficient evidence to…"

"Hang the evidence," said Quinlan, slamming his hand down on the desk. "I don't care about the evidence. Those men should have been in Solitary as soon as you found out who they were. As an example, if nothing else. They were in all probability making Pruno right under your noses. Now I want those men out of here. I'll sign the transfer papers; just put them on my desk. Find a reason. Any reason. Be creative. That's part of your job. If they're guilty, get rid of them. This is not old John Alexander behind the desk now. This is Robert Quinlan. The new posse is shaping up and we're about to run some bad hombres out of town…" He paused to chuckle. "If you're doing your job, you'll find that I'll back you a hundred percent. I want those men in Folsom by next week. Understand?"

"Yessir!"

"Good. The records also indicate numerous incidents without proper disposition. Numerous. A certain inmate by the name of Voodoo keeps turning up. Just who in the hell is Voodoo?"

"That's inmate Jefferson," said Hebner. "George Jefferson."

"Might I suggest that future reports indicate this Jefferson by full name and A number. We don't need all this...jigaboo stuff."

He glanced quickly at Powell, who continued to stare at Quinlan without changing expression.

"What do we know about the Vargas killing?" said Quinlan.

"No leads yet," said Hebner.

"There was no next of kin?"

"No."

Quinlan leaned forward and put his elbows on the desk.

"Well, don't waste too much time on the investigation. Finding convicts who are making Pruno to the detriment of everyone here is one thing. But finding convicts who kill other convicts is not high on my priority list. We have a hundred and two men in this institution who have been convicted of murder, and God knows how many others who were just never convicted. I view this as a process of natural selection more than anything else. Survival of the fittest. We are not dealing with future teachers and doctors here. This is more like pure genetics at work. A Darwinian world, if you will. You're familiar with Darwin? Origin of the Species?"

"Of course," said Hebner.

Powell had a dazed expression on his face.

"So unless this gets out of hand," said Quinlan, "and becomes a matter of public record, this convicts-killing-other-convicts thing, we won't waste a lot of manpower trying to solve what is essentially an unsolvable crime...and may not be a crime at all. I mean in the grand scheme of things. Of nature."

Quinlan returned to the Incident Report.

"There is one truly troublesome report here about an inmate striking an officer. The report indicates some gobbledegook about the officer provoking the inmate. How does an officer provoke an inmate? Think about that for a minute. An officer provoking an inmate? Simply not possible. And the disposition? Thirty days in the Hole. Thirty days? Not even a slap on the wrist...I'll see that man in hell for striking one of my officers. Discipline, gentlemen. Discipline."

He cleared his throat and straightened his tie.

"Powell, your position here is somewhat unique. You are one of the few colored officers to have attained the rank of lieutenant. Very commendable. A credit to your race, as the saying goes. And other than a few minor incidents, your record has been excellent."

"Thank you, sir."

"Now your...color may be of some advantage here," said Quinlan, "gaining the confidence of the Negro inmate. Infiltrating, so to speak, to obtain information. I would like you to make that your special bailiwick, establishing a communications network. Finding ways to..."

"Snitches, sir?" said Powell, attempting to indicate his grasp of the concept.

Quinlan frowned.

"That's a convict word, Powell. Snitch. We don't need that word here. I am speaking of a communications network to gather useful information."

"Of course," said Powell, looking at the floor.

"For your part, Hebner, I would hope that disciplinary measures would become more...stringent. One-fifteens and one-twenty-eights haven't gone out of style for some reason, have they? You might inform your subordinates of that fact. The indeterminate sentence works in our favor in those areas. We hold the keys, gentlemen. The ship is ours. Let us not relinquish control."

He stood up to terminate the meeting.

"I have every confidence in you two men. We hold the high ground; let's keep it that way. Together, I believe we can make Fremont a prison that the people of the state of California can be proud of...That will be all for today."

Quinlan made brief notes on the meeting and then dialed his home number. His wife answered.

"Hi, Lil," said Quinlan.

"Hi, Bob."

"Listen hon, don't hold dinner for me tonight. I'm more than likely going to be held up in that six o'clock meeting. You know, they always run long."

"Oh, Bob. . ."

"I know, I know...and I'm sorry, but..."

"It's okay," she said. "I don't mean to complain. And I know it's rough getting things started on a new job."

"Just takes time," he said. "Don't wait up. No telling how long this thing'll last."

"Okay. Love you."

"Love you, too," he said.

He broke the connection with his index finger, waited a moment, then dialed another number.

"Lambert Lighting," said a breathy female voice.

"Julie?"

"Spea-king."

"This is Adam. . ."

"Eh. . .Mr. Lambert is not in right now, sir."

"I see. Can't talk, eh?"

"That's correct, sir," said Julie. "Would you like to leave a message?"

"How about dinner tonight?"

". . .I think that can be arranged."

"Six o'clock? The usual place?"

"That will be fine, sir. I'll inform Mr. Lambert."

"Good," said Quinlan. ". . .Mister Dinky is ready for action."

"And so is Miss Muffin."

She giggled and hung up.

He was smiling as he set the phone down. He took a deep breath and flicked the intercom on.

"Call records and get me the file on inmate Jefferson," he said.

"There are eleven Jeffersons here, sir," said the inmate clerk. He appeared to be familiar with the request.

"George," said Quinlan. "George Jefferson."

"There are three George Jeffersons...You mean Voodoo?"

"I-mean-George-Jefferson," he said evenly.

"I'll have the files sent right down."

"And also Leonard. Dave Leonard. How many of those we have?"

"Only one Dave Leonard."

"Thank you," he said dryly.

"Anytime. . . sir."

Preacher continued his tireless crusade.

*I, who am also your brother and companion in tribulation, heard a great voice as from a trumpet, saying, I am the Alpha and the Omega. I am Quinlan, ruler of all. What thou seest, write in a book. . .*

# CHAPTER 9

The main corridor in the Guidance Center was fifty feet wide and four stories high. The first thing Stan noticed was the noise; harsh and strident, it ricocheted off the walls and seemed to come from everywhere—the sharp metallic clanging of cell doors opening and closing, the dull thud of Santa Rosa hightop boots pounding on the concrete floor, the loud voices vying for attention. He stopped and tried to get his bearings.

His cell assignment was in Palm Hall. He had no idea where it was and he was afraid to ask anyone. Convicts leaning against the far wall seemed to be staring at him, sizing him up. He thought he saw Toasty out of the corner of his eye, but he dared not look. He slung the small cloth sack over his shoulder and started walking, trying to appear casual, to act as if he had done this before, as if he knew exactly where Palm Hall was. But he was clumsy in his new ill-fitting shoes and baggy pants, and he knew his long hair marked him as a Fish, a newcomer. He did not look in the direction of the catcalls and whistles; perhaps they were not meant for him. He looked at the floor and kept walking, his heart pounding in his ears.

He saw PALM HALL stenciled on the wall above a steel door near the end of the long corridor. He entered, walked quickly up the steel stairway to the third tier and found his assigned cell. The door to 324 was open; he went in and put his bedding on the bottom bunk, grateful that there was no bedding on the top bunk.

A few minutes later a buzzer sounded and soon the tier was filled with convicts returning to their cells for noon count. Several glanced in his cell. Only one stopped.

"Hey, boy," he said softly.

Stan didn't look up, but it didn't sound like Toasty. The man moved on a few moments later.

"If you touch me I'll kill you," Stan said under his breath. "I'll stick a knife in your fucking heart. Swear to God." Just saying it made him feel better.

The cell doors rattled noisily for a few seconds before they began to slam closed. The eerie silence that followed the last loud claaaaang was interrupted by the flushing of a solitary toilet and the soft squeak of Sergeant Frankel's crepe soled shoes as he padded swiftly along the tiers, stabbing a stubby pencil at each convict, tracking the count with a rotary motion of his rubbery lips. Somewhere, someone was crying. Stan gripped the bars and stared out at the shattered windows in the Palm Hall wall.

**...Time...**
*...I have no choice but to sentence you as the law proscribes....*

In an unremembered moment, the course of his life had changed forever. In front of him, a tunnel of time that stretched endlessly into a future without hope. There would be no going back. Five to life... Five years to life. How long is forever? Like the distance between earth and the nearest star, the notion was beyond him; he could not fathom the idea of spending that much time in prison. Each of the days since his arrest had seemed interminable, filled with fear, apprehension and dread. What would several thousand of those days be like? How would he possibly endure?

He remembered the line from the Rhubiyat...The moving finger writes, and having writ, moves on...And on and on. Forget it, he told himself. It's done. But he couldn't forget it. One day he was Stanley Smith, ex-altar boy, dutiful son, scholar, a student of exceptional promise, engineering graduate cum laude, husband of the lovely Bonnie Aldridge Smith. Next day he was Stan Smith, Cold Blooded Murderer...Nor all your piety and wit can lure it back to cancel half a line, nor all your tears wash out a word of it...

**... Tiiiiiiiiiiiiiiiiiiiiime...**
*Till death do us part...*
*... I hate you, Stan Smith, and I hope you die...*

He blinked away the tears and stood dutifully at the bars as Sergeant Frankel made his rounds. He was a number now: A83534. How ironic, he thought. He'd always been good at numbers; now he was one.

It was a warm winter with little rain. Nearly every afternoon there was a softball game on the small patch of grass behind the main cellblock. Stan watched, but he was careful to find a different vantage point every few innings. It seemed important to keep moving, not to present a stationary target. Sometimes fights broke out and Officer Farnsworth in the West gun tower fired off a few rounds from his thirty-caliber carbine. He enjoyed that a great deal, seeing how close he could come to the combatants without actually hitting them, though he had on occasion inflicted a flesh wound when his aim was a little off. Shattered Marvin Johnson's ankle last year, but mostly there were flesh wounds. Then he got after them with his bullhorn.

"You boys cut that out, heah?"

He loved using the bullhorn; it gave him a sense of power. What with the carbine and the bullhorn, he got people's attention. He liked that; he thought attention was the same thing as respect. He looked like a chipmunk, but nobody laughed at him when he had his carbine and his bullhorn and all his police gear. No siree. Officer Farnsworth was from Russellville, Arkansas. His grandest dream was to shoot him a nigger someday. Kill one. Nice and legal. It was something he thought about often.

Stan watched the games, the convicts, the cops, everything. Knowledge is power, he told himself. Knowledge is safety. If I know enough I'll be okay. But he wasn't sure if it was true. He kept moving and watching, moving and watching, learning as he went, filing events and scenes as if it were a movie, wondering what Bogart or Cagney or Edward G. Robinson would do. Surely Brando would know. Each morning he got up and constructed the day in his head. Sometimes it read like a movie script:

*Smith moves across the Yard with that powerful stride.*
*His expression is hard, determined; he gives no indica-*

*tion of his destination. The men on the Yard move out of
his way; Smith is not a man to be taken lightly. . .*

After breakfast he walked from Palm Hall to the gym to the main
corridor to the Yard (though he varied the routine slightly every few
days). Then two or three turns around the Yard, hands in his pockets,
denim jacket collar turned up against an imaginary wind, practicing
his icy stare. An occasional grunt sufficed as a greeting, though he
talked to no one. He was the loner, always moving, always watching,
always afraid. He thought that people might be following him. He
devised elaborate schemes to double back and expose them, though
he had no idea what he would do if he actually discovered that
someone was following him.

He made up stories about some of the men he saw, imagined
himself involved with them in bank heists, jewel robberies, high
speed chases, all-night celebrations of life when manhood was challenged and never found wanting. Just call me Duke, he said to his
imaginary gang of international jewel thieves. And they did.

During the empty hours of the night, he dredged from the musty
cellar of his past memories filled with regrets, old wounds that had
never healed, things he had not thought about in years. One of his
earliest memories (he couldn't have been much older than three or
four), vague and bewildering, was of a little brother who appeared
briefly in his life and then vanished. In later years Stan would wonder
if he had just dreamed it. His mother assured him that he never had
a little brother…Wouldn't we tell you if you did?…Yet he was often
haunted by a small pink face that always seemed to be crying. And
something (or someone?) that was carried from the house one night
wrapped in butcher paper, smelling of blood.

He remembered when he had to shoot the family dog because
the dog had distemper and his father had decided that the best thing
to do (the most-humane-thing, his father had assured him) was to
kill the dog so it wouldn't suffer. It's the best thing, his father had
said. Would you want to suffer if you were sick from some incur-
able disease? And stop crying, for chrissakes. Grow up. You're nine
years old now—it's just a dog. He made it sound like a minor event.
But it wasn't; Stan knew that much. Every time he thought of that

Cocker Spaniel looking back at him with those sad eyes just before he pulled the trigger, he remembered how sick he felt inside. But he pulled the trigger anyway. He wanted to be grown up more than he wanted to spare the dog. He wanted to be grown up, to be Real, more than anything. He wanted to be a man, whatever that was. He thought later that his father would have killed the dog anyway, so what difference did it make? But it was later when he thought about it—not then. And it did make a difference.

He remembered the day in grade school when he got into a fight with someone who said his mother looked like an ugly old toad. It was Thomas Keneally. Fat Pig Thomas Keneally, who he hated with all his heart. He took a swing at him but all he got for his troubles was a bloody nose, a split lip and the humiliation of getting punched around in front of half the school who had gathered to watch. Fat Pig Keneally sat on his chest and made him say, I give up, Mr. Keneally five times before he let him get up. He hated it but he did it anyway; he thought he was going to die because he couldn't breathe. And then, feeling that he had betrayed a sacred trust of some kind, he cried. That was the worst part. He cried in front of everyone. (He couldn't imagine any of his movie heroes crying.) If he'd been told once, he'd been told a hundred times…Big boys don't cry.

His solace, his comfort, he found in books. Hiding in the thick stand of bamboo back by the chicken house, he escaped into the wonderful world of Tarzan, or Pinocchio, or Winnie the Pooh. He spent hours traveling the Hundred Acre Wood with Winnie (Sing Ho! for the life of a Bear!) and Tigger and Piglet and Eeyore and the rest of the gang.

But it was Pinocchio that he recognized as a kindred soul, always getting into trouble no matter how hard he tried to be good (despite his best intentions and the efforts of his conscience, Jiminy Cricket). All Pinocchio ever wanted to be was a Real Boy, but he was always running into people like Stromboli, or J.Worthington Foulfellow, or Lampwick who lured him to places where bad things happened. The Blue Fairy told him that if he would be brave, truthful and unselfish, someday he could be a Real Boy. Stan didn't know if his chances of becoming Real were all that good. Considering how things were.

Recent memories were no better. Bonnie paraded naked in his head, mocking and taunting, opening and closing her thighs like butterfly wings, luring him to despair. Put it right here, Wimpy. What there is of it...After lights out, he masturbated until he was exhausted. Every time he came into that soiled sock, the ghost of Father Samuels' florid face rose like a hunter's moon in the night-time sky to remind him that with each impure thought, with each impure act he was driving nails into the hands and feet of Sweet Jesus, who loved us so much that He died for our sins. For us. All of us. Imagine. Sweet Blessed Jesus...

> *...O Lord I am not worthy, that Thou should come to me...*

He, young Stanley Smith, hammer in one hand, penis in the other, was standing by the cross, driving nails into the body of his Redeemer who loved everyone. Still...consumed by the guilt that was his relentless shadow, he prayed for forgiveness even as he waited impatiently for the next erection that he believed would somehow lift him out of the ashes of despair. Just once more. Peace was just a few strokes away. Or a shot of whiskey away. A few pills perhaps. It never worked. The promise was always empty, the hope always hollow and unfulfilled. But it never stopped him from trying. Just once more. Always just once more. This time it'll be different. It was that way with everything. Drinking, sex, drugs, Hershey Bars, gambling, everything. Even books; somewhere, in a musty tome on a back shelf in a tiny bookstore he was sure he would find The Answer (even though he remained unsure of the actual Question). He always thought that someone would come along and fix him. Maybe even something. A book. A bauble. A boxcar. A babe. Fill that empty place inside. Stamp his ticket. Make him okay. Set him free. Bonnie did for a while, but of course it didn't last. He should have known. Nothing ever did. Ever lasted. Not the Heaven Hill Straight Kentucky Bourbon. Not the drugs. Not anything. Not for long. But he never stopped looking. Was else could he do?

During the long nights he pondered his plight. Like a rat in a maze he explored the possibilities but found no solutions, no exit doors, not a glimmer of light. He knew it was only a matter of time before someone discovered his presence and took advantage of him. He had seen it. Other people walking the Yard seemed to know one another; he didn't know anyone. He was alone. He prayed for guidance, something he hadn't done in years. He apologized to God for his long absence from church, his various obsessions, his bad behavior, his propensity to indulge in all things sinful. He promised to do better, to sin no more, to try and pray, to never even look at his penis unless it was absolutely necessary. But even as he swore fidelity to high-minded principles, he was already reaching for the same old handy solution. He listened for the still small voice of the divine, but all he heard were the clanging of cell doors, the loud voices of other convicts and the abrasive whine of Sergeant Frankel's early morning wake up chant:

> . . .*Wakey, wakey, wakey, convicts. Time to drop those cocks and grab those socks. Time to get up and do some more time, time, time.* . . .

Frankel traversed each tier on his morning rounds, rattling the bars with his night stick like a truant boy past a picket fence. Annoying everyone.

Soon the tests began. He took the Minnesota Multiphasic Personality Inventory in a room full of other convicts, some who never bothered putting pencil to paper, preferring to sleep through the hour.

He had an interview with a psychiatrist who wanted to know if he felt bad about what he had done. (Yes, he lied. If I did what they say I did, I really feel terrible.) How would he have handled the situation differently? (He said he would have confronted Mr. Loughlin and suggested constructive dialog. But in his heart of hearts, he knew that was a lie.) Would he describe himself as a happy person? (...Mostly, he hedged.) Had he ever thought about killing anyone before? Did he like sex? Did he think about having sex with other men? Did he masturbate? How often? Had he ever thought about having sex with animals? Did he have trouble urinating...He fielded the questions as deftly as possible, supplying answers that seemed appropriate, being vague when he was unsure.

When the questioning was over, he told Doctor Bloom that he thought there might be some people following him, intent upon doing him harm...What kind of harm, Mr. Smith?...Stan said he thought bodily harm of some sort...Bodily harm?...Yeah. You know. Bodily harm...You think someone might try to violate you? Take advantage of you sexually?...I've seen it happen, sir. Twice now...Is that so?... Twice...And how does that make you feel when you see things like that?...Makes me crazy...Crazy?...Well, not really crazy, but...fearful I guess...You often think people are out to get you, Mr. Smith? Out to do you harm? Injure you?...Dr. Bloom had wild red hair and a beard more gray than red. He even had hair sprouting out of his ears. He talked without ever looking up from the pad he was writing on...No, said Stan. Just since I've been here...I see. Well, we'll talk again, Mr. Smith. Explore this in more detail. Your fears and so forth. Unfortunately, our time is up now...What if those people catch me and hurt me? ...Unfortunately, our time is up now...

Medical and dental exams were cursory. The dentist who examined his teeth reeked of alcohol, made notations about several cavities, then painted his gums with an evil-tasting purple substance. He was so short he had to use a Johnny Step to work on his patients. The medical doctor took his blood pressure, checked his pulse and pronounced him fit.

Thanksgiving passed without notice. Christmas approached with little fanfare, though there were large mesh stockings filled with soft oranges and hard candy, thanks to the Salvation Army. Father Zelinski said Catholic mass in a small classroom off the main corridor, unaware that someone was getting a blow job in the back row. Stan attended, somehow comforted by the familiarity of it, though he had not been in years. He repeated the Latin phrases to himself and asked God to deliver him from this fucking valley of tears.

Protestant services were held in the gymnasium and much better attended. Reverend Daniger extolled the virtues of Je-sus and told them that Je-sus loved them no matter what they'd done. Je-sus, he assured them, was a guy you could depend on, a guy you wanted at your back when the action came down. A stand up guy, this Je-sus. He told them that they could be happy even during these difficult times, knowing that Je-sus loved them, one and all. There was even a song about it.

There were bland, sectarian words over the P.A. system by Warden Spellman who thought it was his duty to mark the occasion in some manner. A small group of Black Muslims attempted to hold services, but were told it was against regulations because the California Department of Corrections did not recognize Black Muslims as a valid religious organization.

"Uppity niggahs," said Officer Farnsworth.

"Yeah," said Officer Kline.

"Next thing you know they'll want some bones to stick in they noses."

"Yeah."

". . .And some drums. Sheee-it. Won't be no end to it."

Visiting was conducted as usual, via telephone, through impersonal panes of bulletproof glass. Dan McCreedy unzipped his wrinkled denims and briefly exposed himself to his child bride, Crystal. She pressed her face against the glass, her eyes big as plums. He tried to work up a decent erection, but was escorted roughly out of sight before it came to much. Crystal stayed and licked the glass for a few moments before she grabbed her purse and hurried away.

Mrs. Smith came to visit on Christmas day. She wore her blue pillbox hat and a spidery veil that clung to her thick pancake makeup. A small gold crucifix glistened on the collar of her tweed jacket. Her face was heavily powdered, her lips Kabuki red. It was as if she had come in disguise, not wanting anyone to know who she was. When she talked, the powder flaked off her face onto the jacket. Gravity seemed to be taking its toll, pulling unevenly at her face. She tried to be cheerful.

"Dad's getting better," she offered.

"That's good."

"You know he was very sick…Very."

"I know," said Stan.

"He'll be coming home soon."

"They kept him a long time."

"He had…other problems."

"Oh." He did not ask what they were and she did not volunteer the information.

"Yes. But Dr. Lerner says he'll be fine. He expects a complete recovery. He has to lose weight, though. Your father. You remember. We always told him."

"Yeah."

Carl Smith packed two hundred and fifty pounds on a five-foot-eight-inch frame. He could lift Stan with one hand.

"And smo-king…" She wagged her finger from side to side like a metronome. "No smo-king. Dr. Lerner was very firm with your father."

"Good. No smoking."

"…How is it, Stanley? In here?"

"Oh…Okay. It's okay."

"Do they…Is the food good?"

"It's not home cooking." He tried to smile.

"And they don't…they don't abuse you?" A sudden frown sent an avalanche of powder cascading through the veil.

"…No."

"You're…safe?"

He nodded that he was, though he was quite sure he wasn't. A week earlier he had witnessed someone being raped as he walked near the gymnasium showers. At first he didn't realize what it was, what was actually happening. There were four Negroes and one white. They had him bent over while one of the Negroes appeared to be entering him from the rear. The white guy made little chirpy noises and struggled a bit, but it wasn't much of a contest. He was about Stan's size.

Stan watched, unable to turn away.

"Get on, muffuckah," said a lookout stationed near the entrance to the showers.

Stan continued to stare.

"Get on, fool, or you be next."

The lookout took a step forward. Stan turned and hurried away.

They ran out of things to say long before the fifteen minutes were up. Their eyes met several times, but neither was able to hold the gaze. She told him that Toby the Smelly Sheep Dog missed his weekend visits.

"Smelly as ever," she said, forcing a smile.

He was relieved when the bell sounded to end the visit. He promised to write. She vowed to make a Novena to St. Jude.

"He'll help," she said, though there was scant evidence that he ever had. "I love you, Stanley. . . .."

She blew him a kiss through the veil; tears had already begun to etch dark furrows in the thick white powder that covered her cheeks. She latched the telephone on the wall cradle and scurried away sobbing into her Kleenex.

"...I love you, too," he said into the dead phone.

It didn't seem to mean anything, saying he loved her. He didn't really know if he did or not, and he didn't know how to find out. When he thought about it, he didn't know if he loved anyone. Had ever loved anyone. Even Bonnie.

# CHAPTER 10

Voodoo was sleek as an otter; even his head was shaved. He jumped off the top bunk and landed lightly on the balls of his feet. He stripped off his pants, wrapped a towel around his waist, walked out of his cell and headed toward the showers at the end of the tier.

Billy 2X stopped mopping the floor long enough to greet his friend with an elaborate handshake. Since the death of Malcolm X it had become the custom among the Muslims to adopt X as a surname. A plethora of names like Leroy and Willie and Earl led to aberrations such as Leroy 5X or Earl 3X. More than one battle was fought about which Earl or Leroy or Willie got the lowest number.

"As-Salaam Aliakum," said Billy.

"Wa-Aliakum Salaam," said Voodoo.

"Voodoo."

"Does slavery make us brothers?" said Voodoo. "Does it bind us together?"

Billy nodded and kept mopping.

"Is the time at hand?" he said.

"Allah will decide," said Voodoo.

"The brothers are ready."

"I know," said Voodoo. "They must remain so."

"They will. . ."

Voodoo looked both ways on the tier.

"Tyrone has betrayed us," he said quietly.

Billy kept his eyes on the mop.

"He has gone to the pigs with names," said Voodoo. "He must pay for what he has done."

Billy nodded without speaking. He understood what had to be done.

Voodoo showered, returned to his cell, donned his kitchen whites and headed for the Officer's Mess. He passed quickly through the system of locks and checkpoints; everybody knew Voodoo. He exchanged the Muslim handshake with the man he relieved at the Officer's Mess and began to make preparations for the evening meal.

First thing he did was discard the leftover mashed potatoes and make a new batch with Redispud and water. When he had whipped the chemical mixture into high froth, he took the metal insert into the storeroom, unzipped his fly, whipped himself up and ejaculated into the mound of spuds. Then he finished fluffing the potatoes, carried the insert back to the steam table and dropped it into the proper slot. Some nice protein for the Pigs, he said to himself.

He stood behind the counter and smiled; he had nice white teeth. With his cook's hat on, he looked a little like Uncle Ben on the Uncle Ben's Rice box. But the innocent smile masked a mind that worked with savage efficiency. Voodoo was a survivor, born and raised on the streets of Watts, schooled in the Projects, quiet and unassuming when it suited him, ruthless for the same reason. The streets had taught him well. He learned long ago that no one was going to give him anything just because he smiled and said please. Not love. Not money. Not respect. Not power. Nothing. What he wanted, he would have to take.

Now, in the heart of darkness, he waited for the proper time. So much depended on striking when the time was right. Malcolm X was gone, but he knew Allah would raise up others to take his place. The time would come, was already approaching, when the forces of righteousness would rise up against the oppressor. The black man had lived in slavery long enough.

Whitey would falter. It had to happen. The white man's soft underbelly would be exposed. History would record the moment and destiny would be his. The racist empire would begin to crumble and Voodoo would be there, riding the crest of blood. Voodoo, Lord of the night, Son of the Great Serpent—Voodoo would be there. And he would show no mercy.

"How's that chicken fried steak tonight?" said Officer Cole.

"Fine, Mr. Cole. Old southern recipe from down your way … Tuscaloosa?"

"Just up the road. Cottondale."

"Mashed potatoes and home-made gravy," said Voodoo.

"Sounds good to me, Jefferson," said Officer Cole, his chubby smile squeezing his eyes into narrow slits.

Voodoo returned the smile and straightened his hat. It tickled him that white folks were eating black sperm.

"Comin' right up, Boss," he said, dropping a healthy spoonful of mashed potatoes next to the chicken fried steak.

And Voodoo would be there when the time was right. He would show no mercy. He would plunge the dagger deep into America's evil heart, then rip open her soft underbelly and bathe in her blood, sacrifice his own life if necessary. For all the years of oppression and pain, for all the humiliations, Whitey would pay. Voodoo would see to it.

# CHAPTER 11

In a few weeks Stan got his assignment to Fremont. It was not unexpected; he had been told that murder was a crime that dramatically increased his chances of being sent there. There were no more appointments to see Dr. Bloom. Or anybody else…We'll talk again. Explore this in more detail…It didn't seem likely. Not then. Not ever.

They left early for the five-hour trip to Fremont; up at four thirty, a hurried cold cereal breakfast, into his traveling whites, on the bus and headed out by 6 o'clock. Chained to his metal belt and shackled to the floor of the bus with leg irons, it was all he could do to sit quietly and try not to scream. He didn't know if the images that came to mind were real memories of actual events or just fantasies…He saw himself bound hand and foot in a dark closet. Rags were being stuffed into his mouth; smelly, foul-tasting paint rags. He gagged and choked but was powerless to stop whoever was doing it. The more he struggled, the worse it got. Finally, just as he was about to lose consciousness, just before he knew he was going to suffocate and die, someone pulled him out of the closet and took the rags out of his mouth. Stan was sobbing hysterically, saying he was sorry, that he'd never do it again, though he didn't know what he was sorry for nor any idea what he had done…Mea culpa, mea maxima culpa…Our Father, who art in Heaven…

Highway 99 was four lanes of concrete, the oldest of California's north-south arteries. Huge oleanders, some as tall as the bus, bloomed in the spacious median that separated the four lanes. He caught occasional glimpses of convertibles, tops down, skirts up, as the bus sped past in the fast lane. Each passing brought forth a chorus of comments and the rattling of chains.

Even after the long bus ride and the processing at Fremont, it was still daylight when Stan arrived at South Block with his bedding. He handed the three-by-five card to the guard on duty.

"Name's Wetzle," said the guard, seated on his chair in the guard shack. "Mister Wetzle to you." He had a face like an old paper bag. "You been here before?"

"Here?" said Stan. "…South Block?"

"No, no, prison," he said impatiently.

"No."

"Then how come you decided?" said Wetzle.

"…Decided what?"

"To come to prison."

Stan shifted the bundle of bedding to his left side. He was so tired he could hardly stand.

"…The court decided," he said.

"But you done somethin'," said Wetzle, referring to the three-by-five card. "Murder second," he read. "Murder in the second degree."

Stan looked down the long cellblock corridor.

"You killed somebody," said Wetzle.

"That's what they say."

"And you? Whada you say?"

"…I don't remember."

"Hah!" Wetzle barked. "I doubt that a great deal."

He pushed himself out of the chair, examined the electrical panel on the back wall and pressed a switch. Somewhere, a cell door slid open. He started up the metal stairway and motioned for Stan to follow him. He was puffing noisily by the time he got to the fourth tier.

"That's yours," he said. "Four thirteen. Last guy had it was a nigra fella. Troublemaker. I can spot 'em. Gotta have this, gotta have that. Rights. That's the deal now. Everybody got rights…I ain't no slave. Course he ain't no slave. We don't have slaves no more. It's illegal, slavery. Since Lincoln. He freed the slaves. S'what that was all about. That Civil War thing. Some people just don't ever get the picture…But this guy was trouble. Caught him with some drugs. Shipped him out yesterday. Folsom. He can try breakin' rocks for a change. Give him somethin' to really complain about. Have time to think about his rights when he's poundin' rocks, makin' little ones outta big ones…Man gives up his rights when he comes to prison. Ain't got no rights here. Not a one."

He looked at Stan.

"You got no rights, boy. Remember that. You give 'em up when you did the crime. You belong to the State of California now. When I say jump, you ask how high. You understand?"

"Yeah."

"Nobody else in your cell," said Wetzle. "Not for now. But it won't be long. Them nigras from the riots be here soon. Everything be crowded again…Only thing I expect is you stay outta trouble. I have inspection every morning. Nine o'clock. Cell's gotta be clean. That's why you got a broom." He pointed to the little dollhouse broom in the corner of the cell. "Bunk's gotta be made. Made right. You don't do it right, I have little white slips I leave as reminders. You get three white slips in a month, you get a one-twenty-eight. A write-up. Goes in your jacket. More than three white slips and, bingo…a one-fifteen. Automatic. Don't wanna get too many write-ups. Understand?"

Stan nodded.

"Okay. Everything you need to know's posted by the guard shack. Chow times. Count times. Lockup…Everything. Just do like you're told. We won't have no trouble."

He looked at the three-by-five card.

"How tall are you?" he said.

"…Five foot eight," said Stan.

"I doubt that a great deal," said Wetzle. "More like five-four. Five-five maybe. Pretty small for a guy your size. So you might need a friend someday. And I might need some information. Keep it in mind. We might be of some mutual good to each other."

"I'll…keep that in mind," said Stan.

"Yeah. Do that…Who'dja murder?"

"Oh…Some guy."

"Just some guy, eh? You walkin' down the street and you just shot some guy? Bang…By mistake maybe? An accidental homicide?"

"…I don't remember," said Stan.

"Course not," said Wetzle. "You got a convenience memory. All'a convicts got that. It's like a disease that only convicts get." He laughed, pleased with the description.

Officer Warren Wetzle was a retired Bos'n Mate who made Chief twice before it finally stuck. He had never been a paragon of virtue; he'd done his share of boozing and brawling and woman-izing in port towns from Norfolk to Pearl City. Despite the fact that he was married, he'd been known to lie abed with a well-greased whore. Even got a blow job at a Benny Boy house in Manila, though he never told anyone.

But he realized that there was a basic difference between himself and those who came to inhabit the murky cells in the long west wing of South Block. And though he would have been hard-pressed to actually define what the difference was, he knew it had something to do with basic decency, with being a God-fearing Christian and an American. He was People. All his kinfolk and most everyone he knew were People. The men in the cells were scum. And worse.

The Negroes, he knew from his Baptist upbringing in Bogalusa, were lazy, shiftless, immoral and dangerous, most barely able to hide their contempt for white people in general and white authority figures in particular. Poor examples of human beings. The whites he saw as trash, all of them, refuse taken bodily from the streets to infest his cells in South Block—useless, long-haired hippie trash. A disgrace to the white race; not much better than the nigras.

He felt there was a certain justice in the fact that they were now locked up in his cells; Warren Wetzle's cells in South Block. He made them keep those cells clean. He was inflexible about it. He was quick to write a disciplinary—too many could put a man in the Hole, add some extra Time to an already lengthy sentence. Nobody wanted that. He left little slips of paper on the bunks that weren't made properly. Murderers, rapist, robbers, he didn't care. If you lived in South Block you made your bed, made it right, or you got a write-up. No exceptions. He was known as Wetzle the Weasel, or just plain Weasel. Or worse. All agreed he was a prick.

"Murder, murder, murder," said Wetzle as he walked slowly down the steps toward the guard shack, idly pulling at his pants.

"Mur-der in the second degree …Just some guy, eh? Well, I doubt that a great deal."

Stan was temporarily assigned to the Grounds Crew. He spent his days picking up discarded papers and dumping fifty-gallon drums of garbage. He worked with Flaco and Chewy. Chewy wanted to know what his beef was.

"Murder," said Stan.

"You murder a dude, man?" He seemed skeptical.

"Yeah."

"Gonna do some big time, eh?"

"Five and up." He tossed it off like it was a long weekend.

Chewy looked at Stan and chuckled.

"Stan the Murder Man. You put some dude in the graveside, eh?"

"Yeah."

"Put his lights out for good, eh man? Alright…And what did this dude do, man, to get put in the graveside?"

"He was foolin' with my old lady," said Stan.

"This chingadera was foolin' with your woman?"

"Yeah."

Chewy went into his bob and weave style of walking, jabbing at shadows, moving lightly from side to side, doing his roadwork, planning for the Big Time when he got out. Jesus "Chewy" Gonzales—El Tigre—had never had any legitimate fights on the street because he was never out long enough to get established. It was always something—drugs, assault, burglary, petty things that kept him locked up in the System. A black watch cap pulled low over his eyes gave him a sinister look.

"So you shoot this gringo?" said Chewy. "…Or did you hit him with your purse?"

"Shot him," said Stan.

"Put some bullets in him, eh?"

"Yeah."

"Put some poison lead in this dude. Alright," said Chewy.

"Al-right," said Flaco.

Chewy reached out and touched Stan's cheek.

"It's too bad, man," he said.

"…What is?" said Stan.

"You got a long time to do, man. And you too pretty. Too little and too pretty. Somebody, maybe a whole bunch of somebodys, gonna make a jailhouse old lady outta you."

"Shit," said Stan.

His hands were shaking as he tried to light his cigarette.

Chewy laughed quietly.

"Come on, Murder man," he said. "We gonna go dump some trash."

When the Grounds Crew got off at three, Stan returned to South Block to shower early. He thought it was an advantage, getting there before the others, showering early. He moved cautiously in the cellblock, observing those around him, thinking that if he was careful no harm would come to him. But there was no way he could have prepared for what happened.

# CHAPTER 12

Dave Leonard waited until the week after Superintendent Alexander's retirement before he had the new copier delivered to the Watch Commander's Office. He thought that with all the confusion following the change of command, no one would think to question it. And if anyone did ask, there was the requisition, in quadruplicate, bearing the apparently authentic signature of John Alexander. Everything legal and above board, except for the fact that Alexander never saw the requisition; his name had been signed by one of the best forgers the State of California had ever produced.

Anyone who knew John Alexander would have known that he would never have spent three thousand dollars on a new copier. He was Budget Conscious. When the State food budget was targeted at eighty-six cents a day per convict, he was feeding his men for sixty-three cents. Feeding them damn well, he declared, a conclusion not shared by the convicts. He was the only Warden in the State who consistently came in under budget. They loved him in Sacramento.

For years an old drum copier in the Watch Commander's Office had been used to print the Movement Sheet and other officially sanctioned memoranda. It was a cumbersome, hand-cranked device that leaked ink and often produced smudged, unreadable copies...And considering what Leonard used it for, too slow and much too visible.

Each week during football season he made out a schedule of college and pro games. Early Monday morning, even as the odd-smakers in Las Vegas were about their business, Leonard was figuring the Betting Line, the Spread, cutting the stencil and running off the first few copies in the Watch Commander's Office. Other copies were later handwritten and distributed by runners. After that, the master and the original copies were destroyed. He kept only a coded record, hen scratches to the uninitiated.

The procedure demanded considerable skill and extreme alertness during the copying phase, cranking the old drum copier with the left hand (the incriminating sheets popped out, face up, on the small exposed tray) while holding in the right hand several recent memos to be dropped on the telltale stack should anyone approach.

Leonard had gone through the Xerox catalog, picked the one he wanted and had Art Falls, a lifer with a key position in Purchasing, order it for him. Art took care of everything—ordering, getting the proper forms, signature, everything. In return he received a full canteen draw of fifteen dollars a month for six months, a king's ransom to a man who had been in prison for twelve years, subsisting mainly on money earned as a medical guinea pig—Pain Tolerance Studies, Bubonic Plague Immunization Study, Scurvy Experiments. All because he killed his daughter. Just a tiny thing and he hadn't meant to kill her. Not really kill her. Discipline was more what he had in mind. He would admit to accidentally dropping her down the stairs in his apartment, an account that lost some credibility when the prosecution pointed out that he lived in a single story apartment building. But after his wife left him, little Amanda Falls wouldn't stop crying. He tried everything. Then there were the cigarette burns; that certainly didn't help his case either. Amanda Falls, pretty as a picture. She looked just like her mother.

So Art got his canteen draw and Leonard got his copier, though he didn't really need it. Could have done the whole thing by hand. Actually did it that way at first. Took a little time, but he had plenty of that. But, after awhile, there was no sense of accomplishment, no sense of beating the system. It was almost too easy. He enjoyed living on the edge where the odds were slim and the call could go either way. That was what made the world go round for Dave Leonard. There was a certain challenge to using the mimeograph machine in the Watch Commander's Office to run an illegal football pool. Their copier, their paper, their prison; it was as if they were subsidizing his efforts. That appealed to him. But eventually he got bored with it. In the end he always got bored.

"The thrill is gone," he said to Greek.

Greek smiled. He knew about things like that.

"Tell me about it," he said.

That was when Leonard started wondering if he could possibly get away with ordering a new Xerox copier. So he did that. And he got away with it. When it first arrived, custodial personnel acted like it was Christmas, oooh-ing and aaah-ing over the shiny gray machine with the multicolored knobs, fascinated by the red nixie tubes that indicated the number of copies run. Superintendent Quinlan was reserved about the acquisition (silently cursing Alexander), but Captain Greer insisted on having his picture taken next to it for inclusion in the next issue of the California State Employee News. He looked like he was standing next to a hunting trophy. All that was missing was the rifle.

There was never enough of anything for Dave Leonard. At least not for long. Yet he was generous to a fault. And if, as some said, he bought his friends, he paid them very well. What he demanded in return was absolute loyalty. It could be dangerous to cross him.

When they took away his freedom, the most natural thing in the world was to rebuild his empire in prison. He had always known that everyone and everything was for sale; all he had to do was find the right price. Simple arithmetic. Despite the expense of a long trial, he still had money. And connections—people he had set up in business who had prospered, who were loyal, people who would literally do anything for him.

He was born in New Jersey (the year before Lucky Lindy flew the Atlantic his mother always said when trying to remember his age), Depression poor, the oldest of three boys. He learned quickly that money was food, money was power, money was what made the engine go, what made everything go, and he made a conscious decision to get as much of it as he could. He was surprised to discover how easy it was. He made himself useful to people who had what he wanted. Physically imposing when he was still young, he went from being a union enforcer to more subtle forms of intimidation and finally to California where, thanks to some underworld connections, he established his gambling interests in Cabazon and eventually set up Garner Investments as a front company.

Prison guards making five hundred dollars a month were not immune to bribes. They merely had to be chosen with care. In the parlance of the Yard, they were Mules. Leonard had a knack for finding the greed in people. One of the men he picked was Jules Reiner, a black man burdened with a limited income and an insatiable appetite for the finer things in life. One of his jobs was to carry correspondence between Leonard and his associates on the street (bypassing the prison censors) and to funnel out the gambling money collected on the Yard. Though he often complained, Jules was well paid for what he did and gladly accepted the role. Perhaps if he had known what he would eventually be asked to do, he might never have started. At least that's what he said to himself later, but by then it was too late.

# CHAPTER 13

Willy and Buck had been watching the skinny white boy ever since he drove up a few weeks before. Willy talked it up with Pokey Brown. They thought they might need a third to get it done.

"Hey, Pokey, you wanna get some stuff?" said Willy.

"…What kinda stuff?"

Pokey was always suspicious. Willy told him so.

"Stuff is stuff, man. You know."

Pokey stuck to his guns.

"What kinda stuff?"

"White boy stuff," said Buck. "We be takin' him to school."

Pokey's smile revealed pink and purple gums and a few random teeth.

"But maybe you too old to get it goin'," said Buck. "Too old for any kinda stuff."

Pokey's smile faded.

"Jive-ass nigger," he said.

Pokey Brown was forty-nine years old; old for prison. His nose was flat, always runny, his breathing labored, his eyes cloudy with cataracts. He had been crowned middleweight champ at San Quentin in 1945, but it was all a joke—they let him win. Pokey couldn't fight his way out of a beauty parlor; everybody knew that but Pokey. He was the Prince of Fools. They called him the Brown Bomber. Pokey, the Brown Bomber. He got out on the streets and told everybody he was the middleweight champ at Q. He was proud of that. But then people started calling him out to see how tough he was. They spread his nose all over his face, knocked some teeth out, put some scars around his eyes. He never did learn how to fight. But he got even; he learned how to do that. Got even with everybody. He learned how to creep on people, come up behind them and do some real damage with a pipe or a tire iron. He liked that a lot better. It took awhile, but he got even. With everybody.

"Jive-ass nigger," he repeated. "You don' worry about Pokey Brown bein' too old."

His mind surrounded the idea of the skinny white boy; only the notion of violence partially roused him. He stared off into space for a while.

"Bring him on," he said finally.

"We goin' to his house," said Willy.

"...Where at?"

"Up on fo'h...He comes in early."

"...When we goin'?"

"Soon," said Buck.

Pokey wiped his nose with the back of his hand. He looked from Willy to Buck and back to Willy; his eyes were so bad he could hardly make out their faces.

"You need me, eh?" said Pokey. "Need the old man?"

"Better with three," said Willy. "Easier."

Pokey smiled.

"I be in my house," he said. "You come get me when school fixin' to start. I bring my shiv. . ."

He slapped his knee and cackled. "Maybe cut me some white meat. . ."

Preacher looked like a scarecrow standing in the Yard. The foot traffic flowed aimlessly around him like water past a rock in a river.

> *...I look and behold a pale horse*, he said, *and on him sat Death, and Hell followed after.*
> *And power was given unto them over the fourth part of the earth to kill with the sword,*
> *and with hunger and with death...A-fucking-men* ...

# CHAPTER 14

Greek Koumantakis had a round, innocent face. Brought up in San Pedro among the hard drinking Greek and Slav fishermen, he had been doing life on the installment plan ever since his first teenage bust for rolling sailors coming out of Shanghai Reds during the War Years. A long-suffering wife, a son (Rocky), and a daughter (Pricilla) shared his brief paroles, but now Ellen was making noises about wanting a divorce, Rocky was doing drugs and Ellen acted like it was all Greek's fault.

He was the Captain's clerk, often seen shuffling behind Captain Greer (who bore an uncanny resemblance to Teddy Roosevelt), steno pad in hand, ready to record an urgent memo. Captain Greer loved writing memos; he prowled the Yard in search of things that needed attention. He was especially fond of writing memos to Shop Superintendent Bennet about the lack of cleanliness in the Shop Area. The Barn Yard, he called it privately. The Captain hated Bennet, though he could never remember exactly why…

> *. . .It has come to my attention that there is still blood on the wall of the Welding Shop from the Vargas incident. Stains. Faint but still in evidence. It has been several months since the Incident and I do not think it unreasonable to expect . . .*

Greek had taken his lumps for a number of different scams, but none as dumb as the one that brought him to Fremont. Looking back, he knew he never should have gotten involved with Eddy Cantril. Anyone with a nickname like Sniffer should have been suspect from the start. But Greek was in the middle of another cash crisis, seriously overextended again, badly in need of some quick funds. By any standards, Cantril was a loser. MacLane had warned him—Cantril ain't playin' with a full deck, Greek—but he hadn't listened. It looked like cake. Easy money.

The hit was a maternity shop—Nest Egg Clothes. Cantril said he knew a woman who worked there. Big bucks, he said. Thousands. You'd be surprised, man. Pregnant broads. Thousands. We hit it before they go to the bank with the weekend take. Big bucks, man. Thousands. Maybe more...Cantril couldn't stop talking. The speed he was taking was eating the enamel off his teeth, turning them black. His gums bled all the time. Ever since Skinny Glaser showed up for a heist at the Red Curtain Club in drag (a red wig and a green cocktail dress), Greek swore he would never do another job with a speed freak. He tried to put the thought out of his head when the day arrived.

Greek took the lead that Monday morning, striding past the racks of billowy Hide-a-Baby clothes and swelling lady shoppers. He leveled the Frontier .44 at the little lady behind the counter with the tortoise shell glasses. Money, he growled. Shaking badly, she stuffed the greenbacks in the bag he provided. Cantril was the cover man; he stood by the front door chewing gum, nervously zipping and unzipping his fly.

Back outside they pulled off the ski masks, walked casually to the stolen Mercury, got in and drove off. Cantril turned the radio on and clapped his hands.

"Hot shit, eh Greek? How much you think we got? Couple of thou? A million maybe?"

"Get real," said Greek, carefully watching the rear view mirror. "Turn the radio off."

"I'll count it," said Cantril.

"Not now," said Greek. "And turn the goddam radio off."

Cantril reached for the paper bag.

"Not-now," said Greek. "You fuckin' deaf, man?"

"Easy, eh Greek? Just like I said. Eddy knows the good scores. Candy from a baby...I'm gonna fuck me about eight chicks tonight. Maybe ten."

They drove along Rosecrans. Cantril lowered the volume on the radio and sang along:

. . .You walked outta my dreams, and into my arms, now you're my angel divine…

Greek spotted a gray Valiant in the rear view mirror.

"I'm gonna count it," said Cantril. "Can't hurt anything. That way we can get an even break. I set this job up, you know. Didn't I set it up, Greek?"

"Will you shut the fuck up," said Greek.

He checked the rear view mirror again—the same gray Valiant. Two guys. One with a coat and tie, the driver with a white hardhat. An unlikely pair, he thought. Cops?…Maybe. He turned right at the next street, then left at the first street. The Valiant followed.

"Oh, shit," said Greek.

"Didn't I set it up, Greek?"

The Valiant started to pass.

"…Pull over! Police!…"

Greek looked left into the barrel of a .45 automatic gripped in two shaking hands.

"Keep your hands on the wheel!"

Greek looked back at the road.

"…Shit," he mumbled, shaking his head.

"…Pull over!"

The voice was loud, filled with fear. Greek began to slow down and pull to the side of the road. Out of the corner of his eye he saw Cantril bend down and reach for the gun.

"Goddamit, Cantril, don't…"

He never finished the sentence. The forty-five that was held in those two shaking hands exploded in his ear. The windshield shattered, spraying his face with slivers of glass. He pulled onto the shoulder of the road and stopped. Cantril sat bolt upright, frozen in position. There seemed to be long minutes when nothing happened—no sound, no movement, nothing…Greek sat with both hands on the wheel. He didn't know if he had been hit.

Some time later, the door was jerked open. A fat man in a coat and tie was kneeling on one knee six feet away, a .45 clenched in both hands, his lips moving rapidly. All Greek could hear was a loud buzzing noise. Seconds later, several black and white patrol cars converged on the scene. The first sound he heard was the dying wail of a police siren. Then the voice of the fat man came through.

"...outta the goddam car. Now!"

Cops crouched behind patrol cars, only weapons and hats visible.

"...not gonna tell you again. Get outta the goddam car and keep your hands-in-sight."

Greek swung his legs out and gripped the top of the door to steady himself.

"Hands behind your head!" said the fat cop.

Greek stood up, put both hands behind his head and squinted into the sun; strange crunching sounds emanated from his forehead.

The cop approached, spun him around and shoved him against the car. He jammed the .45 behind Greek's ear.

"Okay, scumbag, why don't you make a move?" he said. "Like try to escape maybe. Save the taxpayers lots of money."

Greek held his breath.

The cop waited a few moments, then growled, "Spread 'em," and kicked the inside of Greek's ankles with his size thirteen, triple E departmental brogans. After the search, he was read his rights. . .

> . . .*the right to remain silent, the right*
> *to the presence of counsel, the right. . .*

Greek sat in the patrol car, hands cuffed behind his back, blood dripping off his forehead onto his khaki pants. He wondered how badly he was cut. His mind went racing through the legal wilderness looking for some ray of hope, but found little in the way of comfort. He had no doubt that he would be identified—the LAPD would make sure that proper memory coaching was available to the ladies at the Nest Egg Maternity Shop. They had the gun and the money. Looked like a piece of cake for the prosecution. And how could he have been so unlucky as to have two plainclothesmen on his tail so soon after the robbery?

"What about the supermarket job downtown," said the fat cop, seated sideways on the front seat, legs out the open door. "Wanna tell me about that one? Or the Ace High Club? Might save you some time later on. Judge might even go easy on you." He looked back at

Greek. "We figure you guys for at least a dozen jobs. A dozen easy. We gonna bury you so deep they'll have to pipe sunshine to you. Ha ha ha…"

It was an old joke; Greek had heard it a hundred times.

"I need a doctor," he said.

"What you need is a lawyer…Better yet you need a fuckin' miracle."

"I'm bleedin'."

"So? I'm supposed to be concerned that you're bleedin'? I got zero interest in your request, scumbag. Zero. No interest. You'll see a doctor when we get ready to have that happen. If we get ready to have that happen. You're lucky I didn't just shoot you awhile back. I could even do that now. Who would know?…Or care."

"Why don't you go fuck yourself, fatso?" said Greek.

The chubby face turned to stare in disbelief.

"Wait'll we get you downtown, freako," he hissed. "We'll play a little ping pong with your head, see what that does for your smart mouth."

True to his word, they put telephone books against his head and beat on them with nightsticks until his head rang and he had no equilibrium. He could not remember if he had confessed to anything. The cuts on his face opened again. Some of the slivers of glass were removed several days later at the jail dispensary; the rest worked their way to the surface by themselves in the months that followed.

Cantril was not at the trial. Greek did not discover till later that he had been set up, that Cantril had been given a suspended sentence in a drug case in exchange for setting him up. He learned that the plan had been to kill him when Cantril reached for the gun and was out of the line of fire, but the fat man was too shaky to get off a decent shot. It was one more score to settle. There was always one more. In the complicated world of justice and revenge, there was always one more. This one would have to wait.

# CHAPTER 15

The Yard was a barren, sterile place; nothing but lies, misery and hate grew on the Yard. It was a place where dreams went to die, where despair was more common than hope, where Time held everyone hostage.

The concrete was darker around the perimeter where convicts had walked for generations (counterclockwise by custom), voices low, fabricating a world where the One Big Score was as close as tomorrow, where junk cars were shiny new Cadillacs, where a dime store robbery might play out like a bank job worthy of Dillinger himself. And the women...Ah, the women—camp followers eagerly waiting to share a bed with a petty thief turned gangster. Pretty Boy Floyd between the sheets. A One Night Fall. The deeds were always deeds of heroes. Memory proved a good, if unreliable, friend in the long nights behind the walls. But it was a world of lies that lived with all the other lies circling the Yard each day. A world where violence was never far away.

Faded white lines marked the handball courts and the one basketball court. The weight area, the domino tables and other territories were unmarked but inviolate. A small white circle painted on the concrete near the Hobby Shop revealed the place where the old men went to play marbles, to pass away the time, some trying to forget, some trying to remember.

The Phantom Crapper left the first of his calling cards that spring, a fetid mound of feces coiled like a serpent at the entrance to the showers on the first tier in North Block. Only threats of major disciplinaries convinced the maintenance crew to clean it up. At varying intervals, similar deposits were discovered on the Hospital steps, in front of the Canteen, in back of the Laundry and outside the Catholic Chapel. There were no immediate arrests. Leonard was making book on when the perpetrator would be caught. The over and under was seven months.

It was not long before another convict was murdered; this one an old timer who had already chewed up the better part of a life sentence for killing a cop. Benny Weir, a loner who prided himself on the fact that he never cut the deal the DA offered him to implicate his crime partner. When the time came, he stood up to the heat, took his number and started walking. A convict's convict.

Leonard read a bootleg copy of the Incident Report about the murder and considered the circumstances. It wasn't so much that a convict had been killed (in an average year, twenty to thirty would die at Fremont) it was the mutilation that followed it. Convict killings were usually quick hits, conducted with almost military precision. The victim was identified, targeted, then taken out in a matter of seconds. One, two, possibly three assailants were all the environment could support; one or two to distract the victim, the third to kill. That's how men died on the Yard. The crowd, the distraction, the hit. Before anyone could react, the target had to be down, the assailants melting into the crowd.

But this one, he thought, like the last one, would have required some time. Both took place after lockdown, when there were very few people out on the Yard. Did Weir have a ducat to go someplace after the Yard was closed? The hospital? The Chaplain's office? Who else would have been out on the Yard? Was it a setup?

His throat had been cut and both ears cut off—that was the piece of the puzzle that didn't fit. It wasn't something that usually happened behind the walls. First the eyes, now the ears; it was a gesture better suited to ritual killing or tribal warfare. And time was always a factor. Unless …unless the killer or killers knew they had all the time they needed.

The Incident report concluded that…

> …Inmate Weir (A-3621) has most likely been
> killed by one of his many enemies on the Yard.
> Case will remain open pending further investigation…

It was signed by Senior Program Lieutenant L.F. Hebner. Leonard folded the copy of the report and put it in the desk drawer.

Funny, he thought. Of all the convicts out walking the Yard, Vargas and Weir probably had fewer enemies than anyone he knew. They were just old line convicts doing time. Numbers. No axes to grind, no scores to settle. Stand-up guys. No ties to the outside world, no visitors, no mail. Maybe that was the key. Nobody to follow up, to ask questions. But then, who wanted them dead? And why?

Preacher stood stoically in the light rain, Bible tucked under his arm, his free hand extended toward the sky. . .

> . . .*Shall not God search you out? For He knoweth the secrets of the heart. Yea, for Thy sake we are killed all the day long; we are counted as sheep for the slaughter.* . .

He lowered his arm and looked sadly at the ground.

"Life is a mean motherfucker," he said. "Blessed is the heart that's clothed in armor."

Moose lumbered by and slipped a piece of paper in Preacher's denim jacket pocket.

"Where's Freddy the Face?" he whispered.

"Back of the Laundry," said Preacher. "The wages of sin is death, Large Man."

"I'll take my chances," said Moose as he hurried off.

"Blessed are the meek," Preacher called after him, "for they shall inherit the earth."

"Fuck the meek," said Moose. "I want some face."

Devil Charley Chiponis circled the Yard trying to memorize the Invocation of Destruction he had found in a Witchcraft Ritual book in the library that had somehow escaped Mr. Oppenheim's watchful eye.

"...Let the mighty voices of my vengeance smash the stillness of the air," he muttered. "I am become as a monstrous machine of...a monstrous machine of...Fuck..."

He took a small folded paper out of his pocket, palmed it and read it while he was walking.

"…of…annihilation to the festering bodies of those who would detain me." He punched the air with his fist. "We got 'em now, man."

Shortly after the Ides of March, Nick the Knife caught Allan Mobley alone by the back door of the Laundry and guaranteed him a lifetime of limited mobility by making powder out of his kneecaps with a ball peen hammer.

"That's for bein' seen with the wrong people," said Nick, but Allan was in too much pain to hear. "Your little friend'll be next."

Leonard sent the Iceman to talk to Hoss. He got right to the point.

"You ain't holdin' out on Leonard, are you, man?"

Ice was so crazy nobody fooled with him. Rumors circulated on the Yard that he had already killed four men behind the walls. What was one more? He got his nickname on the street because several of his victims were found with icepicks buried in various parts of their anatomy. What led the police to him was the fact that he always used square handled ice picks that were clearly stamped:

### JENSEN TOOL AND ALLOYS
### (213) 624-8123
### Distributors of Industrial Hand Tools

A single stakeout found him lumbering toward Jensen's Tools on South Main one afternoon under a heavy load of Tokay to purchase more tools.

"You kiddin'?" said Hoss, trying to act offended without getting the Iceman mad. "You talkin' to Hoss Criner, man."

Iceman's face was a mass of contradictions; even his eyes appeared to be looking in different directions.

"You ain't holdin' out, are you, man?" Word for word, just like Leonard told him. He remembered. The eyes settled for a brief moment and focused on Hoss. Hoss looked away.

"No fuckin' way," said Hoss. "I always been straight with Leonard."

"…Better be." The voice was a monotone, most of the brain cells immobilized or destroyed by too much exposure to gasoline fumes and air conditioning refrigerant. He went spinning through life in his own mad world, accountable to no one, operating on the limited information supplied by a faulty memory and the shadows that surrounded him. The shadows and the voices.

"I cut it right down the middle," said Hoss. "Like we agreed. Half of what I collect."

"Better be…" Iceman felt like hurting him anyway; he didn't like Hoss. And hurting people made him feel better. He didn't know why and it didn't last long, but it made him feel better, gave him some sense of relief, of purpose even, like he was doing something important. At least for a little while. But he remembered that Leonard just wanted him to talk to Hoss, let him know they were watching. Just talk. This time.

Billy 2X and Delray walked up behind Tyrone and grabbed his arms. Before he could begin to struggle, Voodoo slipped the fourteen gauge electrical wire around his neck and slammed him back against his own body. His mouth was close to Tyrone's ear.

"Ty-rone gonna die," he hissed. Like a snake.

Tyrone struggled to get free, but they held him tight. He opened his mouth, but no sound came out; his windpipe had been crushed. His eyes were bulging, filled with terror. His mouth worked furiously and his body began to dance. Billy and Delray tightened their grip.

"Tyrone gonna die for goin' to the Man," Voodoo whispered. "Tyrone never gonna talk to the Man again. Give him names. Give up his brothers. Ever. Ain't gonna talk to nobody. You gonna die, homeboy."

As if an electric current were being passed through his body, Tyrone went into spasms every few seconds. Voodoo tightened the garrote…The spasms grew weaker and weaker and finally stopped.

Billy and Delray were both surprised; it hadn't taken all that long. They relaxed their grip. Voodoo held the body up for a few seconds then disdainfully pushed it away and let it fall.

"Fool," he said.

# CHAPTER 16

Stan knocked on the Program B office door at nine o'clock sharp for his appointment with Mr. Banner.

"Come in, come in."

Stan opened the door.

"Ahhh…Smith, isn't it?"

Stan nodded. The man behind the desk was thin and bald, his lips curved like a scimitar.

"Well, sit down, sit down," said Banner, motioning toward a wooden chair on the convict side of the desk. "I'm your counselor, Smith. Name's Banner. I'm here to help. That's the first thing you need to know. I want you to feel free to contact me anytime. Anytime. Let me know how things are, how you're doing. I'm here to help. Don't fall for that Convict Code horse pucky that you hear on the Yard. You know…Do your own number. Nobody goes to the Man. That kind of thing. You can talk to me. I'm here to help."

The delivery seemed rehearsed, the words dull, lifeless.

Donald Banner was an ex-postal employee, holder of an Associate of Arts degree from Pierce Junior College, most recently employed by the Eagle Rock Probation Department; a gaunt, socket-eyed man of fifty-three. He was a man who liked to get to the Heart of the Matter, to the Bottom of Things, a man of modest intellectual and emotional means who leaned heavily on Positive Thinking and tried and true American Bromides. He was reared in a lean Democratic home during the Depression where he learned the value of a dollar and the turn of a phrase from a father well versed in both. He fought in the Second World War when Might Made Right, when Japs and Germans were recognizable enemies, when John Wayne and Bob Hope made people glad to be Americans.

He opened Stan's central file and scanned the first page.

"Well, well…Quite a story here," he said. He placed his fingertips together and gently bounced the index fingers off his lower lip. "Murder in the second degree. With malice aforethought, Stanley Smith did unlawfully kill another human being…Care for a smoke?" He pushed the pack of Pall Malls toward Stan.

Stan took one and lit it.

"Murder indicates an abandoned and malignant heart," said Banner. "That's what it says in the California Penal Code. About murder…Interesting description. You think you have an abandoned and malignant heart, Smith?"

Stan just shrugged; he didn't know how to respond.

"You know what a malignant heart is?" said Banner.

"…Evil?"

"Poisonous. Evil…Aggressively malicious. And abandoned. Not a good combination."

"Oh," was all Stan could think of to say.

"You have a college degree," said Banner, pointing to an item on the page. "I never made it all the way through myself. Just two years. Had everything going for you." He made a pistol out of his hand and pointed the index finger at Stan. "Then, bang bang you're dead. What was that all about?"

He lowered the gun to the desk where it became a hand again.

"College boy," he continued, without waiting for an answer. "Good grades. Smart as a whip it seems. How in the world does someone with your background wind up doing such a thing." He seemed disappointed.

Stan watched the smoke curl up from his cigarette. More than a year after the murder and he still didn't have an answer that satisfied anyone, even himself. And everybody asked: lawyers, psychiatrists, counselors, everybody. He always wanted to say, Because he was fucking my wife. Don't you get it? But he never did. The Incident (he had come to refer to it as the Incident, rather than the Murder) certainly wasn't without provocation. He didn't just go out and shoot somebody at random. But nobody wanted to address what Jeffrey had done. Or what Bonnie had done. The fact that Jeffrey had taken from him the person he loved and cherished most in the whole world was something that didn't seem to enter into the equation. Everybody had taken the high moral ground. Smith is a cold-blooded killer. Guilty as charged. . . *Case closed.*

"I don't know," said Stan. "It just…happened. I don't remember doing it. Don't remember the…shooting."

"Drugs?" said Banner, twisting his mouth into a sour shape.

"…Some sleeping pills. A few. They gave them to me. The doctor did. After she left…I couldn't sleep."

"Alcohol?"

"…A little," he lied.

"How much is a little?"

"Oh…A few bottles of beer occasionally. Eastside. Lucky Lager. Some wine with dinner maybe."

"Hard liquor?"

Stan looked at his hands and wondered where the conversation was going.

"…Hardly ever," he said.

"You think you have a drinking problem?"

"No."

"Your arrest record indicates two arrests for drunk driving, Smith. That might lead me to think you had a problem."

"…Well…I…"

"We have resources here, you know. A.A. comes in twice a week. Holds meetings. Father Sweeny is the moderator. Very effective I understand. The meetings. You might want to think about attending."

Banner made a notation in Stan's central file.

"You bought the gun?" he asked.

"We had it. Bonnie thought we ought to have one. For protection. We kept it in the closet."

"The best laid plans of mice and men," said Banner, shaking his head. "…And then?"

Stan looked up.

"…And then what?"

"That's what I'm asking. And then what happened?"

"She left with Loughlin."

"He forced her?"

"Not…physical force."

"Psychological…persuasion?" said Banner. "He deceived her?"

"He was older. A war hero. She's young. She doesn't understand any of that."

"I see. So you got even," said Banner. "Revenge. An eye for an eye." He arched one eyebrow; light gleamed off his bare scalp. "You got your gun and got even. Bang bang, Mr. War Hero. You're dead. Stanley Smith just killed you."

"…At first I just thought about it, about getting even. Maybe blowing up his car. Or his house. I don't know. Something. But I was just thinking about it. Imagining it. I never meant to shoot him. Not really shoot him…I wanted to scare him. I mean how would you feel if someone ran off with your wife?"

Banner pictured a wheezing, overweight Matilda Banner squeezing out the back door on her bad leg with some mysterious stranger, perhaps the plumber, wrench in one hand, Matilda in the other. The thought did not displease him. But he said he would feel bad about it.

"See?" said Stan, as if he had made his point.

"You ever think about shooting her?" said Banner.

"No," he said, though he had.

"So you had a few drinks, a few pills, drove over to his house and killed him. Just like that."

"That's what they say," said Stan. "I don't remember any of it."

"Don't remember," said Banner, making additional notes in the file. "Almost inconceivable. Nothing much doing tonight, think I'll go kill somebody."

Stan leaned forward.

"I mean I was just thinking about it, about doing him some kind of harm…not killing him or anything. Never that."

Banner cleared his throat and leaned back in his chair.

"No," he said. "Of course not. But that's all after the fact, isn't it? Water under the bridge, so to speak. Spilt milk. If you had planned it, as in premeditation, you'd be here on a first-degree charge. Doing life. Straight life. Maybe the Green Room."

He rubbed his head.

"But we're dealing with today, Smith. I'm not here to judge you. That's what we have courts for. As far as I'm concerned, it's yesterday's news. We're at square one, you and me. Everybody's at square one. That other part, the murder part, is over and done with. History. We simply have to accept the judgment and move on...Where are you working now?"

"The Grounds Crew."

"The-Grounds-Crew," said Banner. "Not much in that for a college boy, eh? You know I never got all the way through college myself. Only two years...Had to go back to work full time. Family and all that. You know. Kids..."

Stan put his cigarette out in the ashtray on the desk.

"...You think I could get a transfer?" he said.

"A transfer...A trans-fer," as if the word was new to him.

"Yeah."

"To where?"

"Another...institution."

"I see. And did you have one in mind? Some other institution?"

"I don't know," said Stan. "Someplace...safer."

"Safer," said Banner. "Well, we'd all like to be someplace safer, wouldn't we?"

Stan waited while Banner fiddled with his pencil.

"You see, Smith, your psychological profile indicates a good deal of instability. More than would be considered normal, even for someone doing time for murder. And the potential for violence? Significant, Smith. Significant. You've already demonstrated that, eh? The violence part."

"I don't know," said Stan. "I was never violent before. I mean never did anything violent...before this."

"It's all here in black and white, Smith." He appeared to be tracing a graph with his pencil eraser in Stan's central file. "Your psychological profile. Very erratic. Looks like a mountain range, all peaks and valleys. Not the best. Keep in mind that you're not here for singing too loud in church. This is murder we're talking about. The unlawful taking of a life. Second degree but still murder. If that's not violence, I'm a drummer in a string band. Transfer to another institution would require..."

"My mother could visit," said Stan. "If I was closer to L.A. This is too far."

"...would require a change in custody status," said Banner. "I have no authority to do that and it's unlikely that..."

Stan pulled another cigarette out of the pack of Pall Malls.

"She's very sick, my mother. And my father's actually dying. He's in the hospital right now. Dying. Heart trouble."

"Yes," said Banner. "I can appreciate that. It's too bad, really. Perhaps in a few years..."

"A few years'll probably be too late," said Stan.

Banner rubbed his hands together as if to dispel the notion.

"Murder is a very serious crime," he said. "Very serious. The most serious there is."

"...Serious," said Stan, then wondered why he repeated it.

Banner leaned forward and put his elbows on the desk.

"We'll soon be having group counseling here at Fremont," he said. "What I think of as e-motional schooling. Sometimes better than the old ABC's. Very innovative—group counseling. Teaches us how to deal with things, eh? Real life things. Conflict resolution. That's the ticket. Get the ghosts out of the closet. The old bugaboos. Get out of there, Ghosts. Strong stuff, Smith. Strong stuff."

He made a fist and shook it weakly.

"What if they kill me?" said Stan.

Banner allowed himself a little smile. He turned his palms up.

"Smith..." he said. "Really."

"It could happen," said Stan.

"And just who is it that's going to kill you?"

"Some people are...watching me."

"Watching you? That's it? Just watching you?"

"Looking at me," said Stan, "like they want to hurt me. I can tell. They're following me. Why would they be following me if they didn't want to...do something? I know two guys got killed in the County Jail. Two guys. In just a couple of months. Strangled ..." He touched his own throat.

"I'm not saying those things don't happen, Smith. Not at all. There's always a few bad apples in any group. And if you're in danger, real danger, we certainly want to know about it. But vague...fears. Perhaps an overactive imagination. Now that's another matter."

"They're going to kill me," said Stan. "I know it."

Banner smiled broadly, revealing teeth too white to be real.

"We can talk about those things in group counseling," he said brightly. "That's what it's for. Get all those bottled up feelings out so we can deal with them. This group counseling, Smith, is going to revolutionize corrections. Mark my words. It's going to break down barriers, help people get together and understand one another."

He seemed delighted at the prospect.

"Now I realize," he continued, "that these are not all Boy Scouts we have locked up in here. And I would guess that being afraid is a normal reaction. Within limits. I mean given the circumstances. Yes...There are some desperate men here. Some even depraved perhaps."

He stroked his head with both hands.

"But that's part of what prison's about, Smith. That's punishment, you see. We don't want to make it so comfortable that you wouldn't mind coming back. We want you to hate it so much that you'll think-twice before you do anything that might bring you back. The more you hate this place, the better, eh?" His right fist shot out of a loose cuff and started going up and down in cadence. "I-hate-prison, I-hate-prison, I-hate-prison...See?"

"They're going to fucking kill me," said Stan. "I just know it."

He felt the shoreline receding, his last few options disappearing. Banner reminded him of the mad Dr. Shivana in the Captain Marvel comics.

Banner made another notation in the file before he continued.

"Now you have a fair amount of time to do," he said. "Seven, maybe eight years. Depending. Could be longer. But you're young," blithely dismissing the years with a wave of his hand. "Twenty-two?"

"...Twenty-six."

"See? Young. You'll only be thirty-four or five when you get out. Forty at the outside. Your whole life in front of you. My God, what I wouldn't give to be thirty-five again. Forty even." He looked off into the distance for a moment. "You could improve yourself in here, Smith. Learn new skills. Coping skills. You're not strong in that department. Think about it. Think about resuming your place in society. What's going to happen if you get married again and your wife runs off with another man. Get a gun and solve it the same way? Not worth it. You know that. The old in-and-outs are great; nobody appreciates a good piece more than yours truly. But murder? Over a piece of tail, good or not? Not worth it. I want you to work on some…stability, Smith. Some coping skills. We'll work on it together. You and me. Work hard. Get in group and talk about it. This is me, group," he thumped the desk with his fist, "and this is what I'm all about…Give the Parole Board something to see. Some evidence that you're changing, making progress, that you're no longer a danger to society. You can make a life for yourself without all this violence. This… shooting people. That's no good, Smith. No good at all."

He stood up abruptly and offered his hand.

"We'll be seeing each other," he said. "I've got a few more years to do myself. Ha ha ha…"

Stan shook his hand; it didn't seem to have any bones in it.

"I look forward to a mutually satisfying relationship," said Banner. "If you need help, get in touch. That's what I'm here for. To help."

Stan released the boneless hand and left the office, sure that his days were numbered.

# CHAPTER 17

Paulson read the May movie list that was posted on the wall in the Inmate Watch Office: *"The Mummy's Tomb, The Mummy's Curse, The Body Snatchers* and *The Mummy's Revenge."*

"What is it with Jenkins and those horror flicks?" said the Count.

"Better him than Tex," said Greek. "Remember Tex? All we got was westerns when he was doin' it. Whoever took him out did us all a favor. I saw *The Star of Texas* four times last year. Four times. With Wayne Morris. That was prob'ly the only movie the guy ever made. I got parts of it memorized…Reach for the sky, hombre…."

"He got killed because he got some bad movies?" said Paulson.

"Don't kid yourself," said Greek. "Pickin' bad movies is a major beef."

"Man…"

"You know, I don't know what to make of all these movies glorifying violence," said Greek, shaking his head. "Like these Mummy movies? Even the westerns. People shootin' each other. Think what it does to young minds."

"What's it do?" said Paulson.

"It twists them," said Greek. "Beyond repair…Like yours."

Paulson smiled.

"Those are probably the kind of movies that this nut case that's killin' people on the Yard was watching when he was a kid," said Greek. "During his…what do you call it—his informative years."

"Just two, Greek," said the Count.

"Two so far," said Greek. "This is what is known as a trend. There'll be more. Trust me."

"…What for?" said Paulson.

"You mean why does he do it?"

Paulson nodded.

"That's the question, isn't it?" said Leonard. "Why would anybody do it?"

"Because this place is full of sick fucks and this guy's just one more," said Moose.

"Too easy," said Leonard. "And too obvious. There's got to be more to it."

"There are guys in here who will do anything," said Moose. "There's a guy on the third tier in North Block who ate people, for chrissakes. Terranova? A fucking cannibal. Killed people and ate them. Jesus. Leave it to the fucking Italians, man."

"How'd you like him for a celly?" said the Count.

"You must live in a really bad neighborhood," said Greek. "You oughta move."

"I live in the worst neighborhood there is," said Moose. "North Block. But I'm thinkin' about movin'."

"Where to?"

"I thought maybe Beverly Hills."

"Let me know if you need any help," said the Count.

"I won't be able to wait that long, man. A year or two and I'll be long gone."

"I'll be ready."

"In a pig's ass you'll be ready. You'll be ready to head back to the Parole Board is what you'll be ready for. You see, all those guys on the Board got kids of their own. Daughters mostly. You think they're gonna be ready to turn you loose anytime soon?"

"Can't keep me forever."

"Fifty years."

"...Fifty years?

"You didn't notice you got a fifty year top? Rape is one to fifty, Countess. Better check it out in one of those law books you been readin'. Time off for good behavior and you'll be like maybe seventy when you get out. You can spend your golden years watching dirty movies and drooling."

"You don't know shit, Moose. You know that? They don't keep people for fifty years on a chicken shit rape beef."

Moose shrugged.

"Well, don't expect Councilman McKeever to run down to the Parole Board and plead your case when it comes up."

"...Who's McKeever?"

"See, you don't even know that Carol McKeever was one of your victims. Councilman McKeever's daughter. From Santa Monica."

"Awwww..."

"Little blonde? About twelve years old?"

"You're really sick, Moose," said the Count. "You know that?"

"I'm just tellin' you how it is," said Moose. "Tryin' to help."

"I'll be out dancin' in the streets long before your big ass hits the bricks."

"Recess," said Leonard, slamming his palm down on the desk to get everyone's attention. "I've decided on the prize for the Fly Killing Contest this year."

"Shoot."

"The prize this year is going to be...a woman to enjoy for an hour or two."

"Awwww..." said Paulson.

"A woman?" said Moose. "A real live woman? In here?"

"Flesh and blood," said Leonard.

"No way, man. Even you can't do that."

"Isn't that what you said last year about the fifth of Jack Daniels?"

"Yeah, but..."

Greek let out a long, low whistle.

"Anybody doesn't want to participate," said Leonard, "just let me know and I'll take you off the active roster."

No takers.

"If you can pull this off," said Greek, "you oughta just get the keys from Quinlan and run the whole show."

"I'm workin' on it, Greek."

"Man," said the Count, shaking his head.

"Anybody even remember what it was like to get laid?" said Moose.

"You talkin' to me?" said Paulson.

"No, Little Man. Why would I ask you a question like that?"

"Because...I might remember."

"That's very doubtful, Paulson. Very doubtful. Unless it was yesterday. You get laid yesterday?"

"…I don't think so."

"See?" said Moose.

"It's like ridin' a bike," said Greek. "One of those things you never forget."

"How did you find out it was McKeever's daughter?" said the Count.

"I can't remember what it was like to hump anything but my fist," said Moose, ignoring the question. "I'm actually having a serious relationship with my hand. Can you believe it? I may even be in love."

"With your hand?"

"Why not? Sometimes it's my right hand, sometimes my left. And the good thing is that there's no law against humpin' your fist. You can even force your fist to give it up and there's nothin' they can do about it. Even if your fist is real young. Under age even. Like eleven or twelve."

"I don't believe there even is a Councilman McKeever," said the Count.

Moose shrugged.

"Suit yourself. Stop by Harvell's in Santa Monica when you get out and I'll buy you a drink. You can get an old person's discount on Tuesdays."

The Count shook his head and walked out of the office.

"What's with him?" said Moose.

> *"St. Paul speaks to us, brothers in sin,"* said Preacher: *"For the good that I would do, I cannot. But the evil that I would not do, that I do. Who will save me from this fucking nightmare? Who will remove this sin from my heart? This lust that burns in my state-issued blues?"*

He held the Book to his chest and bowed his head.

> *"Only the Warden has this power, homeboys. Only the blessed Quinlan. He holds the power of life and death,*

*freedom or incarceration. So let us pray...Our Warden who art in Control, hallowed be Thy name, Thy prison come, Thy judgments done, on earth as it is in Fremont. A-men..."*

He closed the book and walked slowly toward the lengthening shadows of North Block.

# CHAPTER 18

Officer Wetzle unlocked the west wing in South Block at two thirty. The Grounds Crew finished at three. Almost everyone else worked until three thirty.

At three o'clock the cellblock was nearly empty. Willy and Buck were there because they worked in the kitchen and didn't have to leave for work until three thirty. Pokey was there all the time; he was on the Maintenance Crew.

Stan hurried to take a shower. He always hurried. He didn't shower every day; it seemed too risky. Very few men were there in the showers that time of day. He lathered and rinsed in a matter of minutes, not daring to look at the others. He felt like he had at his first high school gym class; they had to force him to take a shower. And of course they all laughed because he didn't have any pubic hair. Just fuzz. A re-tard, said Angelo Lucas, football star who was shaving at fourteen and had hair all over his body. Everybody but Stan had pubic hair. Everybody. He thought there must be something wrong with him.

Now he had pubic hair, but his shoulders were narrow, his chest nearly concave, his meager penis dwarfed by the masculine members he saw dangling between muscular thighs. He was a person of little substance, slender as a reed, surrounded by men of frightening proportions. He suspected everyone; trusted no one. Left to wander, his mind created terrifying scenes of torture and pain.

He finished his shower and hurried back to the safety of his cell. He didn't think to look before he entered; it hadn't occurred to him that anyone would be there. But as he entered, someone slapped a hand over his mouth and propelled him toward the rear of the cell. A wet voice whispered in his ear:

*You make a noise, muffuckah, I cut yo' throat...*

A sharp blade probed the side of his neck. The towel around his waist was ripped off and he was forced to his hands and knees. Someone grabbed his hair and pushed his head down. His knees were pulled apart.

He tried to move forward with the first painful thrust, but his head was pushed into a smelly groin. Strong hands gripped his hips and pulled him backwards. He fought to tighten his sphincter muscle but it did no good; he was entered in short, painful increments. He struggled to breathe. The prodding continued—thick, relentless. The tempo increased. His intruder grunted rhythmically. Stan was certain he was going to be sick.

It seemed to go on for a long time, though it may have been only a minute or two. The final thrust and withdrawal was accompanied by a low animal sound. Then the same voice behind his ear:

> *You a fool, boy. You know that? You mine now, white boy.*
> *All mine…*

He wiped himself with a towel and tossed it at Stan.

> *You go to The Man, you dead meat. I be back, boy…Don'*
> *fo'get.*

Then they were gone, all of them, and the only sound was his heart pounding noisily in his chest. He crawled under the bottom bunk and curled up as tight as he could, knees against his chest. But he knew he couldn't stay there; he would have to get up. He forced himself out from under the bunk and struggled to his feet. He reached for the towel; it was covered with blood and feces. He threw up in the toilet. He wiped himself carefully with his shorts, tried to sit down and pull his pants on, but it was too painful to sit. He labored into them, his legs shaking so badly he could hardly stand. He put his shirt on, splashed water on his face and leaned heavily on the sink. Tears stung his eyes.

A sweet, sickening smell filled the cell. Later he would identify it as Dixie Peach Hair Dressing. Conk, they called it. For the Distinguished Man. Thick as axle grease, sweet as marmalade. The

Negroes used it to straighten their hair. That and Royal Crown. They had used it on him.

In a few minutes, he noticed a wetness on the inside of his thigh. He cleaned himself again; he was bleeding. He folded some toilet paper and used it as packing. The burning sensation was worse than ever. He didn't know if he could even walk. He took a position at the rear of the cell, leaned on the top bunk and stared out through the bars without seeing them.

I'm okay, he said to himself. I'm okay. But he knew it was a lie even as he said it.

His scalp tingled. His mouth was dry, his breathing shallow. He didn't realize that he was sweating profusely. His mind spun through the sequence of events, but would not stop to examine any of them. Scenes from the past formed and vanished before he could tell what they were. It was like a movie that was running too fast. He struggled to remain conscious.

At three thirty the cellblock began to fill with men returning from work or the Yard. They talked and jabbered as if nothing had happened. Stan wondered if he should tell someone—Wetzle, Banner, the Chaplain. Somebody. Go to the hospital maybe. But he couldn't move. And what difference would it make? He didn't know who they were. They were black; that's all he knew…And how could he possible tell anyone?

Dead meat. That's what they said. Dead meat if you go to The Man…He touched his neck where the knife had scratched. You mine now. I be back…Stan took a few shaky steps toward the front of the cell. It made him sick when he thought about it, about what they had done. He felt soiled, violated, humiliated. And they said they'd be back. That was the worst part. It was going to happen again. And again. What would he do? What could he do?

The bell rang for count. The cell doors slammed shut, tier by tier. He felt safer when his finally closed.

He stood at the bars and listened for the sound of Sergeant Frankel stumping along the tier for count.

For the first time in his life he thought about suicide.

# CHAPTER 19

Voodoo knew that the black man and the white man would never live together in peace. He had suspected as much when he was growing up in the Projects; now he was sure of it. The white man wanted to own the black man—to enslave him, take his freedom, his women, his dignity, punish him for being black, for being the dark side of his own sick soul. Mister Charley had the money, the power, the juice. It was a perfect example of what Voodoo had learned about the Golden Rule:

*He who has the gold makes the rules.*

He viewed the Civil Rights Movement as a joke—pitiful Uncle Toms laboring under the illusion that once white America saw how poorly black America was being treated, they would raise their voices in protest. Fat chance. Truth was that white America already knew how badly black America was being treated and they weren't the least bit concerned. They hadn't cared for four hundred years; why would they begin to care now? What they saw on the evening news might as well have been taking place on another planet. Dogs and fire hoses and Bull Conner...*Look what they doin' to the niggers, Martha*...Sit-ins and marches. Big deal. Film at eleven. Who cares?...*Pass the butter, Frank...and change the channel...*

A few white college kids with nothing better to do during summer break than head south, participate in some civil disobedience pranks, then go back to Yale or Harvard for the winter and tell their friends that they were in the vanguard of the new Civil Rights Movement. Black folks with a jug band and a blind guitar player. Soul, baby. Got to have soul. All of a sudden white kids wanted to have cornrow hair and wear dashikis. And how those kids loved a good Negro spiritual …Come to Jesus, nigger. You gonna fetch your re-ward in the sweet by and by…While officially passing legisla-tion to right previous wrongs, America would continue to ignore the Negro problem until it showed up on their doorstep. And Voodoo planned to do just that, to bring it to them in living color—blood red.

"How about a hamburger, Jefferson?" said Officer Hedges, sliding a metal tray along the railing in front of the steam table.

"Yessir, Mr. Hedges," said Voodoo. "Medium well, heavy on the mayo?"

"Right on, bro," said Hedges, who looked like an aging Howdy Doody. Officer Hedges liked to keep up with the latest slang; he thought it helped break down barriers between custody and the con-victs. The convicts just thought it was stupid.

Voodoo slapped a thin hamburger patty on the grill and peeled off the paper like a man who enjoyed his work. He had a wide dis-arming smile and straight white teeth. He knew the white folks liked to see him smile; they always felt safer if the niggers were happy. He hummed Old Man River and tapped his spatula on the grill. Hedges grinned and tapped his foot. For the briefest of moments they were in sync.

Voodoo flipped the patty and removed the buns from the toaster with his free hand. He applied a liberal layer of mayonnaise, a limp lettuce leaf and a slice of tomato to one half of the bun before sliding the greasy patty onto the other half. A handful of potato chips and a sweet pickle completed the offering. It wasn't much, but it was only thirty-five cents. Prison guards didn't make much money.

George Jefferson was a dreamer; he'd always been one. First it was dreams of things he didn't have, things he'd seen on the street, in store windows or on teevee. Later, when he discovered how things got to be the way they were, he dreamed about revenge.

It was Hambone who first told him that the White Folks put the Black Folks in the Projects, not to help out or to give them a place to live like they said, but so's they'd know where they was all the time. Be easier to cheat them if they was all in one place. Easier to keep track. The White Folks bought up all the businesses around the Projects, jacked up the prices and put some Uncle Tom nigger behind the counter so everybody would think it was a black-owned store.

The Poor Folks, the Black Folks, didn't have no money for cars or busrides so they had to shop close by. At the high-price stores. That the White Folks actually owned. Man…(Hambone shook his head). White Folks got rich cheatin' Black Folks. It was a known fact. A math'matical certitude, said Hambone.

Voodoo liked to listen to Hambone tell about puttin' the Man in a trick bag and hustlin' him. Like mailin' letters? Hambone never used stamps; he was too slick for that. He said you just put where you wanted the letter to go to in the return address place and drop it off at the post office. Mailman sees it ain't got no stamp, so he sends it back to the re-turn address. Hambone laughed. He was slick. He was a player. He got respect. He be whippin' his game on the foxes, gettin' some steady trim. He drove a big old Caddy. A hog. He just come to the Projects to see Luana Simpson. He said he was two hundred pounds of soul waitin' to explode inside some lucky pussy. That's what he said, but Hambone didn't weigh but a hundred and fifty with twenty pounds of rocks in his pockets.

Slowly, George Jefferson began to learn how the world worked. It was run by White Folks; that was easy enough to see. Didn't seem to be any important people who were black. And the world could be a very dangerous place; those who didn't learn how to take care of themselves were doomed to an early death. Respect was important. Man with a Cadillac got respect. Man with a gun. Power got respect. You hit some fool and take him down, you got respect. George liked that, having people be afraid of him.

"Anybody can be a nigger," said Hambone. "Takes a man to get respect."

White man didn't need a Cadillac to get respect; he got it just because he was white. Some black men thought havin' a white woman meant respect. But George didn't like white women; they had little asses and skinny legs. He liked a good brown-skinned woman with fine big legs.

But he got respect, Voodoo did. When he got older he got a gun and he got some respect. He became a skilled practitioner in the art of intimidation, first in the Projects, later in the wider world surrounding the Projects. He discovered that if people were afraid of him, they did what he wanted. No fuss. No argument. They just did it. Fear was a useful thing.

His introduction into the mysteries of Islam began with his first trip into prison while he was still in his teens. Rufus Johnson sat him down one day on the Yard at Preston and explained to him about the Prophet Farad and the Nation of Islam and the Reverend Elijah Muhammad ...and Yacub's History...

"The very first humans (said Rufus) was black people who lived in the holy city of Mecca. Everything was goin' fine until along comes a man by the name of Mr. Yacub. That man be born for trouble. He began preachin' a evil doctrine in the streets of the holy city, so they banished him and his followers to this little island called Patmos. Now this Patmos Island was all rock, man. Didn't nothin' grow. It was a stone cold mothafuckah. So this Mr. Yacub, he cursed Allah and decided to create him a devil race—a bleached out race of white people.

"Now Yacub was a educated man. Went to all the best schools in Mecca. And they had some fine schools in those days, not like now. He was a bio-physicist. You dig, man? He knew about some chemistry. And genes, them little things that make people look like they do. He knew that the black man contained both black and brown genes, and even though (Rufus wagged his index finger), even though the brown was the weaker gene, every third or fourth baby would be on the brown side. That's the way a recessed gene is. That's the way they do.

"But instead of lettin' nature be the way it supposed to be, they nursed them little brown suckahs along and they'd only let brown ones marry other brown ones. You dig? So the mothafuckahs got lighter and lighter. And more and more evil. If a baby was black, they had a midwife stick a needle in its brain and kill it. But they took care of them brown babies. Yeah. Fed 'em. Sent 'em to school. Treated 'em real good.

"So after two hundred years everybody was brown. Another two hundred years and everybody was red. Two hundred more years and everybody was yellow. And two hundred years after that they was all white. On that island, that pitiful little mothafuckin' island, they was nothin' but blond, pale-skinned, blue-eyed devils. Then they come to the mainland settin' black against black with all kind of lies and triggeration. That's how it all got started."

"What happened to Mr. Yacub?"

"Oh…" the gesture was vague. "He died. He was the most evil man who ever lived."

"Worse than Hitler?"

"Huh," he snorted. "Hitler didn't do nothin' but kill him a few Jews. Just think what Mr. Yacub done, man. He changed the history of the whole mothafuckin' world. Think what he did to the first brothers, man. The very first humans. Wasn't for Mr. Yacub, wouldn't be no mothafuckin' white dudes. Wouldn't a been no slavery. Think on that for a while. That's evil, man…"

With Johnson's help, George Voodoo Jefferson began his study of Islam and black history. Between prison terms he returned to the Projects, developed his Game, commanded respect, became a consummate Player.

Behind the Walls he raged against the system that enslaved him. He got a reputation with Custody as a Troublemaker. Along the way he picked up the name Voodoo when it was learned that a man he put a curse on died a week later. He did not deny the story or the obvious implication. He discovered books, developed a sense of history and his place in it. He pictured himself as part of an ancient lineage that stretched back to the warrior priests of East Africa. (His mother told him he had been born with a full set of teeth, a sure sign of spiritual power.) Noble, wise and courageous, the warrior priests had ruled a kingdom for a thousand years. He read of the slave ships sailing across the Atlantic with their cargo of human cattle to satisfy the white man's greed, starving black bodies that came to haunt his dreams and cry out for vengeance. He read Marcus Garvey and W.E.B. DuBois. The struggle began to take shape in his mind. He heard the voice of Malcolm X:

*The only way to end oppression is with power. . .*

When he discovered the writings of Frantz Fanon, he found a soul brother whose hatred of whites was equal to his own. He read and reread his contraband copy of *The Wretched of the Earth*. This was no separatist manifesto; this was a call to exterminate the white race. When he tried to get a copy of *Black Skin, White Masks*, the prison librarian explained it was considered revolutionary material and would not be allowed inside the prison. Regulations, he said, as if that explained everything. Voodoo feigned surprise at the nature of the book he was requesting. The librarian, a tiny humpback of a man with bushy gray hair, assured him that it was so and recommended *The Great Chain of Being* as a substitute. Voodoo smiled but declined, instead imposing upon Officer Wallace, who owed him several favors, to bring him a copy. He underlined and memorized his favorite passage:

> *He who is reluctant to recognize me, opposes me. In the savage struggle, I am willing to accept the convulsions of death...*

*...In the savage struggle...*He looked back with a sense of pride when he remembered the smoldering ruins of Watts, his city of origin. Though the violence had unfortunately been misdirected, at least his people had risen against the oppressor. He was familiar with the corner of 116th and Avalon, where it all started, had shopped at the nearby A&J Market, attended the Grace Temple Baptist Church up the street, knew the businesses along 103rd that were torched. His vocal support for the rioters came close to starting additional violence in the prison dayroom when the evening news was aired that night. The white convicts grumbled but did nothing. Only the fledgling Aryan Nation began to make plans to take action.

He had come to accept the fact that it might be necessary to forfeit his own life in the struggle to come; sometimes he even longed for it. In the meantime he fought the rage that boiled within him. To express it in petty ways was a waste; he had already done it far too often and spent useless weeks in the Adjustment Center, the prison within a prison. It was important that he remain in control, that he be able to marshal the forces at his disposal. It was his duty to instruct the brothers, to be their leader.

He would choose the time and the place. What Shaka had done to fuse the Zulu nation into a fighting force at the beginning of the nineteenth century, he would do for the black men at Fremont, and by example the black men of America.

Voodoo, Dreamer of Dreams, Drinker of Blood, Son of the Great Serpent ...Voodoo had a message for white America. The message would be written in blood and it would be so terrible that all would be forced to listen.

# CHAPTER 20

Quinlan watched the Yard through army binoculars from the third floor of the Control Building, the powerful lenses magnifying everything, drawing him closer to the turbulent surface below. He peered intently at the faces that slid in and out of focus, faces he recognized as evil. He sometimes pictured himself as the captain of a ship with a mutinous crew who were eager to defy authority, to overthrow the existing order and replace it with chaos. His job, the job of The Captain, was first of all to put down the mutiny, then mold the men into useful citizens before he allowed them to go ashore and live in a free society.

Some of them, he knew, were without reason or compassion, unwilling to differentiate between right and wrong. He did not believe they were unable to differentiate between right and wrong—just unwilling. He made that distinction. He thought that psychological word games implying diminished responsibility due to the inability to tell right from wrong were so much hogwash. Mumbo jumbo. Poor upbringing my ass, he said. (He was fond of pointing to Booker T. Washington as a man who had risen above his surroundings. And a nigger at that, he said, but only privately.)

With the right kind of treatment, he believed that basic attitudes could be changed. Distinguishing right from wrong wasn't all that hard. It was something that could be taught. And having learned the difference, teaching them to choose the right shouldn't be that difficult. You made choosing anything but the right extremely painful. After all, even rats (and flatworms, if he remembered the article correctly) had been taught to negotiate a complex maze on the pain-pleasure principle. Surely convicts could be taught as much. The Prison Director's Rules regarding rehabilitation were very specific:

*. . .Use discipline in order to develop self-reliance and
self-control. . .Instill in each inmate the desire to conform to the accepted standards for individual and community life in a free society. . .*

Simple enough. He would use discipline—his own brand—to
instill a desire to conform. Still, he knew there were some men who
would never get the message and should never be released. He had
already found several at Fremont. George Lincoln, a mountain of
a black man, had raped a white woman, defecated on a table and
forced her to rub it on her face, then stabbed her repeatedly in the
buttocks with a small penknife. A hundred and thirty-seven puncture
wounds. Fortunately, she lived to testify against him. Unfortunately,
there was a good chance he would someday be released from prison.
His prior record indicated that chances were excellent he would
repeat his aberrant behavior.

Andrew Green was another. He had chopped off a woman's
hands prior to raping her. Miraculously, she too had survived to
identify her attacker. The picture of a woman waving bloody stumps
around while being raped filled Quinlan with disgust. What kind of
a man would do something like that? What kind of an animal? Of
course it wasn't always the Negro who committed the most heinous
crimes. Not always. He realized that, took that into account. But
there did seem to be a disproportionately large number, considering
the percentage in the general population. That told him something.

He wanted to be fair about it, about his judgments. After all,
he believed in fairness. He also believed that Negroes were infe-
rior. He viewed that conclusion not so much as a judgment, but as a
biological fact that seemed difficult to refute. Studies by Crimmins
and Geary lent scientific credence to it, and twenty years in the
Department of Corrections had only deepened his conviction. It was
not a personal issue; he did not blame the Negro for his inferiority.
But he took it into account. He knew it was not a popular stance (he
shared his views with only a few, realizing that they might well be
politically unwise). And while bleeding-heart liberals were calling
for shorter sentences and conjugal visits, he was left to deal with
men who would cut your throat or shatter your kneecaps for a pack

of cigarettes, men who would rape another convict in the recovery room of a prison hospital.

And the recent trend toward militancy certainly hadn't made his job any easier. The Black Panthers were organizing. The Nation of Islam was a rising force. The Aryan Nation was gaining strength. Even the Mexicans were banding together.

And of course they all wanted something. The Muslims wanted validation as a legitimate religious organization; they wanted meals without pork (Don't want no muffuckin' hog, is what their spokesman said). The Black Panthers wanted recognition as an Afro-American self-help group. They argued that if the Seventh Step Foundation and Alcoholics Anonymous could have weekly meetings and outside visitors, they should be allowed the same privileges. Quinlan denied the requests, even put a stop to the Seventh Step Foundation (which he considered a Communist front organization). Only Alcoholics Anonymous was allowed to continue (the rumor mill had it that someone high up in the Department was actually a member), though outside visitors were required to get clearance three months in advance, effectively reducing the number of visitors and the attendant custody problems.

Robert Quinlan was not a man who succumbed easily to pressure. It irritated him that the new and supposedly enlightened programs that had come tumbling out of the vast bureaucracy in Sacramento recently often contained detailed directives about program implementation. The Hows and Whens and Why-Fors. He considered that the worst kind of bureaucratic meddling. And the latest abomination out of Sacramento? Group Counseling. God, what would they think of next? A further source of irritation was the fact that the people charged with devising these programs were not real Corrections people, not line officers who had walked a post or manned a gun tower in Folsom or Quentin. No, they were people with graduate degrees in Sociology and Criminology. Theorists. Soft people. Pansies. None had ever walked by a cell and had urine or feces thrown at him just because he was wearing a khaki uniform. None had ever been physically attacked by some deranged convict.

And now the theorists and the pansies had decided that Group Counseling was the answer. The answer to what? he wondered. To violence? To crime itself? Recidivism?

Quinlan was not so naïve as to think that any kind of group counseling would put much of a dent in the crime problem. (It's going to help to talk about it?) Proper discipline might, but he could hardly imagine that group counseling would have much of an effect on the type of men they had at Fremont. Besides, he knew far more effective ways of dealing with the George Lincolns of the world.

And to top it all off, the latest rumor out of Sacramento was that they were considering women for work in corrections. God… Women. Dykes and Do-Gooders, he thought. He didn't know which would be worse. What could they possibly be thinking of?

He moved the binoculars slowly across the Yard; he liked the idea of watching without being observed. A few men lounged on the old wooden bleachers in front of East Block. Two groups were playing dominoes on the tables on the north side of the Yard. Negroes at one table, whites several tables away. The Weight Area was equally segregated, the weights and benches for negroes clearly marked with yellow paint.

It was as it should be, he thought. He saw nothing wrong with segregation. The races didn't want to live together; people seemed to overlook that simple fact. Left to their own devices, they would segregate naturally. But once again the courts, and the Sacramento theorists, and the ACLU Lawyers had gotten involved and decided that desegregation should be the Law of the Land. Never mind that hardly anybody wanted it. Quinlan had never met a Negro who wanted to live in a white neighborhood or go to a white school. Not one. In all his years in corrections. He thought it possible that some might want to visit long enough to steal something or get into some mischief, but he never met one who really wanted to live there.

The idea of whites and Negroes living together implied sexual congress; a notion that was especially abhorrent to him. He thought of his wife, Lil, and his lovely teenage daughters, Pamela and Peggy. Black faces next to theirs filled him with distress. Black bodies next to theirs? God help us, he thought.

The two handball courts were occupied by the Mexicans; it was their game. Occasionally an Anglo would be allowed to play, most often a drug connection from the streets, but it was rare. They kept the courts to themselves. Territory. Turf. No Trespassing.

Quinlan spotted someone he thought was Dave Leonard leaning against the wall near the hospital entrance. A huge convict who appeared to have no neck stood nearby. Though they weren't facing each other, he had the feeling that Leonard was talking to him. That must be Criner, he thought. An informant had called him Hoss. There they were—the Hoss and the Boss. (Quinlan had already managed to find several informants eager to relay information for small favors and a chance to be remembered favorably to the Parole Board. Quinlan was careful to make no promises.) He made a mental note of seeing them together.

His secret search of the Yard revealed other faces he had come to recognize. Voodoo was one of several Negroes gathered by the benches near North Block. (Even Quinlan had begun to think of him as Voodoo.) Billy Jordan was there. Quinlan wondered if that was the Billy 2X he had been hearing about. The conversation was animated. Voodoo seemed to be the center of attention, the man they deferred to. A black inmate joined the group and was greeted by each man in turn with an elaborate handshake. In a few minutes, another departed to the same ceremonial ritual.

Quinlan wished he could listen in. More than just Yard talk, he guessed. More than just talk about a stable of brown beauties and a big Caddy. No, these men had other concerns. They were part of a new group of radicals who considered themselves political prisoners. Well versed in the history of revolution, they were organizing. Quinlan knew he would have to see to it that they didn't get too well organized. An informant inside the group would be invaluable, but so far officer Powell had been unable to establish any kind of network of informants, let alone one that would reach the inner circles of the Black Muslims. (He thought it possible that Powell's clumsy overtures might have had something to do with the death of Tyrone Jackson.)

Harry "Ice" Burgess stood off by himself, hands in his pockets, staring blankly across the Yard. Quinlan focused the binoculars and shuddered without realizing it. Ice was not a big man; standing there in his baggy pants, he looked like some transient who was down on his luck. But if even half the rumors were true (and he had a feeling they were), Burgess was one of the most dangerous men on the Yard. Fortunately, it was only other convicts he killed now, an undertaking that Quinlan thought quite forgivable. Perhaps even laudable.

Little Joe Manning was walking past the Hospital with Junior Grimes, the Catholic Chaplain's clerk. Little Joe was a dwarf who seemed to have a hand in everything; no one suspected him of being Quinlan's man. But it was Little Joe who bugged the Catholic confessional for him. Quinlan's only regret was that it wasn't much use with the Negroes, since few of them were Catholic. Still, he got enough information to justify its use. And he had no qualms about using it. He was a Methodist who believed that the Pope was the anti-Christ. Besides, he understood that Father Sweeny had a serious drinking problem and more often than not would be half in the bag when hearing confessions.

He lowered the binoculars, returned them to the desk drawer and looked back at the Yard. A different perspective without the glasses; there were no faces, no visible expressions, just shapes moving across the Yard. Bodies of different sizes and colors. Children of the State, its own divisive offspring, locked up for safe-keeping. And he, Robert Quinlan, was the Keeper of the Keys, the public's appointed guardian. Society had entrusted him with that task, and he held that trust in high regard.

He couldn't see the hate in those hooded eyes from that distance, but he knew it was there. He could feel it. But it was not a concern; whether they loved him or hated him was immaterial. The myth of Warden Duffy and his love affair with San Quentin was just that—a myth. Plenty of convicts hated Duffy, would gladly have cut his throat. There were always plenty of convicts who hated anyone in authority. Quinlan's own initial experience in Corrections included being sucker-punched and badly beaten by three inmates who got him into the cell on the pretext that one of them was having a heart attack. It was a mistake he never made again.

Quinlan realized the value of discipline; consistent, fair, even-handed discipline. John Alexander's main shortcoming was his failure as a disciplinarian. He starved them on rations and let the drug traffic flourish. The prison was in shambles. Men were making Pruno in the Laundry. Having sex in the gymnasium. But Alexander was only interested in coming in under budget; he thought that made him a good superintendent. And so did Sacramento.

Quinlan had different ideas; Fremont would be his testing ground. There were ways to make inmates more tractable, more manageable. Once they realized that punishment for wrongdoing would be swift and certain, he was sure that attitudes would change. The Adjustment Center, the AC, prison within the prison, could be used for the most difficult cases. Disciplinary write-ups implying the threat of additional time were an effective tool. Fear could be a powerful motivator. Prolyxin and Anectine therapy were possibilities. Perhaps even neurological treatment for violent inmates, though that was officially discouraged.

The goal was to return rehabilitated men to a free society; everyone agreed on that. Only the methods differed. He realized that his methods might appear harsh to some, but when the theorists and pansies in Sacramento saw how well they were working, they'd soon jump on the bandwagon.

He was well aware that he'd come in for his share of criticism early in his career for shooting an inmate under what were termed questionable circumstances. The incident involved an inmate who was trying to escape. In Quinlan's eyes that made him fair game. The Board of Review absolved him of any formal blame, though comments regarding his judgment (or lack of it) were duly noted. (What they failed to note, he thought smugly, was that escape attempts were drastically reduced during the following six months.) But he had no regrets, no doubts, and no second thoughts. He was even a little surprised at how good he felt about the whole incident—how empowered he felt firing the gun, actually shooting someone, seeing the inmate fall from the fence. He had come very close to emptying the entire clip.

He sat at his desk, closed his eyes and took a deep breath. So much to do, he thought. He had considered moving inmate Leonard to some menial job, but decided against it. Leonard would be more likely to incriminate himself in his present job; best let him operate thinking he was unobserved.

He applied the same rationale to Voodoo; leave him alone to fashion his own noose. And Quinlan was sure that he would. When the axe fell on Voodoo's schemes (Quinlan could only guess what they were—most likely something to do with being political prisoners), chances were good that new charges could be filed and his sentence lengthened accordingly. And if there was a shortage of evidence, he could always arrange to have some manufactured. That had never been a problem.

You fight toughness with toughness; convicts don't understand anything else. He learned that from his father, a tough San Francisco cop who ate his gun one gray November day.

Tomorrow he had a surprise shakedown scheduled for West Block. He would cut late Yard movement to a minimum. Tighten security. There was no reason to have convicts out wandering around the Yard after the evening meal. There were holes to plug— he was willing to concede that there might be some rotten apples in Custody. There was contraband traffic to deal with. Drugs. Pruno... All in good time.

He picked up the phone and dialed.

"Lambert Lighting."

"Julie?"

"Spea-king..."

"This is Adam."

"I'm sorry but Mr. Lambert is not in at the present time, sir."

"We on for tonight?" said Quinlan.

"Yessir. As per our agreement, a representative from our staff will be sent to your place of business."

"Good. I'll tell Mister Dinky."

"...Miss Muffin will be waiting, and," she added breathlessly, "open for business."

# CHAPTER 21

Chewy noticed it right away.

"You walkin' funny, Murder Man."

Stan straightened up and tried to walk normally.

Chewy smiled.

"Hey, Flaco," Chewy said to his partner. "Some dude got to the Murder Man."

"I don' beliv' it," said Flaco.

"Me too," said Chewy, shadow boxing his way across the Yard. "This dude have a big chorizo, Murder Man? This guy who got to you?" He held his hands a foot apart. "This big, homeboy? Some hammer got to you?"

Stan tried to walk faster, but it was too painful. He didn't know what to say.

"You gonna be a jailhouse mama now," said Chewy, jabbing the air with a left, following it with a right uppercut. "Somebody's old lady. They be linin' up at your cell now, homeboy. Waitin' to get some pussy…From you, homes. Pussy from the Murder Man."

He stopped and stood in front of Stan.

"You want that?"

Chewy pushed him lightly with both hands.

"Hey, I'm talkin' to you," he said, raising his voice. "You want that? Bein' a jailhouse old lady? You want that?"

Stan looked away.

"Hey!…"

Chewy slapped him across the face with an open hand. Stan blinked; his lower lip trembled. Chewy turned away in disgust. He jerked his thumb over his shoulder.

"How did this puto ever kill somebodys?"

Flaco squinted at the sun and smiled.

"…Maybe he keess him to death."

Flaco chuckled at his own joke. Chewy doubled over with laughter. After a few moments he stood up, threw a few phantom punches and turned back to Stan.

"We gonna call you Putoman now, eh? Like Superman. Only you gonna be Putoman."

"Faster than a spiding bullet," said Flaco. "Able to lip tall chingaderas…"

"Puto-man," said Chewy.

He slapped Stan hard across the face, first with his right hand then with his left. Stan made no effort to retaliate.

"You better go see the Padre, man," said Chewy. "Padre Joe. He can fix you up with Jesus. Then you and Jesus can be homeboys. You can say your prayers while your new daddy be humpin' you…"

Stan wiped his nose on his sleeve.

"Ahhhh…" said Chewy, grabbing him by the arm and pulling him along. "Come on…We got work to do, Murder Man."

They continued on toward the Mess Hall and the fifty-gallon drums of garbage.

After lunch, Stan approached Officer Wetzle.

"I'd like to see the Chaplain," he said.

Wetzle's eyes narrowed.

"People in hell want ice water, too," he said. "You got a ducat?"

"…No."

"You know the rules, Smith. Gotta have a ducat to see the Chaplain. Gotta have one the night before. None of this same-day crap."

"This is an emergency," said Stan.

"Yeah? What kind of emergency we got here?"

"Personal."

"Yeah? What kind of personal?"

"…Private."

"Huh," said Wetzle. "We got rules and regulation for things, Smith. Like civilized people. Rules to follow. Not like where you come from."

"…Please?"

"I'd have to bend some of those rules, Smith. Make an exception. I don't like to do that. Pretty soon every asshole in here wants a favor."

"It's important..." said Stan.

Wetzle rubbed the side of his face and thought about it.

"Well," he said finally. "I might be able to do it this one time. But I'd expect you'd be willin' to cooperate in case I needed some information about certain things might be goin' on. I could count on you to do that, eh? Get some information?"

Stan nodded.

"Good," said Wetzle. "Now we just might be able to get you a ducat. I suppose it's the Catholic Chaplain."

"Yeah."

"Figures."

He picked up the phone in the guard shack.

Stan looked around to see if anyone was watching. Most were walking slowly to their cells after lunch. Only an old Negro with milky eyes seemed to be staring at him. Stan had seen him before; he worked on the Maintenance Crew.

"Bledsoe? This is Officer Wetzle in South Block. Make out a ducat for Smith to see the Chaplain. Stan Smith...No, the Catholic Chaplain. Father Joe. Get the Watch Commander to sign it. Leave it at the Control window. I'll send Smith down after count to pick it up."

He hung up the phone and turned to Stan.

"You know where Control is?"

"Down by the handball courts?"

"That's it," said Wetzle. "You owe me, Smith. Don't forget."

Stan mumbled thanks and hobbled away.

"You hurt?" said Wetzle.

Stan shook his head without turning.

"Huh," said Wetzle.

Pokey squinted, trying to make out the figure near the guard shack. It looked like the little white boy, but he couldn't be sure—not from that distance. And getting any closer might just be inviting trouble. Still, if the white boy was going to The Man, they might all be in trouble. He fretted with his mop for a few minutes, then went to find Willy and Buck.

Father Sweeny's office was located in the Education Area next to the classroom that served as a chapel. There was a shiny brass plate on the door:

**Fr. Joseph Sweeny**
**Catholic Chaplain**

Stan's timid knock was answered by a hearty invitation to enter. The office was small, cluttered, overly warm; magazines and books were stacked on every available flat surface. A stocky priest with a shock of red hair closed the book he was reading, stood unsteadily and offered his hand. Stan took it and glanced at the book—a blue hardcover with large white lettering on the dust jacket: **Alcoholics Anonymous.**

"Here, hand me those," said Father Sweeny, indicating a stack of magazines on the only other chair in the room.

The top one was The Pastoral and Homiletic Review. Stan guessed by the yellow covers that there were some National Geographics mixed in. Father Sweeny took the magazines and set them on the floor. The lopsided grin seemed permanently affixed. He offered Stan the empty chair with an open palm, then sat heavily in his own. Stan sat down carefully.

"Stanley Smith," he said, looking at the ducat Stan had given to him. "How may Father Joe be of assistance?"

"...I wanted to talk to a priest."

"Well...Here I am. Father Joe Sweeny. At your service."

Neither spoke for a few moments. The silence amplified the sounds of breathing, enriched the smell of wine that lingered in the air. Stan began to feel dizzy.

"And what was it you wanted to talk about?" said Father Joe.

"Oh...Some things..."

"I see...Things. What kind of..."

"I haven't been to confession in a long time," said Stan.

"Would you like to do that? Go to confession?"

141

"I don't know. I don't think I have much faith anymore, Father. I used to believe a lot more. Believe in God a lot more. When I was younger. I was an altar boy...I still believe in God sometimes, but I have doubts. It's more like a habit—believing in God. I don't know if I really do. Or even if there is one."

"I see...The substance of things hoped for; the evidence of things not seen," said Father Sweeny. "That's what St. Paul says about faith. About belief. That's his definition."

Stan glanced quickly across the table, then went back to staring at the floor.

"You go to church, Stanley?"

"Sometimes. Not often. I was married in church...The Catholic Church. I went to a Catholic high school—Loyola. Then I..."

"Church is important," said Father Sweeny, slurring church slightly so it sounded more like chursh. "The sacraments and all. Very important. Avenues of grace. Divine grace. We all need that."

"...I killed somebody," said Stan.

"I see," said Father Sweeny. His eyes were watery, set close to the bridge of his nose; bushy eyebrows cast them in shadows.

"It was my wife's..." he could not bring himself to say lover, "...my wife's boyfriend."

"Hmmmmm...Murder," he said, rubbing his hands together. "Murder."

"Only second degree...And I don't even remember."

"...Don't remember what?"

"Doing it. Shooting him. I don't remember that part."

Father Sweeny leaned back and looked at the ceiling.

"God sees all things," he said. "He reads your heart. What does your heart say, Stewart?"

"I don't know," said Stan. "I don't think it says anything. They were sleeping together, Father. My wife and this...guy. Why would God let something like that happen?"

Father Sweeny took a sip from the coffee cup on his desk. His hands were shaking.

"We must be careful not to blame God for things that are a matter of..."

"I never cheated on her," said Stan. "Not once. All I ever did was drink a little too much sometimes…I mean I worked hard, had a house, car, good job…Now this."

"Who can know the will of God?" said Father Sweeny, turning his palms up and shrugging his shoulders. "Divine justice is often something beyond our ability to compre…"

"And I masturbate, too," said Stan. "Sometimes…"

Father Sweeny squinted at him without speaking.

"That's a sin, isn't it?" said Stan. "Masturbation? I remember that's what they told us."

Father Sweeny was slow to answer.

"…Usually," he said, rubbing his chin. "Would you like to go to confession…Did I ask you that already?"

"I've been…raped," said Stan, suddenly close to tears.

Father Sweeny's eyebrows flickered momentarily.

"I see…Have you reported it?"

"No. They said they'd kill me if I told anyone."

Father Sweeny sat up in his chair and took another sip from his coffee cup.

"Father Joe's seen it all, Stewart. Fifteen years. Fifteen years in this place. More than most lifers. You're not the first. No, not the first. And you certainly won't be the last." He glanced up at the ceiling. "Sometimes I ask God why? Why this? Why here? Why now?"

He closed his eyes and lapsed into silence, his forehead rippled in a reflective frown.

"…What should I do?" said Stan.

Father Sweeny opened his eyes.

"Do?…About what?"

"About…what happened."

"Cast your lot with Jesus."

"What if it happens again? What if they come back? They said that, that they'd be back."

"There is no sin," said Father Sweeny. "You were an unwilling participant. There is no sin."

"But what do I do?"

"Do?…Go to the authorities."

"They'll kill me."

"Who will?"

"The people who did it."

"Oh…"

Father Sweeny stared at his coffee cup.

"Prayer is the answer," he said.

Stan closed his eyes and shook his head.

"Fuck…"

"That's not necessary, Stewart," said Father Sweeny. "That type of response …We all have our crosses to bear. Our burdens. The big horses get the heavy loads. That's what Father Jurgelitis told us in the seminary. I never forgot it. And it's true, of course. …I wanted to be a parish priest when I was ordained. I ever tell you that?" He paused for a moment, forefinger to his lips. "No, of course not…I wanted a small parish. Young people. Old People. Families. Marriages and baptisms. Just people living their lives. I wanted to be like the Curé of Ars. Remember him? St. John Vianney. I prayed for the gift of discernment, that I might read men's souls, to better serve our Lord. For the greater glory of God. Instead I got this." He waved weakly at his surroundings. "Fifteen years of it. I offer it up. That's what I do. For the greater glory of God. Ad majorem Dei gloriam. I pray that He will give me strength to do His will. To overcome … temptation."

He touched the coffee cup with both hands.

"Heavy crosses," he said.

He leaned back in his chair and closed his eyes.

"Be a big horse…Go in peace."

Stan waited. A cold chill crept up his spine. No place to run and no place to hide…Can't be doin' no big time less you gets yo mind right…Walk slow, boy, keep yo prune tight and yo back to the wall…Penitentiary wisdom. They would find him and kill him. Or brutalize him so badly he would wish for death. And there was nothing he could do about it. Nothing. Flight was useless; the pursuit would be relentless. They would find him and kill him no matter where he went.

He stood up and left the room. Father Sweeny was slumped in his chair, snoring softly.

On his way back to his cell, another convict fell into step beside him. Stan instinctively moved away.

"Just keep walking," the convict said quietly. "Act like we know each other. Just before we hit the Yard, I'm gonna slip something into your jacket pocket."

"…What is it?"

"A little medicine for your sore ass," he said.

Stan turned to look at him for the first time. He was older, paunchy, a little taller than Stan with a rubbery face and sparse brown hair.

"That supposed to be funny?" said Stan. He felt something drop into the pocket of his denim jacket as they turned out onto the Yard.

"I don't know…You tell me."

"…What do you want?"

"Name's Doc," he said. "D-o-c. Just like it sounds."

"How do you know about what happened?"

"No secrets on the Yard, kid. Even as we speak, there are those who are watching, wondering what we're talking about, trying to make some connection."

"Why the medicine?"

"Can't help myself. All those years of training."

He shook a cigarette out of a pack of Pall Malls and offered it to him. Stan took it and thanked him.

"Don't mention it," said Doc. "Anyway, the worst part's not physical. In case you haven't already discovered that. Rub the ointment on twice a day, morning and night. It'll speed the healing process. It only feels fatal. If you get caught with it, it's contraband. Should anybody ask, you found it…With me so far?"

"Yeah."

"Now, about the…incident. Don't go to the hospital and don't go to The Man. If you go to the cops, they'll want you to name names."

"But I don't know who they…"

"Not relevant. If you tell them you don't know, they'll think you're lying. If you do name names, then maybe, just maybe, they'll put you in Protective Custody, where they will be less than diligent about protecting you."

"But…"

"Try to get over the illusion that these people care about you, Smith. About what happens to you. You're a number to them. That's all. No more, no less. The State pays them so much per prisoner. They want you to shut up, do your time and not cause trouble. That's all they want. Forget rehabilitation. As far as they're concerned, you're the scum of the earth, not worth rehabilitating, whatever that means. You're here to do time, to satisfy a concept of justice which demands that you be punished for violating the rules. They don't care if you come back. All things considered, they'd rather you did come back. You're job security.

"Now…anything of a sexual nature that gets into your central file will only cause trouble every time you see the Parole Board. Guaranteed. Board members seem to have a prurient interest in that sort of thing. Mad Dog Owen's favorite line is, That your deal, Mister? Takin' it in the ass? Calls everybody Mister. Very formal. Then he's likely to hand out a three-year denial. He's ex-Rampart Street Robbery Division who was wounded during a robbery. Not a nice person. And of course he hates convicts. All convicts."

Doc nodded to several people as they made their way across the Yard.

"If you don't learn to fight back, Smith, your life's not going to be worth living. Believe me."

"But they…"

Doc held up his hand.

"I know," he said. "Don't give me chapter and verse on the circumstances. I've heard it a dozen times. Listen carefully…If you don't fight back, it won't be long before you'll be wishing you were dead. If you do fight back, even if it's not much of an effort, you'll make it difficult for them. You have to be more trouble than you're worth…You afraid?"

"…Yeah."

"Good. Use it—it's a great motivator."

"They said they'd kill me," said Stan.

"They won't. You're not worth it. They may punch you around a bit, break a few bones maybe, but then they'll go find somebody who won't fight back. Plenty of those…Going to see Father Joe was a waste of time unless you wanted to sit around and talk about what a good guy Jesus is, or how we all have our burdens to bear, or listen to him whine about having to spend all this time here when he just wanted to have a small parish with all those people coming to him for advice, telling him how wonderful he is. Anyway, you'll have to catch him sober to get even that much out of him. And that's not always easy. He's a lush. But then, you probably figured that out already."

"...You really a doctor?"

"Really a doctor."

"What are you doing in here?"

"Time," he said dryly. "Same thing you are...Had a guy in here last year who worked on the Manhattan Project. Atomic physicist. Helped develop the A-Bomb. Turned out he had five wives... unfortunately all at the same time. The State takes a dim view of polygamy. But then, we all have our little weaknesses."

"I killed somebody," said Stan.

"I know that. Do yourself a favor and don't volunteer information about anything. The less people know about you, the better. Given a choice, lie."

They passed Preacher delivering a sermon on the Yard:

> *Babylon is fallen and destroyed. Howl*
> *for her, take balm for her pain that she*
> *may be healed.*

Doc touched his index finger to his right ear. Preacher nodded, closed the Bible...

> *...And the Father, who seeth in secret,*
> *will reward thee openly...*

...and set off hurriedly across the Yard.

"You see," said Doc, gesturing toward the Yard, "this is all about fear and intimidation. About establishing power, humiliating people, getting a place a little higher up on the food chain where it might be safer. You'll see guys on the iron pile four, five hours a day. Getting big. Getting tough. They figure if they get big enough, strong enough, tough enough, nobody'll fuck with them. That's one of the ways you get respect."

Doc slowed briefly to pass something to another convict walking by.

"If somebody owes you something, they have to pay. That's one of the rules. If they don't, you have to hurt them, maybe even kill them. That's the way the system works. Because if someone can beat you for a pack of smokes, they can beat you for two, or a box, or anything you got. You're a chump. And chumps have no standing in this community of ours. You get no respect. You slip a couple of notches on the food chain. That's why people get killed for a pack of smokes. It's not the smokes; they're incidental. It's the idea; it's what they represent. You owe, you pay. Simple. Otherwise you're just another meal way down on the food chain.

"Place is full of guys who started out strangling puppies and setting cats on fire for kicks when they were kids. Psychopaths. Sociopaths. Don't have a clue about right or wrong. Only thing they understand is power, force. In lots of ways they're just like the cops; the reverse side of the same coin. You got something they want, they take it. You resist, you get hurt. You resist a lot, you may get killed. Or they might leave you alone, figure you're too much trouble to deal with...It's very basic. And simple. The strong survive. The weak often don't. And I'm not just talking about physical strength. You have to be mentally tough. You've got a lot to learn, kid, and if you don't start soon, you won't make it."

"Any suggestions?" said Stan.

Doc shrugged.

"You'll think of something."

"What if they come back?"

"What'd Father Joe tell you to do?"

"...Pray."

"That's Father Joe—he thinks prayer is the answer to everything."

"So what do I do?"

"Beats me," said Doc.

"I thought you were helping."

"Wrong. I pass out medicine, maybe give a short indoctrination course on how things work. The rest is up to you. But you're no dummy. Be resourceful."

"Maybe I could grow another six inches and put on a hundred pounds."

"Maybe…And maybe you could stop feeling sorry for yourself and get on with it."

"With what? With this?"

"With life. With doing your number. You think you get excused from life because somebody ripped you off? Because somebody got to you? If you don't get on with it and come up with something, I can assure you those guys'll be back on a regular basis. They'll bring friends. You're easy, Smith. A pushover. A pretty kid. You should pardon the expression, but you're an easy fuck. Pretty soon you'll be doin' blow jobs and maybe they'll knock all your teeth out so you won't bite. They do that sometimes. Makes it nicer for them."

"They're going to kill me," said Stan.

"Probably not."

"…I don't get it," said Stan.

"Get what?"

"Any of it. What you're doing. Why the medicine. Anything…"

"You don't have to get-it," said Doc. "There are people in here who are interested in you. You don't need to know why."

"They wanna fuck me, too?"

Doc looked over for the first time, his mouth twisted in an odd grin.

"Touché," he said. "But don't kid yourself—you're not that pretty."

"So am I supposed to do something now?"

"Watch and wait. Learn. Preacher always has an interesting message. You might want to check it out. In the meantime, walk slow and keep your back to the wall."

"Guy in the County Jail told me the same thing when I was there."

"Convicts been saying the same dumb things for the last hundred years," said Doc. "Nothing ever changes behind the walls… But it's not bad advice."

"You suppose if…"

Doc suddenly veered off and disappeared into a crowd of convicts milling around the Yard during lunch break. Stan watched for a moment, then turned and headed back toward South Block.

# CHAPTER 22

Someone was making up the top bunk in his cell when Stan returned.

"Name's Hawk," he said, without turning.

"I'm Smith," said Stan. "Stan Smith."

"Smith," he snorted. "Jesus…Smith. That your real name?"

"Yeah."

Hawk was close to six feet tall, wiry, dark hair, his body a bundle of energy. He made up the bunk with a series of karate chops, vaulted into it, leaned back against the wall and looked at Stan for the first time. His face was stone gray, narrow as a hatchet, the eyes buried in tunnels of darkness.

"The Hawk's in for Robbery Two," he said. "What's your beef?"

"Murder," said Stan. "Murder Two."

"Couple of deuces. We might be here for a long time, you and me."

"…Might be."

"Fuck it," said Hawk. "Ain't no big thing. Gotta do time, might as well do it here." He leaned forward and lowered his voice. "I'm gonna be up front with you, man. I hear you been haulin' coal. That's what the grapevine says. That shit don't go with me, man. If you're into it, I'm gonna find me a new celly. I ain't cellin' with no dude likes to get his shit packed. You dig?"

"…I was…forced," Stan said weakly.

Hawk shook his head.

"Man…First thing you learn is that you gotta fight for what you believe in. For what you got. Don't make no never mind what it is… Dope. Chicks. Country. God. Whatever. Man don't fight for what he believes in, for what's his, he ain't nothin'. Ain't even a man. Ain't even a pimple on a good man's ass. Some fool come along and take everything you got. Know what I mean? You don't wanna give up your prune, you gotta fight for it. That's how it is, man. Plain and simple.

...Am I right, man?"

"Right," said Stan.

Hawk pulled a pack of Pall Malls out of his shirt pocket and set it on the bunk.

"What's mine's yours," he said, tapping the pack of cigarettes. "That's the law. Ain't no big thing...The Hawk's a good man to know, a good man to have on your side when the shit comes down. Knows his way around. Been doin' time since juvey. Thirteen years, man. Lucky thirteen. You want somethin' done, you come see the Hawk."

He lit a cigarette and blew the smoke out of his nose.

"The Hawk can fly, man," he said. "Flies at night when nobody can see him. Been doin' it for a long time. Someday he's gonna fly right outta here." He waved at the smoke in front of his face. "If you get my drift."

He jumped off the bunk and faked a jab at Stan's face. Stan backed toward the front of the cell.

"No, no, man. Don't run. Block it. See?...Like this."

He demonstrated how to slip a punch and come in under it.

"See, man. Come in under it. Bam bam bam...to the ribs. Always comin' in. You gotta learn, man. No runnin'. Runnin's for sissies. And cocksuckers. You wanna be a cocksucker?"

Stan shook his head.

"I just decided," said Hawk. "The Hawk's gonna teach you how to fight. Yeah...I decided just now. This very fucking minute. Must be your lucky day. Give me somethin' to do till I fly away."

He jumped back up on his bunk.

"No big thing," he said. "You know I was the lightweight champ at Nellis. You ever been to Nellis?"

Stan opened his mouth to say no, but Hawk raced on without waiting for an answer.

"Fred C. Nellis, School for Boys. My mother sent me there. Said I was incorrigible. I been incorrigible since I was a baby. I was the only kid in fourth grade who could spell it—I-n-c-o-r-a-g-i-b-l-e. See? Still can."

"Yeah."

"One cold motherfucker, that Nellis. We used to make the Fish eat come. The new guys? Rub in on their faces. In their hair. You ever do that? Eat come?"

"…No."

"Me neither. Queers do. Women…Swallow it. Jeez. Makes you sick thinkin' about it."

He dangled his feet over the side of the bunk and tapped his heels together.

"Coach Pryor at Nellis said I had a great left hook. All the great ones had the left. That's what he said. Jeez…Only thing wrong with Pryor was he was a cop. Said I could prob'ly turn pro. Work out some, have a few amateur fights, then turn pro. Wouldn't that be somethin'? Me turnin' pro? Jeez. But I never trained. I hit the streets, it's bye bye baby. I'm off and runnin'. Trainin'? Forget it, man. The Hawk's flyin' by this time. Free as a bird. But I can still fight. Twenty-eight ain't too old. Prob'ly have to fight middleweight now, but I could still make it. Get out and start workin' out. Hey, no problem. Change my name…Irish Jack. Like it?"

"Yeah. Irish Jack." Stan was beginning to warm to his new cellmate.

"Irish Jack Motherfucker…versus Jigaboo Jones at the Olympic Auditorium. I'd start there, then to Vegas and the big money. Vegas is big time, man. You ever been there? To Vegas? Great place. And chicks? Jeez …All about ten feet tall. Big tits. Pussies like little pillows. They got a machine turns 'em out by the dozen. You wanna dozen chicks? Comin' up." He cranked an imaginary handle. "Fuckin' Vegas. Where you from?"

"L.A.," said Stan.

"Where in L.A.?"

"The Valley."

"The fuckin' Valley," he sneered. "The Valley's horseshit, man."

Stan's shrug said he couldn't help where he was from.

"I'm famous," said Hawk. "In Venice. Helluva place, Venice. Santa Monica, too. Everybody knows the Hawk in Venice.

Everybody. You could ask anybody, Hey, you know the Hawk? Yeah, man. Everybody knows the Hawk."

Hawk rubbed the blanket with his right hand.

"My mother tried to kill me when I was a kid," he said. "...Somethin' else."

"Your own mother tried to kill you?"

"Twice...The Lady Hawk didn't fuck around. She was serious business."

"...You call the cops?"

"She was my mother, man. You don't call the cops on your mother. You don't call the cops on anybody. Jeez, man. Wake up."

"What happened?"

"I ran away. Hit the road. Bye, bye, baby."

Neither spoke for several minutes.

"They tell me the Voodoo Man's here," said Hawk.

"...I don't know who that is."

"Voo-doo. Me and Voodoo had a run in one time at Preston. I jumped his black ass. Whipped him good. He ain't nothin', man. Thinks he's a big deal, but he ain't nothin'. A ze-ro. The Aryan Nation fixin' to put him out of business anyway. Permanent. Hog gonna do it himself. Fuckin' Hog, man. He's somethin' else. You ever see Hog?"

Stan said he didn't think so.

"Weighs in about three twenty, arms this big around. Mean, man. Dirt mean. Hog'll kill a man easy as look at him."

Hawk talked until evening chow release. Though he claimed to know many men at Fremont, he greeted no one in the Mess Hall. After chow he continued to talk about his adventures, chain smoking on the upper bunk, twitching nervously every few minutes.

Stan was both repelled and fascinated by his new cellmate. Perhaps they could be friends, he thought, though he realized they had little in common. Still, it might be possible. Stan had never had any close friends, never been really close to anyone (except maybe the people in the books he read). There were acquaintances like Robert and Jason, but never anybody he could call a close friend, anybody he could confide in. He was afraid of most people, even people his own age, though he often called the fear by other names.

Careful. Cautious. He had lived in the shadow of the Elder Smith all his life (even after he moved out), dwarfed by his judgments, fearful of his wrath.

His mother had nurtured his developing psyche with terrifying tales of the things that could happen if you weren't always careful, always vigilant…You never know, she said, shaking her head and wagging her finger like a metronome. She was a long-suffering woman, skilled in her role, waiting stoically for some cosmic event that would snuff out their fragile lives and demonstrate to a pagan world the undeniable love and destructive power of the One True God and His Only Son, the Lord Jesus Christ. She suffered Carl, a monster of a man, who tortured her frail body with his incessant sexual demands. She feigned indifference to his advances; he didn't seem to notice. Nearing fifty-five now, she thought it would abate. But it seemed to be getting worse; he exercised his waning virility at every opportunity.

His heart attack, she knew, was an answer to a prayer. In one bold stroke, her body, and possibly his soul, had been saved.

God knows, she said, anointing her forehead with holy water from Lourdes, giving thanks to the Blessed Mother. And not a moment too soon.

Stan lay on the lower bunk and read his library copy of *Moby Dick*, following Ahab and Starbuck on their long sea journey until the sounds of the cellblock were replaced by the snap of the wind in the sails and the slap of the sea on the wooden hull of the Pequod. He fell asleep before lights out at ten, only to be awakened twice during the night when the upper bunk shook violently for a few moments, then stopped as suddenly as it had started.

When he was somewhat healed and the agony of his first bowel movement was only a memory, he and Hawk began to meet at the gym each afternoon for his boxing lesson. The first day, Hawk bloodied his nose. Stan wanted to stop right then, but Hawk kept throwing punches and yelling at him to fight back. After Stan threw a few awkward punches, Hawk let him stop long enough to wipe the blood away. Stan could hardly breath. He was sick from swallowing blood, but Hawk made him fight for another half-hour. He was exhausted. The second day was a repeat of the first.

"I changed my mind," said Stan, after they had finished on day number two. "I don't want to learn how to fight. Wasn't my idea anyway."

"Too late," said Hawk. "We already started. Can't stop now. Forget the bloody nose; ain't no big thing. I might need a backup some day. Gotta pay your dues, man."

"Honest, Hawk. I'm through. Washed up. I can't do this."

Hawk knocked him down with a straight right hand.

"Fuck that," he said. "You can't be through. Not allowed. And if you cry, I'm gonna beat you to death right here. You're gonna learn or else. And someday you're gonna thank the Hawk. Remember that. Thank you, Mister Hawk."

Sometime during the second week, Hawk threw a roundhouse right that broke Stan's nose…Then he told Hawk he honest-to-God had to quit because his nose was broken and he couldn't breath. Honest-to-God. Hawk told him if he tried to quit he'd kill him. Strangle him in his sleep. Stan didn't know whether to believe him or not.

In the days that followed he watched the dark circles form under his eyes and the bloodclots cloud his vision.

"You look like you been out kissin' a gorilla," said Hawk. "A gorilla with a bad attitude. Ha ha ha…"

"That's really fuddy, Hawk," said Stan. "Really fuddy…"

He started throwing more punches when he discovered that his nose was safer when he was on the offensive. One day he caught Hawk with a left jab that bloodied his nose. Hawk was furious.

"Fuckin' lucky punch," he fumed, wiping his nose on his forearm. "No fuckin' Valley wimp's gonna give the Hawk a bloody nose. No fuckin' way…'cept luck. You're the luckiest fucker I ever seen, man. You know that? We oughta take the gloves off right now so I can beat the shit outta you."

Stan apologized, but Hawk tore into him with a vengeance anyway. Still, Stan caught him a few more times; it didn't seem all that hard. He was getting the hang of it; slipping punches, using the jab, planting the back foot to get more power behind his punches. Hawk wouldn't even talk to him when it was over.

It had never occurred to Stan that he might be able to fight, to defend himself. He had always thought of himself as weak, inept and clumsy. His father had chuckled good-naturedly at his first attempts to play baseball.

"Never be a ballplayer," he announced, closing the issue. "Not with those itty bitty hands."

It went without saying that Carl had been a ballplayer, though he often said it anyway. Wide as a door and tough as rawhide, he'd been the starting left guard on his high school football team (before the sissy face masks, he always said), and the catcher on the baseball team. He showed Stan his high school yearbook—there he was on the varsity sports page: Carl Smith, man among boys.

Stan's initial foray into the sexual jungle only reinforced his feelings of inadequacy. His first experience ended almost before it began, eager sperm filling his jockey shorts long before the ceremonial thrust. Wise old Martha told him not to worry; at thirty years of age she had learned a thing or two worth knowing. She pushed his empty face between her plentiful thighs and played upon his desire to please. He did not find it particularly pleasant, though Martha seemed to enjoy it and he was not without some sense of power as she groaned her way to gratification. Other trysts followed similar patterns; his timing was always off.

Bonnie, his own sweet Bonnie, pressed his face to her muff like a poultice to a wound. She held him with urgent hands until she spasmed, but would not reciprocate. She found his member (she said) unattractive. She didn't mean it in a personal way. So she said, though it seemed to him to be personal enough since the member in question was his.

He examined the offending appendage with a magnifying glass, noting the irregularities, the tiny bumps decorating the length (where did they come from? he wondered), the unsavory folds of skin, the other unpleasant artifacts that bloomed under the ledge where the shaft joined the head. He had to admit that it was not all that attractive. He didn't blame her for her lack of enthusiasm, though he secretly wished for more of an effort. He suggested that she close her eyes (that's what I do, he said...after all, how pretty

157

are vaginas?). She replied that since she already knew what it looked like, closing her eyes wouldn't help. He couldn't fault the logic.

The fear of his surroundings gradually lessened as the days passed and there were no more incidents like the one in his cell. A creeping sense of confidence began to replace the terror that had been his constant companion. Though the fear was still present, it didn't dominate every waking moment. He even entertained the idea that he might be able to defend himself if confronted by the men who had attacked him. He didn't know what he could do against all three, but perhaps Hawk would help.

He made an effort to walk near Preacher at least once a day to listen for some possible message. What he heard were biblical quotes and misquotes, warnings about sin and repentance…

…Come to me you who are heavy burdened and I will lighten your fucking load…I will give to thee a wheelbarrow to carry your burdens…

He saw Doc several times on the Yard, but made no attempt to speak to him. On the one occasion that their eyes met, Doc looked away and shook his head. Not now, he seemed to say.

A few more weeks and Stan was close to holding his own with Hawk. He began to look forward to the afternoon sessions in the gym, but Hawk appeared to be losing interest; he had other concerns. He was becoming more active in the Aryan Nation.

"We got plans," he said. "Big time plans, man. Shit gonna come down. Things gonna change." His eyes gleamed with excitement. "You oughta join now. Get in while you can. None of them jungle bunnies be fuckin' with you if you was part of the Nation."

With his ear to the heartbeat of hate, Voodoo heard it all. There was little he did not know. The word went out to watch Hog Beaumont, Arkie Panier, Bingo Pierce, and the new guy, Hawkins. Voodoo and Billy 2X assessed the situation and decided upon a plan of action.

"The Hawk can fly," said Hawk, standing outside his cell one night after the evening meal. "Bet your ass the Hawk can still fly. Money in the bank. Don't forget it." He hit the air with two left jabs and a right hook. He gave a mean look to two Negroes who jostled him as they passed on the tier.

"Fuckin' niggers," he said, then went back to shadow boxing till the cell doors opened for lockdown.

The following night, as the cellblock was filling with men returning from the evening meal, the same two Negroes approached swiftly, lifted Hawk over the railing and dropped him from the fourth tier. It hardly seemed to take any effort at all. And only an instant in time. One moment he was standing on the tier, the next he was hurtling toward the floor forty feet below. Hawk didn't make a sound; not until he hit, head first, like a giant hardboiled egg hitting the concrete at gravity speed. Stan, walking a few paces behind, watched him fall. No windmilling arms, no screaming for help, no frantic effort to right himself and land on his feet—almost as if he was already dead the moment he left the fourth tier. The sound he made when he hit was sickening.

He looked like a giant swastika lying on the floor, arms and legs at odd angles, a pool of blood spreading under his head. Those near the body drew back, as if proximity would be incriminating. Those near the flight path on the tiers moved away from the railing. Officer Wismer wheeled around on the gunwalk and leveled his carbine.

"Hold it!" he barked. It was the only sound.

Wetzle took one look and called the Goon Squad.

Hawk's left leg quivered for a few moments. None of it took very long. It was quiet enough to hear his bowels empty when he died.

Someone spoke from the second tier.

"That muffuckah shit-his-pants, man."

Then the noise began.

"Hold it!" shouted Wismer. He fingered his carbine nervously.

In a matter of seconds, Officer Cheswick and the three other members of the Goon Squad came blustering into the cellblock. Convicts melted into their cells. Cheswick, his baton raised to begin the symphony, found no one to hit. The four stood around the broken body, methodically slapping nightsticks into open palms. Stan was the only one outside his cell. He stood at the railing on the fourth tier and stared at the body, unable to move.

Cheswick nudged the body with his foot and wrinkled his nose.

"Stinks," he said.

"Dead?" said Wismer.

"Got himself an early parole," said Cheswick.

"Should we call Doc Dorfield?" said Wetzle.

"Can't hurt," said Cheswick. "Make it legal."

He looked up and saw Stan.

"Hey you! Get down here."

Stan walked slowly down the four flights, playing the scene over and over in his mind, listening to the sound as Hawk hit the floor, trying to grasp what it meant.

"You might want to think about movin' it along, Mister," said Cheswick. "I got other things to do besides watchin' you stroll down the stairs."

Stan stood by the body shaking his head. He was close enough now to smell the blood and the body waste. Could it really be Hawk there on the floor? He didn't seem to be breathing. But how could that be? He had been alive and breathing just a few minutes ago. Talking. Shadow boxing. Eating dinner...Hey, man, everybody knows the Hawk...

"You know this guy?" said Cheswick.

"Yeah."

"Who is he?"

"Hawkins."

"You push him off the tier?"

"No."

"You see who did?"

"...No."

Cheswick was built like a linebacker; when he got mad his face turned red.

"You didn't see nothin', eh?"

"No...(Is that you, Hawk?)

"You suppose he just jumped off? Thought he could fly maybe?"

Stan shrugged...(Hawk? This guy doesn't know you can really fly. Hawk?)

Cheswick waved a hand in front of Stan's face.

"You see okay?"

"Yeah."

"But you didn't see nothin' up there, eh? On the tier." His face was getting redder.

"No."

"He come off the fourth tier?"

"...I didn't see."

"Another blind convict," he fumed, turning to Wetzle. "Call Doc Dorfield and make out a report. Try and get some witnesses. Then clean up this mess ...And call the cook and tell him there'll be one less for dinner tonight. Ha ha ha." It was Cheswick's idea of a joke. He pointed his nightstick at Stan.

"What's your name?"

"Smith."

"A number?"

"...Eight three five three four."

Cheswick pulled a small notepad out of his shirt pocket and wrote it down.

"I'll remember you, Smith. I got a really good memory for convicts who don't cooperate, for assholes like you." He put the notepad away. "Better count 'em," he said to Wetzle, implementing conventional Custody wisdom—When in doubt, count.

The Goon Squad formed up and left in formation, two by two.

Stan was left standing near the body.

"Thank you, Mister Hawkins," he said, then turned and walked slowly back up the stairs to his cell. He faked a left jab and came in with a right uppercut, the way Hawk would have done it. A feeling that he didn't recognize stirred inside him. Maybe, he thought, Just maybe.

*...All things are possible*, said Preacher, *to him who believes.*

# CHAPTER 23

Bugs Petrocelli died that summer, his throat cut, his mouth clumsily shredded, the third victim of an unknown killer whose presence was beginning to cause some degree of anxiety among the convict population. The strange aspect was that, though the rumors were plentiful, nobody seemed to know who was doing it. A lone wolf acting on his own? A random killing by someone truly deranged? Revenge murders? The grapevine had no real information.

Bugs lay buried under several bales of hay at the prison Dairy for a day and a half before anyone found him. Lt. Wotek made Nelson count North Block three times before he finally accepted the short count with Bugs missing. Moose had a fit because chow was an hour late and he just knew it was Nelson who had the count screwed up again.

How Bugs got to the Dairy was another mystery; it was an area outside the walls, open only to Honor Block inmates with less than a year to serve. Bugs didn't fit into either category. Dairy trucks were carefully searched coming and going. All the guards knew Bugs by sight; there was no way he could have sneaked out on a phony Honor Block I.D. card. Yet there he was, dried alfalfa stuck to his eyes and a gaping hole where his mouth had been. Bernardo "Bugs" Petrocelli, dead in the Dairy of all places, surrounded by real cows he had never once even seen while he was alive. Tony Shoes and Jimmy the Fist wouldn't have believed it in a million years…Bugs in the fuckin' dairy? With the cows? Bugs don't know cows from cannoli…

Though the late summer heat was oppressive, Preacher manned his post on the Yard and continued to spread the Word:

*...I beheld a great beast coming out of the earth; and he had two horns and he spoke as a dragon. And he made fire come down from heaven and scorch the earth. He had the power to give Paroles or to cause death, often exercising the latter and denying the former...He was a prick...*

Father Joe remembered Bugs in his prayers for the dead, adding yet another name to the long list he kept in his heart, poor lost souls who had forsaken this world for Another, who dwelled in the Land of Nod, to the east of Eden. After morning Mass on Monday, he wrote a note to remind himself to order two more cases of sacramental wine. For some reason, the supply seemed to be dwindling faster than usual.

Summer brought the wanna-be boxers out in force, hooded figures jogging around the Yard early in the morning, getting in shape for the monthly matches at the gym where smokes, machismo and reputations rode on every punch. Bragging rights to South Block or West Block where often on the line, things of no small consequence. Sometimes a fighter from the Free World would come in for an exhibition match. In July, Scrap Iron Jones, a washed up heavyweight, came in and punched Bulldog Davis into submission early in the third round. Scrap Iron knew how it was behind the walls; he'd done time himself. When they told him it was just an exhibition, he said, Exhibition, my dick. Some convict gonna pay his dues to old Scrap Iron...

Chewy was out doing his roadwork, scowling brown face framed by a white towel draped over his head and tucked under the collar of his jacket, Santa Rosa high tops thumping methodically on the Yard, shadow boxing his way to the Big Time. Flaco was never far behind. Every now and then, Stan did a double take at one of the boxers who looked a little like Hawk with his wiry quickness. But then he remembered...The Hawk's gone, man. Done flew away...Besides, Hawk never did any roadwork anyway.

The Saturday night movie was announced over the P.A. system:

*The movie for tonight is* Drag Strip Girl *with Fay Spain and Steve Terrell…*

"Didn't we see that a couple of months ago?" said the Count.

"Last year," said Leonard.

"How times flies, eh?" said Moose. "That the one about the chick who falls for the race driver?"

"I think," said the Count.

"With the big tits?"

"…The guy or the girl?"

"You been here too long, Countess," said Moose. "Take a break and give yourself a hand job tonight. Get some strange stuff. Try it left handed."

"I'm good with either hand."

"Lucky you," said Greek. "I can hardly wave goodbye left handed."

"Plus the fact that your dick don't get hard anymore."

"Hey, Moose, come sit on this, willya? See if it's hard or not."

"Forget it," said Moose. "If you're into somethin' strange, maybe Paulson here can give you a hand job. Won't get much stranger than that. Ha ha ha ha…"

"Awwww, man," said Paulson.

"Besides, if you don't hurry," said Moose, "this guy that's slicing people up might come along and slice your dick off. Then it won't make any difference. You won't even care."

"Tell you what," said the Count. "I'll always care. Even when I'm dead. Even after I'm dead a hundred years, I'll still care."

"That because you're a vampire and vampires never die?"

"No, it's because I'll always care about what happens to my dick."

"Even after you're dead?"

"Even after I'm dead."

"…Jesus."

The Aryan Nation began planning the retaliation for Hawk's death, not particular about who they got as long as the skin color was black. They had a few favorites, but in a pinch most anyone would do. Hog took out his list and checked the names. He knew they needed to balance the scales of justice as quickly as possible… and two for one seemed like just the right balance.

Hoss Criner took up his position by the Laundry and collared those who owed him. Reno dropped two boxes of Big Reds on the bench and kept moving. He had a sizeable scab on his cheek. Hoss took a long drag off his tailor made cigarette and exhaled slowly. A slight smile pulled at his mouth.

"Thanks, Reno," he said. "See you next week, eh? Only two more. Don't be late, old buddy. 'Cuz you know what happens if you're late."

Gimpy made a mark in his notebook. Reno kept walking.

It ain't fair, he thought. No fuckin' way it's fair. At this rate he'd never catch up. The original box had already cost him eleven.

Fat Tony prowled the Yard seeking someone to violate.

The Iceman walked the perimeter alone, collar up, chain smoking Bull Durham cigarettes that he rolled himself. He could have had all the tailor-mades he wanted (all he had to do was ask Leonard), but he preferred the Bull, the Dust; it suited him better. His memory had grown dark and unreliable in the shadows behind the walls. He had conversations with people he remembered from his childhood, people from comic books and old movies. He saw things that no one else saw, things he could not name. He simply called them Things, as in, I seen some Things today. Some came, took human shape and threatened him. They had to be killed. There was no other way. It was kill or be killed. Self-defense. Survival. He understood that… Hour after hour he walked, lost in his own world.

Many walked the Yard with newspapers or magazines wrapped tightly around their ribs, subtly hidden under chambray shirts and denim jackets—such was the violent nature of the Yard. An attack might come at any time, from any direction. Even though no enemies were known, an attack might be a case of mistaken identity. Howard Taylor died that way, his misfortune being that he bore a close resemblance to an undercover drug agent. A sharpened plastic toothbrush entered his ascending carotid artery one sunny afternoon and his life gushed away in a matter of minutes as he rushed around the Yard in a frenzy screaming for help. Everyone gave him a wide berth, lest they be identified with the victim. Fat Tony giggled hysterically; it was the funniest thing he'd ever seen. Taylor looked like a wind-up toy run amok. It was a lucky hit, even Tony knew that. He didn't think he could do it again if he tried a hundred times.

Young convicts, some still in their teens, hardened graduates from the spartan training camps of Preston, D.V.I. or Tracy, stepped across the Yard with a slow, disdainful strut, each step an invitation to violence, heads tilted back to allow limited vision through half-closed lids, arms swinging slowly, deliberately, jackets on and buttoned to the neck no matter what the weather...Walkin' the Walk. Talkin' the Talk. Spoilin' for a beef...

Most drifted in a loosely defined circle around the Yard, hands deep in denim pockets, shoulders hunched, bearing some unseen burden. A few made plans for the future, though most lived in the past, fabricating lives from a junkyard of memories when high times were always the order of the day. Those were the days, man. They all agreed. Those were the fucking days, man...

In a continuing effort to kill his crime partner (who had turned State's evidence) long distance, Devil Charley Chiponis faithfully repeated the Invocation to Destruction each day...

...and the great shapes shall rise from the pits and vomit forth their putrescence into his puny brain...

He continued his daily recitation and waited eagerly for news of his crime partner's death. When none came, he turned his attention to someone closer (Hoss Criner) with the hope that speeding Criner's demise would at least relieve him of a portion of his burden of debt.

George Lincoln patrolled that portion of the Yard where the brothers were playing dominoes. Lincoln was the best; nobody could beat him. Put some bones in his big black hands and he was king. Though he and Voodoo seldom spoke on the Yard, Voodoo had initiated several private meetings in hopes of uniting the black convicts for the coming Revolution. As always, Lincoln was on the lookout for the best offer.

Stan was reassigned from the Grounds Crew to the Watch Office shortly after Hawk's death. He found the change order on his bunk when he came back from work one day:

**FROM:** **Grounds Crew**
**TO:** **Watch Office—clerical**
**Effective immediately.**


He had to ask Wetzle where the Watch Office was.

"Control," said Wetzle. "Where you picked up your ducat."

"How come I got a job change?"

Wetzle shrugged.

"It happens. They lost a guy to parole awhile back. They need someone who can type. You type?"

"A little."

"Huh…Used to be only fruits could type."

"Things change."

"Some do, some don't."

Stan turned to leave.

"By the way, Smith," said Wetzle, "I was real disappointed you didn't come through about Hawk. Real disappointed."

"…Come through with what?"

"Information about who did it. I thought we had a deal—I let you see the Chaplain, you return the favor when I need a little help. You didn't hold up your end of the bargain. Cheswick wants those guys real bad. Wants 'em out of here. You could help. Might be doin' yourself a favor at the same time."

"I'd help if I could," said Stan, "but I didn't see anything."

"Bullshit."

"I was on the stairs goin' up to the fourth tier when it happened. You know Hawk, always in a hurry. Beat me back to the cell every time."

Wetzle tapped his pencil on the desk in the guard shack and shook his head.

"Well, I hope you don't need any help in the future, Smith. Hope there's no…accidents up there on four. Takes a real long time to get all the way up there from way down here. A real long time. Might even have trouble getting' anyone to respond at all, far as it is up there…Be terrible havin' one of them crazy guys get all over you, hurt you real bad, maybe even cut your throat and not have anybody to help. Person could die up there. Be a goddam shame."

Stan lowered his voice.

"I just need some time," he said. "I'll work with you."

Wetzle got up from his chair and moved a step closer.

"That's better," he said. "I want you to let me know what you hear on the Yard. Who's makin' the Pruno, what's up with the nigras, drugs, anything you hear about I want to know."

"I haven't heard much so far."

"You will," said Wetzle. "Everything goes through Control and the Watch Office. That goddam Leonard knows shit before the Warden does. Just keep your ears open…And you know, Smith, it don't hurt to have somebody put in a good word for you when your parole hearing comes around. Your counselor wants to know how you're doin', he comes to me. Any problems? Does he get along? Cooperate? I can go either way. Bein' a fuck-up obviously don't help your chances. But if I say you're a responsible person who is willing to come forward with information about illegal activities, that goes a long way toward convincing the Parole Board that you might be ready to return to society, a completely rehabilitated person. See what I'm gettin' at? This can be a mutually good thing."

"I see that. I'll keep my ears open and let you know what I hear."

"Yeah. You do that, Smith. You just do that…"

Leonard introduced him to the Watch Crew when he got to Control.

"You gonna be around awhile?" said Moose.

"Probably."

"How long?"

"Five to life."

"That's awhile. Robbery?"

"Murder Two."

"You don't cheat, do you?"

"…Cheat at what?" said Stan.

"Anything. Last guy we had in here cheated all the time. Carson. He'd rather cheat than eat. Cards. Dominoes. Everything. Fuckin' guy murdered his mother, for chrissakes."

"I don't cheat," said Stan.

"Good," said Moose. "You didn't kill your mother, did you?"

"No…My wife."

Moose sounded relieved.

"Maybe we caught a break, Leonard," he said. "Fuckin' Carson even cheated on the Fly Killing Contest."

"...What's that?" said Stan.

"It's very complicated," said Greek, "but basically we have millions of flies that show up here at Fremont during the summer months to feed on the shit in the dairy. Or whatever they feed on. It's like a vacation for them. Disneyland for flies. You can't imagine how many there are. And it's our job, partly because we think of it as a civic duty, and partly because Leonard decided it was a way to pass the time, to try and eliminate as many flies as we can. So the person who kills the most flies gets a prize."

"Too late for you anyway," said Moose. "You'll have to wait till next year. I won't even tell you what the prize is for this year."

"...Why?"

"It'll just make you crazy that you're too late to get in the contest."

"Oh," said Stan.

"You type?" said Leonard.

"A little. I'm slow."

"Not to worry," said Greek. "We're in no hurry."

"Officially your job is to work for the Records Officer," said Leonard. "Unofficially, we need a runner, somebody to deliver messages from time to time. Pick up a few things. Low profile. You're not known on the Yard yet. Think you can handle that?"

"I can learn."

"You get along okay with Hawk?" he said quietly.

Stan hesitated before he spoke, wondering what they knew.

"...We did okay."

"Good. You learn anything?"

"Yeah."

"Like what?"

"How to slip a punch and come in under it."

"Might be the most important thing you learn here," said Leonard. "Hawk was ten to one to die in prison, kid. No other way it could've happened. Close the case and forget about it."

"You know I don't cheat, Leonard," said Moose. "You know that."

"I do?"

"Absolutely."

"I'm grateful," said Leonard, "that we have someone around here with a little integrity."

"And Moose has got as little integrity as anyone," said Greek.

"Go fuck yourself, Greek."

"Oh, if I only could."

"You like jute balls?" Paulson said to Stan.

"Yeah."

"Me, too," said Paulson. "That's what we got for dinner tonight. Greek says they put rat turds in 'em."

"Fact," said Greek. "Dried rat turds. Cheap and nutritious. Lots of protein. Taste like those rice crispy things. It's not a well-known fact, but ounce for ounce, rat turds have more protein than steak."

"Awwww, Greek," said Paulson.

"Just keep eatin' 'em, little man. Won't be long before you're growin' a tail."

"This is the best place in the whole prison to work," said Paulson. "Better than the Laundry or the Furniture Factory even."

"Welcome to Disneyland," said Leonard, pushing his glasses up on the bridge of his nose. "Hope you haven't forgotten all your engineering skills."

"Not all of them."

"Never can tell when they'll come in handy," said Leonard. "We may need to splice into a phone line some day. Know any engineers that could handle something like that?"

"Possibly."

"Good...Now back to business. Greek, who you like in the Packer, Bear game?"

"Home field for the Pack," he said. "Take the homeboys and lay the six."

Leonard made a notation.

"How come you're so smart?" he said.

"For one thing I don't eat the jute balls. That helps."

Three days later, Stan's new cellmate arrived, so big that the bedding rolled up under his arm looked like a brown towel.

"I'm Big," he said. Heavy eyebrows formed a dark V just above his nose.

"I can tell," said Stan, shifting toward the front of the cell to make room. "...I'm Smith."

"That your real name? Smith?"

"Yeah. And you? Just Big?"

"Eddy Big. They call me Big Eddy. Backwards 'cuz I'm so big."

"Makes sense."

Big Eddy tossed his bedding on the upper bunk, dropped to the floor and did twenty quick pushups. "I can bench press three seventy."

"Great..."

"I keep workin' out I'll be Mister fuckin' America."

"You got my vote."

The five-by-eight cell suddenly seemed much smaller.

"I hate this fuckin' place," he said. "Folsom was better. Guy could jerk off in peace."

"Yeah?"

"Yeah. Single cells...Too many guys gettin' killed when they double up. Know what I mean? Long nights. No witnesses. Who knows what happens. Comes morning only one of 'em's alive. Self-defense."

"Figures," said Stan.

"Cops can't be everywhere," said Eddy.

"Right...Only so many cops. Can't watch everything."

"Cops are fuckin' worthless."

"And then some..."

"You ever think about killin' yourself?"

"Not for a while," said Stan.

"I have," said Eddy, wiping the stainless steel mirror over the sink with his towel. "Maybe take a hundred reds and go to sleep forever. Big time Z's. Know why I don't do it?"

"No, why?"

"I think about all the chicks I haven't fucked yet. Keeps me goin'. You know there's millions of women in the world."

"I heard that."

"Millions and millions. Think about it. You know how many that is?"

"More than just a couple," said Stan.

"Better believe it. I figured it out one time. Round numbers. Just to fuck a million, just one million, you'd have to plug about sixty a day for fifty years. That's a lot of pussy."

"...Big time."

"Sixty a day. I figured it out one time...That's more than three an hour, eighteen hours a day. Guy'd hardly have time to eat."

"Hey, who needs food with all that pussy."

"Gotta keep your strength up. Wheat germ. Vitamin E. Gotta have it."

"Right."

"Still...Sometimes it don't seem like it's worth it."

"...What doesn't?"

"Anything...Sometimes I think it'd be easier to kill somebody in here and have 'em send me to the gas chamber. Get it over with. They tell me those cyanide pills smell like peach blossoms. Not a bad way to go."

"What about the chicks?" said Stan.

"Chicks." He shook his head. "Them chicks'll give you the blues, man. Guaranteed."

He glanced at Stan, then bent over the sink, looked into the stainless steel mirror and attempted to squeeze one of the larger pimples near his nose.

"Wouldn't bother me to kill somebody," said Eddy. "Be easy..."

Stan didn't say anything.

"Food in this place gives me zits. All fuckin' grease. Makes me crazy."

Big Eddy splashed some water on his face and surveyed his wavy reflection.

"That guy that got shoved off the tier was your celly, eh?"

"Yeah."

"I heard two niggers did it."

Stan glanced at the guard on the gunwalk.

"I don't know," he said. "I wasn't close enough to see."

"I thought you was right there when it happened."

"No. I was still on the stairs. Didn't see it."

"Somebody said it was two guys…Willy and Buck."

"…Coulda been. I didn't see it."

Eddy dried his face and set about making his bed.

"I gotta tell you…warn you about this terrible temper I got. I get really crazy sometimes. Just snap. Like that." He snapped his fingers. "I'm gone. Loony tunes. Serious crazy."

"That's weird," said Stan. "I got the same deal. One crazy motherfucker." He looked straight at Eddy's chest. "They used to call me Crazy Stan, the Hamburger Man."

"I remember one time," said Eddy, "I hit this guy with a baseball bat. Creamed him. Right across the bridge of the nose. Goodbye nose. Blood like you wouldn't believe. Dropped him like a rock."

"Born to lose," said Stan.

"I'm gonna end up killin' somebody someday. Sure as shit. Can't help myself." He slammed a fist into his open palm several times.

"Tell me about it," said Stan, leaning against the bars and facing his cellmate. "Couple a years ago I had to kill a guy who was fuckin' around with my old lady."

Eddy stared at him for a moment.

"You killed somebody?"

"Had to. This lame motherfucker was bangin' my stash. I had to take him out. Flush him. Send him to Long Beach."

"…How'd you do it?"

"Put a few holes in him with a .357," said Stan. "So long, loser."

"Your old lady there when it happened?"

"Caught 'em in the act."

"You caught 'em together? Doin' it?"

"On the couch."

"…Whadja do to her?"

"Made her watch while I blew him away…Then made her go down on me."

"After you killed her Sancho, you made her go down on you? Jesus, man. That's the coldest thing I ever heard. What'd it feel like, man. I mean after you did him?"

Stan shrugged.

"Great," he said. "Guy got what he deserved. If I had to do it over I'd just make it slower. He didn't suffer enough."

"Crazy Stan, the Hamburger Man, eh? How'd you catch the name?

"Oh…I put a guy's hand in a meat grinder once. Wasn't a big deal. He only lost a couple of fingers. Guy named Freddy. Boston Freddy. From Boston. Cheatin' a little heavy at cards. Freddy'd rather cheat than eat."

Eddy chuckled.

"Rather cheat than eat, eh?"

Stan turned toward the bars; a smile pulled at the corner of his mouth.

"Ain't no big thing," he said quietly. "No big thing."

Pokey talked to Willy and Buck outside the Mess Hall. He was animated; the prospect of violence had him going again. Willy and Buck smiled at the old man's enthusiasm.

"Soon," they told him. "We be settin' it up soon."

"I be getting' my stuff this time. Pretty white boy stuff."

Pokey flapped his arms like a chicken.

"The Hawk done flew away," he said. "Flew the coop fo' good. I be sure to get me some white meat this time."

They all laughed.

Voodoo emerged from North Block like a panther from his lair; he even stretched like a cat. He looked at Hoss, checked the Iceman's location, watched Hog and Bingo and Arkie stroll across the Yard as if they didn't have a care in the world. He raised himself up on his toes and rubbed his shaved head with both hands.

Another day, he thought. One day closer. Merry Christmas from the Voodoo Man…Look out, sweet baby Jesus, Voodoo comin' to get you. Gonna drink your blood…You and all those other blue-eyed honky motherfuckers.

# CHAPTER 24

Though far different in appearance, Hebner and Powell were both men of ambition who sought positions of power. Quinlan knew all about men like that; he was one himself.

Hebner, whippet thin and weasel mean, was born in Bakersfield, California, second son of a Sweaty Hardhat and the Little Woman, possessed of a certain inbred cruelty that prompted him to tear the tails off squalling cats and set fire to small grounded birds. He grew up second best in everything—sports, school, romance. His older brother got the trophies, the girls and finally the piece of shrapnel that tore his chest open and ended his life during an assault on Heartbreak Ridge in Korea. Young Mark Hebner was not noticeably unhappy about it.

Powell had the appearance of dark apple butter, soft and pliant. Underneath, he was made of sterner stuff, a self-indulgent mercenary cleverly disguised as a shuffling darky, clawing his way up the corporate ladder.

His imagination roamed toward the promised promotion to Captain. He would be the first Negro in the Department of Corrections to reach that position. At least in California. Captain Powell. He snapped a salute to the mirror in the bathroom ... Yassuh, Cap'n Powell. Cap'n, Cap'n Powell...All he had to do was to get some of the brothers to talk. Sounded simple, but it was proving far more difficult than he had imagined.

The Escape (or the Collins Caper as it became known in the Watch Office), took place late in the summer. As Senior Program Lieutenants, both Hebner and Powell had to share the blame.

It all seemed like such a good idea at the time, this new and progressive program. Powell envisioned it as a stepping stone to Captain, Superintendent, perhaps even Director of Corrections.

The present Director, Ray Procunier, couldn't last forever. He was rumored to be in poor health, and even if only half the rumors were true, he surely wouldn't last much longer. Powell could possibly be the first Negro Director of Corrections. The first anywhere in the country. Director Powell.

The cause of their mutual embarrassment began with a small group of convicts who called themselves the Prison Preventers. It was the brainchild of Bradley Collins, a child of affluence who, against all odds, managed to spend most of his adult life in the penitentiary. He was a distinguished looking man, graying at the temples, crushing the life out of his late fifties, walking off his fourth prison term. There were stock swindles, bad checks, pigeon drops, schemes gone awry and long stretches of very bad luck; not much for a man raised on Chaucer, Joyce and the Cavalier Poets.

Collins conceived the idea during long empty nights behind bars, his restless mind always in pursuit of some new scheme. Prison Preventers was to be a group of convicts who would go into the community to speak at local high schools, Rotary Clubs, Moose Lodges and Women's groups, lamenting the wasted years of misconduct, recounting tales of innocence lost and wisdom gained, sharing moments of enlightenment and futures now bright with the heady glow of true repentance. As a group they would deter would-be criminals and save lives. Simple enough.

Collins presented the idea to Powell and Hebner. Since his attempts to establish a communications network among the Negro inmates had met with little success, Powell was eager to demonstrate to Quinlan that he was capable of implementing a bold new program.

Hebner was openly suspicious, wondering what sinister plot lay behind this seemingly altruistic gesture. He was sure of only one thing; the program had not been prompted by any humanitarian concern; he knew Collins far too well to believe that. But Powell was persuasive and Hebner reluctantly agreed. Together they brought the idea to Quinlan.

Quinlan listened with his back to them, staring out the French windows at the interminable procession of junk cars that rattled in and out of the visitor's parking lot...He was thinking about Julie. He had never known a woman who shaved her genitals. He found it all strange and wonderful. He pictured her applying lime-scented lather and shaving. God…It was a whole new perspective. He wondered if she ever got razor burn. But then maybe she used an electric razor. For some reason neither one of them ever mentioned it; as if a bald muff were the most natural thing in the world. Bzzzzz…Bzzzzz. A Little Miss Muff shaver…Hello, Miss Muffin, this is Mister Dinky. I see you trimmed all the bushes in front of your house. Can I come in and play?

"…What's that, sir?" said Hebner.

"Oh…Nothing," said Quinlan, swiveling around in his chair to face the two lieutenants.

Powell spoke forcefully about the public relations value of having rehabilitated men speak to schools and civic groups.

"Showing that the system works, sir."

Quinlan nodded at appropriate times, though his mind was not always on the subject at hand (something he would later regret).

Powell pressed on with a brief description of each man. Collins, he said, was a Harvard man.

"Those are real credentials, sir," said Powell.

Quinlan grunted, wondering to himself if the public really cared whether they were being swindled by Harvard men or high school dropouts.

Powell continued the lineup. There was Phillip Morgan, a youthful forger with an angelic face; Barney Olson, a wrinkled old thug, given to tears of gratitude when speaking of his rehabilitation and his friendship with his new buddy, Jesus; Tank Coulter, the token negro, considered too old and too addled to be an escape risk.

"A cross section," said Powell, summing it up.

Quinlan turned it over in his mind. There were risks, but he did not consider them substantial. There was always the danger of escape, but with these four it was not likely. The benefits? Proven rehabilitation…Superintendent Quinlan has those men out in the community talking to our young people about the evils of a life of crime…An increase in public trust; vital to a career in politics. His own personal visibility as an effective administrator. Fair minded. Forceful…VOTE FOR QUINLAN…That's what politics was about—getting the edge. Name recognition. He would be perceived as an innovator who was actually doing something about crime; returning men to society as useful, productive, and yes, taxpaying citizens. Robert Quinlan had done that. Robert T. Quinlan. Governor Quinlan. Now get out there and vote…

He allowed himself to be convinced, stressing the need for success.

The first appearance of the Prison Preventers took place at the San Luis Obispo Elk's Club. Civic minded men had tears in their eyes as they listened to improbable stories of shattered homes, virtuous young lives somehow gone bad, the harsh but loving hand of Justice that guided them back to righteousness. Paradise miraculously regained, courtesy of the California Department of Corrections.

Collins planned his escape for the third outing, the evening they were to speak to the Modesto Women's Club. Using his privileged position as the Protestant Chaplain's clerk, he kited a letter to Stump Kowalski, a long time business associate, detailing the escape plans.

Collins spoke last that night, leaning heavily on the part of his story that included being regularly beaten by a cruel stepfather. In the confusion that followed his presentation, Collins managed to slip through the crowd of well wishers and out the side door. The guard who had escorted them, Officer Harper, intently explaining his role as public guardian to several ladies, did not notice his absence for several minutes.

Out on the street, Collins looked for Kowalski's green Ford coupe. It was not on the side street where it should have been. Collins ran toward the rear of the building, along the back and up the other side, frantically trying to locate the Ford. Near the front of the building he collided with Officer Harper rushing out the door in pursuit. Harper threw him to the sidewalk and pushed his distinguished face into the pavement.

"Asshole," said Harper.

Badly winded, Collins did not reply.

Stump Kowalski was, at that very moment, buying another whiskey sour for Thelma Mauer, her stiff platinum hair highlighted in the back bar mirror at the Circus Room, his mind far from the important rendezvous with Collins.

Inside the Women's Club, the ladies clustered around the participants, unaware that an escape was in progress. There was a sense of excitement in the air; none of them had ever been this close to real live convicts, actual criminals who had done terrible things. They tittered with anticipatory dread.

Phillip Morgan bummed a tailor made cigarette from a lady with high morals and low cleavage, sprinkling his conversation with goddams and fucks because the ladies seemed both horrified and pleased by it.

Barney Olson stared at the mole on Mrs. Chasen's neck without blinking, the soft whir of his mushy brain barely audible above the background noise.

"Jesus is my friend," he said in answer to her question about when he would be released from prison.

She nodded and asked if he had learned a trade while incarcerated.

"Jesus is my friend," he replied, smiling broadly.

Mrs. Chasen returned the smile and wandered off in search of more intelligent game.

It was several minutes before Tank Coulter caught on. First he noticed that Harper was missing. Then he noticed that Collins was gone. Hurriedly putting two and two together as best he could, he bellowed something unintelligible (later interpreted by the ladies as the F word, or possibly the MF word) and headed for the door, scattering wooden chairs and well-dressed ladies as he went, his eyes wild with a vision of freedom. He blundered out the door, across the street and into the night, never to be seen again.

Harper returned with Collins in tow, only to discover that Tank had escaped. Rather than risk losing the others, he had one of the ladies call the local authorities and report the escape.

Stump Kowalski did not remember his important mission until the following morning. He woke next to Thelma Mauer, her mechanical hair now matted and somewhat less lovely in the sunlight that hammered into the bedroom.

"Jesus," he said.

"What'sat, hon?" said Thelma.

"Jesus... What's today?"

"Mmmmm... Saturday?"

"The date," he said irritably. "I need the date. The number."

"Mmmmm…the twentieth?"

"The twentieth?"

"…I think.

"You sure?"

"No," she said, pouting at his tone, turning the famous Mauer posterior toward him. Her mother told her that all the Mauer women had derrieres that men would kill for.

Stump glanced at the brown spots on her back. He tried to read the date on his watch, but he couldn't see without his glasses. He looped his left arm over in front of her face.

"Can you see the date?" he said.

She moved his wrist away and squinted.

"The twentieth…I think."

"You think?" he snapped. "It's either the fuckin' twentieth or it's not, for chrissakes."

"Then read your own goddam watch," she huffed, pushing his arm away. "And don't use that kind of language."

"Well, sor-ry, Miss Emily fuckin' Post. Musta been some other lady I was pumpin' in here last night."

"You are without doubt the most crudest person I have ever met," she said. "No class Kowalski. Takes the ladies to bed with his watch on. So you tell how long you can keep it up? Big time lover boy. You'd do better with a stopwatch. Speedy Gonzales. You remember to take your shoes off, Speedy?"

"Fuck…Where's my goddam glasses?" he said groping around the bed.

"If they were up your ass you'd know where they were," she said, pulling the covers over her head.

He struggled out of bed and found his glasses on the chair.

"The twentieth," he said. "Holy shit…the twentieth."

Thelma wouldn't leave it alone.

"Now I know why they call you Stump," she said. "You oughta put an extension on that thing so you can find it in the dark. Either that or a light."

"Jesus," he said. "The fuckin' twentieth."

Quinlan was furious. The Modesto *Courier* had not been kind in their assessment of the incident, calling it...foolish...liberal to the point of stupidity...Accompanying the scathing editorial was a cartoon of a robed figure passing out keys to a group of convicts. The caption read:

## GO AND SIN NO MORE

Quinlan was very sensitive about press coverage.

He had the two program lieutenants in his office for nearly an hour, railing about their stupidity, their lack of judgment, their inability to fathom something as shallow as the criminal mind.

"It helps to be smarter than they are," he said. "The convicts. Helps a great deal. The average I.Q. out there is less than a hundred. A good deal less. Somewhere in the eighties. Wouldn't seem like too much to expect you to be a little smarter than that...Would it?"

"No sir."

"No sir."

Hebner and Powell stood stiffly at attention, their gaze fixed on the front of Quinlan's desk, stoically accepting the abuse. Quinlan reminded Powell of his inability to establish a communications network, a simple communications network...Not a world wide spy network, Powell. Just a communications network. Right here at Fremont...He called it disappointing in a tone of voice that made it sound much worse than disappointing. He mentioned that Hebner's subordinates did not seem to be writing many disciplinaries... Perhaps you haven't explained our position on this...He indicated that quite possibly only one Captain would be needed next year. Maybe not even one. Or perhaps they could find other candidates, more qualified candidates, from other institutions.

He dismissed them with a wave of his hand, then turned and looked out the window. They saluted and backed out the door. The squeeze was on.

# CHAPTER 25

The Aryan Nation swiftly took revenge, killing Durrell Jackson outright and putting Jerome 3X in the hospital for a long stay with a punctured lung. Though they weren't high on the hit list, they were accessible. Easy targets. Black targets …Hog and Bingo sat back and waited for the next move.

"How about we get Hog and send that fat muffuckah to Hog Heaven," said Billy 2X, who wanted to start a war right then.

Voodoo said no, choosing instead to file the incident for future reference. And of course he knew that when the time came to avenge the attack, they would have to take care of it themselves; Custody would expend very little energy searching for those responsible for the killings—black convicts counted for even less than white convicts, though neither counted for much. At one time he had hoped that the few black officers in Custody might be of assistance in some way, but he had come to realize that the likes of Powell, Jules Reiner or Wardell Hughes were so busy climbing the ladder of social respectability and eating scraps from Massa's table that they had little time for anything having to do with black convicts. Oreos, he called them, demeaning the cookie of the same name.

He recognized the Aryan Nation as just one of many cancers festering in the soul of White America—a cancer that would have to be cut out. So the killing would continue because the doctrine of white supremacy that had spawned the Aryan Nation and all the groups like it would have to die. You didn't reason with it; you ripped it out by the roots and killed it, destroyed it so it would never grow back. Scorched Earth. Burning Spear…One for one. Two for one. Ten for one. What was the difference? It was just arithmetic. If every member of the Aryan Nation had to die, so be it. The killing would continue as each side retaliated in turn. An eye for an eye. More arithmetic. The killing always continued. Death and struggle were the lot of oppressed people everywhere.

Voodoo understood that freedom, real freedom, would not come from just randomly killing members of the Aryan Nation (necessary as that might be at the moment), or having more laws enacted in Washington, or having people talk about it around long mahogany tables at high level conferences dealing with racial equality. Real freedom would be won at the barricades where it had always been won. Power to the People...And it would be on the Yard at Fremont that the first blow would be struck. From there to the cities and towns across America until it was a gaping wound so wide and so ugly and so obvious that none would be able to ignore it...Let freedom ring, mothafuckah...The final days of liberation would begin with a spark ignited by men living in the darkness of prison, black warriors who would unleash the violence and command the attention of the world by their willingness to die rather than continue to live in slavery. And if they had to sacrifice their own lives in order to gain that freedom, so be it.

"How about we kill both them muffuckahs?" said Delray. "Hog and Bingo."

"The time will come, my brothers," said Voodoo. "The time will come."

While Voodoo saw Quinlan as just one more white bigot in a position of power, he also recognized him as a formidable adversary. Experience had taught him that the worst thing he could do was to underestimate his enemies. The prison grapevine told him that Quinlan was ambitious and ruthless. From D.V.I. to Soledad to Quentin the stories were the same...(He don't like no black skin, Cletus Drummond told him. And he don't like no nigger like you be shavin' his head and walkin' around like he own The Man's penitentiary).

Though Quinlan was relatively young to be a Warden, Voodoo knew he was Old School, a throwback to the times when guards carried cane sticks and corporal punishment was the order of the day. Certainly Quinlan was too smart to start openly flogging prisoners again, but the Adjustment Center, the Hole, the Strip Cells and Drug Therapy with all their attendant excesses were alternate methods perhaps even more effective. He knew Quinlan would use whatever methods, legal or otherwise, he deemed necessary to maintain control. Absolute control—that would be Quinlan's way. And since all the mail entering and leaving the prison was censored, there was little opportunity for convicts to report abuses. The few reports that trickled out via family members, parolees or an occasional lawyer, were treated as sour grapes, querulous ramblings from chronic malcontents. What would you expect from convicted felons?

Voodoo listened to the Yard; it told him everything. The Yard was his mother, his father, his home—its concrete surface his playpen, school and teacher. It had a rhythm, a heartbeat that he recognized as his own. It was his Song of Songs, the lullaby that rocked him to sleep each night. Like a river that ran through his life, he knew the currents, the turbulence, the shallow pools and the deep water.

He awakened each morning to listen to its message, knowing that freedom, whenever and however it might come, was one day closer…Nigger man, proud man, gonna rise up and smite his oppressors. Let freedom ring, mothafuckah …The idea sustained him and forged his will into iron. He took comfort from the fact that nearly half the three thousand convicts at Fremont were black. His brothers. His warriors…When the time was right, the time to strike, the Yard would tell him.

Voodoo was known by nearly everyone. Loved or hated, feared or admired, few were indifferent. When he walked the yard with his lieutenants, he was noticed. He moved with the grace of a jungle cat. He had power. When he said the word, people got hurt. Some got killed…Put a curse on some dude and he was dead a week later…So the grapevine said. And at six foot two, two hundred and ten pounds of finely chiseled black steel, he was an imposing figure. He carried himself with a certain regal bearing (as he imagined a Masai warrior might carry himself) that infuriated white convicts. He knew they called him Nigger and Jigaboo and Spook behind his back, but he also knew that at least from some he had earned a grudging respect because he had done his time, held his mud, and stood in open defiance to a common foe—the Police.

Billy 2X and Delray were anxious to strike back, to even the score, but Voodoo counseled patience, thinking that Quinlan might be looking for a reason to break up the nucleus of the Black Muslims. If violence on the Yard began to escalate too quickly, Quinlan might take steps to cool it down. Of course he could do that anyway, break up the Aryan Nation and the Muslims, ship the leaders to other prisons to slow the cycle of violence. But he could have moved Voodoo out of the Officer's Mess and into some menial job at the Laundry if he had been so inclined. Since he hadn't, Voodoo's guess was that he wanted him close at hand so he could keep an eye on him. That's probably why Leonard and Hog still had their soft jobs; Quinlan wanted the convicts to think it was business as usual.

And then maybe The Man wasn't interested in minor rules infractions. Maybe he had his sights set on more serious crimes, ones that would stand up in a court of law and add more time to an already lengthy sentence. Perhaps a lifetime, as in the Habitual Criminal Act—The Bitch...Voodoo looked out across the Yard, then closed his eyes and listened to the rhythm...Something wasn't right, but he couldn't tell what it was. Not yet.

Early darkness in the late fall gave Quinlan an excuse to curtail Yard movement at five thirty, right after the evening meal. (Movies were already down to every other Saturday.) Preacher, looking like a scarecrow in his loose fitting denim jacket, stood in the fading light to broadcast his relentless message to the lengthening shadows on the Yard...

> *...And behold a pale horse, and Death sat upon him and Hell followed after. And power was given to them over the fourth part of the earth, to kill with sword, and with hunger, and with death, and with the beasts of the earth...*

Later he would return to his cell to dine on a small can of Vienna sausages courtesy of Dave Leonard, who supplied him with a limited canteen ration in exchange for information and running an occasional errand. He was one of many on the payroll.

That afternoon Devil Charley Chiponis came to taunt him.

"Jesus was a weenie, man," said Charley.

"...Thou shall worship the Lord thy God with," said Preacher.

"A dick head..."

"…Whoever shall smite thee on thy right cheek, turn to him the left…"

"Hail fuckin' Satan," said Charley, raising a fist to the sky.

"…Love your enemies," said Preacher. "Bless them that curse you, do good to them that hate you. For your heavenly Father maketh the rain to fall upon the just and unjust…"

"Rain on this, Preach," said Charley, grabbing his crotch.

Preacher lowered his Bible and spoke quietly.

"You keep fuckin' with me, man, and I'll have someone bury you. I'll have Leonard put a number on you and you can sit around and wait till it comes up. Then we'll bury you. We'll have a little ceremony. Get it?…Bye, bye, Charley. Won't take long. So the best thing you can do right now, cocksucker, is take a hike. Surprise yourself—use some good sense."

Charley grumbled briefly, but wandered off without another word. Preacher continued his warning:

> *…And I saw an angel in the midst of heaven saying with a loud voice: Give glory to Him for the hour of judgment is come…And another angel who said, Babylon is fallen because she made all nations drink of the wine of wrath…*

Since Hawk's death and his own transfer to the Watch Office, Stan had been in the habit of taking a brief walk around the Yard before going to work. He followed the perimeter, plodding along as thousands of others had done before him, watching the concrete pass under his feet, letting his mind drift from fear to fantasy to hope…He thought about Hawk, about some of the things he had said…*Man don't fight for what he believes in, he ain't nothin' … Some fool come along and take everything you got…Runnin's for sissies. And cocksuckers…* Stan took some consolation in the memories. He thought…Maybe. Just maybe…

One day Doc joined him.

"How's it goin', kid?"

"…Fair."

"Your visitors return yet?"

"No," said Stan.

"They will."

"…How do you know?"

"I'm a student of human nature," he said. "Helps pass the time. You're easy. They'll be back."

"I may not be so easy next time," said Stan.

"They don't know that. Far as they know, you're the same old pushover."

They walked in silence for a few minutes.

"Custody wants you to finger the guys who killed your cellmate," said Doc. "They need a witness if they're gonna make anything stick in court. The Warden wants them so bad he can taste it and he thinks he can squeeze you for the answer…And your new guy? Your new cellmate, Eddy Big?"

"Yeah?

"Most likely a plant. Assignment didn't come through the Watch Office, which usually means that someone higher up made the decision. Never a good sign. Just be careful what you say. Snitches have an extremely short life expectancy around here. And regardless of what Custody may tell you, they won't protect you. Most likely, when they get the names they want, they won't even try to protect you. You'll be tossed back on the Yard with a snitch jacket. Like bait. Then your life expectancy goes down to days or weeks instead of years."

"I got it."

"So what do you think about all this?" said Doc.

"…About prison?"

"Yeah."

Stan just shrugged.

"Was it worth it?" said Doc.

"You mean what I did?"

"Yeah."

"…I don't know. Sometimes it's like looking at an old movie newsreel. A guy who looks like me is shooting Somebody. Then Somebody falls down and the guy who looks like me walks away. End of newsreel. I don't really have any idea if it was worth it. They told me what happened so often I think I know. But I don't. Not really. I'm just a spectator."

"You were what...drunk?"

"Yeah."

"The blackout defense?"

Stan ignored the question.

"When I look close at the guy in the newsreel," he said, "he starts to fade, like maybe he's not real...And I wonder how I should feel. I don't think I feel bad. I don't think I feel anything. Sometimes I wish I did. It just seems stupid now. Why did I make such a big deal out of it? Why couldn't I just let it go? Let her go?"

"Well," said Doc, "better work on a little guilt and remorse before you go to the Parole Board. They're partial to it. Makes them feel better about what they're doing. Can't be rehabilitated unless you show a little guilt and remorse. Says so in all the textbooks. And they're very big on rehabilitation. The old time convicts have it down to a science; they can manufacture real tears while the violins are playing in the background. But you won't find more than a handful out of three thousand who are really sorry for what they did. They're all sorry they got caught, but that's about the end of it."

"You, too?" said Stan.

Doc frowned.

"Sure, I'm sorry I got caught. You think I should be glad?"

"No."

"I'm no crusader," said Doc, running a hand through his hair. "I did abortions because there was a lot of money in it. Simple case of supply and demand. The American way. That's what free enterprise is all about. I was providing a service...Happened to be illegal, that's all."

"Just your luck."

"I don't think it was wrong. Never did think that. Just illegal. Someday we'll get smart and change the law."

"Then what?" said Stan.

"Then I'll do something else. Maybe something legal."

Doc offered Stan a cigarette and lit one himself. His hands were small and delicate.

"You know Caryl Chessman was here," he said. "At Fremont. Before they took him to Quentin and gassed him. You remember Chessman? The Red Light Bandit?"

"Sure."

"Probably walked the Yard right where we are. Dr. Finch, too. Did his old lady in so he could run off with a young redhead. Carol something…Then there was L. Ewing Scott. They convicted him and never did find his wife's body. Hormones can be a terrible thing."

"Yeah."

"You got people on the outside. Friends? Family?"

"My folks," said Stan. "Couple of guys I grew up with."

"Anyone visit?"

"Every few months my mother comes. I don't think she likes to, but she comes anyway."

"She can't help herself. It's in the genes. It's what mothers do. They suffer. They have a need to suffer."

Stan nodded his agreement.

"…Your ex?" said Doc.

"Not likely she'll show up anytime soon."

"She blame you for what happened?"

"…Who else?"

"If she showed up today and asked, maybe begged, would you take her back?"

"…You takin' a survey, Doc?" The questions were beginning to make him nervous. He hadn't had a conversation this long since he'd been locked up.

"It's research. I'm gonna write a book about all this when I get out and I need some insight into the criminal mind."

"I don't have a criminal mind."

"Okay. Some insight into a sick mind."

"I don't have a…"

"Just answer the question, Smith."

"Would I take her back if she asked me to?"

"I believe that was the question."

Stan didn't say anything for a few moments.

"…Maybe."

"Jesus, Smith…Here, take the dunce cap and go sit in the corner for a couple of years. And you don't think you have a sick mind?"

Stan shrugged.

"I said maybe…"

"Just the fact that you would even consider the remote possibility is a strong indication that you're not all that well. You're thinking with your dick, Smith. And believe me, that's not always the most reliable source of information."

"Not to worry," said Stan. "I don't imagine she's ready to show up anytime soon."

"Good. If you're lucky she'll marry somebody else, move to China and make his life miserable."

"She said I was the worst person she'd ever met."

"Possibly an exaggeration."

Little Joe and Junior Grimes sped by, obviously in a hurry.

"The odd couple," said Doc. "You ever get a chance when you're in Records, take a look at Junior's file."

"Interesting?"

"Mild mannered Junior Grimes turns out to be an axe murderer. Killed people and dismembered them. Used a Boy Scout hatchet. The official kind. I always thought that was a nice touch—an official Boy Scout hatchet. Put the body parts into green plastic lawn bags and delivered them to various dumpsters all over town. Some here, some there, a little flesh mixed in with the lawn clippings and empty microwave boxes. Probably never would have caught him except he had this thing about hands; threw everything away but the hands. Just the right hands. Kept them in a drawer in clear plastic bags. All labeled. Very neat. Annie Parson's Hand…Mrs. Elrod's Hand…The story is that he took each severed hand, wrapped it around a short piece of broom handle and kept dipping it into shellac until it hardened. Like dipping candles. From the smell, the neighbors thought he was refinishing furniture…That Grimes boy. Always into something… Somewhere in the process out comes the broom handle and the hand is left to harden like a claw. He hung them by a thread from a clothesline near the basement heater."

"Man…"

"He even kept one in his car. Of course, eventually somebody spotted it."

"Careless."

"Maybe not," said Doc. "All killers want to get caught."

"That's not what I heard."

"Reinforces the belief that they're really terrible people. You weren't exactly hiding when they caught you."

"I didn't even know they were looking for me...So what did he do with the hands."

"You don't want to know. Imagine the sickest thing he could do...and it's worse than that."

"Jesus..."

"Your beef is definitely minor league, Smith. You work for the Record's Officer. Check the files on Magoo, Roadrunner, Ice, Nick the Knife, any of those guys. That's the big leagues...And if you want real gruesome stuff check the people over in East Block where Custody has its own Little Shop of Horrors. You haven't heard of John Misner or Butcher McCloud?"

"No..."

"A sad gap in your education, Smith. Unfortunately, just one of many. You ever wonder who's slicing up convicts and butchering the remains?"

"Yeah."

"Try this...Maybe Custody gives a guy a ducat to go see the Program Lieutenant or the Chaplain and then lets one of the crazies from East Block out to hunt him down and kill him. Gives him a straight razor and tells him, Cut his throat and cut the ears off...Or the nose. Or the eyes. It's worth a canteen draw for a whole month."

"...Why would they do that?"

"Lots of reasons...Generates fear. Gets rid of certain convicts they don't like. Undesirables. Maybe people the other convicts respect. Nobody feels safe."

"Doesn't make sense," said Stan.

"You're so logical, Smith. And naïve. You still think it's supposed to make sense. You probably still believe that policemen are your friends. I'm sure you heard that in grade school. I'm Officer Bill and I'm your friend. Forget it. After you've been here awhile you'll stop expecting things to make sense. And you'll learn that it's not about logic, it's about control, about who has the biggest hammer, about who's going to come out on top of this human garbage heap. Don't automatically assume it'll be Quinlan—Fremont has driven more than one high-powered, Department of Corrections guru into early retirement."

"Crazy."

"Now you're getting it," said Doc. "Fear is just another weapon in the arsenal. Think of it as a military campaign. Quinlan has the heavy artillery, but we have a big edge in ground troops. Plus the fact that most of our troops are not playing with a full deck. Believe it or not that actually helps."

The announcement for the movie came over the P.A. system:

...The movie for Saturday night is *The Hard Guy* with Jack Larue and Mary Healy...

"That's me," said Stan, doing a little shadow boxing.

"Where'd you learn that routine?"

"From Hawk. My celly. We worked out at the gym every day."

"Forget it," said Doc. "You want protection, get a shank or the right friends."

"I can handle myself."

Doc put a hand on Stan's shoulder and squeezed lightly.

"I hope so," he said. "We wouldn't want to lose you."

Stan coughed and looked across the Yard.

"Well," he said. "Gotta go...Work time."

Doc squeezed his shoulder again.

"Don't be such a stranger," he said. "I might be able to make life a little easier for you. Look me up when you get a chance. I'm right down the street in South Block, two forty-seven."

"Sure. Okay," said Stan, hurrying away.

"Who in the hell is White Eagle?" said Quinlan.

Lieutenant Powell stood in front of the desk shifting his weight from side to side, fussing with the knot in his tie.

"That's inmate Moore, sir."

Quinlan waved the piece of paper he held in his right hand.

"What's all this...gobbledygook about a sacred elk and a ritual dinner?"

"They want to have a ritual dinner to commemorate some... event. Something of a religious service, I believe."

"What religion might that be, Powell?"

"Eh...I'm not sure, sir."

"And who are the they we're talking about?"

"The Indians, sir."

"Ah, yes...The Indians. They want to have a sacred elk shipped in here for this dinner?"

"Yessir," said Powell.

"Hard to believe," he said, shaking his head. "They must think this is the Reservation Country Club. Did they by chance tell what event this was? The one they want to commemorate?"

"Sand Creek."

"Sand-Creek," said Quinlan, drumming his fingers on the desk.

"During the Indian Wars," said Powell. "Evidently some Calvary were involved in the massacre of...non-combatants."

Quinlan winced.

"Massacre," he said. "Those people were savages, Powell. You don't massacre savages. You just kill them. You do what's necessary. We offered them places to live. Reservations of their own. They just wouldn't accept them. They were trying to fight progress."

"...Of course."

"Convicts are like children, Powell. You should know that by now. They're always testing to see how far they can go. If you give ground they'll just keep pushing and pushing. That's what children do. Doesn't mean they're bad...necessarily."

"Yessir."

"How many Indians do we have here?"

"Ten, I believe."

"Ten little Indians...What are the odds of that?"

"...Of what, sir?"

"Oh...Never mind. Well, we can't bow to pressure groups. You know that. If we do, we'll have three thousand people telling us how to run the prison. The Muslims want special diets. No pork. The guy who wrote *My Shadow Ran Fast* was in here the other day offering advice on how to run things. Bill Sands. A.A. wants to have more meetings. Now Narcotics Anonymous wants to start a group. Dope fiends. Jesus…What do they care; they don't have to pay for the extra Custody. The taxpayers do. More meetings my ass. What they could all use is a little more backbone, not another social night… And now the Indians want a ritual dinner. Pretty soon we'll have the ACLU in here telling us it's okay for them to take those drugs, those…peyote things because it's actually a religious ceremony. The Redskins Church of Dope."

Powell chuckled along with Quinlan.

"Here's how I'd like you to deal with those requests in the future," said Quinlan, crumpling the paper and tossing it in the wastebasket. "Deposit it in the round file."

"Exactly my sentiments," said Powell. "I just wanted to be sure we were thinking along the same lines. I'll take care of them in the future."

Quinlan smiled thinly.

"Good," he said. "And by the way, it's ca-valry, not calvary."

Powell looked blank.

"…What is?"

"You know, the horse soldiers."

"…The what?"

"You said the cal-vary was involved in this Sand Creek business. It's ca-valry. Cal-vary is the thing with Jesus. You know. The Hill… You a Christian, Powell?"

"Oh, yessir."

"Then you know about all that, the hill and everything. People get the words confused. It's a common mistake. Anyway, I appreciate you bringing this issue to my attention. But in the future, just ignore them. We don't want to set a trend, do we?"

"Certainly not, sir."

"Before you go," said Quinlan, "what do you know about an inmate known as Freddy the Face?"

"Freddy-the-Face," said Powell. "That would be inmate Schaeffer."

"Why do they call him the Face?"

194

"He's...eh, a homosexual, sir?"

"That the way they refer to homosexuals here?"

"No sir," said Powell, giggling nervously. "Freddy is particularly notorious for taking it in the face, so to speak."

Quinlan seemed puzzled.

"Taking it in the face?"

"You know, sir...Blow jobs."

"Ah," said Quinlan, nodding. "Blow jobs. I see. Sucking dicks, as it were. And what makes him so...notorious at these blow jobs?"

Powell shrugged, nibbling nervously on his lower lip, looking for a way out of the conversation.

"I'm told by my informants," he said cautiously, "that Freddy has been know to start at one end of the tier and go from cell to cell giving these...blow jobs."

"While the men are locked in their cells?"

"That's what I've been told."

"And just how does he do that, Powell?"

"Through the bars, sir. I'm told. The men hang their...things out through the bars and Freddy..."

"Their things?"

"... Penises."

"Cocks?"

"Yessir...Cocks."

Powell went back to fussing with his tie.

"So Freddy just goes along from cell to cell offering sex to anyone who wants it?" said Quinlan.

"That's what I'm told, sir."

"And we allow that to continue?"

"We have not been able to catch him...in the act. If it were not for my extensive network of informants, we probably wouldn't even know about..."

Quinlan slammed his fist down on the desk.

"Goddamit, Powell, everybody in the system knows about Freddy. The men in the print shop at Folsom printed flyers saying SEND FREDDY TO FOLSOM. I am...disappointed, to put it mildly, that we continue to tolerate that kind of behavior here at Fremont."

He flipped open the one thick file on his desk.

"I see that inmate Schaeffer is a tier tender in North Block. That's like the fox in the henhouse. A perfect opportunity to ply his disgusting trade. Need I remind you that oral copulation is still a crime in this state, defined in section 288a of the Penal Code and punishable by up to fifteen years in prison?"

Powell worked on his tie with both hands.

"I'll look into it immediately," he said.

"It's your responsibility to check work assignments?" said Quinlan. "That correct?"

"Eh...Yessir."

"Odd that you would let someone like Schaeffer be a tier tender."

"I don't recall seeing that assign..."

"Gives him access to all the inmates when they're locked up... Maybe even the staff."

"...that particular assignment," said Powell, his voice trailing off. "You were saying, sir?"

"I said, Maybe even some of the staff...You ever have sex with a man, Powell?"

"No sir," he said quickly. "Definitely not."

"I've heard that once you've had a man give you a blow job, you'll never go back to women...You suppose that's true, Officer Powell?"

"I don't know, sir. Doesn't seem likely. At least not to me."

Quinlan leaned forward and spoke softly.

"If I ever hear that you're involved, I'll have you charged and personally see to it that you're convicted. And when they send you to Fremont, I'll turn you loose on the Mainline to see how long you survive. We'll run a friendly office pool and see who comes closest to the actual time of your demise...Do I make myself clear?"

"Absolutely, sir."

"Good. I want this business stopped and I want it stopped now. I don't care how you do it, but I want the career of this Freddy the Face to come to a halt. I won't have him turning my penitentiary into a brothel."

Quinlan leaned back and smiled pleasantly.

"That'll be all, Lieutenant. I'll expect a report in two weeks."

"You shall have it," Powell said grimly.

# CHAPTER 26

The Watch Crew was gathered in the office for the final hours of the Fly Killing Contest. Only the Count, far out of the running, had gone to the movie.

"How many I got, Chief?" said Paulson.

Leonard glanced at the tally sheet on his desk.

"Five hundred and fifty-three," he said. "Same as the last time you asked."

"Five hundred and fifty-three?" said Paulson. "Not sixty-three?"

"Why'n the fuck don't you write it down?" said Moose. "So's you don't have to ask every five minutes. You must have shit for brains, man."

A moment later, he spied a fly buzzing close to the window. With amazing speed for such a big man, he was off the stool, across the room, backhanding the fly with a folded newspaper. The fly, stunned in flight, looped in a small arc and fell to the floor. Moose went down on one knee, raised the newspaper over his head and crushed it in one swift motion.

"Gotcha," he said triumphantly. "You might be the one that wins old Moose a piece of tail. Just think of it as sacrificing your life for a worthy cause...How many's that, Leonard?"

"Whyn't you write it down?" mimicked Paulson. "So's you don't forget."

"Get fucked, willya, Paulson."

"That's five hundred and sixty," said Leonard. "I'll read the whole list. Count is hovering around the four hundred mark, give or take a fly..."

"No wonder he went to the movie."

"I've got five ten and Greek's got five seventeen."

"Give it up, Greek," said Moose. "You're out of it. Besides, if you won, you'd have to work some kind of a miracle to get a hardon."

"Close your eyes and open your mouth," said Greek. "I've got a surprise for you."

"So it looks like Moose and Paulson down the stretch," said Leonard.

"What about me?" said Stan.

"Too late," said Moose. "Didn't I tell you that? You're gonna have to wait till next year."

"I been keeping count on my own," said Stan, "and I've got five forty-seven."

"Sure," said Moose. "And how would we know that?"

"I counted them," said Stan.

"Oh…You're on some special honor system?"

"Well, I…"

"First of all, you gotta know the rules before you can play. That's primary. And we got this rule, Smith, where you have to have somebody watching when you kill a fly. Somebody has to watch just in case you might be tempted to fib a little. Like that fuckin' Carson, who always cheated. Now on my special honor system count, I got one million, four thousand and one hundred and twenty-three dead flies."

"Consider it practice for next year, kid," said Greek. "Who knows, Leonard might be givin' out paroles by then. Or government jobs. Anything's possible."

"I'm already workin' on it," said Leonard.

"See?"

"Since you're down seven with only a couple of hours to go, Paulson," said Moose, "why don't you just give up? Save yourself the hassle. Make one of those I-give-up speeches and I'll accept. Make it easy on yourself."

An unsuspecting fly, lured by a small spot of jam, landed atop the filing cabinet to inspect the sticky mess. Paulson killed it with an awkward stroke.

"Only six down," he said, flicking the remains off his folded newspaper.

"You know," said Leonard, doing some quick calculations, "we've each been killing about a hundred and fifty flies a month."

"That a record?" said Stan.

"I don't know. I'd have to look it up."

"Just think of all the time we could be doin' for fly-murder," said Greek. "Thousands of years. You suppose fly-murder carries the same penalty as people-murder?"

"Maybe in fly-court," said Leonard.

"You guys hear about the chick who was afraid of flies till she opened one?" said Moose.

Nobody responded.

"You gotta come up with some new material," said Greek.

Paulson smashed another fly against the side of the desk.

"Five," he said, grinning at Moose.

Leonard opened the newspaper he was using as a fly swatter and read the headlines from the first inside page.

"...Mother throws baby off freeway overpass..."

"Somethin' like that shoulda happened to Hebner," said Greek. "Or Powell. Where were those mothers when we needed 'em?"

"And Nelson," said Moose. "How about stupid fuckin' Nelson?"

"Maybe they didn't have freeways then," said Greek.

"They had bridges," said Stan. "Bridges been around forever. Could've thrown him off a bridge."

"Good point."

"...Violent crime up seventeen percent..."

"Jeez," said Paulson. "And I go to the Board soon."

"Who you kiddin'?" said Moose. "You like it here. They ever let you out you'll have to go pull another rubber-gun robbery so you can get back in."

Paulson crushed a fly that landed on his knee.

"They're comin to me now," he said. "They want me to win."

"That's it, Paulson," said Moose. "The flies are coming to you on a suicide mission because they love you and they want to sacrifice their lives for you. My goal in life is to have all the flies love me. Jesus...You take a shower once in awhile it wouldn't happen."

"Here's something by President Johnson," said Leonard.

"Johnson?" said Greek. "What happened to Roosevelt?"

"Go back to sleep," said Moose. "We'll wake you if anything important happens."

"Johnson says the war will get worse before it gets better."

"There's a war someplace?" said Greek.

"Vietnam," said Leonard.

"Vietnam? Where's that?"

"Go down to Santa Barbara and turn right. You can't miss it."

Moose lunged off his stool and smashed a winged creature on the corner of the desk.

"Gotcha, sucker."

"Oh, no," said Paulson. "You're not gonna tell me that's a fly."

"Wasn't no fuckin' turtle, man."

"That's a moth. That thing's been flyin' around in here for an hour."

"Moth my ass. That's a large, overweight fly. Big as it is, I should be able to count it for two."

"You saw it," said Paulson, appealing to Leonard. "Tell him it was a moth."

"Does that look like a moth?" said Moose, pointing to the gooey mess on the desk.

One oversize wing was still fluttering. Moose tried to brush it away with his newspaper.

"Wait!" said Paulson, grabbing his arm. "Flies don't have wings that big. Look, Chief."

Leonard and Greek got up and examined the fly.

"Moth all the way," said Leonard. "Take a look, kid."

Stan bent over and looked.

"I don't want no goddam Fish makin' these important decisions," said Moose. "I have no clue if this guy can be trusted."

"He's an engineer, for chrissakes," said Greek.

"So? Engineer's supposed to be extra reliable? Wasn't Hitler some kind of engineer? Besides, it don't mean he knows jack shit about flies."

"I'm votin' moth," said Greek.

"Moth," said Leonard.

"Moth," said Stan.

"The fuckin' Rules Committee strikes again," said Moose. "Decent person don't have a chance anymore."

"I told you," said Paulson.

"And fuck you Paulson shit-for-brains. I'm gonna win anyway," said Moose. He slapped his thigh with the rolled up newspaper and scanned the room for flies. "Honesty is always the best policy, Paulson. Remember who it was told you that."

"Here's a guy," said Leonard, back in his chair with the newspaper, "who killed fourteen people in Texas."

"Too many people in Texas anyway," said Greek.

"Boy Scout Leader," said Leonard. "Model citizen… Engineering student."

"See?" said Moose. "What'd I tell you about engineers?"

"Too much education," said Greek. "Brain drain. Makes you crazy. Ask the kid."

"Any of 'em niggers?" said Moose.

"…Doesn't say," said Leonard. "Killed his mother first…"

"Hey, this is your kind of guy," said Moose. "Sounds like Carson all over again. Maybe we can get him transferred up here to work in the Watch Office."

"…then climbed up in the University Tower, killed thirteen people and wounded thirty more."

"Any of the wounded niggers?" said Moose.

"Doesn't say. Just says people."

Moose shook his head and continued wandering around the room.

"You know there's different kinds of people," he said. "There's regular people—white people. Then there's the others—niggers and spics and those types. They're not regular people. You seen 'em."

"For one thing they're different colors," said Greek.

"And they smell," said Moose. "You ever notice that?"

"They smell bad," said Greek.

"You can say that again."

"…They smell bad."

"Jesus."

"…Jesus."

"Listen to this," said Leonard. "...Dear Abby: I am fifteen years old and my boyfriend is forty-one. He is married but says his wife doesn't understand him. He says he is going to get a divorce and marry me, but it's been a year and a half and he's still married to her. What do you think I should do?"

"Man," said Moose, shaking his head. "That's illegal for chrissakes."

"Fifteen's too young?" said Greek. "Or is forty-one too old?"

"See," Moose said indignantly, "they got guys out there doin' that shit, and I'm in here for smoking a little non-habit-forming weed. Nature's own product. Where's the justice in that?"

"None," said Greek. "Zero justice."

"You can say that again."

"None. Zero justice..."

"...Man...How did I ever end up in a place like this?" said Moose.

The talk continued on into the night. Leonard typed the Movement Sheet. Greek got the dictionary out and corrected the spelling on Captain Greer's latest memo. Greer, who loved to write memos, composed several every day. Moose occasionally filed a housing card while being on the alert for flies. Stan retyped the agenda for the Correctional Facilities Meeting to be held in December. Paulson made the coffee, heating the water with a contraband stinger readily available on the Yard for three packs of Big Reds.

Leonard glanced at the clock on the wall every few minutes, noting the position of the hands and the slow, laborious passage of Time. Sometimes he wished they'd just take the clock away. But as long as it was there, he was powerless not to watch it. The days, the calendar days, were bad enough. But the hours? Minutes even... He knew the trick was to keep busy, keep the mind occupied so it would not spiral down and lock onto the slow procession of minutes. Do the Time...Don't let it do you. Playing bridge helped, but there weren't many bridge players in an institution where the median level of education was the sixth grade. Collins was the best, but he was gone now, transferred to an institution of higher security after his escape attempt. The library was a joke and poker interested him only as a source of income. The football and baseball pools were the only things that held his interest for any length of time.

He wondered what his sons were doing. Were they out on dates? Were they even old enough to go out with girls? (He made a mental note to ask Esther.) At their age he hadn't been allowed such freedom. His parents were old country Jews. Poor but honest, his father was fond of saying, not without a certain amount of pride. Poor but honest. He seemed to glory in their poverty, to see it as a special sign of g-d's favor. Leonard hated it.

A familiar sound alerted him to the fact that he was grinding his teeth again.

"My mind is turning to mush," he said.

"Don't worry," said Greek. "Soon as it goes completely, they let you out on parole."

"I don't think so, Greek. You happen to talk to Ice or the Organ Grinder lately?"

> *...Attention on the Yard! Attention*
> *on the Yard! Movie release. Return*
> *to your housing units immediately...*

"I wonder if anybody knows we're here?" said Greek.

"Here?" said Stan. "In the Watch Office?"

"Here in prison."

"The fuckin' bulls know," said Moose, pointing to the Watch Commander's Office across the hallway. "Guaranteed. That's why they count us five times a day. Be sure we stay here. Job security."

"I mean real people," said Greek. "Free people...Maybe there's nobody out there anymore. You ever think about that? Maybe they've all gone somewhere. Maybe they're all dead."

"You can see 'em on teevee," said Paulson.

"That's just teevee," said Greek. "You don't know if that's really real."

"There's millions of people out there," said Moose. "Where you think they all went?"

"I don't know," said Greek. "How about Mars? The moon maybe. Anywhere. All I'm saying is we really don't know for sure if anybody's out there anymore."

"My mother's out there," said Paulson. "She knows we're here. She writes me every week."

"Good old Mom," said Leonard.

"You check the postmark?" said Moose.

"…No…Why?"

"Next time you write," said Moose, "tell her she oughta be grateful she didn't have a son like Carson."

Correctional Officer Burton came in to have the Watch Crew sign the outcount sheet.

"Hi, boys," he said. "Just sign on the dotted line."

Burton was a quiet, gentle man, close to retirement, one of the few that nearly all the convicts liked.

"You catch the movie tonight?" said Greek.

"No. I was on the Pruno Patrol."

"Find anything?"

"No. Clean as a whistle. You guys got a new hiding place?"

Officer Dunsmore was in charge of a program implemented recently to discourage the manufacture, sale and consumption of a crude homemade brew known on the Yard as Pruno. Quinlan called it the Stamp Out Booze program—S.O.B. The mission was to seek out and destroy all fermenting batches of alcohol and arrest those responsible. Dunsmore made up several signs lettered in purple crayon:

> *I pist in this one and one other.*
> *Guess which one.*
> *Ofc. C. Dunsmore.*

He placed the signs near the evidence of home brew, knowing that the rest of the batch, no matter where it was, would be dumped by suspicious convicts who would never know just how much of the brew he had found.

"This one's okay," said inmate Peterson one night after the Pruno Squad had raided the Laundry.

"You think?" said Leach, looking carefully at the mason jar that Peterson was holding.

"Yeah. Go ahead and drink it."

"…You sure?"

"It was behind the main vat, for chrissakes. No fuckin' way he coulda found it."

"Whyn't you drink it?"

"For chrissakes, man, how the fuck could he find it behind the vat? Huh?…He's too fat to even get back there to look. Much less piss in it. Don't be a pussy, man."

"I dunno," said Leach, shaking his head. "I don't wanna drink nothing some cop pissed in."

"Shit," said Peterson. "Use your head, man. There's no way …"

"I dunno…"

But they finally poured it out, neither willing to take a chance.

"We're stashin' it in the chapel now," said Greek. "Behind the altar. It'll be safe there as long as Father Joe doesn't find it."

"Good place," said Burton.

"Yeah. Don't tell anybody."

"Not me. Just more paperwork."

"You're up on all this legal stuff," said Moose. "Tell these guys it's illegal to fuck a chick under eighteen."

"Or a guy," said Leonard.

"…A what?"

"Never mind."

"True," said Burton. "Commonly known as statutory rape."

"What if you don't know how old she is?" said Paulson.

"No excuse."

"What if she likes it?"

"Too bad the Count isn't here," said Moose. "This is stuff he prob'ly needs to know."

"The law doesn't recognize her emotional response," said Burton. "Let me see that old California Penal Code book you got stashed."

Leonard retrieved it from the back of the filing cabinet and handed it to him.

"Here it is. Section two sixty-one...Rape is defined as sexual intercourse with a woman not your wife..."

"It's okay to rape your wife?" said Paulson.

"How can you rape your wife, dummy?" said Moose. "She's supposed to put out. How can you rape somebody who's supposed to be doin' it? Wake up, man."

Burton continued.

"...a woman not your wife under one of the following circumstances. First, if she's under eighteen."

"I mighta done that," said Greek.

"Me, too," said Stan.

"Yeah, but you still look like you could be seventeen or eighteen."

"Everybody gets lucky once in awhile," said Leonard.

"Unfortunately," said Greek. "I am now in the Dirty-Old-Man category."

"...Second, if she's crazy," said Burton.

"Fuckin' a crazy chick is rape?" said Moose.

"Makes you stop and think, don't it?" said Greek.

"Third, if you force her to do it...And fourth, if you do it while she's unconscious."

"Huh," said Moose. "What if she's dead?"

"What-if-she's-dead," said Burton. "...I don't think that's covered in this section."

"Prob'ly be okay, though," said Moose. "Long as she was dead. I mean, what would she care? Dead's dead."

"Moose is doin' time for possession of a sick mind," said Leonard.

"Just a question, man."

"You ever fuck a dead chick?" said Greek.

"Some of 'em didn't move a lot, but I don't think any of them were actually dead."

"How do you tell if it's rape?" said Paulson.

"They ask the woman," said Leonard. "Unless she's dead. Then they ask Moose."

"I mean do you actually have to...eh..."

"The law calls it penetration," said Burton. "Any penetration, however slight, is sufficient to complete the crime."

"You're safe, Paulson," said Moose. "They cut an inch off yours, you'd have a hole there."

The Count returned just in time to sign the outcount sheet.

"How was the flick?" said Moose.

"Shitty...Same as last time."

"This the one with the gorilla?"

"Yeah."

"Fuck. That's the second time I missed it."

"Don't worry. It'll be around again. Jenkins loves it."

"How's it end?" said Moose.

"You really want to know?"

"Now why would I ask if I didn't really want to know?"

"The gorilla gets the girl," said the Count.

"Does he fuck her?"

"Moose, this gorilla is about eighty feet tall."

"What's that got to do with it?"

"He's prob'ly got a dick five feet long."

"Man...Wish I had a dick five feet long," said Moose.

"What would you do with a dick five feet long?"

"Same thing I do with the one I got now...Play with it. Ha ha ha."

"Jesus," said the Count. "Who's got the lead in the Contest?"

"The Big Guy," said Stan.

"Onward Christian Soldiers," said Moose. "The good guys are winning again. That's how God planned it."

The count is cu-lear...The count is cu-lear...

The ten o'clock count was cleared. Three thousand, one hundred and twenty-eight convicts all present and accounted for...Murderers, rapists, robbers, junkies, forgers, and assorted deviants—Enemies of the State. Violators of state and federal laws. All present.

Night watchmen prowled the perimeter, carbines at the ready, dogs on leashes, aware of the presence of desperate men. Guntower guards, alert to the movement of shadows, drank lukewarm thermos coffee and spoke of wives grown soft and fat with age, of children ungrateful for the gifts so graciously bestowed by loving parents.

Convicts lay awake on narrow bunks remembering the twangy sounds of the streets, tall draft beers and twelve stool bars, honky-tonk songs and tough talking women, the rush of the chase, the sorrow of tomorrow, the 7 A.M. Never-Again Blues.

Some recalled wives and dime-store sweethearts, tender embraces and lesser moments. More than a few stroked their manhood under rough wool blankets, stoically pumping semen into state issue handkerchiefs. Some could only remember the squalor of the Projects and the stench of the street, a ten-cent ride with a two-ton load. Some watched the gunwalk guards with murderous eyes, plotting revenge.

> *Re-lease for medication...*
> *Re-lease for medication...*

Medication release, always late on movie nights, brought forth a gaggle of escorted convicts to drift like ghosts across the lighted Yard, eerie chalk figures in the searchlights, ten milligram dreamers, supplicants at the Pharmacy of Hope, stone cold addicts of the blues.

At ten thirty Moose proclaimed his victory by a margin of five.

"Okay, Leonard," he said. "When do I get laid?"

"Plans are being made," said Leonard.

"You're not goin' to back out on this, are you?"

"...Trust me. The wheels are already in motion."

"If you're good, Paulson," said Moose, "I'll let you smell my dick when I'm through."

Paulson turned his back and opened the newspaper.

"Maybe even lick it," said Moose, smiling wickedly. "If you're really good."

# CHAPTER 27

Junior Grimes claimed no memory of the crimes that shocked Piedmont County and compelled Judge Osborne to proclaim them the most heinous crimes he had heard of in his thirty years on the bench. After his insanity plea was rejected, Junior stood trial and was given a life sentence. He was in his fourteenth year of that sentence, perhaps even within sight of a parole date, though the Board traditionally did not take kindly to axe murderers, and relatives of the dismembered would most certainly clamor for continued incarceration.

Junior was a model prisoner, mild and soft spoken, often the lone attendee at Father Joe's morning Mass. Ignoring the directives of the recent Vatican Council, he intoned the responses in Latin. Father Joe liked that; he knew Latin was God's language.

Junior's cellmate was Mark Hartford, a young degenerate afflicted with severe acne and a bad temper. They had not been cellmates long. Young Mark could sometimes be seen in the upper bunk, sighing heavily and ejaculating into a soiled handkerchief. He made little effort to hide his habit, claiming a strong sexual nature that made resistance impossible.

Through it all, Junior smiled pleasantly.

On the morning of December tenth, only Junior Grimes awoke in the cell in North Block. He was singing his favorite Latin hymn in a soft tenor voice: O salutaris hostia…Young Mark had expired sometime during the night, a victim of numerous stab wounds. It appeared that some effort had been made to cut off his hand. Junior claimed self-defense, describing in detail how he had been attacked in the middle of the night by his demented cellmate, exhibiting a small cut on his finger as evidence. There were, of course, no witnesses; even the gunwalk guard had been unaware.

Quinlan read the report, scanned Hartford's rap sheet and concluded that perhaps Junior Grimes had done the State of California a favor. Besides, in the absence of witnesses, a trial would be inconclusive. And expensive. Hartford had no close relatives, no one to initiate an investigation. Quinlan penned his agreement with the theory of self-defense and marked the file CLOSED. Across Junior's file he wrote:

### Single cell placement.

No use chancing it again.

# CHAPTER 28

After months of fruitless investigation into Hawk's death, Stan was called in for questioning by Hebner and Cheswick. Hebner made it clear that he wasn't buying Stan's story about not knowing who did it. Seated to the right and slightly behind Hebner, Cheswick huffed and puffed like a train pulling a grade—few of the sounds he made were words.

The Lieutenant worked his way around to the notion that Stan's life might be in considerable danger if those who were guilty of the killing suspected him of being a snitch, of going to The Man with information. He suggested that a story just like that might somehow get circulated on the Yard. Those things happened. Could be dangerous, he said. Possibly fatal.

When he got no reaction, he presented the argument that seldom failed.

"Wasn't but a bunch of niggers," he said. "You know that. Think of what they did, Smith. To you. Think about that for awhile. And you're protectin' them?...Turn the tables and they'd give you up in a minute. Prob'ly less."

"I remember you," said Cheswick, folding his face into a frown.

The knot in Stan's stomach had been there for a long time. His life had become an emotional roller coaster of highs and lows, though the highs were not very high, and the lows (that tended to be very low) were the dominant part of the cycle. Sometimes he just wanted to cry, though he couldn't bring himself to do it even when he was alone. Other times he wanted to scream at the top of his lungs, but he had the feeling that if he ever started he wouldn't be able to stop. Instead, he set his jaw, put one foot in front of the other and kept walking. Walk slow and keep yo' back to the wall. He tried not to get sidetracked like Pinocchio did. One more goddam day. And then another goddam fucking day.

There were nights when he prayed that he would go to sleep and not wake up, when his despair was deeper than anything he had ever known...Now I lay me down to die...only to be jarred back to reality by the noisy 6 A.M. klaxon horn sounding in his ear like a giant bee, and the unmistakably sour smell of Big Eddy filling the small cell. Reluctantly he would fight his way back to the surface to begin another day. One more day. And how many more after today? Most mornings he went to the gym and punched the heavy bag until his arms ached and his knuckles bled; the pain seemed to keep him focused. He returned day after day to repeat the performance, punching the bag till his knuckles bled, taking some solace from enduring the pain and knowing that it connected him with Hawk. Somehow, it made him feel better. He began to walk with his head up. Even Chewy noticed when they happened to meet on the Yard.

"You takin' care of bi'ness now, Murder Man?"

He faked a left-right combination. Stan blocked the left and taped him on the cheek with an open hand before Chewy could bring the right around. Fast.

"Takin' care of business, homeboy," said Stan.

"...I remember you," growled Cheswick.

"You prob'ly be next, Smith," said Hebner. "Niggers'll kill you. Wouldn't that be somethin'? You protectin' them and they kill you. Serve you right."

Stan shrugged.

"Swan dive off the fourth tier," said Hebner. "Just like your buddy, Hawkins. Splat!...So long, Smith. Nice knowin' you."

"You ain't shit," said Cheswick. It was his standard observation.

Hebner made several notations in his spiral notebook. Smith was an important witness; with his eyewitness testimony they might be able to file charges and get a conviction. Convictions were hard to come by behind the walls; witnesses were always scarce. But it was the kind of thing Quinlan would appreciate—busting convicts, filing new charges, giving them more time behind bars where they belonged. His kind of police work. And it certainly wouldn't hurt his own chances of becoming a captain.

"See, we already know who did it," said Cheswick. "Your testimony would just help a little, that's all. But we don't need it. Or you. We got other witnesses. You could just make it easier on yourself by cooperatin'. Guy like you might need some help from Custody someday. Know what I mean?"

Stan stared at a spot just above Cheswick's head.

Hebner watched with a growing sense of futility. He could see it coming; the kid was going to stonewall them. It didn't take long before they all learned the standard Convict Code: See nothing, hear nothing, say nothing.

Hebner sat back in his chair, lit a cigarette and pushed the bill of his cap up with his thumb. Though he was in his early thirties, he looked barely old enough to shave.

"Sarge is right," he said. "You ain't shit. Just another stupid convict who doesn't know what's happening. When are you guys ever gonna learn?"

Stan didn't respond.

"The thing is, Smith, you're holdin' out on us. I happen to know that for a fact, and that doesn't show me any respect...See, a guy like you doesn't deserve to be out on the street with decent people. You're scum. You and the rest of your buddies. That guy you killed was a Marine veteran—a fucking patriot. My brother was a Marine. A hero. Got killed in Korea. Making the world safe for assholes like you. Jesus, you guys piss me off."

He flicked his ashes on the floor without taking his eyes off Stan.

"You're gonna be here a long time, Smith. A long, long time. By the time Voodoo and his friends get through with you you'll be beggin' to tell me everything. Beggin'. They'll be lined up outside your cell every morning, waitin' for you to wake up...Hey, Smitty baby, it's your homeboys. Get up and bend over."

He leaned forward.

"Now you can do hard time...or you can do easy time. It's up to you. You cooperate, we see that things get better. We see that nothin' bad happens to you. And the thing is, Smith, nobody has to know about it. Nobody. This is just between us."

The statement hung in the air. Hebner puffed hard on his cigarette until a cloud of smoke nearly obscured his face. No one spoke for a few moments. Stan coughed.

"...We don't have to know right away," Hebner said finally. "Next couple of days is okay. Think about it. This is a very important decision for you. Gonna make a lot of difference in your life. A lot. Remember that." He dismissed him with a wave of his hand.

"You ain't shit," growled Cheswick.

Stan left the room.

"Fuckin' convicts," said Hebner. "They just don't get it, do they?"

"Ain't none of 'em shit," said Cheswick.

Stan knew who it was that had attacked him in his cell that day. Not their names—he didn't find that out till later—but who they were. It was the way they looked at him; like they owned him. And he knew they'd be back; he'd always known that. Even before Doc told him. What surprised him was how long it took.

His mind turned the incident over and over until he had seen it from every possible angle, then began to turn it over again, like an endless loop. His imagination constructed elaborate schemes of revenge—strangling them with piano wire, poisoning them so he could watch the slow, agonizing deaths, driving rusty nails into their eyes.

Hawk had given him some measure of confidence, had stirred within him the idea that perhaps he could take care of himself. After all, he had been holding his own with Hawk at the end, getting in some good shots. And Hawk was no slouch. Ask the guys at Nellis.

After the rape, his tenuous sense of himself as a man all but vanished. First Jeffrey took Bonnie. She was part of what he was, part of his maleness. Lying beside her at night he would think that anyone married to Bonnie Aldrich must be a person of some substance, a man of some substance. She certified his fragile manhood, stamped his ticket as a Red Blooded American Male. Capable and Virile. Able to satisfy the most insatiable sexual appetite. (Look here what I got, baby. I am Ozymandias, King of Kings.) He was comforted by her presence. Reassured. But he worried about whether he was big enough, strong enough, man enough, worried about whether she really loved him. Worried about everything. And because he felt most like a man when he was with her, he thought she knew something about maleness, thought she could teach him. But she didn't; she knew little enough about being a woman.

And when she was gone, when he knew in his heart that she was really gone, all he wanted to do was get even. (Doc told him he must have been thinking that pussy was more important than freedom, but he never thought about it in those terms, not either-or like that. Besides, it was about a lot more than just that.) He became much more interested in revenge than in possible reconciliation. It became a matter of principle, of honor, of...manhood. Something he prized very highly had been taken from him, stolen from him (he seldom allowed himself to think that she had gone freely). Another man had done that, had challenged his manhood and found it lacking. He saw revenge as his only vindication.

Yet, Jeffrey had not been the first to enter his life and take something from him. There were women who just walked in and walked out because they thought he was boring or stupid or uninteresting. Just walked away...See you later, Stan. You don't fill the bill...He took all rejections very personally.

But when he finally got his revenge, it was not at all like he imagined it would be. It just made him feel empty inside. There was no satisfaction, no feeling that Justice had been done, that he had been vindicated. Though he told himself he had not intended to kill Jeffrey, not really kill him, it alarmed him that he had even been able to entertain the thought. Still, most of the sorrow he saved for himself, for his predicament, for the time he had to do. He settled much of the blame on alcohol and the pills he took to change his world...I didn't know, he thought. How could I have known? I don't even remember...Now, more than two years later, he wasn't so sure. Perhaps he did know...did remember.

His own rape had stripped away what little vestige of self-respect that remained. It seemed foolish to think of it as losing his virginity, yet that's the way he thought about it. He had been entered, violated. In the nights that followed, he sometimes lay awake and examined his feelings. He tried to identify them. (Dr. Harwood's Psychology class: Sad? Mad? Bad? Glad? It seemed to trivialize all the emotions.) There was fear; even thinking about it made his heart race. But there had always been fear in his life. He was brought up in a house that was emotionally booby-trapped; he never knew where the next explosion would come from. He had never known a life without fear. He could like it or dislike it, but he always had to deal with it. Then there was the shame and the guilt. The one notion that bothered him more than the others was—Maybe I liked it…At first it seemed absurd. How could he have possibly liked it? Yet, beyond the fear and the shame and the pain, he remembered it as erotic. Sick as he had been, he had an erection when it was over.

His fantasies alarmed him. Did he subconsciously want them to come back? Organs of considerable size had begun to spiral through his dreams. Without wanting to, he reached for them, touched them, brought them to his lips. Perhaps he was a homosexual after all. He had worried about that very thing when he was young, wondered why he was so fascinated with male genitalia. Were other boys? Of course he never asked.

After Stan left Control he continued on across the Yard toward South Block.

*…We are the seed of Abraham,* said Preacher, *ministers of Christ, some wheat, some chaff…surely revenge is sweetest when blood is shed on hallowed ground…*

Maybe he could put up a decent fight if they came back. When they came back…He didn't have long to wait to find out.

# CHAPTER 29

Leonard set up a meeting with Correctional Officer Jules Reiner by slipping an official looking envelope into the mail slot marked Ofc. J. Reiner. The note was typewritten, unsigned:

*Meet at the usual place.*
*3 pm Thursday.*

The usual place was the cavernous Laundry with its long counters, bins of dirty clothes, noisy presses and double-load industrial washers. It was where they conducted business. They met at the counter farthest from the door, Leonard behind the counter sorting socks and shorts, Jules in front, his back to the counter, casually smoking a cigarette. He was a stocky black man with slick, wavy hair. A wisp of a moustache accented his upper lip. He was neither young nor old.

"I need you to get a woman in here for me," said Leonard.

Jules coughed and sputtered.

"Come on, man," he said. "Get serious."

"I am serious."

"…Come on…"

"One more time. I need to get a woman in here."

"Shit, Leonard." He dropped his cigarette on the floor and stepped on it. "I can't get no goddam wo-man in here. You crazy? You think I just go out and get some woman and bring her in here? Just like that? Pardon me, but I got to bring this woman in here for one of the convicts. Shit…"

"Reiner…"

"You want some whiskey, too. How 'bout some hair-o-in…We might's well get it all while we gettin' it. Shit, man…"

"You through?" said Leonard, folding a pair of shorts and setting them on the counter.

Reiner shuffled his feet and lit another cigarette.

"Now," said Leonard. "I need you to find a way to get a woman to the back door of the hospital. We'll need her for about two hours."

Reiner took a deep breath and shook his head.

"Man oh man…A woman. If that don't beat all. This muffuckah wants a woman in here," as if he were talking to a third party. "A woman."

"Right," said Leonard. "You gettin' the idea now, Reiner. A woman. They're the ones with the tits. You'll know as soon as you spot one."

"How'm I gonna get a woman in here?"

"You'll find a way. I pay you to be resourceful."

"Man…"

"There's money in it."

"Hope to shit they better be money in it…Big money."

"There is," said Leonard.

"How much?"

"…Plenty."

"I can't use no plenty to figure my bills," said Reiner. "Plenty don't mean nothing. See what I'm sayin'? Got to have a number with it so's it means somethin'."

"What do you think it's worth?"

"Oh," said Reiner, rubbing the back of his neck. "I'd say about a thousand dollars. Round numbers. Maybe more."

"Jesus, Reiner, I don't need Miss America. Just a woman; somebody not too ugly who's got all the right plumbing."

"She for you?"

"That make a difference?"

"…Might."

"No, she's not for me."

"Risky," said Reiner. "Awful risky. Quinlan's not old man Alexander. He be payin' attention to what's goin' on."

"Many women as you know, this ought to be a piece of cake."

"Plen-ty risky."

"Three hundred's as high as I go," said Leonard.

"You been locked up a long time, man. They's inflation goin' on out there. Be eatin' a man's paycheck up somethin' bad."

"Three hundred, Reiner. That's half a month's salary for a few hours work."

"Might cost me my job."

"That's not the only thing that could cost you your job."

"…What's that supposed to mean?"

"Just a comment."

"You can't go to The Man with what we been doin', Leonard. I figured that out a long time ago. You'd get busted, too."

"In case you haven't noticed, I'm already busted." He pushed the glasses up on the bridge of his nose.

"You talkin' blackmail, man?

"Lightweight stuff," said Leonard. "Maybe another year or so. Might be a little different for a correctional officer, though. Walkin' the Yard. Some people might have hard feelings. I mean guys like Hoss, the Organ Grinder…maybe even Ice, might be offended by your presence on the Yard. You know how convicts are, how upset they get over little things."

Reiner ran his hand through hair that glistened with Royal Crown Hair Straightener.

"I could maybe make an exception and take five hundred," he said. "Just this once."

"I pay you too goddam much as it is," said Leonard.

"Make me an offer."

"I already did…Three hundred."

"You ever hear about negotiatin', man? That's the way people in bi'ness do. I make an offer, then you make an offer…Like a counter-offer. Then we negotiate. We reach a compromise…"

"Three hundred," said Leonard.

"That's it?"

"Top dollar."

Reiner exhaled slowly and sagged against the counter.

"No wonder you in the penitentiary," he said.

"We got a deal?"

"…Yeah."

"Wait for the first rains," said Leonard. "Next big storm. Bring her in in foul weather gear. Custody gear. All bundled up. Nobody'll notice. Get her to the back door of the hospital. She'll be out before anybody knows she's been here."

"I get my money this month?"

"Next month…If everything goes right."

"I need some up-front money, man. At least half. Heavy bills this month."

"Later," said Leonard.

"You a crook, man."

"Surprise, surprise," said Leonard. "Who said you guys in Custody weren't smart?"

"What you gonna do with her?"

"…We need a fourth for bridge."

"Say what?"

"Never mind."

"You not gonna hurt her?" said Reiner.

"No."

Leonard dipped into the laundry bin for more clothes.

"Try to get a nice looking one, eh?"

"Sure. Three hundred dollars? Ought to be able to get Cleo-fuckin'-patra for three hundred big ones. Jesus…"

Reiner pushed off the counter and started to walk away.

"Reiner?" said Leonard.

He stopped without turning around.

"Yeah?"

"I wouldn't want anything to go wrong. This is important. You know what happens when things go wrong."

"Yeah. I know."

"You remember last time?"

Reiner just nodded.

"We won't have to do that again, will we?" said Leonard.

"No."

"Good. Well, see you in the funny papers, Officer."

Reiner pulled a pack of cigarettes out of his shirt pocket as he walked toward the door. His hands were shaking as he lit one.

# CHAPTER 30

They were waiting for Stan in his cell when he came in from work early that afternoon. The same three. They must have known that Big Eddy never returned to the cell until after the evening meal. He didn't see them; he just knew they were there because he had begun to sense the presence of those around him without actually seeing them.

It all happened so fast he didn't have time to think about it. When Willy reached for him, he turned and swung as hard as he could. Pure reflex. It surprised Stan as much as it did Willy. He buried his fist in Willy's stomach. Willy's eyes went wide and white as he doubled over and sank to the floor.

Buck grabbed Stan from behind and Pokey closed in from the front, nostrils flared, gums exposed. His nose was running. Stan brought his knee up hard between Pokey's legs.

"Muffuckah," he moaned, grabbing himself and backing away.

Stan slammed his elbow back into Buck's ribs. He heard the ooof and felt the grip loosen.

The next thing he remembered was pounding someone's head against the cell bars. It was Buck; his face had the appearance of raw meat. The eyes rolled randomly, and blood ran from a number of cuts.

One of the Goon Squad pulled Stan away and held him. Cheswick put his face up close to Stan's.

"I remember you," he hissed.

Stan's heart was pounding in his ears. He struggled to get loose, but strong hands held him tightly. The smallest man on the Goon Squad outweighed him by eighty pounds.

Buck slid down the bars and sat heavily on the floor. Pokey and Willy were nowhere in sight.

"Wetzle," said Cheswick, "call Control and get somebody to take our friend Buck to the hospital. Tell them no hurry. If we're lucky he'll die on the way and we'll save the taxpayers some money."

He turned to Stan.

"I think you and me better take a trip down to see the Lieutenant."

Hebner thought it was funny.

"What'd I tell you?" he chuckled. "Those guys tried to kill you, Smith. Just like I said. First Hawk, and then you. When you gonna wake up?"

Cheswick made a sound that might have been a laugh.

Stan nodded but didn't speak. He was filled with an unfamiliar sensation that was warm, visceral. He, Stan Smith, had actually done something—fought off his attackers, defended himself, acquitted himself with what he believed could be considered some sort of honor. Wimpy Stan had done that. With those itty bitty hands.

"...Didn't I tell you?" said Hebner.

Loughlin's death had left Stan in an emotional limbo, uncertain about the part he had played, his feelings vague and undefined. Only later, in the long nights that followed, did he begin to recognize and acknowledge the fear, the self-pity, the anger, the despair that had always been with him, begin to realize how little of his life had been his own. As a skinny, underweight child, his mother had done for him (raw eggs and brandy, vitamin pills and shots). The Runt, Carl called him, as if Stan's size was a personal affront to his own manhood.

When he was older, Bonnie had done for him, opening her arms and her legs, cradling his senseless root like a child in heat. He cast a shadow only when he was with someone else. In between, teachers indulged him, defended him against predatory classmates, encouraged his intellectual pretensions, suggested that he was among the best and the brightest. He had allowed it, savored it, eventually discovered that he couldn't live without it...Stamp my ticket. Make me okay...He was what people believed him to be, a Master Chameleon so unsure of what he actually was that he instantly became what others believed him to be. And when Jeffrey came and took Bonnie away, Stan's world went with her. There was nothing left. No shadow, no substance—nothing. So he got even. It was the only thing he could think of to do.

"Didn't I tell you?" Hebner said again.

"Yeah," said Stan.

"Those were the guys, eh?"

Stan gave no indication that he had heard the question.

"...Weren't they?" said Hebner. He was still smiling.

"Weren't they what?" said Stan.

"Weren't they the guys who killed Hawkins?"

"Oh...I don't know. I didn't see the guys who did it."

Hebner's smile collapsed.

"Goddamit, Smith. You think this is some kind of bullshit game?"

He jammed a cigarette in his mouth and lit it before he continued.

"We can burn your ass, Smith. Believe me. And we will if we have to. If you don't cooperate. Don't doubt that for a minute. You're here on a murder beef. Murder Two. Violence. The Board doesn't like violence...We bust you on this deal and we might be able to file a new beef. How does assault with intent sound? On top of murder. You'll be a hundred fuckin' years old before you walk outta this place. A hundred if you're lucky. If you live that long. You won't be able to buy a hardon, you'll be so old...Now I want those cocksuckers who killed Hawkins. I want names, and you're gonna give 'em to me."

He eased back in his chair, inhaled and blew the smoke out of his nose. He moved his head but kept his eyes on Stan.

"What do you say?"

"...I didn't see anything...sir."

Cheswick made strange hissing sounds, like a snake choking on a mouse.

Hebner got to his feet, placed both hands on the desk and leaned forward. His expression was pained.

"You're telling me no-deal, Smith? No-fucking-deal?"

Stan nodded.

"You ain't shit," growled Cheswick.

Smoke poured out of Hebner's nose.

"That gets you a write-up, Smith. A one-fifteen. You got a bad attitude, kid. You know that? A really bad attitude. So we're gonna send you to the Adjustment Center for awhile. See if we can adjust that lousy attitude you got. Got a guy down in the Adjustment Center who eats his own shit. Lives on it practically. You'll like it real well down there. They're your kind of people—assholes. We'll try the thirty-day treatment to start with. If that doesn't work, we can always fix you up with a longer stay. Maybe even till your eyesight improves and you can remember seein' who it was tossed your buddy Hawkins off the tier.

"We got plenty of time. As a matter of fact that's all we got here. You could think of this place as a kind of Time Factory. We manufacture time. We can make more time or less time. We can make easy time or hard time. All kinds of time. We can do anything we want and you can't do anything about it. You could think of us as gods here. Especially as far as you're concerned…I got a long time to go before I retire, Smith. Years. And you got a life top. You might still be in the Adjustment Center when I retire. I'll be getting' a gold watch and you'll be down in one of the strip cells havin' a spoonful of shit. Breakfast of champions." He smiled at the prospect. "We got guys been down there a long time. Can't seem to adjust. Jerkoffs… Like you."

He straightened up.

"Fighting is a very serious offense, Smith. Very serious. We may have to file additional charges."

He motioned to Cheswick.

"Take this man to the Adjustment Center, Sergeant. I'll do the write-up."

He sat down at the desk and pulled open a side drawer.

"You're the worst kind of convict, Smith. You know that? You're the kind who should know better. You got an education. Your parents are prob'ly decent people. Working people. And you? You're a fucking disgrace. So I'm gonna bury you. Me personally. I'm gonna make that my job, my vocation. Every day I want you to get up and think about me—Lieutenant Hebner. I want you to think how much you hate me, how much you'd like to kill me. Because that makes me feel good. Any time a convict hates me, I know I'm doin' my job."

He took a one-fifteen form out of the drawer, set it on the desk and began to fill it out.

"Prob'ly would have been easier if you'd just gone ahead and let 'em fuck you, Smith. In the long run."

# CHAPTER 31

It was never completely dark in North Block; safety lights that burned twenty-four hours a day sliced between the bars and cast long, gridiron shadows on the cell walls. Each night the same dreary pattern, the same number of bars, the same false moon in a fixed and barren sky. Night after night Voodoo counted the bars. He knew where they intersected, where they ran diagonally down the wall to meet and bend at the floor. He knew the number of rivets in the cell wall seam, small round bumps with shadows behind them, innocent as pimples, smaller than the shadows would suggest. He knew the feel of the coarse wool blanket, had grown accustomed to its smell.

He had schooled himself to endure, to be unaffected by his surroundings, to be in control of his responses. He was a warrior, as his ancestors had been warriors. They had killed and been killed, fighting for what belonged to them, for what they believed in—that was the way of the warrior. But he also knew the cruelty of time, and he knew that time was slipping away.

It was after late lockdown and lights out at ten o'clock that he prepared himself for the battle that was to come. It was then that he mentally made the match and moved the players around like pieces in a chess game. The pawns were known—they were expendable. The Rooks were here, the Knights there, the Bishops ready to slice diagonally across the board, the all-powerful Queen a decoy. And of course the King. Though the King was restricted in his movements, not as mobile as some of the other pieces, you couldn't win unless you captured the opposing King. He was the key...Check... Checkmate...Victory.

Voodoo lay awake and listened. It was quiet; even the most disturbed eventually drifted off into some kind of troubled sleep.

He closed his eyes and pictured his own face—the broad nose, full lips, smooth dark skin. Black skin. Black is beautiful, he said, but deep in his heart he didn't know if he believed that. Sometimes he hated his blackness. He had been imprisoned by it long before his first jail sentence. And where did it come from, this hatred of what he was, of his own color? Was it so deeply imbedded in his psyche, so much a part of his consciousness, so much a part of his racial heritage, that he couldn't escape it? Didn't they call one another nigger as a term of derision? Nigger this and nigger that...Why?

It was in those late hours that his mind seemed to have a mind of its own. It appeared to work independently (often he just watched, sometimes alarmed, sometimes amused), examining issues and drawing conclusions he was often not ready to accept. At times it betrayed him, revealing selfishness he had not suspected, doubt that hid in the shadows. Untethered, his mind roamed freely over scenes of madness and destruction, creating episodes yet to come. And more than once it told him he was a fool, that he best leave the business of revolution to those more qualified. A black fool at that.

He kept a small notebook with excerpts from the writings of Frantz Fanon. The words soothed him, renewed his sense of purpose. He had committed some of his favorite passages to memory:

> *...The colonized man will manifest his aggressiveness against his own people...*

The prophecy was being fulfilled in the riots taking place in black ghettoes across the country—Detroit, Los Angeles, Newark —black men destroying their own communities.

> *...Colonialism loosens its hold only when there is a knife at its throat...*

A knife at its throat...Voodoo's hand closed on the metal bunk railing. He mentally recited the passage he had delivered yesterday to a small group of brothers on the Yard:

> *...So the pimps, the hooligans, the unemployed and the petty criminals shall throw themselves into the struggle for liberation...And they will discover, by militant and decisive action, the path that leads to freedom. The prostitutes, too, and... all the hopeless dregs of humanity, all who turn in circles between suicide and madness, all will recover their balance and once more go forward and march proudly in the great procession of an awakened nation...*

The brothers liked it so much, they had him repeat it. He was eloquent, forceful, caught up in the moment. They nodded, voiced their approval. *Right on, Blood. Right on...*Questions about how and when did not arise. Was it so abstract, so Pie-in-the-sky that they could not conceive of it actually happening? Was it, after all, just so much talk? Or was it that they trusted him completely, that they knew when the time was right, Voodoo would lead them? And all would be revealed in good time.

He left them with a final passage from *The Wretched of the Earth*:

> *...For if the last shall be first, it will only be after a murderous and decisive struggle...*

Voodoo rubbed his arms and his torso, comforted by the strength of his body. He was a strong black man. A brave black man. A warrior.

Officer Macon's crepe-soled shoes betrayed his approach on the gunwalk. Voodoo lay perfectly still as the tongue of light flicked briefly into his cell and moved on.

The dream was like a volcano inside his chest, just waiting to erupt. It was a dream about justice, about making right what had been wrong for so long. And it would not be denied. He knew that everything in his life had been a preparation for the days that were to come. He had studied the history and prepared himself mentally. He had fashioned himself into a spear, a burning spear, a weapon of liberation and retribution. Like Jomo Kenyatta, he would strike terror in the hearts of those responsible for the long years of oppression.

There would be killing; he understood that. Bloodshed. He knew that he might die. He wondered how many of the brothers would follow him if they knew what the chances of survival were? A few, he imagined, but only a few. Blinded by rhetoric and hatred, they believed. At least for now. The struggle gave meaning to lives that had none, hope where there had been none. They embraced it eagerly. Right on, Blood. Right on...But how many would stand with him when the time came? And for how long?

Many will die, he thought. Scenes of white men lying in pools of blood filled him with satisfaction. Some he had already chosen. Moose Rankin, three hundred pounds of racist pig, would drown in his own blood. Voodoo would see to it himself. He would carve him, gut him, perhaps even present him to Quinlan as an offering. Several members of the Aryan Nation had also been chosen in advance...

*...The last shall be first only after a murderous and decisive struggle...*

They would take arms, such as they were, and fight. For freedom. For justice. (There was no doubt in his mind that he was a political prisoner.) To the barricades. To the cellblocks. They would kill. And be killed.

And they would take hostages.

When they took over the prison, when national attention was focused on Fremont and millions of television sets blinked on all across America to catch the five o'clock news, he would take the stage and present his list of grievances, his list of demands, his Freedom Manifesto. They would include not only Fremont, but the entire United States of America. And America would listen and watch, horrified. (Lookit all them niggers, Bobby Joe! What they doin'?) They would all be his captives then. And if he was not heard, if his demands were not met, he would kill the hostages, one by one, each to atone for a thousand black men and women slain for the color of their skin. Strange fruit, black fruit hanging from southern magnolias. Billie Holiday and the blues. From the plantation to the ghetto, four hundred years of slavery. (Fo' hunnut muffuckin' yea's o' slav'ry, said Billy 2X.) One by one, begging for mercy, the hos-

229

tages would die, blood spilling to atone for the sins of the white race...Voodoo took pleasure from the scene.

And the world would remember. Generations would remember. His name would be mentioned in the same breath with Marcus Garvey, Frantz Fanon, Jomo Kenyatta...the Voodoo Man, Son of the Great Serpent, Black Avenger—his name would be writ large on the pages of History.

He stretched and turned over on his side. A smile formed on his lips.

"Look out, white boy," he whispered. "Heah come the Voodoo Man. Gonna cut yo' throat. Gonna drink yo' blood."

He grasped his flaccid manhood in both hands, took a deep breath and began to count the rivets in the cell wall seam. In a few minutes, he was sound asleep.

# CHAPTER 32

"Break his legs," said Hoss.

"Both of 'em?" said Hunter, crouching unsteadily on the top bunk in Reno's cell.

"Jesus, Hoss," said Reno, trying to control his voice, "not both of 'em. That ain't humanly."

Red and Nemo held him down on the floor, legs extended, heels on the bottom bunk a foot above the floor.

"You owe eight boxes, Reno. Been owed too long. Way too long."

"I paid some, Hoss. You know that. Ten, twelve boxes already."

"But late, Reno. Every fuckin' week you're late. You got some bullshit excuse about next week you gonna straighten me with the whole deal. It never happens, man. You makin' me look bad."

"We been walkin' the Yard a long time, Hoss. You and me."

"This is business, man."

Hoss looked at Gimpy standing watch outside the cell. Gimpy gave him the okay sign.

"But to show you I'm a right guy, I'm only gonna break one leg. Which one you want broke?"

"Oh...Jesus," said Reno.

"Quit whinin'," said Hoss. "I'm givin' you a break...Hey, that's funny. Givin' you a break, eh?"

Reno didn't even smile.

"You right-handed?" said Hoss.

Reno nodded.

"Simple. Then we break the right leg. That way you can hold yourself up on that side."

Without a word, Hunter jumped off the top bunk and landed on Reno's left knee with both feet, bending it backward out of its socket, slamming it hard onto the concrete floor. Nemo had a hand over Reno's mouth to stifle the scream. He held it there until Reno's eyes went white and he passed out. Hunter hobbled away holding one of his ankles.

"Sprained my goddam ankle again," he moaned.

"You ain't landin' right, man," said Red. "I tole you that last time."

Hoss looked at Reno slumped on his side, one leg bent backward at the knee, the other bent forward.

"Hold up your right hand, Hunter," he said.

Hunter hesitated for a moment, then held up his right hand.

"And your right foot?"

Hunter lifted his right foot.

"Good," said Hoss. "So how come you broke Reno's left leg?"

"Shit," said Hunter. "...I was lookin' down at him, Hoss. From the bunk. Facin' him. So I thought, right leg here, right leg there. Shit. We was facin' each other. I got the wrong leg, man."

"No shit," said Hoss.

"It's not like an arm, Hoss. It's not like he's gonna have to learn to wipe his ass with a different hand. It's just a leg. He can limp either side it won't make no difference."

"How about if I break your fuckin' leg?" said Hoss. "You care which one? I mean right leg, left leg, it's all the same?"

"I was just sayin'..."

"Well, don't. You startin' to give me a big pain in the ass, Hunter. You get a couple of packs of Big Reds for two seconds work and you can't even get that right. And then you sprain your fuckin' ankle. I could get an idiot would do a better job. Jesus, man..."

Marv Fletcher left the canteen with his monthly draw in a brown paper bag—three cans of Bugler tobacco, two large jars of Folgers Instant Coffee, two boxes of sugar cubes, a box of Saltine crackers and a large jar of Skippy Extra Smooth Peanut Butter. Almost fourteen dollars worth, but it would last him the whole month. If he rolled them tight, he could get a whole carton of smokes out of a can of Bugler. Eighty cents for a carton wasn't a bad deal. Especially since he had to watch his money. The Furniture Factory job paid him nine a month, and Gwen could only afford to send six. It was close, but it worked out okay.

He turned the corner of the Laundry on his way back to North Block and walked into Snake and Okie. Snake bumped him hard and knocked the bag out of his hand.

"Watch where you're goin', asshole," he said.

Marv made eye contact for just a moment, then bent down to pick up the bag. Okie pushed him out of the way and picked it up himself.

"I do believe this is my bag of groceries here," he said. "Don't this look like my bag, Snake?"

"It does, man. Just like it."

"I set it down to take a piss and somebody ripped it off." He looked in the bag. "Bugler, peanut butter, coffee...Yep, this is it."

Marv looked at Okie, then at Snake; he knew who they were. Snake was the little guy with the leathery face and beady eyes, Okie was his slab-shouldered partner who did the heavy work. Okie had Don't Stare tattooed across his forehead.

"...It's mine," Marv said weakly, though he knew there was little chance he'd get it back.

"You starin' at me?" said Okie.

Marv shook his head.

"Four-eyed fuck," said Okie.

He took Marv's glasses off, dropped them on the concrete and crushed them with the heel of his Santa Rosa high tops.

"Can't stare so good now, eh?"

Marv shook his head again.

"We got a deal for you," said Snake. "We runnin' low on supplies at the old corral and we figure you'd like to help us out...We figure right?"

Marv looked across the Yard; he could hardly see without his glasses.

"I'm talkin' to you, asshole," said Snake. "We figure right about you wantin' to help out?"

Marv nodded slightly.

"Louder," said Okie. "So we can hear you."

"Yeah," said Marv. "Sure."

Snake slapped him on the back.

"That's it, man. The deal we got is that we let you keep half your canteen draw every month. We get half and you get half. Can't ask for no better deal than that, man. Fifty fifty—right down the middle."

"…Half?" said Marv.

"Half," said Snake. "Just half. And we ast nice and polite. We coulda just took it. All of it. Some people woulda done that."

"What if I don't like the, eh…deal?" said Marv. Even as he spoke, he knew it was the wrong thing to say. But he couldn't help himself; he felt he had to say something to protest. "What if…"

Okie hit him in the face with a right hand that knocked him down. It happened so fast, he didn't have time to react.

"That would really be a bad choice," said Snake. "Okie doesn't like people like that—disagreeable people. People who don't cooperate. That's why we have wars, man. You ever think about that? We have wars because people just can't seem to get along. Whole fuckin' countries can't get along. So they have a war and lots of people get killed. Actually get killed because of a stupid war. What a fuckin' waste…You coulda saved yourself a punch in the face with a better attitude, man. A little cooperation."

Marv touched his lip where it was bleeding and looked at his hand. He got up slowly.

"…Right," he said.

"So we got a deal, buddy?"

"…Sure."

"We'll give you a list of stuff to get," said Snake. "Like this Folgers Coffee? We don't like Folgers Coffee do we, Okie."

"It's like horse piss," said Okie. "No self-respectin' white person would drink it."

"So next time get Maxwell House," said Snake. "And instead of the Bugler, get us some Big Reds for our half."

Marv was about to say he couldn't afford to buy tailor-mades and Bugler, but then thought better of it.

"We'll be in touch, old buddy. Let you know how things are goin' at the ranch, what supplies we need. Stuff like that. And just in case you thinkin' about goin' to The Man with some kinda complaint or somethin', I'm tellin' you it would be a very bad idea. Very bad. You followin' me?"

"Yeah…I got it."

"Good. So, see you around, eh?…We'll keep these supplies here," he pointed to the bag Okie was carrying, "till the next shipment. We're a little short at the ranch. You don't mind, eh?"

"Well, I was…"

"You don't mind, eh?"

"No. But I thought maybe you could leave one of the cans of Bugler."

"You want to borrow a can of Bugler?"

"I…Yeah. Borrow a can."

"You know if you borrow a can, you owe two next month. Doubles every month. That's the way it works. Same deal everywhere."

Marv couldn't envision life without cigarettes. Not now. And he was sure he could come up with two cans by next month. After all, it was only eighty cents a can. He was sure he had that much money on the books.

"No problem," he said. "Two cans next month."

Okie reached in the bag, grabbed a can of Bugler and tossed it to him.

"Two for one," he said. "Don't forget."

"No problem," said Marv.

But it was. It was more complicated than it seemed. There was no money on the books. A buck sixty. Three twenty. More…Eventually it almost cost him his life.

# CHAPTER 33

They made Stan take off his belt and remove his shoelaces before they put him in the Adjustment Center cell. Regulations, they said. Lessens the chances of suicide. Big problem, suicide. Lots of paperwork. It was dark and foul-smelling inside. He tried to breathe evenly and not panic.

Though the ceiling seemed higher, the cell itself was narrower than his regular cell; he could stand in the center and easily touch both walls with the palms of his hands without straightening his arms. The front of the cell, even the door, was solid plate steel. A narrow slot in the center of the door slid open just enough to admit a small food tray. The only source of light was a small opening high on the wall.

In the dim light he could barely make out the shape of a toilet. There was nothing else in the cell—no bunk, no wash basin, nothing. In the evening, sometime around nine o'clock he guessed, a thin mattress was tossed in. No blanket, just the mattress. The nights were cold. The mattress was removed each morning.

He did not eat at all the first day. He had heard the stories about ground glass and dog food and fecal matter being put in the meals that went to the Adjustment Center. (Hawk insisted that he had seen Custody put dog shit in it...I seen it, man. Dog shit. Swear to God. Can you imagine how sick those fuckers are?)

Each morning, when the guard left the breakfast of one orange, a cup of water and a bowl of cold mush, he also left the daily ration of toilet paper—ten sheets. Tough, industrial grade toilet paper. Never more and never less. Stan counted them in the dim light. He wondered why only ten sheets? In the days and weeks that followed, he had ample time to ponder the subject.

The following morning he ate the orange. The soup that was lunch smelled like rotten cabbage. By the time dinner arrived it was dark. He explored the contents of the bowl with his fingertips; it had the same consistency of the breakfast mush, though it smelled worse. He stirred it with his plastic spoon, but could not bring himself to eat it. He munched on the dry bread and drank his cup of water.

On sunny days, morning was heralded by a sliver of light from the small window. As the day progressed, the light moved slowly across the floor, widened briefly into a rectangle, then became thinner and thinner until it finally disappeared sometime in the late afternoon. Tiny particles drifted through it, illuminated for a moment, then plunged into darkness on the other side. Stan watched for hours, trying to count the particles.

He inspected his hands in the light, unzipped his pants and examined his penis. Nothing new, he decided; same old shaft. He wondered if life wouldn't be easier without it. It seemed a shame that, years ago, just when he had begun to discover the new and unexpected pleasures the appendage could provide, Father Samuels had appeared on the scene to inform all the wide-eyed freshmen at Loyola High School that solitary sex was a depraved, sinful, immoral activity. Self abuse, he said, with obvious disgust, was an evil, sinful habit that led to…spilling the seed…an act so closely akin to murder that, unrepented, would lead directly to the gates of Hell. And beyond.

In a few days, the diet of oranges and little else left him with a bad case of diarrhea. He asked the guard for more toilet paper. The guard laughed. When the ration of toilet paper was gone for the day, he wiped himself with his shorts, rinsed them in the toilet and hung them over the edge of the bowl, hoping they would dry. They didn't; the cell was cold and damp. He tried waving them around, thinking the wind might dry them out, but it didn't help much. He used them damp. It was better than nothing, though not much. Without warning, hemorrhoids appeared.

He asked the guard about showers. The guard didn't answer. Guards didn't answer questions, weren't supposed to talk to the convicts. Regulations. He learned later that once a week he would be allowed to shower, shave, change clothes and have fifteen minutes of exercise out on the small Adjustment Center Exercise Yard. Regulations Concerning Solitary Confinement of Inmates—section 3, para. 4.2. Exercise alone. So the violent inmates wouldn't try to kill one another.

Winter darkness came early; it was already too dark to see when the evening meal arrived. The darkness frightened him. With nothing to focus on, his mind created monsters and gargoyles, Hieronymous Bosch demons who danced across the sinister landscape of the night. (As a child, he always slept with the light on. His father made fun of him, called him a sissy, but Stan just knew it was safer with the light on. He'd always known that. It seemed so obvious.)

His mind informed him that the mattress that was tossed into his cell each night was filled with cockroaches. No stuffing—just cockroaches. When he went to sleep, they would come out and crawl all over him. In his ears, his eyes, his mouth, everywhere. Just thinking about it made his skin crawl. He tried sleeping on the floor at the rear of the cell, far away from the mattress. He even tried to sleep sitting up on the toilet, but that never worked for more than a few minutes; every time he dozed, he started to fall off. Eventually, cold and shivering, he was driven back to the mattress where he would fall into a fitful sleep and dream about cockroaches. He hated them. He never recalled even seeing one until he got to the Old County Jail. The men there would try to corner them and burn them with cigarettes, shouting triumphantly when one succumbed. It wasn't all that easy to get one in a corner; it often took four or five men with lighted cigarettes. The cockroaches were fast. Survivors from another age, they were quick and resourceful. But the men had a grudging respect for the bigger ones, ones they assumed had been around for awhile. Some even claimed they could identify cockroaches they had seen six or seven years ago. (Yep, that's old Whitey. And Gus over there. You still doin' time for that phony parole violation, Gus?) They were almost family. They made up crimes for them (Biting, Disturbing the Sleep), held court and always sentenced them to death. Just like family.

The most telling sounds were the slamming of cell doors; everything else was muffled, indistinct. Late at night he thought he could hear somebody howling, but he was never sure. When he strained to listen, all he could hear was a faint heartbeat and the blood rushing in his ears.

The solitude played tricks on his mind. He was haunted by childhood memories of someone stuffing rags in his mouth. Had he done something wrong? Been crying? Wet the bed again? It seemed he was always doing something wrong. All he could remember were the rags and the awful sense of suffocation. He still couldn't bear to have a piece of cloth near his mouth, or even touch anything wool.

The memories were fragile, vanishing even as he reached for them. He dimly recalled having a little brother when he was very young, though his parents always denied it...No. Don't be silly. Wouldn't we have told you if you had a brother?...He even thought he remembered the name (Larry) and the small pink face that always seemed to be crying...Maybe they killed him, he thought. Stuffed rags in his mouth so he wouldn't cry, then wrapped him in butcher paper and buried him out behind the house. Two acres of land; they could have buried him anywhere. Maybe they fed him to the dog. They had a Doberman named Caesar that Stan was sure would have relished eating a baby. He dug holes in the back yard, looking for his brother. Carl wanted to know Why the hell he was digging up the back of the house? Stan told him he was looking for buried treasure and Carl said loud and clear that there wasn't any goddam treasure buried there and he better stop diggin' right now if he didn't want to get his butt busted. So Stan stopped but he never forgot; he buried Larry deep in his heart where he kept the things he couldn't bear to look at.

One night he heard Bonnie's voice, a thin, plaintive wail informing him that he was the worst person she had ever known. Possibly the worst person who had ever lived. In the movie that ran constantly behind his eyes, she appeared naked on a big white bed, smiling wickedly, her pubic hair on fire. Here, she said pointing to the fire...Pretend it's a weenie roast...He wondered how he could possibly have loved her as he had (and maybe still did?)... She spread her legs and fanned the flame. Here it is, she said. Your Burning Bush...He shook his head, hoping to dislodge the image, but it remained, indelibly etched on the blackboard of his memory.

When he discovered that he was growling, he put his hand over his mouth.

He began to shout at the guards when his meals were delivered:

*...I am Jean Valjean, the galley slave! Nineteen*
*years in the galley at Toulon...*

The guards ignored him.

"Here is the real criminal," he said, unzipping his pants.

Later he began to pray. He didn't believe in prayer, but there was nothing else to do (he'd already been through all the poetry he knew). He said all the prayers he could remember; some that he learned in high school he could still recite in Latin...Pater noster, qui es in coelis...He closed his eyes and joined Jesus on Golgotha. Just the two of them, Stan and Jesus, suffering together. The Messiah and the Murderer. He listened for some message, waited for some miracle of deliverance, but when he opened his eyes he was still locked in the same gloomy cell. He said the Jesus Prayer over and over until the words had no meaning. He had read somewhere (Salinger? *The Way of a Pilgrim?*) that saying it had the power to transform one's life. He begged and pleaded. All things are possible with God. That's what Father Gallagher always said. But then, maybe not. Maybe it was just another lie.

Make the cockroaches go away, he prayed. In Thy divine mercy, kill the fucking bugs. Make it warm at night...Simple things...A decent meal. More toilet paper...Not much to ask of Someone who had created the earth and the stars and the universe out of nothing. What's a little toilet paper to You? It certainly didn't seem like too much to ask.

But even in the midst of prayer, he was often consumed by lust. He saw dog and pony shows with well-known religious participants (the Virgin Mary doing unspeakable things with the head of John the Baptist). Halfway through the Our Father, he was compelled to masturbate. Compelled. Out came the Criminal and soon it was done. Then, guilty and remorseful, he stuffed his spent member back in his pants and continued his prayer...Our Father who art in heaven... Pater noster qui es in coelis...After awhile nothing made sense.

He sang to himself—sad songs, love songs, a few hymns. He liked Adeste Fideles. His voice was weak but true. He did the scales: do re me faaaaa…He imagined a cathedral, a chorus of hallelujahs. Handel. It was Christmas; they were singing the Christmas liturgy.

*Rejoice! Rejoice! Today a Savior is born…*

He had often gone to Midnight Mass with his parents. They always had to arrive early. So we can get a good seat, his mother said. Were there bad seats in church? he wondered. His father was like a ship of state—huge, regal. People deferred to him. He smelled of tweed and pipe tobacco. Familiar, if not actually safe.

*Rejoice! Rejoice! Unto thee a Savior is born…*

He held his breath and counted the seconds. One, two, three, four, five, six…Time. What was it? He tried to keep track of the days by leaving a scuff mark on the floor with his shoe, but he could never be sure if he had left one or two for that day. Memory often betrayed him. He watched the sunlight crawl across the floor in its rectilinear box of light, slowly changing shape, a noiseless accordion silently wheezing the minutes away, wheezing his life away… Take five. Take twenty. Years. Second degree murder, homeboy. Take your time. Take the A Train. It's about tiiiiime.

He took his shoe off and stared at his big toe as it passed from light to shadow. The sun moves. Or is it the earth? If the earth didn't move, if there was no day or night, would there still be Time? His foot looked strange, alien, like it was beginning to decay. The light moved on, unaware of its place and importance. On and on, until it vanished; until it, too, became part of the darkness…and darkness was upon the face of the deep, and the Spirit of God moved upon the face of the waters… Then the long night. Not even shadows; just inky darkness…I am Jean Valjean, the galley slave…

He thought about how wonderful it would be to smoke a cigarette. How satisfying. He pictured himself inhaling deeply, then tunneling the smoke out of his nose. He relived his last shower— warm, soothing water (a week ago? a month ago?). He shaved with a sealed safety razor (no chance of getting the blade out in case he was thinking of suicide). The guard watched. Regulations. Wouldn't take his eyes off him. Then the clean clothes. Even socks. He lingered in the sunlight on the small Yard as long as he could, but it wasn't very long. Regulations. Fifteen minutes and he was back in his cell, back to watching the little aquarium of light swimming with photons until it vanished and the darkness returned. Then the night. The long night.

He started doing pushups and situps. It hurt to do the situps; he was badly chafed and the diarrhea lingered. But it was something to do. He kept at it; every day a few more.

His mind foundered in seas of uncertainty, sometimes racing, sometimes so lethargic that the simplest act of reasoning seemed far beyond him. He had fleeting glimpses of deep philosophical insights, but they were gone before he could capture them and set them to words, before he could explain them, even to himself. He couldn't remember how old he was. He recalled his birthday with some clarity, the day and the year, but he could not calculate his age from it. Odd, he thought. Shouldn't be that hard to do…But he couldn't. He wondered if perhaps he was asleep and didn't know it. Maybe even dead.

Characters from old movies wandered through the waking hours. Gangsters mostly. Cagney. Bogart. Raft…Nails Nathan. Cody Jarrett. Johnny Friendly from *On the Waterfront*. Tough guys. Like Stan always wanted to be. He pictured Brando in the back of the taxi with Rod Steiger…

> *I coulda been a contendah. I coulda been somebody…
> 'stead of a bum…*

His own brother, Charley the Gent, sold him down the river. Jesus…

Bonnie hated it when he did his gangster imitations. She put her hands over her ears and refused to listen. He did Bogart and Cagney, memorized whole scenes from his favorite movies, played them out endlessly when he was drunk. A few glasses of wine and he went on and on and on. Couldn't shut him up.

The box of light moved slowly across the floor, getting thinner and thinner. His mind skipped from thought to thought like a flat rock on a pond.

He recalled a picture of himself as a little boy with boxing gloves on. He was six or seven at the time. His John L. Sullivan pose—one foot forward, both hands up. A classic bare-knuckle pose. Another unsuccessful attempt by his father to lure him into the mysterious world of men, of manliness. He looked bright, cheerful, eager to please. Who shall I hit? he seemed to be saying. Yet he did not like it when his father arranged a friendly match with another boy who hit him in the face. That didn't seem right. And it hurt. Nobody told him about that part, about how it would hurt if he got hit. And the other boy was bigger. Much bigger. Couldn't his father see that? Practically a giant. Stan cried and would not continue. His father pleaded and cajoled and then threatened, informed him that he would never be a man, never ever, not a real man, unless he continued the fight. Stan felt betrayed. By the time he was through, his face was a mess. How could his father have done that to him? And then seem so satisfied that Stan had blood all over his face? It was one thing to put on the boxing gloves and have his picture taken, quite another to get smashed in the face.

His hemorrhoids itched something terrible, but he dared not scratch them; it only made it worse.

"…Hello, Stanley…"

He turned toward the door, though he didn't think it was time for dinner yet. Besides, the guard never spoke to him anyway.

"…It's me…"

Stan peered into the darkness. He couldn't tell where the voice was coming from.

"…Who's me?" he said.

"God…"

Stan backed up against the wall; it was solid, reassuring. He held his breath and strained to hear—just prison sounds, muffled as always. Yet he sensed something; there was an unmistakable presence in the cell.

"…Who?" Buying time.

"God. You remember…"

The voice was plain, ordinary he remembered thinking later. Common. It might have been anybody's voice. Or nobody's.

"Nobody's in here," said Stan.

"...I'm here..."

"Can't be," said Stan. The hair on the back of his head felt as if it was magnetized. He was afraid to move. "...I can't see you."

"You're not looking in the right place."

He was startled when the partition in the door opened and the food tray was shoved onto the inside ledge. The guard tapped on the cell door with his club.

"Who you talkin' to in there?" he said. "Case you ain't noticed, you're in there by yourself."

The guard chuckled. The partition closed. Stan slammed the door with the palm of his hand as hard as he could.

"You're not supposed to talk to me!" he yelled. "Asshole!"

"So tell the Warden, Ding Dong."

Stan's heart thumped noisily in his chest. He strained to pull from the darkness some other sound—motion, breathing, anything. He did not move for a long time.

Finally, he whispered:

"...Hello?..."

But there was no reply. Of course not. He shook his head. The cell was completely dark.

"Shit," he said quietly.

He groped for the tray. It felt like the same evening meal—stale bread, mush, a cup of water. He sipped the water and munched on the bread; it tasted like cardboard. His teeth ached; he was sure his gums were bleeding. He could hear himself chewing inside his head.

When he finished he sat on the floor and leaned back against the wall. It was already cold; he began to shiver...Could the voice have been real? He didn't know; didn't have any way to find out. But the longer he thought about it, the more convinced he became that it couldn't have happened. It was too bizarre...

> *...Rejoice! Rejoice! I bring you*
> *tidings of great joy...*

He put his fingers to his lips and discovered that they were moving. Had he been doing it all along? Talking to himself and thinking it was someone else?...He felt hollow, empty. And what difference did it make? What difference did anything make? Another night stretched out in front of him like a long dark penance...*Mea culpa. Mea culpa. Mea maxima fucking culpa* ...The same old refrain...*My fucking fault*...He had begun to look forward to meal time, not for the food, which remained uniformly awful, but for the presence, however briefly, of another human being. Even a guard. Alone, his mind suggested only hopelessness.

He thought about freedom, tried to picture it, what it would be like to be free, to come and go as he wished. He could not remember what trees looked like. When he tried to picture them, his mind showed him cartoon trees, badly drawn. Black. Grey. Not one of them green.

His hemorrhoids itched so badly that he finally had to scratch them. He knew he shouldn't, knew what would happen if he did, but he scratched them anyway. He couldn't help it.

> ...*For I know that the sufferings of today*, said Preacher, *are not worthy to be compared with the glory which shall be revealed*...

# CHAPTER 34

Time.

Few envisioned the turmoil that lay ahead. Only Voodoo, with his hand on the pulse of the prison, had any inkling.

That winter, Quinlan began reading a series of medical studies that Dr. Dorfield had given him concerning the use of anti-androgens to reduce the sex drive in males. Preliminary studies indicated that blocking androgen receptors through the use of cyproterone acetate significantly reduced the male libido. Quinlan wrote it all down in his notebook, along with a note to remind himself to ask Dorfield where he could get some. He also made a note to check with Pollard in the Mess Hall to see if it was possible to get the necessary 100 milligram per convict daily dosage into the mashed potatoes or the jute balls or the oatmeal. (According to the article, it came in some kind of powder form.) The contraindications, the possible side effects of fatigue, depression, apathy and constipation seemed to Quinlan to be nearly as beneficial as what it was primarily designed to do. Either way it was a plus. Make them more tractable, he thought. More teachable (after all, weren't they supposed to be teaching inmates new ways of living?). Help keep their peckers in their pants. At least it was a start.

Quinlan cancelled the traditional Christmas Show with outside entertainers, citing the need for discipline and the prohibitive cost of the extra custodial personnel to provide coverage for the event. (This isn't a goddam country club, he said to Hebner.) There were the usual number of complaints and death threats scribbled on pieces of paper and left on the bulletin boards for guards to find:

*I am gona kil fuckin wardin Kwilin…*

Quinlan responded by closing the Yard fifteen minutes earlier, so no one would have a chance to be out, even briefly, after the evening meal. He knew how to deal with malcontents…I'm in charge here, he said to his empty office. And don't forget it.

The winter was dry, promises of rain unfulfilled as one year ended and another began. Preacher continued to hold forth with exhortations and warnings under skies as gray and somber as the day he was born.

> *…I heard a great voice out of the temple saying to the seven angels…Go forth and pour out the vials of the wrath of God upon the earth…*

Freddy Schaeffer, alias Freddy the Face, was killed at the dawn of the New Year, a harbinger of evils to come, his body, sans genitals, found near the Hobby Shop by Officer Cole shortly after the nine o'clock count failed to clear.

"My honey's dead," said Nick the Knife when he found out, scratching his crotch as if to reassure himself.

Preacher closed the Bible and held it to his chest.

> *…Thou shalt lie down with mankind as with womankind,*
> said Preacher, *when no womankind is available…*

"Neither shall thou make enemies among those on the Yard, Freddy," he said under his breath. "Nor fuck with those in power … But it's a better place you go to, homeboy. Believe me. Though there are many who will miss your sweet lips through the cold, gray steel. Rest in peace."

Leonard cranked up the rumor mill and filled the Yard with fabricated details of Freddy's murder. The grapevine buzzed with reports of a ritual satanic slaying, cannibalism, race reprisals, mutilation, his heart as well as other significant parts removed and eaten. The evening meal of franks and beans encouraged further discussion.

"Here be Freddy's dick," said Dice Jablonski, holding up a cold frankfurter, displaying his humorous side for the flunkies who gathered near the High Power table every night hoping for a few crumbs of wisdom or favor to fall their way.

Speculation about who was responsible helped fuel the mill— even Moose got a mention.

"No fuckin' way," he said indignantly. "What do I look like, man?"

"A three hundred pound dope fiend," said Leonard.

"Right," said Moose.

"Perhaps you were swept up in the passion of the moment," Greek suggested.

"Gimme a break."

"You were seen entering the Laundry following Freddy last week," said Greek. "Doesn't look good, Big Guy."

"He wasn't killed in the Laundry, asshole."

"We're establishing motive for the jury. We already know you killed him. And don't talk unless we ask a question. Right, jurors?"

"Right," said Paulson.

"Right," said Leonard.

"Right," said the Count.

"Jesus," said Moose.

"Now, to continue," said Greek, hands behind his back, pacing back and forth in the small office. "You were obviously in love with The Face. You confronted him about giving head to Voodoo... Voodoo Jefferson of all people. Your arch enemy. You couldn't deal with the infidelity. It was too much. You waited for him outside the Hobby Shop and zap! you got him."

"I think you have serious mental problems," said Moose, tapping his temple. "Something's bad wrong up here."

"You cut his heart out and ate it. Then you cut off his..."

Moose got off his stool and started across the room.

"Just kiddin', Big Guy," said Greek. "Just kiddin'."

The Saturday afternoons that Quinlan spent at the prison on the pretext of catching up on his paperwork were actually spent in the empty office on the third floor of the Control Building listening to Catholic confessions via the bug that Little Joe had installed in the confessional. The small device picked up both voices with amazing clarity; only occasionally were the voices too faint to hear.

Quinlan found the idea of confession repugnant; he only listened because it sometimes proved a valuable source of information. (More than once he found himself wishing that Voodoo was a Catholic; perhaps then he'd be able to get some decent information on what the Muslims and Black Panthers were up to. If he waited for Powell to establish a network, he'd be retired before anything useful came through.) The only way to identify the voices was to write down the exact time of each confession, and have Little Joe, ostensibly praying at the rear of the chapel, record the name and the time each man entered the confessional. It made Quinlan uneasy to be collaborating with someone like Little Joe. He was offended by the big moon face and the ugly little dwarf body, the odor of sweat and menthol that seemed a permanent part of him, the air of familiarity he cultivated, as if they were equals, co-conspirators in some grand scheme...Shall we synchronize our watches, Mr. Quinlan...Jesus. Obviously he'd been watching too many old war movies.

Quinlan knew the confessional form by heart...

>...*Bless me, Father for I have sinned,*
>*blah, blah, blah, blah...*

Sins. Quinlan called them by their proper name—crimes. Theological gibberish about sin and redemption aside, he knew what they were.

He learned that Dennis Jakelli (Big Deuce) had indeed raped his stepmother as initially charged, then forced her into other heinous acts. A plea bargain by a slick lawyer brought him to Fremont on a lesser charge where Father Sweeny extended his slurred blessing and the forgiveness of the Church of Rome. God, the arrogance. Nice and neat. Absolution for that bastard while Mrs. Jakelli, abused and betrayed by the stepson she raised as her own, was left to grieve by herself. What was the goddam Pope and the Catholic Church doing for her while Jakelli was solidifying his claim on Eternal Life by doing a penance of ten Our Fathers and ten Hail Marys?

He discovered that Bonaru Billy Tesik was masturbating four or five times a day. A day. Quinlan wondered where he got the energy. (He made another note to talk to Dr. Dorfield.) Honor Block inmates working at the Dairy were getting drunk at least once a week. Quinlan had suspected as much; what he really wanted to know was where they were making the brew. But of course Sweeny never asked. Whose side was he on?

Several of the homosexuals made weekly confessions, always sorry, always repentant, always back the next week with a new supply of similar sins (wasn't it the idea that they were supposed to stop doing those things after they confessed them?). Freddy the Face had been a frequent visitor to the confessional, detailing his list of blow jobs and other disgusting activities, his weak lisp as recognizable as Father Sweeny's alcoholic mumble. Quinlan drew a line through the name. At least that's over, he said to himself. Sweeny's counsel was a mix of pop psychology and old time religion. Through it all, Jesus continued to love them. It was the one constant, though it didn't seem to deter any of them from future sins. Or crimes.

The Fremont basketball team, bolstered the year before by the additional of "High Yellow" Jackson, Junior College Player of the Year, and "Big Hands" Murrell, all-city center from Crenshaw High, continued to burn up the Industrial League. Visiting teams had to contend with convict refs (often with a wagering interest on the outcome), time-keepers with variable speed timepieces, and the slippery concrete floor (purposely waxed in certain areas) in the old quonset hut gymnasium. General Dynamics, I-5 Trucking and several other industrial firms with some good ex-college players made the trip at the start of each season with high expectations. At least for the first trip; after that they understood what they were up against. The score was apt to change without warning (and without a basket being scored by either side), several minutes might be added or subtracted from the clock, depending on the game situation. Visiting teams soon learned that if the home team scored the go-ahead basket late in the fourth quarter, the buzzer would most likely go off and the game would be over, regardless of how much time was left on the clock. Correctional Officer (and coach) Joe Randolph (Fat Black to most everyone on the Yard) waved off the protests with his big smile, waddling out on the court to assure the visitors that the time keeping was proper and that any discrepancies were most surely in the minds of the visitors. When all else failed, he went into his Ain't nothin' but a bunch of poor convicts routine, suggesting that anyone who would insist on victory at any cost over a group of misunderstood young Negro men was surely lacking in some basic human quality. Like compassion. There was perhaps (he hated to mention it) even some racism at work. Hard to imagine, but still possible. Haven't they suffered enough? he seemed to be saying, arms open, palms up, head cocked to one side. Haven't they suffered enough? More than anything, Fat loved to win. How he accomplished that wasn't particularly important, a concept shared by his players.

Ice Burgess looked up at the threatening sky, lit another home-rolled Bugler and said to no one in particular:

"No rain, man. I hate the rain. Sleepin' in it. Remember? Cold. Wet. Jesus...Ice don't like the rain, man."

Time.

Few envisioned the turmoil that lay ahead. Only Voodoo, a true Child of the System, had some idea. Its fate was linked to his own. The signs were there for those who could read them. It was only a matter of...

T-i-m-e...

# CHAPTER 35

A Pacific storm moved toward the California coast early in February. Heavy rains were predicted.

Leonard talked to Reiner.

"This is it," he said. "Storm's due Saturday."

Reiner looked bored.

"U-huh," he said.

"Bring her in on the third watch. It'll be almost dark by then. Bundle her up in foul weather gear. Hat, coat, everything. Nobody'll notice. There's a movie that night. Take her to the north side of the hospital. The door'll be open. Go to room twelve and let her in. Be sure she locks herself in. When she hears four taps…taptap… taptap…like that, she can open the door. Not before. Got it so far?"

"Yeah, yeah."

"What's the number of the hospital room?" said Leonard.

"Eh…twelve?"

"Don't fuck this up, Reiner. I wouldn't want to have this deal go sour."

"Nothin' goes wrong on my watch," he said, with a lightness he didn't feel.

"Be sure it doesn't. Somebody'll show up at six twenty. That's movie release. Movie starts at six thirty and lasts an hour and fifty-seven minutes, so be back at the hospital no later than eight twenty-five. People will be out on the Yard for a few minutes, so that'll help your cover. Take her back and send her on her way. Easy, eh?"

"Sure, you think it's easy 'cuz you don't be doin' nothin'," said Reiner. "I gotta do the stuff. Put my career on the line. Looks a little harder from where I am…Who's the guy gonna be with her?"

"You don't need to know that."

"But it's not you, right?

"I already told you that," said Leonard. "It's not me…Why?"

"Nothin', man. Just checkin'…When do I get paid?"

"If everything goes okay, I'll give you a number to call. Couple of days after that, you'll be two hundred dollars richer."

"Three hundred, man. Three hundred."

"Right, three hundred. Slipped my mind."

"I bet…No wonder you in jail, man."


The day Leonard told Moose to get ready to collect his prize, he headed for the Mess Hall to see Spike Freeman about getting some pills.

"What'a you got for a party?" said Moose.

"We got streamers and big red balloons," said Spike. "Chocolate cake. Whad'ja have in mind?" He had a mouthful of big jagged teeth.

"You got some whites? Some dexies?"

"Shipment ain't come in yet."

"What'a you got?"

Spike closed his eyes for a moment.

"Only thing I got is some Stelli's, some Dilaudid, a few Daprisals. Like I say, the shipment won't be in for a few days."

"What's Daprisals?" said Moose.

"Pain pills…For minstrel cramps."

"For what?"

"For chicks when they have their periods. You know."

"I ain't gonna have no fuckin' period," said Moose.

"Never can tell," said Spike. "Least you'll be prepared."

"They uppers or downers?"

"Mostly downers. Pain pills. A few days, we'll have some whites."

"Can't wait."

"What kinda party you got goin'?" said Spike.

"…What if I told you I was gonna get laid?"

"You and your hand got a date?"

"What if I told you it was a real broad?"

"I'd say you been out in the sun too long. You got heat prostation maybe. Since there ain't much sun I figure you got a lockup disease. How long you been in?"

"Three plus."

"That's about when it starts."

"When what starts?"

"The dellucinations…Like thinkin' there's real broads here. Thinkin' you're gonna get out next time you go to the Parole Board. Stuff like that. Dellucinations."

"Shit," said Moose. "S'all you know. How much you want for the pills?"

"Five packs for ten of 'em."

"Five packs? For ten fuckin' pills?"

"You think I get 'em at the canteen?"

"I know, man. But five packs…man."

"Listen, Romeo, anybody who can get a real broad into the penitentiary shouldn't have no trouble comin' up with five packs of smokes."

"Fuck," said Moose, when he returned to the Watch Office to wait for the count to clear. "A Jayne Mansfield flick and I gotta miss it."

"I'll take your place," said the Count. "Wouldn't want you to miss a good flick."

"No," said Moose, his face flushed, pleasantly buzzed from the pills. "A deal's a deal. I gave my word…Anyway, man, you should be here studyin' that Miranda thing you got goin'. I know nobody ever read me my rights. They just came in, slapped the cuffs on and took me away. I have most likely been…wrongfully detained all this time."

"Most likely."

"Sure hope she shows up," said Leonard.

"What'a you mean, hope she show up. This a done deal or what?"

"Well, the retirement home doesn't like to let the older residents…"

"Retirement home…"

"I mean she has to have her heart medication, hemorrhoid treatments…you know."

254

"Man," said Moose, shaking his head.

"Anybody'd fuck a dead chick can't be too worried about a few hemorrhoids," said Greek.

"I never said I fucked a dead chick," said Moose. "Will you guys get it straight? I just wondered what would happen if…"

"Least she'll be warm," said Greek. "Won't she, Leonard? The one you got comin' in? You think she'll still be warm?"

"Warm," Leonard said thoughtfully. "Warm's a very subjective thing, Greek. What's warm to you might be cold to somebody else."

"Fuck you guys," said Moose. "Hey, Paulson…I'll be sure and get plenty of pussy on my dick so you'll have somethin' to lick when I get back."

Paulson didn't even look up.

"How you gonna get plenty on somethin' that small?" he said.

Greek laughed out loud.

*Movie release. Movie release. The*
*movie tonight is* The Wayward Bus,
*starring Jayne Mansfield…*

Moose headed for the hospital without another word.

…taptap…taptap…

The door swung open. Moose quickly stepped inside and closed it. At first he didn't see her; she was leaning against the wall behind the door. When he did turn toward her he was startled by the sight of a khaki uniform. She smiled, took off her floppy foul weather hat and shook her head.

He squinted at her.

"I'm Nay-o-mi," she said, her voice like smoke.

"…Jesus," he said. "You're…you're…a…"

"A colored person," she said.

"Man…"

"You di'n 'spect no colored person?" she said, smiling broadly. Only a slight twitch at the eyes betrayed any emotion.

"No."

"Oh…"

He shoved his hands in his pockets and stared at the light fixture on the ceiling.

"Man," he said.

She continued to smile. Her lips were caked with magenta lipstick, her hair wiry, the color somewhere between blond and orange. She seemed slim and shapeless in the baggy khaki uniform. He coughed and looked at his shoes.

"Man…What'a you know."

"Oh, not much," she said brightly.

But it wasn't long before his initial reaction began to fade. For some reason he did not equate her color with his hatred of Negroes. (Only men were niggers—that seemed obvious enough.) But he had no experience with black women. And very little experience with white women either. Most of his sexual encounters had taken place in a state of chemical dementia; he had difficulty recalling any of them with any clarity. His posturing on the Yard and around the office belied the fact that he was ashamed of his ponderous body and could never remember consummating a union without the aid of drugs or alcohol.

Now, confronted by a woman for the first time in more than three years, he wished for a few more pills, a drink perhaps, something to take the edge off. Anything.

"Well, here we are," he said.

"You wanna go to bed? Do some jelly roll?"

"Sure," he said, moving toward the bed on legs that felt like wooden stumps. "Jelly roll. That's for me."

He pulled back the covers and sat on the edge of the bed. She stood in front of him and started to unbutton his shirt.

"Uh…You know, we don't really have to do this," he said. "This is sort of a joke we played. You know. On this guy that…"

"I likes to do it," she said, rubbing the inside of his thigh. "Don't you?"

"You kiddin'? Jelly roll? I fuckin' love it."

She continued to unbutton his shirt. He reached for her shirt front and patted tentatively for the presence of breasts. She pushed toward his hand. He felt a small squishy breast in his palm.

She pulled his shirt off.

"Mmmmm…" she said.

She flicked his belt loose with one deft motion, then quickly unbuttoned his pants.

"Stan' up," she said cheerfully.

He struggled to his feet. She jerked at his pants; they collapsed to his ankles. He sat down, naked to his shoes, glistening in the light like a great pale whale. His thick white thighs hid his genitals. She popped off his shoes and peeled off his socks. He gave his legs a weak wiggle and she pulled off his pants.

"Mmmmm," she said. "You got some fine big legs."

He folded his hands in his lap as she quickly shed her clothing.

Her upper body was slim, her thighs and hips bulky. Her breasts sagged like loose shirt-pocket flaps, nipples pointed down, almost a feminine afterthought. She turned around slowly.

He licked his lips and tried to swallow; the pills made his mouth dry. She pushed him back on the bed and rubbed his stomach, then reached between his legs and gently fondled his limp remains. The next thing he felt was her lips down there. He squeezed his eyes shut.

"Ohhh…" he said.

In a few minutes he was fully aroused. She moved up to straddle his thighs, and began to tap a rhythm on his ample stomach with her soft pink palms.

"Oh, rock me, mama, rock me one mo' time…"

She moistened her index finger with saliva, slowly wiped it between her legs, then moved forward and lowered herself onto him.

"Ohh, daddy, you too big," she lied. "You almos' hurt mama," though she quickly slid down the short shaft as if it were greased.

"Ohhh," said Moose.

"Talk to yo' mama…"

She began to rotate her hips.

"Rock me, mama," she crooned, "Till you can't rock no mo'… Oh, rock me, daddy, till you can't rock no mo'…I got fo' hungry chillun and a no good lazy man…"

She swayed from side to side, eyes closed, her shirt-pocket breasts half a beat behind the measured ticking of her torso. Moose felt a tingling begin to creep across his abdomen, nerve endings reaching for bliss.

"Ohhh...slow down."

She smiled.

"Oh...rock...me...da-ddy...till..."

She stopped for a moment and contracted her vaginal muscles.

"Feel that?" she said.

"Yeah...Yeah...How'd you do that?"

"Mama knows," she said. "Mama knows how to do things with her money maker."

He felt the contractions speed up and slow down.

"...Wow."

"You wanna be on top?" she said.

"Yeah...Great. I'll be on top," he said, as if the idea were new and radical.

They shifted in small increments until she was under him. The top of her head barely came up to his chin.

"Don' squash mama," she admonished.

He looked like a bleached leviathan, beached in the throes of mating with his dark brown partner. The colorless cheeks of his considerable posterior quivered with preorgasmic tension.

"Ohhhh..." he said.

"Oh, rock me, daddy," she sang, her voice a plaintive blur, her lips only inches from his chest, "...till you can't rock no mo'."

She wrapped her legs around his thick hips and began to beat a tattoo on his buttocks with dry, scaly heels.

"Oh...rock yo mama...till...you..." Faster and faster but ever so brief.

"Ohhh..." said Moose, his voice a rising crescendo of excitement. "I'm comin'," he wailed. "I'm comin'...Look out."

"Come on," she said. "Come ahead on."

The callused heels of her feet thumped on his plump cheeks.

"I'm...Ahhhhh..."

"Mama be ready."

The motion slowed and then stopped. Less than three minutes from start to finish.

"...Ahh..." He slipped down on his elbows.

"Don' squash mama," she scolded.

He rested for a moment to catch his breath, then abruptly withdrew and sat on the edge of the bed.

"You okay, daddy?" she said, still flat on her back, knees up, both hands between her legs.

"Oh...yeah."

"Was mama good?"

"Great," he said flatly.

She frowned.

"You wanna do some mo'?"

"Oh...not now," he said.

He pulled his pants on, walked across the room to the wash basin, bent down and looked at himself in the small mirror. He could see her reflection over his shoulder. The hands between her legs were making small stroking motions. She made soft, warbling sounds as the motions quickened, then slowly subsided. Her laughter was rich, musical. She rolled over on her side, propped her head on the palm of her hand and smiled as he returned to bed.

"You sho know how to do it, daddy," she said.

"...Yeah?"

"U-huh. You can flat do some jelly roll. And that big thing you got could hurt some po' girl."

"Really?"

"Mama don' tell no lies."

He looked at the clock on the wall—ten minutes to seven. He was exhausted. He yawned.

"Ti'ed?" she said.

He nodded.

She slid over to the far side of the bed and patted the blanket next to her. He lay down and drew his knees up toward his chest. In a few minutes he was asleep. He looked like a giant fetus. She raised herself on one arm, peered over his shoulder, then got out of bed, both hands cupped between her legs, and tiptoed awkwardly toward the bathroom.

"Hush," she said as the toilet gurgled noisily.

She returned and covered him with his shirt, singing softly.

"…I'm a one-hour woman, got me a five-minute man…Oh, I'm a one-hour woman, got me a five-minute man…"

She slipped into her baggy khakis and rummaged through the small dresser. In the corner of the top drawer she found a Bible and a frayed deck of playing cards. She removed them both, sat on the floor and opened the Bible. On the inside cover was a penciled message:

## JESUS SUCKS

She shook her head disapprovingly and thumbed at random through the Book of Matthew. She placed a long red fingernail on a page and started to read, slowly mouthing the words:

"…Love your en-e-mies…bless them that curses you…do good to them that hates you…"

Moose slept fitfully, moaning and grinding his teeth. Naomi read for awhile, then played solitaire, finally leaned back against the wall and drifted into a light sleep.

They were both awakened by the loudspeakers on the Yard.

> *Movie release. Return to your housing units immediately.*
> *Count will commence in ten minutes…*

Moose sat up and tried to get his bearings.

"Count!" he said. "Count! Jesus."

He put his shirt on as Naomi scrambled to her feet.

"What'sat?" she said.

"Get your stuff on. We gotta get outta here."

He stood up, stuffed his shirttail in, and got into his shoes without bothering with the socks. She donned her raincoat and put on her hat. He listened at the door for a moment, then opened it and peered up and down the hallway.

"Come on," he said, reaching back for her hand.

She took it and followed, her free hand clutching the raincoat to her throat. They hurried down the hallway toward the back door. She squeezed his hand and released it before they went out on the Yard.

"Bye, daddy."

He didn't answer.

Jules Reiner stood in the light rain just out of sight, watching as they emerged from the hospital. He shook his head.

"Moose Rankin," he said under his breath. "…If that don't beat all."

Moose hurried off, moving quickly down the walkway in front of the hospital, joining the stream of convicts returning from the movie.

*Count in five minutes…return to your housing units immediately…*

"What a movie," said Duke.

"What tits," said Red. "That chick has the greatest tits in the world."

"The greatest," said Tony.

"Humungous," said Duke.

"Man," said Red.

He spotted Moose.

"What'a ya think, big man? Was them tits or was them tits."

"Tits," said Moose. "Not bad pussy either."

"Dream on," said Duke.

"Helluva flick," said Red.

"Yeah," said Moose, smiling. "One helluva flick."

# CHAPTER 36

Moose swaggered into the Watch Office, took a seat on his stool and leaned against the wall. He glanced at Leonard and wondered if he knew about the woman, about her being black. But Leonard's face, as usual, gave no hint; it always had the same hard look, the same stoic expression behind glasses that seemed to view the world through prisms of ice. You could never tell...But he decided that, no, Leonard probably didn't know. And if Leonard didn't know, the only one who did know was the contact in Custody who smuggled her in, someone obviously on Leonard's payroll, someone who (if he wanted to stay healthy) would be smart enough to keep his mouth shut.

"Well?" said the Count.

"Well what?" said Moose.

"The chick. The babe. Come on, man..."

"Was it a real one?" said Greek.

"Greek," said Leonard. "How could you doubt?"

"She had tits and a pussy and a real high voice," said Moose. "I'm guessin' she was real."

"You mean," said Greek, "that Leonard actually got a real live woman into this place?"

Leonard's shrug said it was no big deal.

"You could use Moose as a reference when you get out," said Greek. "You gotta figure a guy who could get a woman in and out of the penitentiary without gettin' caught ought to be a real business asset."

Moose started to unzip his pants.

"Hey, Paulson," he said. "Wanna smell it?...Maybe lick it?"

Paulson turned away.

"Some people are very sick," he said. "Very sick."

262

"What was she like?" said the Count.

"Oh, about so tall. Big tits." He cupped his hands a foot in front of his chest. "I mean big tits, man. Monster tits. Blond hair. Blue eyes...Fuckin' beautiful."

"How many times you...do it?" said Paulson.

"Do what?" said Moose.

"How many times you...give it to her?"

"You mean how many times I fucked her?"

"...Yeah."

Moose counted on his fingers.

"Five," he said.

Greek groaned.

"Moose," he said. "Come on, man."

"You gotta be kiddin'," said the Count.

"I'm fuckin' tellin' you," said Moose.

"Five?" said Paulson.

"I bet you never got laid five times in your whole life," said Moose.

"Well, you lose," said Paulson, although he knew the number might not be much higher.

"You musta used somebody else's dick," said Greek.

"Wait a minute," said Moose, counting on his fingers again. "I lied. It was only four...four and a blow job."

"How long were you with her?"

"Couple of hours maybe."

"Couple of hours and you fucked her five times?"

"Four and a blow job."

"The Animal," said the Count. "They oughta put you in a cage."

"Whadaya think this is?" said Greek.

"Or the circus," said Leonard.

"There is no way I'm gonna believe this story," said Greek. "No way."

"I wouldn't expect an...older person to understand," said Moose. "First of all, Greek, you have to be able to get a hardon. That's the way you get started...Then..."

"Remember that guy in East Block, Leonard?" said Greek. "Nevins? Needledick the Bug Fucker? That's the kind of shit he'd come up with."

"On my mother's grave," said Moose.

"I thought your mother gave you up for adoption when you were a baby," said the Count.

"Don't mean I didn't love her," said Moose.

"Lucky you're not doin' time for lyin'," said Greek.

"…She had muscles," said Moose.

"In her head?" said Greek

"Your mother?" said the Count.

"No man, the chick," said Moose. "In her pussy. She could squeeze your rod with 'em. She just about fucked my brains out."

"Might not a been all that hard," said Greek.

"She said my dick was almost too big."

"For what?" said Paulson.

"Where were you tryin' to put it?" said the Count. "In her ear?"

"Everything looks big to midgets," said Greek.

"She wasn't no fuckin' midget," said Moose. "I'm not into midgets."

"Lucky for them."

Moose rolled up a newspaper and slapped it on the desk.

"Well," he said, "I'm ready for next year. Same prize, Leonard?"

Leonard pushed his glasses up on the bridge of his nose and looked around the room.

"Maybe," he said. "Maybe somethin' better."

"Better?" said Moose. "Shit…Ain't nothin' better."

# CHAPTER 37

Stan was released from the Adjustment Center after 30 days. The sunlight hurt his eyes as he walked across the Yard toward South Block. Several convicts that he knew caught his eye and gave him the high sign. Preacher looked his way as he passed.

> *Rejoice in hope,* he said. *Be patient in tribulation, constant in prayer…*

Stan paused for a moment to listen…

> *…And the third angel poured out his vial upon the rivers and fountains of waters and they became blood…Beware the fools in South Block, homeboy. …Not all love the Baby Jesus…*

He nodded and walked away. The Iceman joined him before he got to South Block. Stan looked at the stubbled face, the eyes that reflected some inner dementia, the mouth down at one corner clinging to a moist home-rolled cigarette. He was about Stan's height, though he appeared smaller in a denim jacket several sizes too large. He might have been any age; most guesses ran to the late forties. Stan shivered, though it was not cold.

"You been in the Hole, eh?" said Ice.

"Yeah."

Ice peeled the cigarette off his lower lip, pinched the head off and stuck the butt in the pocket of his jacket. Each quadrant of his face seemed to harbor a different emotion. He had the quick, cold eyes of a snake; they darted around the Yard, taking in everything.

He shuffled along breathing heavily, the cuffs of his pants dragging on the ground.

"Be careful," he said. "Hebner needs names. He don't get names, he'll set you up, make you sing the blues…"

Stan scanned the Yard as if it would provide an answer …some place to run, some place to hide. But he knew better by now; of course there was no place to run, no place to hide. This was the penitentiary with Rules all its own. And the Yard was where it all came down—one on one or five on one, it all happened on the Yard. Small and large moments of truth. Gut checks. Trials. To fail one was to be assigned to a lower level on the Food Chain; to fail several was to be relegated to the communal trough where anyone could come and feed…Meat. Parade pussy.

"Watch your back," said Ice. Without another word, he veered off and disappeared into a crowd of convicts.

Stan didn't have long to wait for things to happen; he never even got to his cell. Wetzle gave him a funny look when he passed the guard shack, but he didn't think much about it till later, when it was over. Then it all began to make sense. But he never doubted that it was a setup; the Iceman had it right. Arky and Hunter didn't just happen to be walking along the tier when he got there. The door to the cell didn't just happen to be open.

Arky, the burly Arkansas trucker doing time for manslaughter, staggered him with a blow behind the ear as he walked past. Then they shoved him into the empty cell and began in earnest. Stan got in a punch or two, but nothing effective. The Goon Squad arrived shortly after Arky and Hunter left. Seconds after. Almost like they were waiting for them to leave so they could move in.

Cheswick's face was a bubble of hostility.

"You again," he growled.

Stan touched his lower front teeth; several were loose. Blood flowed from his nose and a badly cut lip. His ears rang from the beating.

"Fightin' again," said Cheswick, shaking his head. "Some people never learn. The Lieutenant will not be pleased."

Stan wiped his face on his shirt sleeve. When he took a deep breath, his side hurt. He wondered if his ribs were broken.

"...Shit," he wheezed.

"Coulda been worse," said Cheswick. "They coulda pushed you off the tier, made a flyer outta you like your buddy, Hawk. Fly away, good buddy...Niggers would'a done that. Least it was white guys, Smith. Consider yourself lucky."

As Cheswick had suggested, Hebner was not pleased, though the frown and the harsh demeanor may have been manufactured.

The Lieutenant said it was sad, very sad, that Stan couldn't seem to be able to cope with ordinary...situations without resorting to violence. It didn't bode well for the future, he said. Not at all. Such behavior, he assured Stan, could only lead to further disciplinary action, prolonged time behind bars. A matter of policy. Stan was well on his way to becoming a Hopeless Case, someone who would have to be locked up in tight security indefinitely. Well on his way. But it was not too late. Not quite. Redemption might still be obtained by sharing with Custody the names of those involved in the killing of inmate Hawkins. That was the good news—there was still time.

Hebner's face, though stern, was lit with an air of expectation.

Stan winced when he tried to take a deep breath. He touched his ribs.

"I'd like to go to the hospital," he said.

"That might be arranged," said Hebner.

He offered Stan a cigarette. Stan shook his head.

"Hurt your ribs?" said Hebner, nibbling a cigarette out of the pack.

"...Yeah."

"Broke?"

Stan shrugged.

"Too bad," said Hebner. "A little cooperation might get you a trip to the hospital. Clean sheets. Mainline food. Better than mainline food."

Stan rubbed his side but didn't speak.

"On the other hand," said Hebner, "a lack of cooperation might get you some more time in the Adjustment Center. We might try sixty days this time. See how the adjustment goes. See if the spirit of cooperation returns."

Stan sucked on his front teeth; all he could taste was blood. His whole body hurt. He wanted desperately to go to the hospital, eat some decent food, take a hot shower, lie down on clean sheets, maybe get his ribs taped. But a glance at Hebner convinced him it was impossible.

"...Well?" said Hebner.

"I think I'll have to pass, Lieutenant," he said.

"You'll have to pass," Hebner said slowly. The pencil in his hand snapped in two. "You'll-have-to-pass."

"You ain't shit," said Cheswick.

"A regrettable decision," said Hebner. "And the wrong one, Smith. I thought you were a little smarter than that...But we'll put it out on the Yard that you cooperated anyway. Gave us some names. Hang a snitch jacket on you. That way, some convict will stick a shiv in you and save us the time and trouble. Somebody like Fat Tony, or Big Deuce, or Hoss. When you least expect it—maybe in the chow line, just walkin' the Yard, anywhere. Somebody'll come by and bang, that'll be it. Snitches don't live long on the Yard; you prob'ly already know that. A box of smokes and you're history. Not a bad deal. I'd even be glad to buy. Convicts aren't entirely useless."

He tossed the broken pencil into the wastebasket.

"In the meantime, Sergeant, take inmate Smith back down to the Adjustment Center. We'll try the sixty-day treatment this time; see if that doesn't improve his memory. Take him by the strip cells on your way. Give him a look at what happens to uncooperative inmates. Especially Misner. Have him take a good look at Misner. It should be...enlightening."

Strip cell occupants were not allowed clothing; the cells themselves were without furnishings, always brightly lit. A small hole in the center of the floor sufficed for toilet facilities. Guards often let it go unflushed as a punishment. At night a waterproof mattress was provided. A small bulletproof window was mounted in the solid cell door so the inmate could be watched.

Cheswick stopped in front of one of the cells and pushed Stan toward the window. He said later that Misner usually threw shit at anyone who stopped to look—today he just didn't have any handy. John Misner hunkered down in the corner of his cell and glared at the window; it's what he did most of the day. Cheswick kept up a running commentary.

"Rubs shit all over himself," he said. "Stinks. God, he stinks. He's pretty clean now. They must have hosed him down after lunch."

Misner's hair and beard were unkempt, his body fishbelly white. A fierce glow burned in his eyes.

"I seen him lick his fingers with shit on 'em," said Cheswick, affirming a curiosity that few had been allowed to witness.

Stan didn't know if Misner could see him through the window, but their eyes seemed to meet and lock for a moment. Stan had to turn his head and look away.

"Ain't he somethin'?" said Cheswick. Like a tour guide explaining Points-of-Interest. "A class-A dirtball."

As if to satisfy their curiosity, Misner ran his hand between his legs and stuck his index finger in his mouth.

"See?" said Cheswick. "Wha'd I tell you?"

Stan closed his eyes.

"That's what happens," Cheswick said smugly. "You spend too much time in the Adjustment Center and the mind goes. You end up like Misner. I see it all the time."

He pulled Stan away and prodded him with his club.

"Don't forget," he said. "Next time the Lieutenant asks a question, think of old Misner back there. Might help your memory some."

It was still daylight when Stan got back to his cell in the Adjustment Center. He sat and stared at the rectangle of light as it moved slowly across the floor, his vision blurred by the tears that made the light sparkle and shine.

When it was dark, he looked into the eyes of John Misner and began to understand something about his own madness and what had happened in that old gray house on DeSoto Street where he grew up.

# CHAPTER 38

Greek pecked away at the typewriter, finishing up another memo from Captain Greer, his third of the day. "I need the typewriter when you're through, Greek," said the Count. "I'm doin' a writ. Miranda. Second Court of Appeals."

"Almost done," said Greek. "Listen to this…

> *Pursuant to Department of Corrections Directive 1203, all night workers will commence group counseling sessions as specified in my memo of last week. All those not working nights will continue their regular group counseling sessions and disregard this memo. And my memo of the 12th."*

"What's it mean?" said Paulson.

"Means we're gonna have to go to group counseling."

"What's group counseling?"

"Therapy," said Greek.

"I was in therapy one time in Vacaville," said Moose. "They ask you about your mother."

"My mother's dead," said Paulson.

"How you felt about her. Things like that. You ever fuck her?"

"…Who?" said Paulson.

"Your mother."

Paulson turned and walked to the other side of the room.

"Can't you do somethin', Leonard?" said Greek. "Get us out of it."

"It's only a couple of hours a week," said Leonard. "Might even do you some good."

"You could find out why you were ballin' your mother," said Moose.

"Why would anyone do that?" said Paulson.

"Do what?"

"You know…What you said."

"About your mother?"

Paulson nodded.

"How would I know. I look like some kind of dipshit counselor?"

*Count. Return to your housing*
*units immediately for count…*

"You ever fuck a sheep, Moose?" said the Count.

"…A sheep?"

"Yeah."

"Why would I want to fuck a sheep," said Moose.

"For practice…You're the one's out fuckin' dead broads, for chrissakes."

Moose shook his head.

"I did once," said the Count.

"You fucked a sheep? A real sheep?"

"How was it?" said Greek.

"Not all that bad."

"I wonder if sheep give blow jobs," said Moose.

"Give 'em enough money, they'll do anything," said the Count. "They're just like people."

"Wait till they find out about you in group," said Leonard. "You'll never get out."

"Actually, I like it in here."

"You like it so much, how come you started doin' all that legal stuff?" said Moose.

"I'm studyin' to be a lawyer."

"Jesus. Just what we need—one more lawyer."

"You should thank me for gettin' into the legal stuff," said the Count. "I'm tryin' to help you guys. Hey, convicts have rights, too."

"Like what?"

"Like the food. You like the food?"

271

"You kiddin'? This shit?"

"We might be able to get better food. The law says we don't have to suffer cruel and unusual punishment."

"That's a law?"

"Like shit on a shingle. And jute balls."

"I like jute balls," said Paulson.

"It's just that most normal people don't, Paulson," said Moose. "You and your buddy Stan the Man. But just so you know, most people understand that they look and taste like bad meatballs with rat turds in 'em ."

"How about the Adjustment Center?" said Greek. "And J Wing?"

"Cruel," said Leonard, "but not all that unusual."

"I still like jute balls," said Paulson.

"Okay, okay," said the Count. "We'll leave your name off the list when we file the lawsuit…Jesus…"

The Group Counseling sessions that the Watch Crew attended were held in North Block every Tuesday and Thursday from two to three in the afternoon. While attendance was mandatory, participation was not, though it was considered beneficial to have active participation in group counseling noted on your preparole board review. Those close to Board appearances tended to be more talkative.

The moderator was Donald Banner, Program B Director. His cheerful greetings were usually met with assorted grumbles.

"Well," he said brightly. "Here it is another fine day."

"Another beautiful fuckin' day in the fuckin' penitentiary," said Nick the Knife. "Makes me wanna come in my pants." Nick didn't care about anything; he figured he was never going to get out anyway.

The chairs were formed in a circle, blacks on one side, whites on the other, always a large gap in the middle where the moderator sat.

"Not to your liking, eh Nick?" said Banner.

"Oh, I just fuckin' love it here, Mr. Banner. You know that."

"You want to talk about it?" said Banner. "Share your feelings with the group?"

"Fuck, no."

Banner sat with his hands clasped behind his head, staring at the ceiling, waiting for someone to break the silence, to bring to the group a problem they could solve as a community. He believed in group counseling, in its therapeutic value. He had read all the studies.

But there were only random gripes, requests to bum a smoke, pass the ashtray...meaningless asides. Most folded their arms and joined Banner in staring at the ceiling.

"What's the movie this week?" said Gabby.

"...Destiny somethin'," said Duke.

"That was last week. Lousy fuckin' movie. About some guy from the slums makin' it in the big time. Total bullshit."

"You don't think someone from the slums could make it?" said Banner, sensing a topic for discussion. "Move up the ladder and make something of himself?"

"Not a chance," said Gabby.

"Why not?"

"Shit...Ain't nobody gonna give you a break, man. That shit only happens in the movies."

"Hey, Leonard," said Duke. "What's the movie for this week?"

"*Nancy Goes to Rio.*"

"God..."

"I know a guy who likes to fuck sheep," said Moose. "That against the law, Mr. Banner?"

Banner thoughtfully stroked his chin.

"Probably," he said, "but I can't remember the statute."

"Everything's against the law," said Nick.

"...How come we get such shitty movies?" said Duke.

"Budget limitations," said Banner. "Cost money to rent movies."

"Cruel and unusual punishment," said Moose.

"Been studying up on the law, Rankin?" said Banner.

"Keepin' my hand in," said Moose. "Convicts got rights, too."

"Indeed they do. Would you like to talk about it, see what the group has to say?"

"Eh...Not at the present time."

"You gotta be dreamin'," said Gabby. "Convicts ain't got no rights."

"We got a right to eat decent food," said Moose. "There's a law about it."

"You don't like the food?" said Banner.

"It sucks," said Gabby. He felt no need to make a favorable impression since his Parole Board appearance was still three years away.

The group lapsed into silence. Reno, still trying to master the crutches he was using, stared intently at the floor. Time inched forward. Gabby pretended to be sleeping. Nick cracked his knuckles; no one wanted to tell him to stop. Voodoo closed his eyes.

"How come no Christmas party this year?" said Duke.

"Budget," said Banner. "Takes extra Custody to put on those things. Costs money."

"What a prick that guy is."

"Are you men angry with Superintendent Quinlan for not allowing you to have a Christmas party?" said Banner.

Silence.

"...Anyone?"

Nobody.

"I'd like to remind you that everything that's said in this room is confidential."

Nothing.

"Anybody going out on parole soon?"

More silence.

"Perhaps some of you have had the experience of being paroled and then returning to prison."

Though nearly all were second or third termers, none volunteered.

"I wonder if them broads'll still be wearin' miniskirts when I get out," said Gabby.

"They'll be wearin' space suits by then," said Duke.

"You see," said Banner, still trying to steer the group toward a meaningful discussion, "everybody has problems. Everybody. Even out there. You remember how it was. The rent. The job. The wife and kids. Girlfriends. Times were tough. Still are." Banner stopped and rubbed the back of his neck. "You know, there's a very big problem out there. Very big..."

"They runnin' low on pussy?" said Duke.

"...The racial problem," he said, ignoring the chuckles that followed Duke's remark. "Ve-ry big problem. Perhaps the biggest. I hope and pray that someday negroes and whites will be able to live together in peace and harmony."

The entire group stiffened.

"I don't wanna live with no muffuckin' white dude noway," said Leroy, a rare display since few of the blacks ever said anything in group.

"Why is that?" said Banner, sensing that he might be on to something.

"Jes' don't," said Leroy.

"I think it would be nice if we could all live together in peace," said Banner, extending his arms in a sweeping embrace. "Like one big, happy family. The Family of Man."

"Why?" said Voodoo.

Banner looked startled; Voodoo had never spoken in group.

"Why?" he said. "I think God intended it that way."

"Which God is that?"

"Oh, I think there's only one God, Jefferson."

"That the one that taught the black man to turn the other cheek? The one that taught him that everything be okay in the sweet by-and-by? That one?"

"Well..."

"Just keep pickin' cotton, nigger. Things be okay in the sweet by-and-by when Jesus come to get you."

"I don't think..." Banner searched for the right words.

"He's comin' early, nigger. Gonna save your sweet black ass and take you up to that white heaven. Comin' early 'cuz you got no food in your belly and you been workin' sixteen hours a day while the white man been takin' your women and your sweat and livin' good. Nigger don't last long doin' that. Good thing they had plenty niggers. God made plenty black folks to work the fields so white folks could live good...That the God you talkin' about?"

"I don't think that's necessarily true," said Banner. "There were some unfortunate..."

"Oh, it's true," said Voodoo. "All of it. Slavery. Lynch mobs. Rape. Still goin' on. You read enough history to know that."

"That's right," said John Lee Hooks.

"You speakin' true, blood," said Billy 2X.

"But there's progress being made," said Banner. "Real progress. You can't expect to…"

"Progress," Voodoo said scornfully. "You call what's goin on progress? Didn't nobody tell Governor Wallace or Bull Connor about progress. Didn't tell 'em down in Greensboro where they turned the fire hoses and the dogs on the brothers and sisters in that lunch counter. Maybe only you white folks heard about it—about progress."

"Tell it, brother," said Leroy.

"And what makes you think," said Voodoo, "that black folks would want to live with white folks? Maybe we just want to…"

"Good," said Gabby. "'Cuz I don't want to live with no black motherfucker either."

There was a general shifting of position as the tension in the room increased. Reno took his hands out of his pockets, sat up and reached for his crutches. Moose rubbed his hands on his thighs.

Voodoo smiled.

"See, there's a man I can understand. I know where he stands. He hates me and I hate him. I hate the color of his skin. I hate him for all the things he's done to my people, for what he's still doin'. I don't want to live next door to him, go to his schools, marry his sister…" The smile never left his face.

"Ain't no white muffuckah gonna tell me what to do," said Billy 2X.

Moose couldn't stay out of it any longer.

"Billy 2X," he sneered. "Sounds like a fuckin' bingo number."

"Now, now," said Banner. "I don't think we have to resort to name calling. That's not what group is all about…I think we can discuss this as mature adults."

"He started it," said Gabby, pointing across the room.

"Fuck you, honky muffuckah," said Leroy.

"And fuck you, nigger."

They were both out of their chairs at the same time. Leroy's first punch, a roundhouse right that missed the mark, sent him sprawling on the floor. All the men were quickly on their feet; a few stood their ground, though most backed toward a wall. Voodoo stood up, folded his chair in front of him and calmly watched the action.

Little Joe slipped out the door and ran to alert Custody.

"Stop! Stop!" yelled Banner, standing and holding his hands over his head.

Leroy scooted away on his hands and knees. As Gabby advanced to finish him off, a chair came sailing out of the crowd and hit him across the bridge of the nose. He fell hard, blood flowing from the cut. Convicts from both sides of the room moved forward to escalate the hostilities.

Banner yelled as loud as he could:

"Help!...Guards!...Guards!"

The sound of a whistle that quickly grew louder froze the action. Sergeant Malkovich was the first one in the room, nightstick in hand, gasping for air. A few minutes later, the Goon Squad burst through the door.

Gabby lay on the floor, moaning noisily, his face covered with blood.

"What's the trouble?" snapped Cheswick, his nightstick at the ready.

Banner took a deep breath and tried to compose himself.

"A little misunderstanding here between..."

"Who started it?"

"...little misunderstanding between..."

"Who started it?" he snapped. He had no use for Banner, a man he considered a meddling civilian, a poacher on correctional territory.

"Inmate Stiles here," said Banner, pointing to Gabby's crumpled form, "and inmate Dee had a disagreement about..."

Cheswick grinned.

"Inmate Dee," he said. "Just can't seem to stay out of trouble, can you, boy?"

He turned to the other officers.

"Get Stiles on his feet and down to Control. Banner, we'll need a report on this right away. Le-roy, you can come with me. This might even get you a little time in the Hole."

Two officers jerked Gabby to his feet and propelled him out the door. Leroy followed, urged on by Cheswick's nightstick in the middle of his back.

The rest of the group moved forward slowly, straightening chairs, breathing easier, sitting down.

"Mau Mau motherfuckers," said Moose under his breath.

Voodoo took his seat, still smiling. This was the new Voodoo—patient and calm. But he knew the brothers would not wait much longer; history was rushing forward to embrace them. In his heart he said, Only a little longer, my brothers. Have patience. Only a little longer...

Banner lit a cigarette, still visibly shaken by the incident.

"Well..." he said. "Well..."

There was a brief silence.

"You know," said Duke, "I had a really interesting experience the other day."

"Why don't you tell the group about it," said Leonard.

"Be glad to. I turned my clothes into the laundry last week and I got them all back. Everything I sent in came back. Amazing..."

"Can't be, man," said Nick. "That ain't never happened to me."

"And best of all," said Duke, "I got a new pair of socks. New... With elastic in the tops."

"You mean to tell me," said Leonard, "that there are socks in this institution with elastic in them?"

"Absolutely."

"Around the tops? To hold them up?"

Duke nodded.

"I find that hard to believe, inmate Perry. I have personally never even seen a pair like that."

"Come over to the house after group. I'll show you."

Banner smoked his cigarette and stared at the floor. He gave no indication that he was listening.

"You think we ought to investigate?" said Leonard. "Might be more of them around."

"Good idea," said Duke.

"Moose," said Leonard, "why don't you check this out and get back to the group next week with a report."

"Uh...I'll think about," said Moose.

"Don't just think about it," said Leonard. "Take responsibility. That's what good citizens do. You want to be a good citizen, don't you?"

"…Of course."

*Release for kitchen workers.*

*Release for kitchen workers…*

The men looked at Banner. Moose stood up and stretched.

"Guess that's it, eh Mr. Banner?"

Banner looked up.

"…What?"

"That's it, eh? Group over? It's three o'clock."

"…Yes. Of course. Group's over."

The men filed out slowly, blacks and whites giving each other a wide berth at the door.

Banner sat chain smoking for a long time after the men had gone. Somehow he wasn't reaching them. It wasn't from lack of effort. God knows, he tried hard enough. But they resisted. He didn't know why. They had no reason to, but they did. Everything to gain and nothing to lose, still they resisted. He tried to draw them out, get them to see patterns of behavior that brought them back to prison time and time again. Destructive patterns. It seemed so obvious. He was trying to help them. For some reason, they couldn't see that. No matter what he did, they couldn't see it.

Nothing made sense. In theory perhaps, in textbooks, in academic circles where they talked about crime at big mahogany tables over cups of Earl Grey tea, but not on the Yard. Nothing made sense on the Yard. It was a world all its own.

# CHAPTER 39

Stan paced back and forth in his cell; even in the dark he knew exactly how many steps to take. Sometimes he took small steps and it was four steps instead of the usual three; it made the cell seem bigger. What a long way, he said to himself. Four whole steps. Sometimes he stopped and pushed against the side walls. Samson in the temple, he thought, though the walls never crumbled. And his Delilah, his faithless Delilah, was far away, perhaps destroying another mere mortal.

But each day the cell got a little smaller and sixty days in a rapidly shrinking cell began to look like an eternity.

Old scenes from the marriage persisted. He tried to wish them away, but they were burned into his memory, etched like acid traces, vivid reminders of a life that now seemed as remote as the Middle Ages. The scenes were painful, full of compromise and duplicity; he on his knees worshipping at the altar of Yin, tossing tantrums like bean bags when he didn't get his way.

His mind, left to wander in the darkness, retrieved bits and pieces of old conversations, snatches of songs, dim echoes of a certain madness that always seemed to be lurking at the edges of his knowing. The seeds of his own destruction gathered like lemmings on the cliffs above the frozen sea of his heart. A bearded, wrathful God, feathered quill in hand, scribbled in the Book of Life, chapter and verse on the short, pathetic life of Stanley W. Smith, a life without merit, plain as the name. A large tombstone loomed in the darkness:

**STANLEY SMITH**
**Murderer 1940-1967**
**R.I.P**

Voices from the pulpit assured him that he would be consigned forever to the fiery pits of Hell, condemned to live for all eternity yearning only for the Beatific Vision (not even a glimpse of Baby Jesus) and a cool glass of water. The wages of sin. (Ain't no pussy in Hell, Rag Man told him. That's why they call it Hell.) God punishes those who disobey Him, said Father Samuels, his eyes dull as bulkhead rivets.

Each childish indulgence, each selfish act rose from the mist like a bloated corpse to taunt him—relics culled from the deep, a chain gang of memories forged together by unbreakable bonds of guilt.

When he discovered the hidden joys his favorite appendage could provide (before he heard the practice denounced as an evil that would eventually lead to blindness, insanity, and worse), he stroked himself until he was sore and chafed and exhausted. Then did it again as soon as he could. As he grew older, additional excitement was provided by giving himself quick hand jobs in public places— restrooms, back alleys, behind the bushes in the park, sometimes barely holstering his tool before some dignified matron hobbled into view. There were many close calls but no arrests.

And what would the Blue Fairy think of it all? Her promise to Pinocchio was that if he could be Brave, Truthful and Unselfish, someday he would be a Real Boy. But Stan saw himself as hopeless; a puppet under siege; Pinocchio with an bad attitude. His chances of becoming Real, while never very good, were rapidly getting worse. Even Jiminy Cricket, his conscience, had abandoned him.

He grappled with images sharpened by hunger and loneliness. His mother appeared, framing his face with her tiny hands, repeating her endless litany of fear and affection...

*I love you...Be careful, be careful, be careful...*

Like a truant boy, he tempered his responses, leveraging control, furnishing only an occasional I love you when it suited his purpose. He knew about the words—what they did, not what they meant. He always had trouble with what things meant. But he knew he spent a nickel and got a dollar. Withheld affection was like money in the bank; horde now, spend later. Easy money. Blood money. He knew that much.

He sat in his cell for hours, sinking deeper into despair, the burden of memory pushing him under each time he came up for air. A supplicant at the Temple of Time, he watched the parade of peccadilloes march across the horizon, tarnished as tin soldiers, the Theater of the Absurd becoming Grand Guignol.

His first sexual encounter with a woman was an epiphany. When he finally managed to achieve union before orgasm, what he remembered was the thrusting, the joyful noise, the smell, the slick, sweaty, belly-slapping rhythm as he plundered his first plump victim. He was convinced in those moments of bliss that forces far greater than any he had ever imagined were at work, that within that magic orifice, that spiral vortex of pleasure, were answers to questions yet unasked. And yet, the feast was nearly always accompanied by the metallic taste of guilt, a sour legacy from the venomous tongue of Father Samuels.

When he was old enough to drive a car, he sometimes drove to Tijuana to visit the houses of prostitution. Bullfights in the afternoon were the prelude, guzzling Tecate beer, sitting in the sun oleing with the other gringos, trying to remember the Spanish names for the cape work he had recently culled from Hemingway's *Death in the Afternoon*. He felt grown up, fascinated by the blood and the bravery, the smell of death that haunted his senses, fabricating dialog in his head to fit the image of a tough young Stan Smith who had come to Mexico to satisfy the whores. Like Hemingway. Papa. He loved the way it sounded when he said it out loud. Whores... Putas...The Gringo with his big Chorizo has come to Mexico to satisfy the whores...Ay! muy grande, Hombre...But he was not able to go often. Mostly he stayed home and practiced with his hand, setting personal bests for Most Orgasms in a Day and Most Orgasms in One Hour.

Waking hours in the cell were filled with voices, nights with dreams. The walls closed in. He felt reality slipping away.

What happened to Larry? he asked his mother.

Hush! she said. Here comes your father.

Jesus, what happened to Larry?...

Carl Smith had a voice like thunder; when he got mad you could hear him two houses away. Dishes rattled when he stomped around the house. He could pick up the Mrs. and toss her around like a toy. Stan, too. Hardly anyone ever came to that sad house on Desoto Street. Carl had an affair with the bosomy blond waitress at Bud's Diner that everybody knew about and nobody talked about. Hardly anybody. At least not in public. One day Carl got drunk, took all his clothes off, went out on the front lawn with his .22 caliber pump action rifle and fired off ten or twelve rounds trying to kill the pesky crows that gathered on the telephone wires across the street. Buffalo Carl Smith, last of the buckaroos. The police came and got him. He went like a lamb. It was downhill after that, slow but sure, as if that was his last hurrah. But he never talked about it; never talked about anything except What time is dinner? and How come this house always looks like a goddam pigsty?

Then the heart attack. Mrs. Smith saw the Hand of God in it; she saw The Hand of God in everything. Carl was dependent on her now. This was the payback. (Who said prayers don't get answered?) Retribution. Big time. He had to ask nicely if he wanted anything. She was generous to a fault, kind and giving and loving, but they both knew it was payback and that she had suffered long enough, hung in there long enough to be declared the winner. She had persevered. Now she had all the cards and she played them slowly, deliberately, with great skill and Christian charity. It had been a long time coming, but she felt it was worth it. He hated it, but there was nothing he could do.

Stan began to curse the guard when he brought the food; the guard responded by shoving the bowl off the narrow ledge and onto the floor inside the cell. Stan screamed at him that he was a no good stupid fucking asshole...But the guard didn't answer. It wasn't long before he began to hear the cockroaches, just a faint rustle at first, then louder and louder, thousands, perhaps millions of cockroaches marching across the floor. An army of them. Stan ran back and forth in the cell, bouncing off the walls, bruising his arms, terrified that they would crawl all over him if he didn't keep moving, ran until his cracked ribs hurt so much he had to stop.

When he showered and changed clothes at the end of the first week, he discovered that both eyes were black, and his nose was slightly off center. Broken, he wondered? He wanted to ask the guard for more than the allotted fifteen minutes out on the exercise Yard, but he didn't.

During the second week he began to hit his head against the wall, lightly at first, an almost pleasant, numbing sensation, then harder and harder until it broke the skin and blood ran down his face. He said to the guard I'm hurt and the guard said So fuckin' what? and shoved the bowl through the opening and onto the cell floor. Stan hit himself in the ribs until it hurt to breathe, sure that he had punctured a lung with a piece of bone from his rib. I'm really hurt he whispered to the guard and the guard said So fuckin' what? and shoved the bowl off the ledge again. Stan felt so sick he couldn't even yell at him.

He asked himself why he was doing it, hurting himself like that, but he got no answer. (He could remember times when he was young that he took a rock and pounded the side of his foot until it was swollen, then went limping to his mother to get some attention.) For some strange reason he seemed comforted by the pain, though he didn't know why. Sometimes he put his head down and walked into the wall, momentarily knocking himself out. His head hurt constantly; the scabs barely had time to form before the cuts were opened again. He stopped yelling at the guard and the guard stopped throwing his food on the floor. It seemed simple enough, but by then he didn't care much one way or the other.

Next time he was allowed to shower (he didn't know how long it was, though it seemed longer than a week), he was surprised at how bad he looked. His face was streaked with blood, his hair matted with it, his forehead cut, badly bruised and discolored.

He took a long time in the shower, carefully lathering his hair with the harsh soap that stung the cuts on his scalp, standing under the hot water as long as he could. He didn't ask to see a doctor and the guard didn't volunteer to send him, though Stan was sure he got more than the usual fifteen minutes out on the Yard. He just stood with his face to the sun and drank in the warmth.

Back in the cell he passed the time conducting conversations with imaginary visitors—Steinbeck, O'Neill, Salinger, Meister Eckhart, Melville, Hemingway (Stan asked him about the running of the bulls in Pamplona and what it felt like to die, but all Papa wanted to talk about were the fishing trips and the big game hunts and the whores and how they all loved him), lamenting his present surroundings, promising better digs when they met next. He had questions for them (What was it about the whale, Ahab?) but remembered few of the answers. Better days are comin', he said, though he didn't really believe it. He decided it sounded too much like a political slogan anyway. He lost all track of time.

A toothless, old, Bonnie Aldrich appeared in the Baby Doll pajamas he bought for their wedding night.

Hiya, Big Boy, she said, lifting her pajamas as the flesh fell away from her bones, revealing only a skeletal cleft and a few random memories.

Stan covered his eyes with both hands.

> *Ay, breach your last to the sun, Moby*
> *Dick! cried Ahab. Thy hour and thy*
> *harpoon are at hand!*

Sounds of a radio dial being spun from station to station filtered through...

> KFWB, Los Angeles with the news at five.
> Pentagon sources report that U.S. military
> casualties have reached a total of...inbound
> Hollywood freeway is backed up to...Station
> KIEV with your Christian Ministry of the air...
> bringing you the good news that Jesus
> Christ Hisself has rose tri-um-phant and...

**WAR HERO SLAIN IN LOVE TRIANGLE**
**WIFE TESTIFIES AT MURDER TRIAL**
**D.A. SEEKS DEATH PENALTY IN BRUTAL SLAYING**

He fought the panic that gripped him in the dark and pleaded with an absent God to bring light, warmth, healing to his ribs and his hemorrhoids. He threatened, cajoled, cursed, lied, and made promises he knew he couldn't keep, wrote letters in his head that started out, Dear God, Fuck You...He visualized the beach at Santa Monica—the rolling surf, warm sand, the women in bikinis, inverted triangles of promise nestled between thighs smooth as marble. The horizon went on forever; the sky was bluer than blue. Sunlight was everywhere. He loved the sun. And the women.

Early on in life he bought into the notion that he was fundamentally defective, that he needed to be fixed and that women were the ones to do it. They were soft, supportive, nurturing and helpful. Or so he thought. At least he was not as afraid of them as he was of men. (Men had always frightened him.) He had plunged his slender member into enough apertures to discover that they all provided a fix for a time. Relief. Respite. Stamp my ticket. Some for days, some for weeks. (In the absence of the Great Looking Chick, he invariably turned to the whiskey and the drugs for solace.) The prettier ones seemed to work longer, Bonnie the longest.

But looking back, he realized that he really had no idea how long that was. Was it weeks only? Months? Had Bonnie left the marriage bed immediately to hike her skirt to the passing parade, searching for something of greater substance to insert between her hungry thighs? Was he, even in the beginning, playing second fiddle in a bad band?

Still, he decided that it would have been worth it, all of it, if he had never known, if she had not been so brazen as to walk out the door into her lover's arms. He could have lived with it all because being with her, just being seen with her, elevated him to a status he could never have achieved on his own. Without her he was Stan, Wimpy Stan. With her he was Stan the Man with the Great Looking Chick. He was Somebody. People looked at him with envy. He was Fixed.

> *Toward thee I roll, shouted Ahab, thou all destroying*
> *whale; to the last I grapple with thee; from Hell's heart*
> *I strike thee...*

The days blended together, separated only by temperature and the slice of light that crept slowly across the floor. Some days went on forever. He spent hours looking into the eyes of John Misner, nodding in response to what he found there. He identified actions rather than the passage of time—sitting, walking, lying down, eating, taking a piss. His Dear God letters expanded to contain challenges. *Dear God, Fuck You. If You really exist, why don't you send a message?*...But there was no thunder, no lightning, no earthquake, no discernible message. Only the silence. Yet, oddly enough, the silence itself seemed to contain a presence of some sort. But when he tried to breach the silence, to surround the presence and find out what it was, it vanished like smoke. He had no words to describe the experience.

He stopped abusing his body and it began to heal. The next time he showered he noticed the darkness under his eyes was disappearing. He massaged his gums with his index finger, hoping it would stop the bleeding. His nose appeared to be permanently skewed, but at least he could breathe through it. Even the cuts on his forehead were healing. And though the ribs were still sore, he could breathe without pain.

Every night at nine o'clock, the guard banged on the cell door, made him stand against the back wall when he tossed the mattress in—the nightly drill. Stan folded the mattress in half, sat on it and leaned against the wall.

Late one night he thought he heard a child crying. In the background, as an eerie counterpoint, a woman was sobbing quietly. He held his breath and listened, but there was nothing for a long time. Then a voice. A whispery child's voice.

"Stan?"

Just the one word.

But the voice carried with it the memory of a small pink face that he was sure belonged to his baby brother (despite what his mother had told him). Stan didn't know why, or how; he just knew that the baby's name was Larry and that he had died very young. Perhaps at the hand of his father—he could imagine an angry Carl Smith throwing the child against the wall in a fit of rage. Maybe shaking him to death. He was capable of things like that. It could have been something else, some childhood disease perhaps, but he doubted it. If it had been, why would they try to hide it?

Stan nodded without speaking.

"They buried me up by the reservoir…Near the walnut tree."

"…Oh…"

"Don't forget about Pinocchio…" But the voice was already beginning to fade. "…and the Blue Fairy. It's your turn to live. Don't forget."

Stan took a deep breath and exhaled slowly.

"…This is a dream," he said finally. "Must be."

He listened intently, but the sound of the woman sobbing and the voice of the child faded to a faint hissss that sounded like tape noise, then finally to silence. As if to punctuate the exchange, a cell door slammed in the background. He touched his eyes to see if they were open. Pinocchio and the Blue Fairy? He didn't know what to make of it. It was another incident in a series of incidents that defied explanation. But for the first time in weeks, he slept through the night.

When he got up in the morning he began doing his situps and pushups; it didn't take long before he could do fifty of both without stopping. He thought about the voice he had heard, but could come to no conclusion about it. His little brother from beyond the grave? And the woman crying? His mother? A figment of his imagination? The result of too many hours in solitary? He didn't know.

But something inside him, some fundamental awareness or attitude began to change. He realized that he could actually die or go crazy or hurt himself very badly in that small cell and nobody was going to care, nobody was going to come and rescue him. All the King's Horses and all the King's Men and all the wonderful women on the beach in Santa Monica wouldn't be able to put him back together again. Hebner and Cheswick would win. To them he would be just another stupid convict who couldn't make it. Couldn't hold his mud. A number…A-83534. Stan didn't want that. He wanted to survive, if for no other reason than to show them he could. And what if he really did have things to do? Was the dream or the voice or whatever it was trying to tell him that he had some special reason to live now? Some mandate to fulfill? Maybe important things—things that Larry never got to do.

He ate his morning mush; decided it didn't taste all that bad. The terrible stench in the cell all but vanished when he stopped focusing on it. Through it all he began to develop a certain inner strength.

He knew there was trouble coming. Maybe it was the dreams, but he really wasn't sure how he knew. But he saw the blood on the Yard and knew that it was going to be bad. Very bad.

There were seven more weekly showers before he was released. He was sure that he had done an extra week or two, but he didn't say anything; it was enough just to be out in the sun.

The first person he encountered was Preacher...

> ...*And the fifth angel poured out his vial upon the beast; and his kingdom was full of darkness and they gnawed their tongues in pain...And why, said Preacher, is there no fucking balm in Gilead? Answer me that...*

Chief White Eagle was doing a war dance near the Weight Area, annoying the Negroes pumping iron.

"Tell that muffuckin' red ass fool to take that shit on down the road," said Willy 5X.

"Yah yah yah yah, Yah yah yah yah..."

White Eagle never missed a beat.

As Stan walked across the Yard on his way back to South Block, he noticed a dark, circular patch on the ground outside the entrance to North Block. It looked a little like a shadow, but when he looked up there were no clouds, nothing to cast a shadow. He couldn't imagine what it might be, the dark patch, didn't know till later, after it happened.

# CHAPTER 40

Leonard expanded his gambling activities into the basketball season. It wasn't as lucrative as football, but he was making money. More than that, it was something to do.

Paulson begged Leonard to let him run off the betting sheets on the Xerox machine in the Watch Commander's Office. Pleaded with him. He took some dummy sheets and ran off twenty copies just to show him he could do it. He even timed himself.

"Less than a minute," he said proudly. "And you don't even need twenty."

Leonard said he'd think about it.

Paulson continued to practice. A week later he ran the entire operation in under fifty seconds.

Leonard finally gave in.

All went well for the first few weeks. But one day, Hebner, suspicious because Paulson rather than Leonard was running the Movement Sheet, crouched behind a tall filing cabinet not four feet from the Xerox machine and pounced on the unsuspecting Paulson just as he was finishing the run. He grabbed one of the sheets and held it under Paulson's nose.

"What's this?" he demanded.

Paulson stared at the floor and said nothing.

"Gambling sheets," Hebner said triumphantly.

Quinlan told Hebner that he was pleased, though his demeanor didn't reflect it. He knew Paulson was just a gopher, a runner, a minor player. Any fool could see that. Leonard was the man they wanted; now they had tipped their hand and he'd be much more careful.

Quinlan suggested that Hebner get Paulson to implicate Leonard. Hebner tried, brought his considerable arsenal of threats and promises to bear, even invited Powell to participate, reasoning in some oblique way that Powell's color might seem ominous, might spur a confession. All to no avail; Paulson was as mute as a carved bee.

Quinlan's decision was to transfer him to San Quentin. A Violation of Section 337 of the California Penal Code was noted in his Central File—Bookmaking, bets and wagers. Quinlan could have taken him to court and tried him for the offense, but trials were expensive (he took pride in his administrative thrift, knowing it would serve him well as governor), and it was punishable by only an additional year in prison. A small notation in his Central File would get him that and more. He was sent to a holding cell to await the transfer. Leonard was powerless to stop it.

A hurried canvass for contacts at San Quentin produced only four reliable names. Paulson, small and vulnerable, would be an easy mark. He would need protection. Letters were kited out via Jules Reiner with instructions that they be delivered as soon as possible.

The night before he was to leave, Officer Burton walked by the holding cell, slipped a paper bag through the bars and continued on without comment. On the outside of the bag were four names and a notation: Look these men up when you get to Q…Inside the bag was a Jolly Burger with pickles and onions.

Paulson arrived in San Quentin in his traveling whites on a Friday. He had lost the bag with the names on it. The letters Leonard sent had not been delivered. (They were still on the front seat of Reiner's car, though he would always swear that he mailed them the same day he got them.) He was processed and in his cell by Friday afternoon.

The visitors came to his cell later that day. He didn't know any of them. His half smile was a shy hello.

They left him badly beaten, scarred in ways he could never have imagined. They made sport of his stumpy body. His mouth was cut, fouled, his body soiled. For a moment he thought it might be a dream, then realized that it was too painful to be a dream.

In less than an hour they were back. Or others like them. He couldn't tell. It didn't make any difference. They pummeled him unmercifully. He wondered where the guards were. He remembered thinking that if his friend Leonard were there, none of this would be happening.

Later that night, huddled in the shadows of the lower bunk, he picked through his state issued possessions—tooth brush, tiny cardboard cylinder with chalky toothpowder, sack of Bull Durham tobacco, twenty cigarette papers, one razor and one razor blade. One blade per week. Regulations. A Gillette Double Edge Blue Blade in a blue and white wrapper...Look sharp and feel sharp...He unwrapped it, held it carefully between his thumb and forefinger and tried to push it into the wool blanket on the bed. It was flexible and hard to hold. He got his handkerchief out and folded it so he could hold the blade tighter. He pushed it into the blanket and made a long cut. Better...

He held out his left arm, took a deep breath and made two long diagonal incisions above the wrist. He was surprised that it didn't hurt much; there was only a slight stinging sensation and a sudden warmth. He watched as the skin parted smoothly and the blood gushed out. It might have been somebody else's arm. In a few moments he felt dizzy and nauseous. He heard his heart flutter erratically. He reached up and began to hack at the side of his neck. It took only a few seconds to find and sever the artery. The last sound he heard was his hungry heart trying to pump more blood. His last feelings were warm and peaceful.

Officer Kerr, a veteran of sixteen years in San Quentin, found him during the ten o'clock count. The gurney arrived thirty minutes later, manned by inmate personnel betraying little emotion, followed by a medical tech with a stethoscope dangling from his neck. Cautiously avoiding the pool of blood, he placed the stethoscope to Paulson's chest, then to the left side of his neck. He looked at the one-way eyes, stood up and confirmed what everyone already knew: Paulson was dead. They placed him on the gurney and covered him with a sheet.

"Early parole," said one of the inmates pushing the gurney.

"You think he's better off?"

"Then he was?"

"No. Better off than we are."

"...Hard to say, man. Hard to say."

The Watch Crew heard about it the following day, though they didn't know all the details for nearly a week. Retribution was neither swift nor complete. Ivory Johnson, one of the participants, was hammered insensible on the Lower Yard at Quentin, but somehow managed to survive. Three months later, a convict known only as Dawg was fatally stabbed in the Laundry. But it took some time and it was never complete. Leonard always regretted that he was never able to get them all.

Paulson's wife took it well. She told the children that Daddy died in the War, grateful that there happened to be a war going on in Vietnam at the time. She, of course, became a War Widow. She liked that; it had a certain noble ring to it. And she knew she was better off, far better off, though she did fret for a time about whether the insurance company would pay off, considering where he was when he died.

Quinlan had been certain that sending Paulson to Quentin would put a stop to Leonard's gambling activities; at least slow them down. Surely the message was clear. But he didn't know Leonard very well; Leonard took it as a personal challenge. Plus the fact that he held Quinlan responsible for Paulson's death. Little Joe informed Quinlan that he had never seen so many betting slips on the Yard.

Leonard mourned the loss of Paulson like he mourned all the losses in his life; outwardly stoic, inwardly seething with rage. He lashed out at Greek one night over some trivial disagreement, and he told the Count to get out of the goddam office and stay out till he was called back. Everyone gave him a wide berth. No one spoke of the incident until he did.

"You know he was a hell of a guy," he said several weeks later. "They tried to get him to roll over on us, to make a deal...but he never said a word."

But when Stan told him how sorry he was, Leonard snapped at him.

"Just the luck of the draw, kid. You been around long enough to know that. You pay your money and you take your chances. Some survive, some don't. Hell, you might be next. Or me. . ." He pushed the glasses up on the bridge of his nose. "Start checkin' records on the Fish. See if we can't find someone to take his place...Then do yourself a favor and forget it."

Quinlan squeezed his snitches for information. Who were the runners? How were the sheets being printed? What did Leonard do with the cigarettes and money he collected? How did he get the money out of the prison?...But he didn't get much useful information. Nobody wanted to cross Leonard. The word was out: If you talk too much, you might not be around for very long.

When Quinlan finally heard the story about a woman being smuggled into prison for the purposes of prostitution, he was furious. His house had been violated. And he had heard it too many times to ignore it. Nobody seemed to know who was behind it. Leonard? Voodoo? High Power? Hog? Could have been any of them.

He called Hebner and Powell into his office and informed them in no uncertain terms that dismissal for failure to perform their duties was not beyond the realm of possibility. Not at all. Incompetence was mentioned several times.

"If this story is true," he said, "and I have heard it too many times to doubt that there is at least some truth in it, then we are the laughing stock of this prison. They," he pointed to the door, "are laughing at us. The goddam convicts. And why not? They've made fools of us. You like that? Being made fools of by a bunch of scum with a sixth-grade education? They bring women in here and they fuck them, pardon my French...they fuck them while we stand around and watch. We're even furnishing the beds. Pretty soon we'll have a waiting list of people who want to get in...You remember the zoo analogy? Remember we talked about that? Well, we are there. We have handed over the keys and we are standing at the bars waiting to be fed. The animals are in control."

He paused to let it sink it.

"And I-won't-have-it!" He slammed the desk for emphasis. "I want the men who were involved in this...this fuck thing...I want the convicts and I want the officers. They are a disgrace to this prison. To the United States of America. The convicts didn't do this without help from Custody. One of our fellow officers has betrayed us. Perhaps more than one. Check your boys, Powell. I understand that the woman was a nigg…a Negro…Now I want results and I want them soon."

He turned his back and walked to the big bay window.

"Dismissed," he said curtly. "Come back when you have something."

"Yessir."

"Yessir."

"I want you to kill me," said Big Eddy, as they stood at the bars for noon count.

Stan gave him a long look.

"…Sure," he said.

"No bullshit, Smith. I'm burned out. Toast. Can't take no more. Fuckin' depressed."

"You don't look depressed."

"So you a fuckin' shrink now, man? Doctor fuckin' Smith, the psycho-guy? What's depressed look like? I don't sleep at night. You're down there catchin' Z's all night while I'm wide awake. I don't hardly sleep at all …What the fuck you know about depression?"

"How you want me to do it?" said Stan. "You want me to shoot you?"

"Don't be funny, man. This is serious shit. I got a shank. I'll give it to you after chow tonight. Hide it under the mattress, then cut my throat when I'm asleep. Right here," he said pointing to the left side of his neck. "That's the big vein."

"I thought you didn't sleep."

"…I got some reds. I'll take 'em and be out like a light. Just make it quick."

"You sure about this?"

"Positive."

"What about all the chicks you haven't fucked?"

"…They'll have to wait."

"Till when?"

"Till…next time."

"Maybe you could just OD on reds," said Stan. "That wouldn't be a bad way to go."

"Too risky," said Eddy. "Besides, I don't have enough reds to OD. Just enough to get to sleep."

"So after it's over, I get to stand trial for murder?"

"No, no," said Eddy. "Plead self-defense. You know the drill. I'll give you a little bruise on the cheek so it'll look real."

Stan shook his head.

"Somehow, this just doesn't sound like such a good deal."

Big Eddy turned and stared at him.

"Then how about if I kill you, motherfucker?" he said. "That sound like a better deal?"

Stan closed his eyes for a moment.

"Yeah. Okay. I get it."

But he knew Big Eddy didn't want to die. He figured Big Eddy for some other scam.

Stan ran it by Leonard that afternoon and Leonard told him to put the shank on top of the mattress at the end nearest the bars just after count and lights out at ten.

Big Eddy came back to the cell after evening chow and handed Stan the shank, a four inch piece of metal wrapped with electrician's tape at one end, sharpened on one side. Stan tested the blade with his thumb and slipped it under his pillow.

"Pretty sharp, man."

Eddy was fidgety and nervous.

"...Wonder what it's like to be dead," he said.

"Prob'ly real quiet."

"Maybe...I had an uncle almost died. Said it was like goin' down a long tunnel with a light at the end."

"The train?"

"...The what?"

"Never mind," said Stan.

Without warning, Eddy lashed out with a right hand, caught Stan flush on the cheek and knocked him back against the wall. Before Stan could even think about retaliating, Eddy held up both hands.

"Hold it," he said. "I'm doin' you a favor. You can tell 'em I attacked you and you had to kill me."

"...You got any ideas about how to explain the knife? How I got it?"

"Easy. You took it away from me when I attacked you."

"Sure, they'll believe that. I just smacked you around and..."

"Who's gonna call you a liar?"

"Everybody," said Stan, sliding into his bunk. "But...maybe I'll enjoy killin' you. Now that you really pissed me off. Maybe I'll sing while I'm cuttin' your throat. You like the Blues, Eddy?...Got the big vein blues," he sang, ' "bleedin' all the time. Got the. . ."

"Don't forget to wait till I'm asleep."

"How will I know?"

"Listen to the way I breathe. When it's slow and steady, I'll be asleep."

"Got it," said Stan. "Slow and steady. And when it stops, you'll be dead...The other thing is, you could just tell me not to do it if you're still awake."

"Right," said Eddy. "I could see you comin' and just say, Hey, I'm still awake. Wait awhile."

After the ten o'clock count, Eddy ran some water in a cup and made a point of telling Stan he was taking the reds. "I'll sleep like a baby," he said, checking his pimples before the lights went out.

"Won't have to worry about those much longer," said Stan.

"Those what?"

"The zits...the pimples."

"Oh...right."

"Say hello to my brother when you get there," said Stan.

"Get where?"

"To...the Other Side. Whatever there is after this."

"Heaven," said Big Eddy. "There's heaven after this."

"You think?"

"Yeah."

"You goin' there, Eddy? To heaven?"

"Yeah."

"...Why?"

"Why not? I been saved, man."

"You and Jesus?"

"Yeah."

"...Anyway, say hello to my brother. His name's Larry."

"What's he look like?"

"He's real little."

"That's it? Just real little?" said Eddy.

"That's all I remember. Just real little."

"I'll ask around…Man, I'm sleepy. Those reds are kickin' in big time."

When the cell lights went out a few minutes later, Stan eased the knife out from under his pillow and set it on the end of his bunk. Sometime within the next few minutes, a shadow moved quickly past the cell. Stan thought it might have been Doc, but he couldn't be sure. When he looked, the knife was gone. He closed his eyes and listened to Big Eddy's shallow breathing.

"Pssst," he whispered.

"Not yet," said Eddy. "I ain't asleep. Gimme a couple of minutes, man."

Soon after, Stan sensed the presence of other men on the tier. Long before he actually heard them, he knew they were there. As if on cue, the cell door slid open and four beefy members of the Goon Squad rushed in together. One of them yanked Stan out of his bunk and slammed him against the wall. Another flipped his mattress over and flooded the steel bunk bottom with his flashlight. He shook the pillow and blankets, then tossed them in the corner.

"Nothin'," he said.

"Where's the shank?" growled Cheswick.

"The what?"

Cheswick pulled him away from the wall, then slammed him back against it.

"That help your memory?"

Stan tried to lift his hand to rub the back of his head, but Cheswick had his arms pinned.

"I'm warnin' you, Smith. You keep fuckin' with us and you're goin' back to the Adjustment Center. Hebner puts you in there again, you'll stay till your memory improves. No matter how long it takes. You might wind up doin' the whole thing in a strip cell. Like your buddy Misner. Or Butcher McCloud. You guys can be roomies. You can eat shit together. What'll we have for dinner tonight, John. How about some shit, Smith? Ha ha ha ha…"

He turned to the other members of the Goon Squad.

"Find anything?"

"Nothin'."

"Okay, let's get outta here," he said. "Convict smell startin' to get to me. Just remember you're on thin ice, Smith. Real thin ice."

After they left, Stan straightened out his mattress and blanket, punched his pillow a few times and got back in his bunk. Big Eddy hadn't moved.

Stan shook the top bunk and whispered, "You asleep yet?"

"Get smart, man," said Eddy. "They already know who did it. All you gotta do is tell 'em you saw it. That's all. They need a witness. For the trial. Don't be fuckin' stupid."

"Sure," said Stan. "Then I can sit around and wait for someone to take me out for bein' a snitch."

"Have 'em take you to P.C.—Protective Custody. Nobody'll get you in there."

"Great. Ten years in lockup."

"Better'n ten years in the Hole. Better'n fuckin' dead."

"What's in it for you?" said Stan.

"Nothin'."

"Fat chance."

"Swear to God, man."

Stan pulled the covers up and propped his pillow against the iron chain that held his bunk to the wall. For a long time he stared at the shadows the bars cast on the side of the cell.

"Well," he said, "maybe you'll get your wish after all."

"…About what?"

"About dyin'."

Eddy didn't say anything for a few minutes.

"What happened to the shank?"

"Shank?" said Stan. "Somebody had a shank?"

Eddy rolled over on his side.

"Be sure you don't get too smart for your own good, Smith. You won't always be able to depend on your hotshot connections."

Stan closed his eyes.

"…I got the big vein blues, da da daaaa…"

It was shortly after the cell shakedown that Big Eddy's transfer took place. Stan didn't ask how or why. A request had gone in, somebody signed it, somebody else signed it, and a week later it was done. Stan didn't know if Eddy had requested it, or if Leonard himself had been behind it. It was never mentioned. Either way, he liked living in a single cell.

In the weeks that followed, Quinlan began to sense the rising tide of tension on the Yard. It was nothing specific, no information worthy of the name. Just general unrest. But the signs were there; he had been around prisons long enough to notice. It wouldn't take much to set it off. Just an incident of some kind. Almost anything.

# CHAPTER 41

Less than a week after Stan was released from the Adjustment Center, he got a ducat to see the prison psychiatrist. It was automatic—two trips to the Adjustment Center meant an invitation to visit Dr. Welbourne.

Dr. Welbourne's office was located in a small room in the prison Hospital (Quinlan was not a great believer in psychiatry as a weapon in the War Against Crime). Most of his time was spent interviewing convicts and preparing Parole Board Reports for those with psychological evaluations specified as a condition for parole, often those prone to excessive violence or deviant behavior. The Board, ever anxious to have a corroborative voice in cases where mental stability or public outrage was at issue, depended upon Welbourne to furnish guidelines and supportive evidence. Most Board members considered psychiatry a definite aid in the decision-making process. Quinlan was not among them; he had seen Welbourne ply his trade.

And though the Board relied heavily on the reports in difficult cases (always eager to have someone to blame in case a parolee turned out badly), lately the reports had been more shadow than substance. Dr. Welbourne had been preoccupied, just going through the motions. His young wife had been staying out late at night; several times she had not come home at all. (Carmela, a young Mexican beauty, was his fourth wife.) She's just acting out, he said, though he wasn't sure what that meant in her case. Or if he should be overly concerned.

He stayed home and tried to cope with Manuel, her two-year-old son by a former lover, who delighted in smearing his feces on the apartment walls. Welbourne drank Silver Slipper gin and told himself that, all things considered, he was managing fairly well.

He was in his late forties, though he could have passed for ten years older, his face a veiny web of worry, his hair (too long for Quinlan's liking) sparse on top, darkened from its natural gray through the miracle of modern chemistry. Several shaving nicks decorated an otherwise uneventful chin. His lips were soft, the color of faded plums. Thick glasses accentuated the dark pouches under his eyes.

When Stan entered he was writing on a yellow legal pad, trying to bring some order to the chaotic life of Elmer "Hoss" Criner. On the desk next to it was Stan's Central File. He looked up and formed his face into a smile.

"Mr. Smith," he said.

On his desk was a plaque that bore the inscription:

## CONFLICT IS THE MOTHER OF MATURITY

It was attributed to Adolph Jackemans.

"Have a seat," he said. "This is just a routine…examination. More an interview than anything, really. Something that Custody requires for inmates who have been to the Adjustment Center more than once. Nothing special. You won't be graded on whether you get the answers right or wrong. As a matter of fact, there are no right or wrong answers. Just answers."

Stan pulled out a pack of tailor-mades. Thanks to the five dollars he had received from his mother, he'd been able to buy cigarettes and a small jar of instant coffee. Her letter said that she was worried about him; he hadn't been writing as often. She loved him. Daddy was as well as could be expected though not really all that well. Daddy loved him, too (though Daddy never wrote and said that himself. Daddy never wrote at all). Everybody missed him. Even Toby the Smelly Sheep Dog…It's what she always wrote. He wrote and thanked her. Said he loved her, too (he had no idea if that was true or not), but things were just very dull and there was nothing much to write about. Told her not to worry. Say Hi to Dad. It's what he always wrote. Nothing ever changed.

"Okay to smoke?" said Stan.

"Certainly," said Welbourne. He reached into his desk drawer and produced a large, ceramic ashtray—Stardust Hotel, Las Vegas.

Stan lit a cigarette and blew the smoke toward his lap. Welbourne took a pack of Luckies out of his cardigan and set it next to the ashtray.

"Now," said Welbourne, leaning forward, long yellow pencil poised over the pad. "A few...routine questions. Do you have trouble remembering things?"

"Not usually."

"Like what month it is? What day?"

"No," said Stan.

"What month is this?"

"March."

"What day?"

"...Tuesday?"

"Tuesday. You sure?"

"...I think so."

Welbourne made a notation on the legal pad.

"That right?" said Stan. "It's Tuesday?"

"Oh...It's not important."

Stan took a drag off his cigarette; he felt foolish about asking.

"Do you like your mother?"

"She's okay."

"Just okay?"

"She's...fine. A nice mother."

"You love her?"

"Yeah," said Stan.

"Your father?"

"...Yeah."

"But you're not so sure about him, eh?"

"No."

"I see," he said, noting the reply.

"Actually, I..."

"No need to explain," said Welbourne. He pinched a cigarette out of the pack of Luckies, placed it in the center of his mouth and noisily lit it. "Have you ever had any homosexual experiences?"

"No."

"None? Ever?"

"Nope."

Welbourne raised an eyebrow and took several short puffs on his cigarette. Stan wondered how much he knew, and how much of The Incident had found its way into official channels. Perhaps none. Perhaps...

"You're in here for murder," more a statement than a question.

Stan nodded.

"You like killing people?"

The question startled him. He had never thought of it like that— liking it or not liking it. It seemed absurd. He wanted to say that he hadn't killed enough people to get a real feel for it, for whether he liked it or not. Instead he said...

"No."

Welbourne referred to Stan's Central File.

"You didn't see who pushed inmate Hawkins off the tier in South Block?"

"No."

"This report says you were close to him when it happened."

"Report's wrong," said Stan.

"Really? Custody was in error?"

"Yes."

"They were lying?"

"They were...in error."

Stan met Welbourne's quizzical gaze; Welbourne was the first to look away.

"Huh," he said, referring to his notes. "I'm going to read a list of words and I'd like you to respond with the first thing that comes to mind... Ready?"

"Yeah."

"Door?"

"Window."

"Closet?"

"Dress."

"Gun?"

"Eh...smoke."

"The first thing," said Welbourne. "...Black?"

"White."

"Dress?"

"Closet."

"Big?"

"…Dick."

Welbourne hesitated for a moment.

"Love?"

"Hate."

"How would you feel if somebody robbed you? Took all your money."

"Bad, I guess."

"Would you be angry?"

"I imagine."

"You imagine, eh?"

Welbourne paused to make a lengthy notation. Stan wondered if he'd been giving the right answers. Despite the disclaimer that there were no right or wrong answers, he had an uneasy feeling about the interview. Perhaps he'd been too confrontational about Hawk. He sat up straighter, and promised himself he would pay more attention to the questions. And his answers.

"How do you feel about Mexicans?"

"They're okay."

"And Negroes?"

"…Okay."

"Homosexuals?"

"Live and let live," said Stan.

"Everybody's pretty much okay with you, eh?"

"Mostly."

"Except maybe Jeff Loughlin. He wasn't so okay, was he?"

Stan looked at the ashtray on the desk.

"I guess not."

"You-guess-not…You're not sure?"

"I don't remember much of it. Of what happened."

"You killed him, Smith. Took his life."

"…That's what I heard."

Welbourne sighed. Last night's load of Silver Slipper gin coursed unevenly through constricted veins. His stomach was queasy. He wondered why he sat in that office day after day, month after month, listening to guarded answers and outright lies from men who were wary and suspicious of everyone, especially those in authority. Was it for the money? Security? Perhaps a little of both, he decided. But he was no longer sure. Of anything.

"I understand that you were sent to the Adjustment Center for fighting. What was that all about?"

"Self-defense," said Stan.

"I see. Some men just started a fight with you? You have any idea why they did that?"

"...No."

Stan waited while Welbourne consulted his file.

"You drink?"

"Some," said Stan.

"You have two drunk driving convictions. Apparently you drink to excess on occasion."

Stan nodded.

"You take drugs?" said Welbourne.

"Prescription."

"What kind?"

"Sleeping pills mostly. Nembutal...Seconal."

"You ever take more than what's prescribed?"

"No."

"You have trouble getting an erection?"

"No."

"You think you're crazy?"

Something in Stan's head said, Be careful...

"No."

"You think murder is the act of a rational human being?"

"No."

Welbourne leafed through the file in front of him.

"Would you say you had a happy childhood?"

"...It was okay."

"Your mother thinks you had a very unhappy childhood and that your father was to blame."

Stan's shrug said he didn't know.

"Do you masturbate?"

"Sometimes."

"Often?"

"…Occasionally."

"Do you feel guilty about it? Like you're doing something wrong?"

"…Sometimes."

"Do you like it?"

"…It's okay."

"Okay, eh?" said Welbourne. "Everything's just hunky dory, eh? A-okay."

"Mostly."

Welbourne rubbed his forehead as if he were trying to erase something. Another one who's learned to play the game, he thought. Sooner or later they all learned; it was only a matter of time.

The years of investigation and the millions of dollars spent on research into criminology and human behavior appeared all but useless when confronting convicts across a small metal desk. Nowhere was there a comprehensive study on crime or criminal behavior that would stand the withering heat of even a week on the Yard. There were genetic and glandular theories, monozygotic and dizygotic studies, theories on role-playing, ethnic affiliations and socio-economic factors; none made any sense in the living laboratory of the prison itself. He was certain that the men who wrote the studies had never lived or worked among convicts. Perhaps never even visited a prison.

He knew he was dealing with men who were interested in only one thing—Parole. Short term goal orientation. Problems with drugs or alcohol were minimized or simply denied. And any actions necessary to get a good parole report were considered fair. Without even knowing the question, all were sure that Parole was the answer.

"Well, it's not okay, Smith," said Welbourne. "You need to get in touch with that. Hasn't been okay for a long time for you. Maybe not ever. You're out there, Smith. Drifting. Not…in touch. Not feeling anything. Humans are sentient beings. They have feelings. Where are yours?"

Stan looked at the ashtray.

"You need to know that what you did is not-o-kay. Not-okay."

He extinguished his cigarette with short angry strokes, causing sparks and ashes to spill out on the desk.. After a moment he stopped, looked blankly at his hand, then picked another cigarette out of the pack and lit it.

"Long day."

"Some are," said Stan.

"I haven't been…feeling well." He patted his stomach. "Ulcers acting up."

Welbourne sat quietly, the only movement the sporadic twitch of his cheek. He seemed lost in thought watching the smoke curl up from his cigarette. It was a long time before he spoke.

"No matter," he said finally. "Water under the bridge. Over and done with. You know…That'll be all, eh…Smith."

Stan stood up to leave.

"Just remember," said Welbourne, "nobody's got it easy. Nobody. Self-pity never helped anyone."

After Stan left, he removed a vial of pills from the desk drawer, shook two green and black capsules into the palm of his hand and gulped them down with cold coffee…Librium. Tiger Tamers. Always did the trick. Relief is just a swallow away, he thought. A drink wouldn't hurt either, but that would have to wait. He leaned back in the chair and closed his eyes.

# CHAPTER 42

"Maybe we should start the Fly Killin' Contest early this year," said Moose.

"Why?" said Leonard.

"It's almost summer, man. Flies'll be here soon. We need to get ready."

"Plenty of time, Big Guy."

"Yeah, but…"

"What did Welbourne want?" Leonard said to Stan.

"Said it was routine," said Stan. "Two trips to the Hole and you get an automatic to see Welbourne. Wanted to know if I liked killing people."

"What did you tell him?"

"Said I hadn't had enough practice to get a real feel for it."

"The stuff of greatness," said Greek. "You're gonna be okay, kid."

"He want anything else?"

"The usual questions about who pushed Hawk."

"And?…"

"I wasn't close enough to see who did it."

"Good answer."

"He want to know if you been gettin' it on with your mother?" said Moose.

"No. Wanted to know if I drank too much and took too many pills."

"Wha'd you tell him?"

"I told him no, of course not."

"You lied?"

"Of course."

"See, you can prob'ly get away with shit like that. You even look innocent. Me, I'm screwed. They take one look and think, Hey this guy must be guilty. You realize, Greek, that we go to the Board next month."

"No big thing. We go to the Board every April. Mad Dog looks forward to seein' us."

"Maybe I won't get Mad Dog this time," said Moose.

"You might get the new guy. Cronin, I think. From Palm Springs. The Postmaster. I think his daughter died of a drug overdose. You can forget about goin' home."

"Awww…"

"I go to the Board in May," said Stan.

Moose snorted.

"Save yourself a trip, man."

"Oh, you never know," said Stan.

"I fuckin' know," said Moose. "You ain't got a chance. You got worse than no chance. A minus chance. I got three years in on a lousy weed beef. Three." He held up three fingers.

"That's three alright," said Greek. "Right on the money. Nailed it the first time."

"Hey, fuck you."

"Second offense," said the Count.

"Mad Dog'll be here in May, too," said Moose. "He'll make fuckin' hamburger outta you."

"Second offense," said the Count.

"Fuck you and your second offense, Mr. Lawyer," Moose snapped. "Don't mean shit. I'm gettin' out this year."

Leonard leafed through a week-old copy of the *L.A. Times*. He was uneasy; he didn't like the things he was hearing through the grapevine. There was trouble coming. Big trouble. The only question was when.

"Here's a guy in London hijacked an armored truck and got away with two million dollars," he said.

"Jesus," said Moose. "Two fuckin' million."

"What would you do if you had two million dollars, Smith?"

"I don't know," he said. "I never thought about it…about having that much money."

"Smith, the Wage Slave," said Moose. "But you know, man, you shoulda never even been convicted. You shoulda got a medal for pluggin' the guy that was doin' your old lady. First thing, though, is you never should have actually killed him. You shoulda shot his bone off so he'd have to go through life without a bone. How about that?"

"Inspired," said Leonard.

"Bone death," said Greek. "The worst kind."

"What's the penalty for killin' a bone, Crisco?"

"...I'd have to look it up."

"Good lawyer'd pro'bly know that off the top, man."

Leonard went back to his paper.

"Here's one," he said. "Man given new heart in Stanford transplant."

"Heart transplant," said Moose. "That for real, man?"

"Page four, Big Guy," said Leonard, holding up the paper.

"Heart transplant," said Moose. "Jesus, what next?"

"Come to think of it," said Greek, "my heart hasn't been all that great lately. You think I could get a new one?"

"No chance," said Leonard. "I have it on good authority that the State is very tired of supporting you."

"Hey, wasn't for us," said Moose, "those pricks wouldn't even have jobs. How about those rights you talked about, Crisco?"

"Rights maybe. But no extra hearts."

"You suppose a guy could get a cock transplant?"

"You havin' trouble with yours?"

"You kiddin'?" said Moose. "I'm havin' trouble findin' some-thin' to stick it in."

"Tried your hand lately?"

Moose ignored the remark.

"That way, when a guy got old and couldn't get it up, they could give him a new one. You oughta look into it, Greek. Might be some-thin' you could use."

"If they could find somebody who wanted to give his up," said the Count.

"No, man. I mean a guy just died."

"You want somebody's dead dick?" said the Count. "Talk about not bein' able to get it up."

"You could use it to fuck all those dead chicks you been eye-ballin'," said Greek.

"You guys," said Moose. "Where you think they get the fuckin' hearts from? You think they go around askin' people, Hey, you wanna give up your heart? I know a guy really needs it. They wait till the fuckin' guy dies, man. Ain't that right, Leonard?"

"On the money."

"Maybe you could just add some to the one you got, Moose. A few more inches you'd have a regular size one."

Moose turned to Stan.

"See what you gonna have to put up with? And you got ten more years of this shit. At least."

Leonard scanned an article on Vietnam.

"Says we got almost a half a million troops in Vietnam."

"Lotta troops," said Stan.

"We winnin'?" said the Count.

"...Doesn't say," said Leonard. "No box score. Maybe it's a late game...Here's a piece about the new governor. Says Reagan's gonna be tough on violent crime. Ve-ry tough."

"Hear that, Smith? Get ready for a long stay."

"Nice room, good food..."

"Speakin' of which," said Moose, "what's for chow?"

"Mystery meat," said Greek. "And road apples, those dumpling things."

"I'll tell you what's a mystery—how I survived all this time on the shit they feed us."

"True," said Stan. "And never lost a pound."

"You know, Smith, you're getting' just like these other pricks."

Stan smiled and went back to filing inmate cards.

# CHAPTER 43

It happened on a Thursday, late in the afternoon.

A news bulletin interrupted Get Smart just as Maxwell Smart was phoning headquarters on his shoe phone. The somber face of Eric Severeid suddenly appeared on the small black and white screen. In dark graphics across his forehead.

### A CBS NEWS SPECIAL

*Today, in Memphis, Tennessee* (he said), *Dr. Martin Luther King, Jr. was killed by an assassin's bullet. As Doctor King and a few associates stood on the hotel balcony discussing plans for a rally on behalf of the city's sanitation workers, a shot rang out from across the alley and Dr. King fell mortally wounded...Martin Luther King was a man who championed freedom and justice for socially and economically deprived Americans of all races...This is one of the darkest days in...*

There was a stunned silence as the report continued, detailing events immediately following the shooting. Dr. King was pronounced dead at the hospital. There were, as yet, no arrests, no suspects.

Black convicts clustered around the teevee sets in each of the cellblock Day Rooms, uplifted faces the color of ashes in the flickering light.

*...Rumors continue to circulate that a white man was seen leaving the area...President Johnson says it is a tragic loss for all mankind...*

Earlier that day, King had said:

> *...We've got some difficult days ahead, but it really doesn't matter, because I have been to the mountaintop...I have been to the mountaintop...*

Tension thick as porridge laced the cellblocks.

Billy 3X raced all the way up to the third tier to tell Voodoo what had happened. He waited, expecting Voodoo to issue an order. But Voodoo displayed no emotion; his eyes flicked from Billy's broad black face to some distant vision beyond the cell bars. It was several moments before he spoke.

"Go," he said quietly. "Tell the brothers that the time is near. Wait until I give the word. Then Allah will be avenged...As-Salaam Aliakum."

"Wa-Aliakum Salaam."

Voodoo leaned against his bunk and thought about what the next few days would bring. Haunted by a sense of time and destiny, he could feel the moment crystallize into history. Though he knew King had not been a true spokesman for his race, he was still a black man who had been murdered. Another black man murdered by the white establishment. How many more would it take?

There was no doubt in his mind that the killer was white. Long before the suspect was in custody, Voodoo knew. It was a Mr. Charley. A White Devil. Four thousand years after Mr. Yacub, the White Devils were still killing blacks. Four thousand years and nothing had changed. Nothing. After all the legislation, the rhetoric, the promises, nothing had really changed.

In order to survive, the black man would have to rise up and throw off the yoke of the oppressor...Stand with dignity and power, said Marcus Garvey...The stage was set. It was time for the Players to enter. They had nothing left to lose.

As if to reaffirm Voodoo's hatred, Moose Rankin walked by on his way to the showers, a mass of soft white flesh that quivered with each step. He whistled a tune, oblivious to his rendezvous with destiny.

Officer Dunsmore furnished the first joke in the Watch Commander's Office.

"You hear they got the guy who shot King?"

"Yeah?"

"Yeah…Arrested him for shootin' coons outta season."

An appreciative audience joined in the laughter.

The days following the assassination were filled with commentaries, news bulletins, interviews and renewed rioting across the nation. President Johnson ordered nine thousand National Guard troops into Washington D.C. in the wake of rioting Negro youths who looted shops and set fire to anything that would burn. Eight people were killed and more than two thousand arrested.

A National Day of Mourning was observed.

The widow King led an orderly march through the streets of Memphis. She urged the crowd to carry on in the spirit of brotherhood and non-violence. One elderly Negro woman died of a heart attack during the speech.

On April ninth, the funeral service was held at Ebenezer Baptist Church in Atlanta. The coffin was drawn through the streets on a mule wagon, followed by fifty thousand mourners. Fifty thousand mourners singing We Shall Overcome.

The attitude among the white convicts was one of guarded disdain. Overt contempt was tempered by the fact that blacks were beginning to move in ever larger groups, some openly hostile.

It was during those days that Voodoo composed his Freedom Manifesto. When it was finished he gave the word and the shit came-down…

The hour of righteousness has arrived, said Preacher, closing the Bible and tucking it under his arm…So beware the jabberwock, homeboys, the jaws that bite, the claws that catch. And beware of false prophets who come in drag to deceive and degrade…

# CHAPTER 44

The takeover was simple.

Five minutes before noon count, when most of the convicts were already in their cells, the guards in North Block were taken hostage at knife point. The hospital was opened from the inside by one of Voodoo's men, and Doctors Dorfield, Masley and a lone guard were also taken hostage. In all, there were eleven hostages. Even Voodoo was surprised at how easy it was.

*Count in five minutes...*
*Count in five minutes...*

Quinlan left the compound a half hour earlier to pursue his petulant piece in the privacy of the Dreamland Motel. In his mind a daytime dalliance was safer; his wife seemed to be getting suspicious of all the late night meetings.

The count commenced in Control with no knowledge of the takeover. Lt. Wotek sat at his desk, outcount and cellcount sheets spread out in front of him. The black conference speaker squawked with background noise.

"Ready to receive the count," he said. "East Block?"

"Wilson in East. Count is seven fourteen."

"Correct...West Block?"

"Nelson in West, sir. Count is seven ninety one."

"...Ninety one?"

"Uh...Yessir...That right?"

"That's correct, Nelson. Just pulling your chain, so to speak."

"Thank you, sir."

"Don't mention it...Why aren't you in North Block?"

"I'm covering for Osborne on a medical. Matuzak's in North."

"Be nice if someone told the Watch Commander," said Wotek. "You'll do that next time, Nelson? Inform the Watch Commander if you're doing musical chairs out there with your assignments?"

"Oh, yessir. Will do. Roger wilco and out."

"Good," said Wotek, shaking his head. "… South Block?"

"Wetzle in South. Count is seven ten."

"Correct. North Block?……North Block?…"

He turned to the Watch Sergeant.

"Comstock, call North Block on the other phone and find out why Matuzak's not on the conference line for count."

Comstock dialed from the phone on his desk. He listened for a few moments, then pressed the receiver to his chest.

"Somebody's there," he said.

Wotek rolled his eyes.

"Well, tell him to push the conference line button on his te-le-phone so we can hear-him. Even Matuzak ought to be able to handle that."

Comstock relayed the message. In a few seconds there was a click in the speaker.

"Matuzak," said Wotek, "you think you could get on board here with the count?"

"Eight."

"…Eight?"

Voodoo put his feet up on the desk.

"Maybe more," he said.

"Who is this?" said Wotek.

There was no answer.

"Whoever you are, you'd better stop foolin' around and put Officer Matuzak on the phone."

"We not foolin' around," said Voodoo. "We got eight of your people. Few more in the hospital. That's the count. Ten, eleven maybe. So far. What else you need to know?"

"Who-is-this?"

"This is the Voodoo Man. Your worst nightmare, white boy."

Wotek sat up in his chair.

"You better quit…"

317

"Listen, fool. We got your people. We own this cellblock. North Block ours now. And the hospital. You want it, you come get it."

Wotek scribbled a message on a scratch pad and handed it to Comstock:

## Get Quinlan

Comstock headed for Quinlan's office.

"You can't get away with this, Jefferson," said Wotek. "If you're smart you'll call this off while there's still time."

"Time for what?"

"...Negotiations."

Voodoo's laugh was forced.

"Too late," he said. "Four hundred years too late."

"How do I know you've got hostages?"

"You think Matuzak just let me use the phone?"

"Let me talk to him."

Voodoo held the phone to Matuzak's ear.

"Matuzak?"

"Yessir, it's me."

"What the hell's going on over there?"

"...Looks like a hostage situation, sir."

"Looks-like-a-hostage-situation," said Wotek. "Jesus Christ, Matuzak, are you a hostage or not?"

"Eh...That's affirmative."

"How did you manage that?"

"It all happened so fast I..."

Billy X placed the point of his knife against Matuzak's cheek and sliced toward his nose. Matuzak screamed.

"Jesus...Help!"

Earl silenced him with a pipe to the head. Matuzak fell like a slaughterhouse steer.

"...tuzak?...Matuzak?"

"Matuzak had a little accident," said Voodoo. "Fell down and hurt himself."

As Sergeant Comstock was knocking on Superintendent Quinlan's door in Control, Robert Quinlan was hovering over the ripe form of Julie Mendlesohn in the Dreamland Motel. His tongue caressed her navel, a tiny jewel-like protuberance bobbing on a sea of stretch marks. Passion throbbed like a hammered thumb between his eager thighs.

"If any of my men get hurt, Jefferson, there'll be hell to pay," said Wotek. "Keep that in mind. I'm holding you personally responsible for…"

"Get Quinlan," said Voodoo.

"He's…on his way."

Wotek looked up as Comstock entered the office and shook his head.

"…Some of your men gonna die, white boy, 'less we get some action."

Wotek swallowed hard and looked around the room at the other grim faces.

"What kind of action?"

"We let you know. When the Boss Man gets there, tell him Voodoo wants to talk to him."

"You can stop this now, Jefferson. Before it goes any further… before it's too late."

"Been too late for a long time, Massah Wo-tek. We both know that. Get Quinlan. Have him call. I be right here. And white boy?"

"Yeah?"

"You don't have much time."

Voodoo hung up.

Wotek flipped the switch that turned off the conference line to North Block and spoke to the other three cellblocks.

"The rest of you hear that?"

A trio of voices mumbled affirmative.

"Okay," said Wotek. "Keep everyone locked down. Official word is that the count hasn't cleared yet. Hang up and wait for orders."

Wotek called Quinlan's house.

"He's not here," said Mrs. Quinlan. "Said he had to speak at the Kiwanis luncheon today."

"Of course," said Wotek. "The Kiwanis luncheon. Here it is on his calendar."

"Anything wrong?"

"No. Just need to get some papers signed. It can wait. Sorry to bother you."

He hung up and frowned. Where could Quinlan be? He dialed Captain Greer's office.

"Greer here." He was beginning to affect a slight British accent.

"This is Lt. Wotek, Captain."

"Yes?"

"We have a hostage situation in North Block."

Greer stroked his mustache.

"Ah...A hostage situation."

"Inmates have taken eight hostages in North Block. A few more in the hospital. We don't know how many all told."

"Ah...Hostages."

Wotek heard him light his pipe.

"Where's the superintendent?"

"Not on the compound."

"What's your appraisal of the situation?" said Greer.

"They're serious...And they want to talk to Quinlan."

"About what?"

"Wouldn't say. They won't talk to anyone but Quinlan."

"Who are they?...Who's the ringleader?"

"Voodoo."

"Voodoo," he said thoughtfully. "A bad nigger."

Wotek nodded.

"Everyone else locked down?" said Greer.

"Yes."

"Good. Alert the Gun Tower guards...And don't let anyone out of the cellblocks."

"What about the hostages?"

"...Stall. Wait for Quinlan. They'll be safe for now. I'll be here if you need me."

Greer cradled the phone and leaned back in his chair. His hands were shaking. He sucked on his pipe, but it had gone out...He thought seriously about early retirement.

Initially, few of the convicts in North Block knew what had happened. Voodoo and the others had entered the guard shack moments after Count in five minutes was announced on the Yard, put a knife to Matuzak's throat and taken over. A similar scenario was being played out on the other wing of the cellblock. Voodoo waited a minute or two for everyone to get in their cells, then rattled the lever and slowly pulled it down. He smiled as the cell doors slammed shut tier after tier.

There were twenty men in the takeover group, fifteen in the cellblock and five in the hospital. They had taken a solemn oath that they would kill the hostages and face death themselves unless their list of demands was met. Yet, none of them had seen the list. If they had, perhaps their response would have been different. But only Voodoo knew.

All the men were armed with a variety of knives and blunt instruments. A small can of gasoline had been stolen from the Vocational Auto Repair Shop. The keys to the pharmacy were obtained and a large cache of drugs delivered to North Block from the adjoining Hospital. Shortly after, the carnage began. Individual cells were opened to release fellow revolutionaries, others opened to brutalize, beat and sodomize inmates selected beforehand. Some were killed to settle old debts long festering in the shadows behind the walls.

With the exception of Moose and Stan, the Watch Crew was outcounting in Control. Stan seldom went in until one or two o'clock in the afternoon, preferring to spend the time either sparring in the gym or walking the Yard. Moose, who would normally have been outcounting in Control, had a dental appointment that made him too late to get on the outcount sheet. He was in cell 326…North Block.

Quinlan returned at one thirty, drained but smiling, his boxer shorts uncomfortable sticky with the residue of recent passion. A stop at the Watch Commander's Office got his adrenaline flowing again in short order. Quinlan paced the floor while Wotek filled him in on what had happened. He cursed himself for not seeing the possibility beforehand, for not taking proper precautions, for not shipping Voodoo and some of the others to Quentin or Folsom. Now that the riot was a reality, he knew he would have to put it down quickly and quietly. The more publicity it got, the worse it was going to be. Political aspirants didn't need that kind of publicity.

"Dial North Block," he said.

Comstock dialed and handed the phone to Quinlan.

"…Jefferson?" he said.

"This The Man?" said Voodoo.

"This is Superintendent Quinlan."

"The-Man," said Voodoo. "Where you been? You got big trouble right here on the plantation."

"What the hell's going on over there?"

"Oh, we got some hostages…Some white folks. Got a list of things need to be done."

"This is the penitentiary, Jefferson. You don't…"

"Yeah," said Voodoo. "Penitentiary pretty much the same way it is on the streets. White folks tellin' black folks what to do, when to do it. Not much different. You got a few oreos now to help out, make it look okay, like a community thing. Good guys against the bad guys. Keep the bad niggers locked up, so's folks will be safe out there.…"

"What is it you want?"

"Black man wants freedom, Boss. Not the bullshit kind you white folks want to hand out. Real freedom. Wants people to hear. America to hear. Bring the teevee people. Radio people…We want the people to know how it is, how it really is. How it's been for four hundred years. We gonna tell how slavery is today—nineteen hundred and sixty mothafuckin' eight."

"…We can't do that," said Quinlan.

"What is it you can't do?"

"Bring teevee cameras, radio people. We can't just…"

"Better learn how. Better learn real quick, because if nobody comes, we gonna start killin' people real soon. Your people, Boss Man. Pretty white folks. That ain't gonna play so good on the evenin' news. People gonna wonder what that fool Quinlan doin' out there."

"You're an intelligent man, Jefferson. You must realize that you can't get away with this."

"Depends on what you mean by get away with it. See, we not afraid to die. Most black folks in this country already dead and don't know it, don't have enough sense to lay down and stop breathin'. Most black folks still slaves, still niggers…Man needs dignity, respect. Man don't have that, he don't have nothin'. He just a nigger slave."

"Respect?" said Quinlan. "You get respect when you earn it."

"Don't play me for a fool."

"Listen..."

"You listen, fool," Voodoo snarled."You not runnin' nothin' now. I be callin' the shots. You hear me?"

"...Yes."

"Good. Governor needs to be here, the newspapers, the..."

"I just can't call the Governor and..."

"Find a way, Boss Man. Find a way if you want to see your people alive again. We gonna kill them pretty white folks one by one. Gonna cut they throats and watch them bleed all that white blood. So find a way. And watch the North Block gate. Don't get too close. Just watch. We got a present for you soon."

Voodoo hung up.

Quinlan held the receiver in his hand and stared at it.

"God-dammit!" he said slamming the receiver down. "Get Hebner and Powell and Cheswick. Who's the maintenance super?"

"Russell."

"Get him, too. Have them in my office in ten minutes. Tell Russell to bring the layout of North Block and the Hospital. The blue-line drawings."

"You want me to call Greer?"

"No," he snapped. "He'll just get in the way."

Voodoo smiled and leaned back in his chair, savoring the moment. He was in control now; Quinlan had no choice but to do his bidding.

He scanned the opening lines of his Freedom Manifesto. It began by paraphrasing the first portion of the Declaration of Independence.

> *When in the course of human events, it becomes necessary for one people to break the chains of bondage, to destroy a system which enslaves and degrades, extreme measures must be taken...*

Extreme measures. It was pure Voodoo, a bitter blend of the old (the Reverend Elijah Muhammad) and the new (Malcolm X) revolutionary rhetoric. He felt sure that the document would inflame the black community, give them the courage to rise up and strike down the white oppressors. He quoted extensively from Frederick Douglass:

> *Those who profess freedom yet deprecate agitation are men who want crops without plowing the ground; they want rain without thunder and lightning...Power concedes nothing without demand. The limits of tyrants are proscribed by the endurance of those they oppress...*

And if George Jefferson, Child of the Projects, Son of the Great Serpent, could take over a prison, command the airwaves, speak to the People, expose the System for what it was, then perhaps other things were possible. Perhaps even freedom. It would give his brothers and sisters the courage to continue the struggle. With the assassination of Martin Luther King fresh in their minds, they would realize how the white world dealt with peacemakers. Force was the only power they understood. His Freedom Manifesto would unite his people and play upon the passions of a nation.

But he knew that his final request would seal his own fate, as well as the fate of those who followed him; that's why he had not shown them the list of demands. The Manifesto ended with the demand that all black political prisoners be released (and in his mind he considered all black prisoners to be political prisoners). They would have to deny him; there was no way they could agree to it...He would then have no choice but to kill the hostages—all of them. He had already accepted his own martyrdom, knowing that his blood would nourish the seeds of the revolution. His hour on stage would be brief; he must make the most of it.

And the others? How would they react if they knew? He could only guess. A few would stand with him. But only a few. For the rest it was a game, a penitentiary game—something to do.

The afternoon spiraled quickly into violence. Massive amounts of drugs were ingested; padlocked years of rage released in a single afternoon. Porcelain toilets and wash basins were torn from their moorings and smashed to pieces. Anything that could be broken, was broken. Mattresses were shredded and burned. The strident sounds of pain being inflicted were mixed with shouts of triumph to form an eerie background symphony.

Bingo Pierce was among the first casualties, doused with gasoline and torched in his own cell. He bounced off the walls and the bars in a frantic effort to escape. He opened his mouth to scream, but the flames ate the words. He finally sank to the floor as if he were melting, clothing and skin like cinder. Leroy got sick from the smell.

"That'a hold a white Aryan Nation muffuckah," said Earl.

Voodoo made no effort to intervene. Late in the afternoon he took several Benzedrine tablets from the pile on his desk. He wanted to be alert when his time came to take center stage.

When the five black convicts came to Moose's cell, he spit at them and called them stupid niggers. But even at three hundred pounds, he was no match for them. Billy 2X was the one who drove the screwdriver into his eye, spraying them both with blood. It was a struggle; death came slowly.

Quinlan talked at length to the station commander of the police department in the nearby town of Fremont, requesting help, but stressing the need for discretion lest the local media publicize this small incident and unduly alarm the community. Captain Ragsdale understood perfectly. By five o'clock that afternoon, several police sharpshooters lay low on the roofs of South Block and the Control building.

At five fifteen, Voodoo called Control and informed Quinlan that the main entrance to North Block would be opening soon. He warned that if any attempt to storm the cellblock was made, all the hostages would be killed. He wanted to know where the reporters were, the teevee cameras, the governor. Quinlan said he was working on it; those things took time. Voodoo told him he better hurry because he didn't have much time left.

At five thirty, the heavy steel grid door slid open and two black men emerged dragging a naked body. They leaned forward, straining against the load, each at the end of a long, limp arm. They pulled the body out onto the walkway, dropped the arms and hurried back into North Block.

Quinlan watched through his binoculars from an office on second floor. The gathering shadows made it difficult to see, but it was apparent that the body was white. Big. Maybe three hundred pounds. Bloody. And dead.

Later, when the body was examined, they found numerous stab wounds, a screwdriver imbedded in the left eye, the shattered end of a broomstick protruding from the buttocks. They identified the body as that of Patrick "Moose" Rankin, A-79724, serving 220 for Possession of Marijuana, Second Offense…R.I.P.

When the phone rang in Control a few minutes later, Quinlan was on the main floor to answer it himself.

"This is Quinlan."

"That was a fat racist pig."

"That was murder, Jefferson."

"No, that was justice. That was one for, what…a hundred? A thousand? How many black babies you make orphans, Boss Man?"

"I won't dignify that with an answer."

"No need to," said Voodoo. "White folks been killin' black folks for so long they done lost count. What's another nigger, more or less?

"…That's not what's at stake here."

"Wrong. That's exactly what's at stake. We talkin' about freedom. About justice. The right to live with dignity. You want to keep us in the ghettoes, in the prisons, locked up somewhere so you won't have to deal with us. Won't have to look at us, black skin and all. That's what we talkin' about. Justice, fool…"

"We can't talk about anything until you release the hostages."

"No way."

"You give up the hostages," said Quinlan, "I give you my word you won't be prosecuted."

"And then it's back to business as usual?"

"You can work within the system to change…"

"Black man got no part of the system," Voodoo said angrily. "We been workin' for four hundred years tryin' to change your system. See, it's a white system run by white folks who don't see a need to change the system, don't see a reason to let the black man outta his chains. Works just fine the way it is."

"The critical point right now," said Quinlan, "is that the hostages have to be…"

"You don't get some news people here real quick, those hostages gonna start comin' out like that fat racist pig—dead. That's how we gonna release them."

"This is a mistake, Jefferson."

"Get some people here," he snapped.

"We're doing all we can."

"It's not enough…And we need some food, white boy. My men don't like waitin' on dinner."

"I'll…have it sent over."

"And Boss Man? You got till seven o'clock to get some teevee and radio people here. Nobody here by seven, the first hostage dies."

"That's less than two hours."

"Right," said Voodoo. "Better get movin'. Not much time left. Your plantation gonna look real bad if you don't hurry." He hung up the phone.

Convicts in the other three cellblocks buzzed with rumors about what was going on. As the light faded, flames could be seen on several tiers in North Block. Burn, baby, burn, came the chant…Just like the long, hot summer of '65…Burn, baby, burn…Burn that muffuckah to the muffuckin' ground!

Stan lay on his bunk and listened to the sounds that drifted across the Yard, remembering the Watts Riots and his own time in the County Jail. A lifetime ago, it seemed. Somehow he had managed to endure it all—the terrible fears, the rape, the humiliation, the physical beatings, the time in the Hole, all of it. He had survived; he took some measure of pride in that. And had he, in the process, become Real, whatever that meant? He didn't know. But he had changed; he knew that much. Somehow, and in some way, he had changed, though he didn't have the words to explain it—even to himself.

He sat up, lit a cigarette and looked out through the bars. Two guards hurried along the gunwalk. Trouble.

### Burn Baby Burn

Big trouble. It was like a Greek tragedy. Chaos waiting for the deus ex machina to descend and solve the problem. There was a time when Stan had dutifully prayed and waited for answers, but no celestial messenger had come to provide them, or to heal his wounds, or to restore his sanity. (He remembered a priest telling him years before—Silence is God's first language. Maybe that was it.) Instead, he'd been left with the madness of being confined like a rat in a maze where the big rats got all the food and eventually killed all the little rats. Nature's own remedy.

Life was fragile behind the walls. Little rats interested in survival developed ways to appear bigger then they were; like puffer fish they added to their stature by being either crazy, fearless, or homicidal. They adapted, doing whatever was necessary to survive. Evolution at its finest.

And what about the Blue Fairy? Did she have the answer? (If you can be brave, truthful and unselfish, someday you'll be a Real Boy.) Geppetto? Jiminy Cricket? For awhile he was sure that Bonnie was the answer. Had he been looking for God between soft feminine thighs all these years? At times it had been the Heaven Hill Kentucky Bourbon, or the pills, or a combination of the two. Fix me. Maybe that's why they called it a Fix. Surely something Out There was going to be his salvation.

But for all his professed resistance to religion, he often found himself in God's Bargain Basement making deals, bartering future conduct for Get-Out-Of-Jail-Free cards.

Maybe the answer (whatever the question) was just the will, or the willingness, to endure, to survive no matter what the price. Maybe the answer was that there was no answer. And maybe, just maybe, God was so cleverly hidden, so deeply immersed in creation itself, in everything (and everyone?), that Stan couldn't find Him (or Her) without examining the world he had spent a lifetime trying to avoid. One of those mystic poets had said as much:

> *God is closer than hands or feet...*

Stan carefully extinguished his half-smoked cigarette and returned it to the pack, then took off his left shoe and sock. He retrieved a small roll of contraband white tape from under his mattress, slit the half-inch tape lengthwise and began to tear it into short strips less than an inch in length. He carefully placed each strip in a rectangular pattern around the painful corn on the fourth toe of his left foot. The corn hurt all the time if he didn't tape it to take some of the pressure off. His shoes never seemed to fit right. Santa Rosa high tops with real leather, either too big or too small. He began to wonder if they even made size sevens…Rome's burning, he thought, and I'm taping my toe…Jesus H. Christ…

Quinlan sat in his office with Hebner, Powell, Cheswick and Russell and studied the blue-line drawings of the North Block-Hospital area. Access through the interconnecting plumbing system was a possibility, though it would be slow; Voodoo would surely have time to kill the hostages before they could get to them.

"We've got to go in," said Quinlan. "A frontal assault. It's the only way."

"No hope for negotiations, sir?" said Powell.

Quinlan's glance was one of contempt.

"You don't negotiate with convicts," he said. "They don't have anything to negotiate with. Convicts don't have rights, Powell. Part of the reason we're in this …situation, is that we've been far too willing to compromise, to be nice. It's not about being nice. They don't understand that anyway. They think that if you're nice, you're weak. You should know that by now. It's about law and order, about being in control, about doing the right thing. Those…convicts will regret the day they challenged my authority."

He rolled up the drawings and got ready to head back to the Watch Commander's Office.

"Cheswick, how long will it take you to get tear gas canisters and twenty men in riot gear ready to enter the cellblock?"

"We'll have to call in some extra men…Say two hours?"

"We don't have two hours. Have them ready in an hour…Bear in mind that there may be casualties. Some inmates may suffer serious injuries. Inadvertently, of course. You don't make scrambled eggs without breaking some eggs. Do you understand?"

Cheswick grinned; he understood exactly what Quinlan meant. And who he meant.

"Yessir. I understand." He held up two fingers in a V sign.

"That's correct," said Quinlan. "Ragsdale, your men are in position?"

"Yes."

Quinlan permitted himself a trace of a smile.

"Good," he said. "Here's what we're going to do. When I get to the entrance to North Block, have…"

During the next hour, the convicts in the other cellblocks began clamoring for food, banging on the bars, chanting, We want food.

"Shall we feed them?" said Comstock.

"Not yet," said Quinlan. "It's only been a few hours since lunch; they won't starve."

He headed for his office to refine his strategy for gaining entrance to the cellblock.

Voodoo called his soldiers together.

"You are my brothers," he said. "We live together and we die together. Soon the free people will be here. Newspapers. Teevee. The governor. The world will be watching and listening; we must conduct ourselves with dignity. Much will depend on how we appear."

He studied the faces. Leroy. Evans. Delray. Billy 2X. Dumont. Hubbard. Cleavus. The others…they were not fully with him yet.

He raised his voice.

"The time is short. We must be ready. Must be. You are the heart and soul of this Army of Liberation; you carry the banner of Righteousness for our people. Stand by me, my brothers. Hear me. The future of the black man in America depends on what we do today and in the days to come."

There were a few half-hearted black power salutes and mumbled agreement.

Was it resentment he sensed? A lack of commitment? Did it seem that now they only wanted to get back to the drugs, the violence and the sleek young boys? Was the rendezvous with history forgotten? He knew he must act quickly to get their attention..

He deliberately chose Dumont Wilson, the biggest of the group, walked up and slapped him hard across the face.

"Stand up, nigger," he hissed. "Stand up straight."

Dumont's eyes flashed for a second, then he stood at attention. The others followed suit; none had any wish to confront Voodoo.

"We speak for the people," said Voodoo, his voice a barely controlled fury. "We speak for the black people who have no voice, who cannot speak for themselves. It is our destiny to be heard. You have been chosen to fight against slavery and injustice. You have been chosen because you are the strongest, the best. We cannot fail. We will not fail....Stand with me now."

It was as close as Voodoo would ever come to asking for anything. They understood that. Voodoo exchanged a handshake with each man, reaffirming their bond.

"We with you, blood," said Dumont.

Voodoo thanked him with a nod.

"Billy 2X, get Dunsmore," he said. "He be the first to die."

Cheswick reported to Quinlan in less than an hour with tear gas canisters and twenty men in riot gear.

"Good work," said Quinlan. He was beginning to feel better about his chances. He briefed the men and deployed them out on a Yard that was now mostly shadows. Their instructions were to approach from the blind side of the cell block, hug the building and make their way toward the main entrance to North Block without being detected. As arranged, he waited ten minutes and then called North Block.

"This is Quinlan."

"I'm listenin'," said Voodoo.

"We need to talk."

"Where the news people? The teevee people? The governor?"

"On their way."

"Dunsmore gonna die real soon, Boss. 'Less you hurry. Correctional Officer Dunsmore. One of your po-lices. Your white po-lices."

"...We need to talk."

"Time runnin' out. Time to say goodbye to a pig."

"Wait," said Quinlan. "I'll come in...in to North Block." His mouth was dry.

"You wanna come in here, Boss Man?"

"Yes. We need to discuss this...this whole thing. Talk about it. Work something out before the reporters and television people get here, before it's too late to…to turn back. I think we can reach some kind of compromise…Avoid a confrontation." He held his breath.

Voodoo smiled. The amphetamine rush made his head spin. His mind surrounded the notion and seized it. He liked it. Of course. They would take Quinlan hostage. Voodoo himself would kill him later, as the world watched, after he had delivered his Freedom Manifesto. White blood spilled in front of a nation. His last act would be killing Warden Quinlan, ensuring his place in history alongside Jomo Kenyatta, Frantz Fanon, Malcolm X and the other heroes of the black revolution.

"Come alone," said Voodoo.

"Of course."

"We search you."

"I know."

"Anything happens, anything goes wrong, you die and all your people die. All the pretty white folks. I say the word and they all die."

"I understand," said Quinlan.

"…Come ahead."

Voodoo told Delray to stay down by the sally port and bring Quinlan back the minute he got there.

Quinlan cradled the phone and turned to Hebner.

"You're in charge during my absence," he said. "Captain Greer is not fit to command. If anything goes wrong with the original plan, storm the cellblock. Use every available man."

"What about the hostages?"

"My orders are to storm the cellblock if anything goes wrong. Are we clear on that?"

"Yessir."

Quinlan turned and walked out of the room. Leonard watched him from the Watch Office across the hall; he could only guess what he was up to. Quinlan stopped near the rear door, took a deep breath and motioned for the guard to open it.

It's now or never, he thought. Be decisive. That's what his father always said. Somebody challenges you, respond immediately. John Quinlan had always been big on decisive action. Even his suicide was decisive. No pills. No long drawn-out scenes. No farewell note.

Just bang! the .38 special slug spiraling out of the barrel, through the roof of his mouth, through the brain cavity, spattering bits of gray matter on the bedroom wall. Decisive. One hand on his gun, the other on his balls.

Quinlan viewed his meeting with Voodoo as something more than just two men locked in a power struggle; in a larger sense he saw it as holding the line between civilization and chaos, as a confrontation between Good and Evil. Black and White (it was certainly no mystery who was causing all the trouble. All you had to do was read the newspaper). And it was his job, Robert Quinlan's job, to see that the line wasn't breached. If people had to die, so be it. Voodoo was certainly expendable. For that matter, they were all expendable. If having one or two fewer convicts (especially Negro convicts) shifted the balance of power in his favor, he was all for it. Courage is acting in the face of fear, his father reminded him from the grave.

The air was cool; he felt chilled. North Block loomed across the Yard like a giant galleon, parallel rows of windows on each of the four tiers glittering like pale points of light. He didn't want to appear hurried; he knew they were watching in the dim light. It might have been a casual stroll across the Yard. But his heart was thumping noisily and his breathing was labored. Each step closer to North Block heightened his fear.

As he approached, he could see the men crouching in the shadows at the base of the North Block walls. He walked by Moose's bloody corpse without looking at it.

He arrived at the main entrance and peered between the even squares of welded iron bars. He could see nothing until a pair of eyes appeared in one of the small rectangular squares.

"It's him," said the eyes.

"Alone?"

"…Yeah."

Sitting alone in the guard shack, Voodoo suddenly realized that it was all wrong. Quinlan wasn't coming in to talk; he was too smart for that. He wasn't a negotiator. If he had wanted to really negotiate, he would have sent someone else in to do it. He was Old School and Old School wardens didn't negotiate; they met force with force. And if they opened the North Block door to let him in, Voodoo knew that only bad things would happen. He grabbed his knife off the desk and sprinted down the cellblock corridor, knowing he had to get to the entrance before Quinlan did.

A beam of light scanned Quinlan from head to foot and finally settled on his face. He blinked and lowered his head. The light went off. He heard a bolt click and the gate began to slide open. It took eight seconds. Quinlan counted them, each one a lifetime. A black hand reached out to grab his arm, the palm pink and faintly luminous in the pale light. He drew back without realizing it. Now, now, he wanted to shout.

But before he could move out of harm's way, Voodoo rushed into the sally port screaming like a man possessed and plunged the knife into Quinlan's shoulder; feeling the blade cut deeply into sinew and flesh. Before he could recover, Voodoo stabbed him again. Had the knife been longer, Quinlan might not have survived. As it was, in the brief time between his attack on Quinlan and his own death, Voodoo believed he had struck the fatal blow. His last few seconds were filled with a sense of satisfaction at having killed his hated adversary. He was never to know he had not succeeded, that even as he was basking in that momentary sense of accomplishment, it was all coming down around him.

Quinlan stumbled back, clutching his shoulder, just as the first tear gas canister whistled by his ear and bounced off an interior wall. Cheswick was the first man in. Before Voodoo could move, Cheswick quickly clubbed him into submission. As he lay unconscious on the floor of the sally port, Cheswick had the final say with his weighted nightstick, visciously beating him until his skull was crushed and brain matter began to ooze through the gashes.

"You ain't shit, nigger," he said, the voice muffled through the gas mask he was wearing.

Looking like men from outer space in their gas masks and riot gear, correctional personnel were inside the cellblock before the startled convicts could react. Tear gas canisters exploded down the long corridors, skittering crazily along the floor. Convicts ran into the few open cells before the onslaught. Some, unable to decide what to do, were bludgeoned where they stood.

Quinlan's guess that the hostages were being held in the first tier Day Room proved to be correct. A four man team sprinted to the end of the wing and took control before any of the guards were killed. Only Officer Dunsmore was seriously hurt, requiring surgery to close deep gashes on his chest and face inflicted by Billy 2X in a fervent display of loyalty and rage.

There was only token resistance; in half an hour it was over. Voodoo was not there to lead them. Only Leroy, Dumont and Delray put up a fight, and they paid for their efforts with serious injuries. Members of the Army of Liberation wandered the corridors blinded and choking from the tear gas, most eventually felled by a nightstick. Few escaped the wrath of Cheswick's expanded Goon Squad, who went about their work with obvious relish, hammering convicts until they were arm weary and covered with blood, keeping the world safe from violence.

All the convicts who were not locked up or crumpled on the floor were herded outside, made to strip and lie face down on the concrete Yard with their hands behind them. Tungsten searchlights swept the Yard. Correctional personnel, barking like dogs, roamed the field of fleshy buttocks, occasionally rapping a convict with a thick oak stick. Gun tower guards relaxed but kept a wary eye on the Yard. The sharpshooters exhaled slowly.

Voodoo's body remained on the floor in the sally port for a long time, his shaved scalp split like an overripe pomegranate in half a dozen places, his head resting in a pool of blood. Later that night, correctional personnel dragged the body out to lie next to Moose Rankin at the entrance to North Block. Those suspected of taking part in the riot were locked up in J Wing. Medical treatment for all the rioters was withheld until the following day.

When they came with the fire hoses to wash away the debris, the Freedom Manifesto, its message neatly lettered in ballpoint pen ink, disintegrated from the force of the water and was lost forever. The final tally was eleven white convicts killed (at least four known members of the Aryan Nation), and dozens injured, some seriously. Three of the Negroes, (including Voodoo) were also killed. There were only a few custodial injuries. Officer Matuzak received sixteen stitches for the cut on his cheek. The one officer requiring extensive treatment was Dunsmore, though it was said that Dr. Dorfield sought medical attention outside the correctional community for injuries suffered from being repeatedly sodomized.

Not wishing to draw attention to his own injury, Quinlan quietly received medical treatment at a local hospital. It seemed adequate at the time, though he never regained full use of his right arm.

And though he was not pleased with the outcome, Quinlan was satisfied that it was not as disastrous as it could have been. He leaked a limited version to the local newspaper; the efforts of the Army of Liberation were recorded for the black people of America on page nine of the Fremont *Daily News*...A racial disturbance, not unheard of in the late sixties...Several fatalities, some injuries. Situation quickly brought under control by the quick action of...

The *News* noted that due to the prompt and forceful action of Superintendent Quinlan, the disturbance was quickly suppressed. When interviewed, Quinlan described the incident as minor, modestly down playing his role. A superficial cut, he said in reference to questions about his injury. After all, he seemed to imply, boys will be boys.

Within the correctional community, where the real story was known, he received mixed reviews. Some hailed him as a hero. The California State Employee Association magazine (*The Watchman*), in an article about the incident, praised his conduct and asked that he...

> ...*Accept the sincere gratitude of the men in khaki everywhere, who daily face*... et cetera et cetera

Most, however, (notably the pansies in Sacramento whom he despised) were more inclined to think of him as an out-of-control gunslinger who was making up the rules as he went along. There was talk that perhaps Robert Quinlan might be better off with a desk job somewhere in the Department. Deep in the Department. Several positions with long titles and little responsibility were mentioned, among them Chief Advisor to the Director of Corrections, a title long on words, and short on substance.

Attempts to reconstruct the incident were unfruitful. The logistics were known; a small group of Negroes had taken over North Block and the Hospital. But the reasoning behind it remained a mystery. None of the men would talk. Quinlan could only guess at the rationale. All he had was a rambling conversation with Billy 2X about the black man getting justice, respect, dignity, freedom, about black people still being slaves. But what had they really hoped to accomplish? Surely not freedom; even with the hostages, they must have known that freedom was out of the question. The idea that it was an attempt to make a statement, an attempt to dignify an otherwise meaningless existence, did not occur to any of those charged with the investigation. Only Voodoo knew and he took the knowledge to his grave.

They were transferred out and later became known as the Fremont Fifteen, languishing in the Adjustment Center behind the walls in San Quentin. Some of them resurfaced in 1971 during the troubles there. Billy 2X and Delray died that year, cut down by a fusillade of bullets from the number four gun tower. The black community suspected that they had been set up, that a gun had been smuggled in to them in the hope that they would attempt an escape. But they took two of the guards with them—Delvecchio and Murray, the two they hated most. It was in all the papers. Front page. Big headlines. Film at eleven.

## SAN QUENTIN INMATES KILLED
## TRYING TO ESCAPE

To prevent further incidents, Quinlan had the Fremont guard shacks renovated. It was expensive, but he considered it necessary (his political future could hardly stand another incident of this magnitude). When finished, they looked like shark tanks. Guards were instructed in strict new security procedures. Several took early retirement, including Captain Greer.

Since Moose Rankin's family could not be located, Leonard had friends claim the body, have it cremated and spread a handful of ashes along Fourth St. in Santa Monica, near Harvell's Bar and Grill. At 2 A.M.

The scars from the Incident never healed. Prisons throughout the system became ever more territorial and dangerous. Several black groups emerged to challenge the Black Panthers. The Mexican Mafia and the Nuestra Familia fought for control of Folsom. The Aryan Nation spawned the even more radical American Nazi Party in San Quentin. The small trust that allowed limited commerce was breached a hundred times a day.

Racial groups closed ranks, manufacturing myths that would stand as history for future generations of convicts. Voodoo's name went down in the annals of penitentiary lore along with Cecil Hightower, Manny Vargas, Alabama Sam, Freddy the Face, and Ice Burgess.

# CHAPTER 45

Easter was late that year; Good Friday followed the Riot by only a few days.

Father Joe drank himself to sleep Holy Saturday night, an event more common than not. His evening companions were often a bottle of Christian Brother's Brandy (might as well support the homeboys, he thought), and the latest *National Geographic*. He studied the pictures of exotic lands and realized his own exile all the more. All for Jesus. All for Jesus, he mumbled, dozing in the large stuffed chair, dreaming of brightly colored parrots and peacocks and landscapes greener than green. And (God help me, he thought) bare-breasted native women.

The troubles on the Yard depressed him. First it was Junior and that unfortunate lad in his cell. What bothered him most was that Junior didn't seem repentant in the least. He went around with that same beatific smile on his face, receiving communion each morning as if nothing had happened. For the first time, Father Joe could picture him chopping up those townspeople with his boy scout hatchet…with that same saintly smile.

And now, along with the normally murderous venue that added to the body count each month on the Yard, bodies were being discovered with their genitals removed. God in heaven. What next?

The Riot itself only added to his depression. What deeds we visit upon one another, he thought. Created in the image and likeness of God indeed. Murder. Rape. Desecration. Now men were killing women and children in Vietnam. Lord have mercy on us. Lord have mercy. Lord have mercy…

But his Irish tenor was rich and joyful as he said Mass on Easter morning, singing praise to Him who gave meaning to his life…He is risen …Hallelujah! Praise Him all ye nations…Ha-llelu-jah…

Attendance at Mass was up, many inmates wishing to display their newfound rededication to Christian ideals in the light of recent events. Even a few Negroes attended.

Though he had been serving as an altar boy for many years, Junior couldn't seem to get the responses right that morning. He even failed to move the Book from the right side to the left side of the altar, something he never forgot. The inside of his head felt like it was filled with cotton. He had been up all night after ingesting an entire Valo Inhaler furnished by a friend. At the elevation of the Host, he had a vision of God. A true vision. Of God Himself. He couldn't move after that, couldn't say any of the responses…Oh my God, it's God, is what he said to himself.

In a brief emotional sermon, Father Joe talked about Peace and Love and Forgiveness. About Brotherhood and the fact that we were all the same in the eyes of God. All God's children no matter what our color or religious persuasion. Or lack of it. Skin color was of no consequence to the Almighty.

A commotion interrupted his reading of the Last Gospel. He turned just in time to see Esteban Garcia being dragged from his pew and out the door by two correctional officers. Esteban screamed Mexican epithets with all the variations of chinga he could think of. Father Joe held out his hands as if to still the troubled waters. When the buzzing subsided, he returned to the Gospel…

> *…In the beginning was the Word and the Word was with*
> *God and the Word was God…*

His step was unsteady as he left the altar. Back in his office, he retrieved the brandy from his desk, slumped in his chair, buried his face in his hands and sobbed uncontrollably. Junior, absorbed in his vision of God, didn't leave the altar for another half hour.

As a result of the Riots, all April Board appearances were postponed until May. Stan and Greek sat fidgeting on the wooden bench outside the Board Room on the second day of the hearings. Board members hearing cases that day were Albert Cronin and Edward "Mad Dog" Owen.

Stan licked his lips; his mouth was dry.

"Think you'll get your time?" he asked Greek.

They both looked at the closed door at the end of the hallway.

"Who knows?" said Greek. "Depends on who you get, how they feel. Is his ulcer actin' up? Is he havin' trouble with the old lady? It's a crap shoot."

"...I don't figure to be goin' anywhere," said Stan. It was almost a question.

"Too soon," said Greek. "You only got a couple in?"

"A little more than three."

"Murder Two, first beef, you'll do seven, eight, maybe nine if you don't keep your nose clean. Not much more...First few years are always the toughest. After that, you get used to it. Forget the streets. Get a routine goin'. You like books, hit the library. Movies on Saturday night. Jute balls on Wednesday. Smokers every couple of months. Throw away any calendars you got. Do it a day at a time—A.M.'s and P.M.'s."

Greek stood up, pulled at the crotch of his pants and sat down again.

"I ever tell you the story of what Eric told the judge when they sentenced him?"

"No."

"Eric had about forty robberies, assaults, suspicions, you mention it, Eric did it. When the judge in L.A. Superior Court found him guilty, he ran all the charges end to end and gave him three hundred years."

"Jesus. Three hundred years."

"Know what he told the judge?"

"...No."

"He told him, I could do three hundred years on the shitter, Your Honor. Three bills ain't nothin' for a stepper..." Greek shook his head. "Can you believe it? The judge didn't even bother with a contempt charge."

"Man..."

"I gotta get my time soon," said Greek.

"What're your chances?"

"...Not great. The priors are gonna kill me...I got kids, you know." He smiled sheepishly as if the notion embarrassed him. "Girl seven and a boy fifteen. Rocky. Helluva kid…My wife thinks he's into drugs. Stayin' out at night, givin' her all kinds of grief. She can't handle him. Wants to know what to do…Hell, I don't know. I was never into drugs. You ever do drugs?"

"…Some."

"I drink," said Greek. "That's it. Maybe too much but that's it. Never did drugs…Maybe if I was home I could do somethin'."

The door at the end of the hallway opened and Hoss Criner emerged. He turned both thumbs down in the traditional gesture of denial and continued past them down the hallway.

Cheswick stood at the door.

"Smith," he growled.

Stan got up and headed for the Board Room.

"You ain't goin' anywhere," Cheswick whispered as Stan walked by.

"Have a seat, Mr. Smith," said one of the two men seated behind the long table. A name plaque identified him as Albert Cronin. The face to his left resembled a Roman death mask. It belonged to Mad Dog Owen.

Stan sat down.

"I see here we have a first degree murder," said Mad Dog.

Stan felt the skin on the back of his neck tingle. He swallowed and cleared his throat.

"…Second degree," said Stan.

"Somebody ask you to speak, Mister? Ask your opinion, fuckhead?"

"…No."

"Then I'll try again. I see here we have a first degree murder. That correct, Mister?…Now it's your turn."

"No, sir…It was second degree."

"Oh, it says here second degree. But we both know it was first degree, obviously premeditated. Doesn't make any difference what you plea-bargained in court, Smith. This is the real court here. The California Adult Authority." He stared across the table at Stan. "Where'd you get the gun?"

"We had it."

"…Did you always have it, Mister? Did Santa Claus bring it? The Easter Bunny?" The guttural sound that followed might have been a laugh.

"We got it from a dealer. A gun dealer."

"Nice and legit, eh? How long ago?"

"Couple of years," said Stan.

"Why?"

"…For protection."

"Huh. Some protection. You know the guy you killed was a Marine."

Stan stared at the table.

"You ever been in the service? Ever fight for your country?"

"No."

"That figures," said Mad Dog. "I did. World War Two. The Marines."

He thumbed through the file in front of him.

"You kill anyone else we should know about? Like some old lady from Pasadena maybe. Blow her brains out with a shotgun while she was pickin' flowers?"

"…No."

"I understand this guy was fu-cking your wife? That correct?"

Mad Dog's eyes were like small, red-rimmed agates. Stan had difficulty breathing.

"…Might have been."

"You ever do that? Diddle somebody else's pie?"

"No."

"You suppose she was giving him head, too. This Marine guy?"

Stan felt a surge of anger.

"I don't know," he said.

"Then comin' home and kissin' her hubby?" An ugly smile settled on his face. "You'd be doin' a blow job by proxy. Know what I mean?…You suppose that coulda happened?"

Stan tried to sound casual but his voice betrayed him.

"I don't know," he said tightly.

"Make you mad, Mister? Thinkin' about that?"

Stan shrugged.

"Hey," was all he could think of to say.

"You're a mistake waitin' to happen," said Mad Dog, turning a page in Stan's Central File. "You can't even stay outta trouble in here. Been in the Hole twice already. Solitary. Three years and you made it twice. Officer Hebner notes that you're uncooperative. You uncooperative, Smith?"

"No."

"This Officer Hebner believes you witnessed a violent act where a man was killed and then refused to identify the men responsible. That true?"

"No," said Stan.

"Officer Hebner is ly-ing?"

"He was…misinformed about where I was when the incident happened."

"You didn't see anything?"

"I wasn't…close enough to see."

"You know," said Mad Dog, "it would seem like a man with a life top would have better eyesight than that. A man with a life top, a man who was truly on his way toward rehabilitation and interested in parole would demonstrate a more cooperative attitude. Because a cooperative attitude might win him a few friends on the Parole Board. And believe me, you need friends. Bad. The right kind of attitude might even lead to a shortening of a sentence, so instead of doing nine or ten, you might do six or seven. Might. You see, we like to see people change, like to see people become willing to live within society's rules, to speak out when they see someone doing wrong. Be willing to stand up for what's right."

He leaned forward.

"Those convicts, those assholes you're protectin' would give you up in a minute if I offered them a deal like this. A minute." He snapped his fingers. "You cooperate on this thing, Mister, and I'll personally see that you get some consideration next year. Serious consideration…What do you say?"

Stan rubbed the back of his neck and looked at the floor.

"…I would if I could, sir, but I…"

"That's it," said Mad Dog slapping the folder closed and pushing it aside. "You're probably the type who will have to spend a long time being rehabilitated. You are what we call a slow learner, a stupid fucking convict who doesn't recognize a break when he sees one. You're probably too stupid to even be on the streets."

Mad Dog opened the next file in the stack on the table.

"Case closed," he said. "Get him out of here."

Stan got up and walked out of the room; he had trouble keeping his balance.

"We'll let you know," said Cronin.

Greek raised his eyebrows.

Stan turned both thumbs down and kept walking.

"Good luck," he whispered.

# CHAPTER 46

The August heat was oppressive. When the wind blew from the east, Dairy smells filled the cellblocks.

Reno lost the first two fingers of his right hand to a table saw in the Furniture Factory. Attempts to reattach them were unsuccessful; they soon turned black and fell off. His requests for additional pain medication were denied. Though the crutches were gone, the limp was permanent.

Preacher looked at the world through the heat waves that rose from the concrete surface of the Yard.

> *Behold, I cry out against wrongdoing, but I am not heard. They have hardened their hearts against me. They have stripped me of my glory and taken the crown from my head...*

He lowered the book and pressed it to his chest.

> *...And I ask the Lord, why hast Thou forsaken me? Where is Divine Justice? And where is my fucking parole, O All Powerful One?*

Quinlan sat in his office sipping a tall bourbon and water, pondering events of the last few months. With the news of Robert Kennedy's death, he had immediately locked down the entire prison, and kept them locked down for a week. Subsequent violence was not extreme, though he worried about the trend. Further measures might be needed.

He looked at the list of names in a small notebook. Four of the ten names had already been crossed out—Vargas, Weir, Petrocelli,

Schaeffer. He was amazed at how easy it had been to eliminate them. (Jefferson and the others were just lucky accidents.) He rearranged the order of the next six, then changed it again. Finally, unable to decide on the final order, he slipped the notebook back into his inside jacket pocket.

But he never got to implement his plan to clean up Fremont and make it a prison that the people of California could be proud of. Before the year was out he was removed as superintendent and assigned to the newly created position of Chief Advisor to the Director of Corrections, due largely to information furnished by the newly-appointed Captain Powell who headed up the committee charged with the investigation of the Riot. Quinlan was given a small office in a small building in Sacramento. Gavin Belson, only five years out of the University of California at Berkeley with a Masters degree in Criminology and very little on-the-job experience, was appointed to succeed him.

Captain Powell was also instrumental in Lt. Hebner's transfer to Folsom, where he was put in charge of the Inmate Adjustment Center in Building 4A.

The Fly Killing Contest was well underway. Todd Hendricks, Moose's replacement, fashioned a huge flyswatter from some contraband mesh screening and a short broomstick, and had jumped out to an early lead, sometimes killing three or four flies with a single stroke. Todd was Involuntary Manslaughter, having accidentally shot his mother-in-law when he mistook her for an intruder. Stan was in second place. He wasn't discouraged; he knew one good streak would get him close. What he missed most about the Watch Office was the presence of Moose and Paulson; it wasn't the same without them. And there was no way Moose would have let Todd use a flyswatter that big. He would have badgered him until he gave it up. He wondered why Leonard let him get away with it.

Leonard was spending most of his time doodling on sheets of copy paper, filling the wastebasket (which Wotek went through late each night) with drawings of stick figures and trees without leaves. He seemed preoccupied.

The Count drifted in and out like a wraith, looking more cadaverous each day, his body bent by some unseen burden. His legal work suffered. Leonard suspected drugs. He was thinking about having him transferred to the Laundry, reasoning that anyone as worried as the Count seemed to be might be willing to buy release from that worry at almost any price, perhaps even betraying his good friends in the Watch Office in a moment of weakness. He finally decided that it would be better to keep him close by.

Greek was there all the time, rearranging his desk so it was neat, drafting letters to prospective employers, cleaning his fingernails with a paperclip, making coffee, in general doing his Time Off For Good Behavior number.

The Riot and the deaths of Moose and Paulson had changed them all. The Yard itself had changed; episodes of violence were escalating, acts of brutality more common. Something in the mindless act of lashing out, of inflicting pain, seemed to satisfy a long festering need to exercise control. It was almost an obligation, a defining act. You can take everything but my manhood, they seemed to say. This is what men do; this is what manhood is about; this is how we know we are men...This is all we have left.

The forest fire that Leonard had been waiting for broke out on a Sunday in September in the Wheatly National Forest. On Tuesday he spent the day in the Watch Office getting updates from Jules Reiner. Some of the County Detention Camps had already been sent out on the fire line. Wednesday morning, Camp Don Lugo went. The Smoke Eaters and other elite firefighting units from Arizona and Utah were called in. The fire, burning out of control, was rapidly approaching the town of Frazier. The Honor Block Firefighters (Honor Block inmates with less than six months to serve) were due to leave for the fire line Thursday morning.

Leonard approached Stan when they were alone in the Watch Office.

"I have a plan, Mr. Smith."

Stan kept filing the disciplinary cards.

"A plan for retirement, Mr. Leonard? A plan to rob a bank?"

Leonard lowered his voice.

"How about a plan to escape?"

Stan stopped filing.

"You interested?" said Leonard.

"...Might be."

"Some of the Honor Block inmates are going out to the Wheatly fire."

"...And?"

"I can get us on the list to go out with them...They're leaving early tomorrow. There'll just be a driver and a guard from Camp James. All he has is names on a roster. He doesn't know anybody. Just I.D.'s and names on a list. I'll type the list for Control and have the Print Shop make us a couple of I.D.'s. All legit."

Stan didn't know what to say. Escape...He'd never given it much thought, other than fantasizing about it when he first went to jail. It had always seemed more like movie stuff. James Cagney in *Jail Break at the Big House*...ramming the front gate with the Laundry truck, tommy gun blazing, cops toppling like tenpins ...Take that, you dirty rat. That was a jail break.

"...Escape," said Stan. "Then what?"

"Somebody'll pick us up."

"Taxi service, eh? Not bad...Only I don't have any money. No place to go."

"Don't worry. I've got connections. Money. You'll be okay."

Stan went back to filing cards.

"It's crazy," he said. "Too simple. Just walk out with the Fire Crew?"

"That's why it'll work. Krasner's on duty that morning. He's got the I.Q. of a small rock."

"Why me? Why not Greek?"

"They as much as told him they'd give him some serious consideration next year. They won't, but he believes it."

"The Count?"

"He's doing drugs. Too risky. Let's just say I like the way you handle yourself. Did your time in the Hole and kept your mouth shut. That tells me something. You might turn out to be a real business asset."

"I'm not much for business. I'm an engineer."

"Might not be too late for a career change."

"I...I just never thought about it. About escape."

"So think about it," said Leonard.

Stan shoved the filing cabinet drawer closed and stood up.

"…You gotta keep running, eh? After you get out?"

"You see too many movies," said Leonard. "You move to another state, get a new birth certificate, social security number, driver's license and you're home free—a brand new person. Pick a name. Any name. The new you. And you're not exactly public enemy number one. They won't have the entire posse out after you."

"And if we get caught?"

"The firing squad," said Leonard.

"…The what?"

"If we get caught they add a few more years to your time. You doing five to life?"

"Yeah."

"So they add a couple of years. So what?"

Stan looked across the room at the big clock on the wall. It didn't take him long to come to a decision.

"…So count me in," he said.

"Good. Two for lunch at the Brown Derby."

"You know, the first thing I thought about when you brought it up was maybe I'd like to stay and see if I could win the Fly Killing Contest."

"See? You've been here too long already. Another year or so, you'll be permanent."

"What was the prize gonna be? You never said."

"I was planning on two women this year," said Leonard. "White women."

"…White women? I don't get it. Wasn't…"

"An inside joke. Moose ended up with a black woman last year. He didn't think anyone knew."

Stan shook his head.

"Jesus. Moose with a black woman. God…"

"Most dicks are color blind," said Leonard. "I don't suppose Moose's was any different."

That afternoon, Leonard let Greek in on what to expect.

"We'll be gone in the morning. Right after breakfast…Gone for good."

Greek looked up but said nothing.

"Be leaving with the fire crew," said Leonard. "Me and the kid. Do the Movement Sheet, anything else needs to be done. We're on the list so count'll clear. Only way they'll know is if somebody actually comes looking for us. And that's a long shot. You'll be clean."

"Escape," said Greek. "Has a certain ring to it."

"Doesn't it, though."

"Well, man…Been a hell of a trip. Like they say, walk slow and keep your back to the wall. I'll miss you."

Leonard nodded.

"What about the Contest?" said Greek.

"Called on account of darkness."

"Todd'll be pissed. He's way ahead."

"He'll get over it," said Leonard. "Tell him ten thousand flies and a few more years and he can get a parole in any state in the union. Besides, anybody who can shoot his mother-in-law and get off with manslaughter ought to be a pretty resourceful guy."

"I'll pass that along."

Leonard walked over to the window that faced out onto the Yard.

"I've got fifty boxes of Big Reds in the Furniture Factory. A hundred at the Dairy. I'll get word to the Maestro to turn them over to you. Give Todd a couple for killin' all those flies. That'll keep him happy for awhile. Keep the rest for yourself. Do what you want with them. Hoss brings in some every month, but I don't know how long that'll last after I go."

"I'll be rich," said Greek.

"And I'll be free."

"I hope."

"Bank on it," said Leonard.

Greek thought for a moment.

"Free is better," he said.

"Every time."

When the roster sheet came in from the Honor Block to be typed, Leonard added two names halfway down the list. Wotek signed it without comment. And without checking it.

The next morning, Leonard and Stan ate breakfast with the fire crew. With newly issued jackets and hard hats, they mustered outside the Mess Hall and marched single file through Control. Krasner was on duty. He checked the roster, the I.D.'s, and counted heads. Collars up, hats pulled low, they were not recognized.

The driver and crew boss were both correctional officers from Camp James. There were no guns, no shackles. After all, these were Honor Block inmates with less than six months to serve; surely none would try to escape.

The small bus sped along the back roads toward the fire. Most of the men had only two or three months to serve; this would be their last chance to earn a little gate money. Fifty cents an hour. Not bad; the top job in the Furniture Factory only paid eleven. Stan made five dollars a month working in the Watch Office.

Less than an hour into the ride, a plume of smoke appeared on the horizon. The convicts cheered. Fifteen minutes later they stopped at Wheatly Junction—two gas stations, a motel, a diner and a gift shop. Blowing smoke transformed the sun into a dull orange ball, and cast everything in an eerie light. The flames were not visible, though smoke billowing into the sky made it appear very close.

They disembarked in a cluster of other buses. Officer Davis called the roster from a clipboard—everyone present and accounted for. They formed a column of twos and hiked up the road toward the fire camp a half mile away.

Captain Edwards of the Kern County Fire Department assigned them to camp duty—cooking, helping with the cleanup, general camp maintenance (experience had taught him that convict crews were all but useless on the fire line itself). Shifts would be twelve hours on and twelve hours off. They were issued army cots and blankets and shown where to set up. Davis informed them that there would only be two counts a day—eight A.M. and eight P.M., when they changed shifts.

"Cover for me," said Leonard, after they had set up the cots. "I've got to get back to Junction and make a call."

"No problem," said Stan. "Anybody asks, I'll tell them you went to get a six pack."

The tone was light, but inside his stomach was churning. There were so many questions without answers; the closer the time came, the more doubts crowded in. What did Leonard mean about being a business asset? Stan didn't know anything about business. And the only thing he knew about Leonard's business was his rap sheet (racketeering, extortion, grand theft) and the fact that he ran most of the gambling and money-lending business on the Yard.

...Move to another state, get a new birth certificate, driver's license and social security number and you're home free—a brand new person...Pick a name. Any name. Was it really that easy? Could Stanley Wayne Smith simply vanish from the face of the earth? And why not? What was so great about being Stan Smith? He tried out several names before he settled on Burgess, the Iceman's official surname. William Burgess. Perfect. Just plain Bill. He wanted to use something out of the Pinocchio story, but he couldn't think of a name that wouldn't draw attention. Geppetto. Cricket. Stromboli. Nothing worked. He tried it out...Hello, I'm Bill Burgess, and I'm from...Hi, I'm Bill Burgess from Toledo and...

"And I'm the fuckin' Tooth Fairy, Bill," said a convict seated on a nearby cot.

Stan put his hand over his mouth, embarrassed at being caught talking to himself. He looked down the fire road that led to Wheatly Junction.

Maybe Leonard was right, he thought; maybe he'd seen too many gangster movies. There were something on the order of two hundred million people in United States; he'd be hard to find. But could he really go through with it? It was just one more thing to add to an already long list. Engineer, husband, murderer...fugitive.

His mind sought the safe refuge of AC Theory or Mathematics where two plus two always equaled four no matter who his cellmate was or whether the count had cleared or whether there was a riot going on in North Block. Algebra and calculus were as certain as the sunrise; the requisite number of knowns would always yield the unknown. Always. It paid off every time.

But life behind the walls was different; it was anything but certain. He couldn't even rely on his own experience. What he had known to be true while he was locked up in the Hole seemed to evaporate in the light of the day. Visions and voices just faded until everything was suspect and the mind said—It never happened, pal. No way. Think about it...And when he did think about it, mentally digest it, he said...You're right. It never happened. How could it?

He thought about his mother, brittle as old china; he'd never see her again. Not that he was so fond of her. But never seeing her again? That was different. He pictured her torturing a Kleenex in her knobby, arthritic hands. She'd never see him again, never know what happened, never know if he was dead or alive.

Still, there was freedom to consider. If he didn't go now, he'd have at least five or six years to do. Maybe more. Walking the Yard. He might not live through it. Some crazy convict might bury a shiv in him thinking he was somebody else. It might be retaliation going all the way back to Hawk. Memories are long behind the walls; convicts never forget...or forgive. Maybe Hebner or Cheswick had already put his name out on the Yard as a snitch. Penitentiary justice. That's what real fear is about—no place to run, no place to hide. Rats in a maze. Five more years of watching his back. Five more years of walking the Yard, listening to Preacher, Doc, Ice, hoping to survive one more day. A.M.'s and P.M.'s. Doin' Time.

> *...I'm Bill Burgess from Toledo, Ohio, and I'm looking for work. Oh, a little electronics, circuit design, light housekeeping, but I'll work at anything, sir. References furnished on request (Ah, here's one from my parole officer)...Hello, I'm Joe the Shmo, from Kokomo. I do this imitation of a Real Person...Hello, I'm Pinocchio and...*

The camp was a mass of confusion. Firefighters, exhausted after a long shift on the fire line, flopped down on the nearest cot when they returned. A row of Coleman stoves was kept hot to feed the men streaming in and out of camp at all hours of the day and night.

Leonard returned to camp with two jackets, SMOKE EATERS stenciled across the back.

"All set," he said, shoving the jackets under his bunk. "We leave at two."

"Today?"

"Today."

Less than three hours. They were divided into two groups, each to work a twelve-hour shift. As luck would have it, Leonard and

Stan drew the second shift; they wouldn't start work until eight that night.

Though the convicts had been told earlier that they could eat whatever they wanted, that stealing and hoarding food was unnecessary and strictly forbidden, the area soon began to fill up with cans of stolen peaches and five-gallon cartons of ice-cream. Old ways die hard; the temptation was too great.

Stan lay on his bunk and stared at the sky, unable to quiet the voices in his head. He wondered what it would be like to be free again. It had taken him a long time to accept the reality that he was locked up, now he couldn't imagine life any other way. Not that he liked the way it was; he just couldn't imagine it any other way.

He'd always taken his freedom for granted; it was like the air he breathed—always there. Then one day it was gone. When he reached back, there was nothing—memories wrapped in twine, paper promises, empty packages. Like so many things in his life, he didn't realize how important it was till it was gone.

Some said freedom was the little things. Taking a shower alone. Not having to watch your back. Having socks with elastic in the tops. Going into a store and looking at things on the shelves. Just looking. Waking in the morning and having the key to the room you're in. Being able to walk out the door anytime you wanted to; just walk out and go somewhere. Anywhere. Not have to worry about missing a count. Just go…Anywhere …Anytime. That was Freedom.

Some said it was the women; that's what freedom was about. And the whiskey, the drugs. But women were mentioned more often than anything else, frequently purchased (as it turned out) at the price of that precious freedom. Get enough Good Pussy while you're out (they seemed to say), and a man could do some time. If he had to. As if woven into the fabric of those brief weeks or months on the streets was the realization that if he got busted again, if he had to do some time, those sweet memories would be enough to sustain a man through any number of long months or years behind the Walls.

This from convicts who had grown up in the System, Children of the State, men doing life on the installment plan, men who knew the ropes, knew how to operate behind the walls, but didn't have a clue about living in the Free World and weren't ever going to learn because they already Knew Everything. Besides, even if they did want to learn, there wasn't anybody to teach them. They always had that run of Bad Luck, that incredible sequence of events that had never happened before and probably never would again in a million years, events that ended with a perfectly good parole being revoked by some Asshole Parole Officer who didn't have anything better to do but to fuck with a guy trying to make an honest living on the streets…Shit, man, wasn't for bad luck, I wouldn't have no luck at all…

At one forty-five, Leonard kicked Stan's bunk and headed down the fire road with his coat on and a shovel over his shoulder. Stan got up slowly, his heart racing, put on his jacket and followed a few yards behind.

Fifteen minutes later they emerged from the hillside behind a small diner. There were several cars parked in front.

"They're here," said Leonard, nodding toward a dirty gray Mercedes sedan.

He tossed his shovel and jacket into the bushes and walked toward the car. Stan didn't move. Twenty feet away, Leonard turned and looked back.

"Come on," he said.

Stan heard himself say, "I'm not goin'."

Leonard pushed his glasses up on the bridge of his nose, walked back and stood in front of Stan.

"Come on," he said evenly.

"I…I can't go."

Stan's chest was so tight he could hardly breathe. His eyes focused on the beads of perspiration on Leonard's upper lip. He didn't see the punch coming. It exploded on his jaw and knocked him down. Without another word, Leonard turned and walked toward the diner. Stan closed his eyes and didn't open them again until he heard the car door slam and the car drive away. Then he sat up; the diner glistened through a moist haze. There was the taste of blood in his mouth. He shook his head, trying to clear the cobwebs.

"Jesus," he said.

He got to his feet slowly and began to walk back up the dirt road toward the camp. His legs were shaking. He rubbed his jaw and worked it from side to side. It hurt, but he didn't think it was broken.

All he had to do was walk to the car and get in. A few yards to freedom…and he couldn't do it. He didn't know why; he just couldn't.

What would he tell them when they discovered that Leonard was missing? Nothing, he decided. They might try to tie him to it, but he hadn't missed a count, hadn't done anything wrong. He had come out with the fire crew because his name was on the list. He was as surprised as anyone. No, he didn't know how his name got on the list. It was just there so he went.

He knew it was far-fetched, but it was all he had. He might get some extra time. Six months. A year maybe. Maybe longer. Maybe he'd get a different shake now that Quinlan was gone and Hebner had been transferred to Folsom. But it didn't seem to matter anymore. He'd do his time and go. He remembered the song Pinocchio sang when he discovered he was Real.

> …*I've got no strings to hold me down, To make me fret or make me frown, I had strings but now I'm free, There are no strings on me*…

He was breathing easier. For some reason his step was lighter and he had a strange sense of being free at last…

www.ingramcontent.com/pod-product-compliance
Lightning Source LLC
Chambersburg PA
CBHW030634020726
47493CB00006B/1706